THE KUKOTSKY ENIGMA

THE KUKOTSKY ENIGMA

A Novel

LUDMILA ULITSKAYA

TRANSLATED FROM THE RUSSIAN
BY DIANE NEMEC IGNASHEV

Northwestern University Press
Evanston, Illinois

Northwestern University Press
www.nupress.northwestern.edu

English translation copyright © 2016 by Diane Nemec Ignashev. Published
2016 by Northwestern University Press. Originally published in Russian as
The Kukotsky Case (*Казус Кукоцкого*), copyright © 2001 by Ludmila Ulitskaya.
Published by arrangement with ELKOST International Literary Agency.

Printed in the United States of America

10   9   8   7   6   5   4   3   2   1

Library of Congress Cataloging-in-Publication Data

Names: Ulitskaia, Liudmila, author. | Nemec Ignashev, Diane, 1951– translator.
Title: The Kukotsky enigma : a novel / Ludmila Ulitskaya ; translated from the
    Russian by Diane Nemec Ignashev.
Other titles: Kazus Kukotskogo. English
Description: Evanston, Illinois : Northwestern University Press, 2016.
Identifiers: LCCN 2016007590| ISBN 9780810133488 (pbk. : alk. paper) |
    ISBN 9780810133495 (e-book)
Subjects: LCSH: Gynecologists—Soviet Union—Fiction. | Abortion—
    Government policy—Soviet Union—Fiction. | Families—Soviet
    Union—Fiction.
Classification: LCC PG3489.2.L58 K3913 2016 | DDC 891.735—dc23
LC record available at http://lccn.loc.gov/2016007590

Truth is on the side of death.

—SIMONE WEIL

CONTENTS

PART ONE

1

SINCE THE END OF THE SEVENTEENTH CENTURY ALL OF
Pavel Alekseevich Kukotsky's male ancestors on his father's side had been
physicians. The name of the first of them, Avdei Fedorovich, appears in a
letter written in 1698 by Peter the Great to the city of Utrecht to a certain Professor Ruysch whose lectures on anatomy the Russian emperor
had attended incognito as Piotr Mikhailov the year before. In his letter the young emperor requests that the professor take on as his student
the son of an apothecary's assistant, Avdei Kukotsky. How the surname
Kukotsky originated cannot be established with certainty, but according
to family legend, the ancestral Avdei had come from the area in Moscow
known as "Kukui" where Peter I had built the German Quarter.

Since that time the Kukotsky surname has appeared repeatedly in
decrees of state honors; it also can be found in the enrollment records
of schools established in Russia following the Decree of 1714. By entering government service upon graduation from these new schools, the
"low-born" gained entry to the nobility. After the Table of Ranks was
introduced, the Kukotskys' meritorious service earned them member-
ship in the "superior senior nobility with all privileges and advantages."
A Kukotsky figures among the students of Dr. Johann Erasmus of Stras-
bourg, the first Western doctor in Russia to teach, among other medical
disciplines, "the midwyf's art."

Since childhood, Pavel had held a secret fascination for the order of all
things living. Sometimes—usually in the uncertain, unclaimed moments
that occurred just before dinner—he managed to slip undetected into
his father's study, where, breathless with anticipation, he pulled from the
middle shelf of the barrister bookcases with their heavy glass drop-fronts
three treasured volumes of the Platen *Handbook of Hygienic Rules of Life*
(the most well-known medical reference book at the time) and settled
on the floor with them in a cozy corner between the tiled stove and the
bookcase. The supplements to the volumes included cardboard paper-doll
figures of a rosy-cheeked man with black whiskers and a comely but quite
pregnant woman with a flap-like womb that opened up to reveal a fetus.
Likely, it was precisely because of this figure, which for most people—no

denying it—was just a naked lady, that little Pavel kept his studies secret from his family for fear of being caught doing something wrong.

Just as little girls tirelessly dress their dolls, so Pavel spent hours assembling and disassembling the cardboard models of the humans and their various organs. Flap by flap the cardboard people shed their outer layer of skin, then their healthy rosy muscles, to reveal a removable liver, lungs that dangled from the pliant trunk of the trachea, and, finally, the bared skeleton, tinted dark yellow and seemingly completely lifeless. It was as if death were always lurking inside the human body, hidden from view by living flesh: Pavel would have cause to ponder this much later.

One day, Pavel's father, Aleksei Gavrilovich, found his son there, between the stove and the bookcase. The boy expected to get his ears boxed, but his father, looking down from his great height, merely harrumphed and promised to bring his son something better.

A few days later his father really did give him something better—Leonardo da Vinci's *Dell Anatomia*, Folio A, eighteen sheets with two hundred forty-five drawings, published by Sabashnikov in Turin at the end of the nineteenth century. The volume—one of only three hundred hand-numbered copies—was more splendid than anything Pavel had seen before. Inside was an inscription by the publisher: Aleksei Gavrilovich had performed an operation on some member of the Sabashnikov household . . .

Placing the book in the hands of his ten-year-old son, Kukotsky senior advised: "Look here . . . Leonardo was the premier anatomist of his time. No one drew anatomical specimens better than he did."

Kukotsky senior said something else, but Pavel no longer heard him. The book had opened up before him as if with a bright light that flooded his vision. The perfection of each drawing was magnified by the inconceivable perfection of the object depicted, be it an arm, a leg, or the pisiform tibialis anterior muscle, which Leonardo referred to lovingly as "the fish."

"Down here you'll find books on natural history, zoology, and comparative anatomy." Aleksei Gavrilovich directed his son's attention to the shelves below. "You can come here and read."

PAVEL SPENT THE HAPPIEST HOURS OF HIS CHILDHOOD and adolescence in his father's study delighting at the incredible articulation of bones in the multisequential processes of pronation and supination, and thrilled almost to tears by the chart illustrating the evolution of the circulatory system—from the earthworm's simple vessel with its thin threads of muscle fiber to the triple-beat miracle of the four-chambered human heart, by comparison with which a perpetual motion machine was remedial arithmetic. Indeed, for the boy the world itself seemed like one enormous perpetual motion machine that ran on its own resources, charged by the pulsating movement of living to dead, and dead to living.

After little Pavel's father gave him a small brass microscope with fifty-power magnification, anything that could not be mounted on a glass slide ceased to be of interest. In the world beyond the field of his microscope he noticed only that which corresponded to the amazing pictures observable under his lens. For example, the pattern on the tablecloth caught his eye for its resemblance to the structure of skeletal muscle . . .

"You know, Eva," Aleksei Gavrilovich said to his wife, "I am afraid Pavlik will become a physician, but he has too good a head for that. He ought to go into research . . ."

Aleksei Gavrilovich himself had spent his entire life bearing the double burdens of teaching and clinical work: as head of the Department of Field Surgery, he continued to perform operations. In the short interval between the two wars—Russo-Japanese and the war with Germany—he labored as if possessed to create a modern school of field surgery, while attempting simultaneously to direct the attention of the Ministry of War to the obvious (for him) fact that the impending war would alter the nature of war in general and that the incipient century would witness wars of a new scale with new weapons and demanding new military medical practices. According to Aleksei Gavrilovich, the system of field hospitals needed a complete overhaul, with priority given to rapid evacuation of the wounded and the creation of centrally directed specialized hospitals . . .

The war with Germany began earlier than Aleksei Gavrilovich had anticipated. And so he departed, as they said in those days, for the theater of war. He was appointed chief of the very same commission he had lobbied for in peacetime, and now he found himself torn in all directions, because the stream of wounded was enormous while the system of specialized hospitals he had devised remained merely a plan on paper: he had not had enough time to surmount bureaucratic barriers before the war began.

Following a fierce clash with the Minister of War, he resigned his commission, maintaining responsibility solely for the mobile hospitals. Set up in Pullman coaches, these operating rooms on wheels retreated through Galicia and Ukraine along with the debilitated army. In early 1917 an artillery shell struck one of the mobile operating rooms, and Aleksei Gavrilovich perished along with his patient and a nurse.

That same year Pavel matriculated to the medical faculty of Moscow University. The next year he was expelled, due to his father having been no less than a colonel in the tsar's army. A year later, at the behest of Professor Kalintsev, his father's old friend and head of the Department of Obstetrics and Gynecology, he was reinstated as a student. Kalintsev admitted him to his own department and took him under his wing.

Pavel pursued his studies with the same passion with which a gambler gambles and a drunkard drinks. His obsession with learning earned him the reputation of an eccentric. Unlike his mother, a spoiled and capricious woman, he hardly noticed material hardship. After his father's death there seemed to be nothing else to lose.

In early 1920 the Kukotskys' living space was "consolidated": three more families were moved into their apartment, leaving only the former study to widow and son. The university professoriate, surviving the best it could under the new regime, could do nothing to help. They too had been reduced to tight quarters, and the scare of the revolution had not passed: the Bolsheviks had already demonstrated that the human life these putrefied intellectuals fought to preserve was not worth a kopeck.

Eva Kazimirovna, Pavel's mother, had an attachment to material things and a knack for keeping them. She managed to stuff almost all her Warsaw furniture, dishes, and clothing into the study. His father's venerable office, once spacious and orderly, turned into a warehouse, and no matter how Pavel pleaded with her to dispose of the clutter, his mother only cried and shook her head: this was all that remained of her former life. Ultimately, though, she was forced to sell, and gradually she bartered away her things at the street market, shedding tears of farewell over every item from her countless trunks of shoes, collars, and handkerchiefs . . .

Relations between mother and son cooled, then soured, and one year later, when his mother married the indecently young Filipp Ivanovich Levshin, a petty railroad bureaucrat, Pavel left home, reserving the right to use his father's library.

He managed only rarely, though, to make his way over to his mother's place. At the same time he attended classes, he worked at a clinic where he spent long hours on duty, sleeping where he could, usually in the linen room, with the permission of the old linen-lady, who remembered not only Pavel's father but his grandfather as well . . .

He had already turned twenty-one when his mother gave birth to a new child. Her adult son only underscored her age, which aggravated the mutton-dressed-as-lamb Eva Kazimirovna. She let Pavel know that his presence at home was not desirable.

At that point relations between Pavel and his mother ceased.

After a while the Medical Faculty was made independent of the University, and appointments were reshuffled. Professor Kalintsev died and was replaced by another man, appointed by the party, with no reputation whatsoever as a scientist. Oddly enough, he supported Pavel and allowed him to remain in the department for his residency. In medical circles the Kukotsky name was no less well known than Pirogov or Botkin.

Pavel's first research project focused on certain vascular disorders that caused miscarriages in the fifth month of pregnancy. The disorder affected microcapillary functions, which interested Pavel because at the time he was fixated on the question of how to influence processes in the peripheral regions of the circulatory and nervous systems, which he considered more tractable than higher-order functions. Like all residents, in addition to his hours at the clinic Pavel did rounds in the lying-in hospital and saw patients twice a week at the clinic.

Precisely that same year, while examining a female outpatient who suffered from systematic miscarriages in the fourth and fifth months of pregnancy, he realized that he could see a tumor in her stomach as well as metastases—one quite visible in her liver and a second, less conspicuous, in the mediastinum. He completed his examination of the patient as if all were normal, but referred her to a surgeon. Afterward he sat for a long time in his office before summoning his next patient, trying to make sense of what had happened and where that full-color schematic image of fully developed cancer had come from . . .

That day Pavel Alekseevich discovered his strange but useful gift. To himself he referred to it as "intravision," and during the first few years he made cautious inquiries to determine whether any of his colleagues possessed a similar capacity, but found no traces thereof.

Over the years his inner vision strengthened, intensified, and acquired a high image resolution. In some cases he even saw cell structures, tinted, so it seemed, with Ehrlich's hematoxylin. Malignancies had a deep purple tint; areas of active proliferation flickered with tiny crimson granules . . . Embryos in the earliest stages of gestation appeared to him as shining light-blue clouds . . .

There were days and weeks when his intravision would recede. Pavel Alekseevich continued working, seeing patients, and performing operations. His confidence in his professional qualifications never abandoned him, but deep inside he felt a subtle anxiety. The young doctor was, it goes without saying, a materialist with no tolerance for mysticism. He and his father had always made fun of his mother's proclivity for attending high society séances with magical table-spinning or dabbling in mystical magnetism.

Pavel Alekseevich regarded his gift as if it were a living thing separate from himself. He did not trouble himself with the mystical aspect of this phenomenon, but accepted it as a useful professional tool. Gradually it became apparent that his gift was an ascetic and a misogynist. Even too hearty a breakfast might weaken his intravision, and Pavel Alekseevich acquired the habit of going without breakfast, not eating until lunchtime or—when he had afternoon hours at the clinic—in the evening. Physical contact with women temporarily deactivated the slightest transparency of his patients.

He was a good diagnostician, and in his practice of medicine had no need to resort to such unorthodox support, but his research seemed to beg for assistance: the hidden workings of capillaries held secrets ready to reveal themselves at any moment . . . It turned out, though, that Pavel's personal life got in the way of his research. So, after breaking up with his on-again off-again heartthrob—a surgical nurse with cold, precise hands—he gently avoided intimacy, was slightly daunted by female aggressiveness, and accustomed himself to abstention. Like anything one does by choice, this was not a particularly onerous trial for him. From time to time he would take a liking to a cute little nurse or young female doctor, and he knew perfectly well that each and any one of them would yield to him at his first beck, but his intravision meant more to him.

Guarding his voluntary chastity was a challenge: he was single, wealthy by the beggarly standards of the time, well known in his field, and maybe not handsome but manly and quite attractive, and for all these reasons— only one of which would have sufficed—every woman who caught his slightly interested gaze would launch such an onslaught that Pavel Alekseevich barely was able to escape.

Some of his female colleagues even suspected that he was hiding a certain masculine defect, which they linked to his profession: what inclinations could a man have if his professional duties dictated that he spend each day groping with sensitive fingers the intimate darkness of womanhood . . .

2

BESIDES THEIR HEREDITARY COMMITMENT TO MEDICINE, the men of the Kukotsky family shared another peculiar trait: they took their wives as if they were spoils of war. His great-grandfather had married a captured Turkish woman; his grandfather—a Circassian; and his father—a Polish woman. According to family legend, all these women were exquisite beauties. The addition of foreign blood did little, though, to alter the hereditary looks of these big men with their high cheekbones and premature baldness. An engraved portrait of Avdei Fedorovich by an obviously German-trained anonymous artist, treasured to this day by Pavel Alekseevich's descendants, testifies to the power of their blood as the conduit over the centuries of the family's traits.

Pavel Alekseevich Kukotsky also had a wartime marriage—hasty and unexpected. Although his wife Elena Georgievna was neither a captive nor a hostage, he first saw her—in November 1942 in the small Siberian town (of V) where the clinic he headed had been evacuated—on an operating table, her condition such that Pavel Alekseevich realized fully that the fate of this woman, whose face he had not yet seen, lay beyond his powers. She had been brought in by ambulance, late. Very late . . .

Pavel Alekseevich had been summoned in the middle of the night by his assistant, Valentina Ivanovna. She was a fine surgeon and knew that he trusted her entirely, but this case was special—for reasons she herself could not explain. She sent for him, woke him up, and asked him to come. When he entered the operating room, hands scrubbed for the operation and suspended in the air, her scalpel had just begun its incision into the pretreated skin.

He stood behind Valentina Ivanovna. His special vision switched on by itself, and he saw not just the surgical area Valentina Ivanovna worked on, but the female body in its entirety—a spinal structure of rare proportions and fineness, a narrow thorax with slight ribs, a diaphragm set slightly higher than usual, and a slowly contracting heart illuminated by a pale-green transparent flame that throbbed along with the muscle.

It was a strange sensation no one could have understood and he could not have explained: the body he saw was one he already knew well. Even the shadow along the top of the right lung—the vestige of juvenile tuberculosis—seemed as dear and familiar to him as the outline of the old spot on the wallpaper near the head of the bed one falls asleep in every night.

Looking at the face of this young woman who was so perfectly structured internally was somehow awkward, but he nonetheless cast a quick glance over the white sheet that covered her to the chin. He noticed her narrow nostrils and long brown eyebrows with a fluffy brush at their base. And her chalky pallor. But his sense of discomfort scrutinizing her face was so strong that he lowered his eyes to where the undulating form of her nacreous intestines should be. The worm-shaped pouch had burst, streaming pus into the intestinal cavity. Peritonitis. That was what Valentina Ivanovna saw as well.

A languid yellowish-pink flame that existed only in his vision and seemed slightly warm to the touch and gave off a rare flowerlike smell illuminated the woman from below and was, in essence, a part of her.

He also could see how fragile her coxofemoral joints were, the result of an insufficiently globular femoral head. Actually, quite close to dislocation. And her pelvis was so narrow that childbirth would likely strain or rupture the symphysis pubis. No, the uterus was mature and had given birth. Once, at least, she had managed . . . Suppuration was already enveloping both strands of her ovaries and her dark stressed uterus. Her heartbeat was weak but steady, while that uterus emitted disaster. Pavel Alekseevich had known for a long time that different organs can have different sensations . . . But how could you say something like that aloud?

Well, no more childbirth for you . . . He had yet even to imagine who exactly might give the woman dying right before his eyes cause to give birth. He shook his head, driving the haunting images from his mind. Valentina Ivanovna had resected the large intestine and reached the worm-shaped pouch. Pus was everywhere . . .

"Clean it all out . . . Remove everything . . ."

They had to hurry. "Damned profession," Pavel Alekseevich thought before taking the instruments from Valentina Ivanovna's hands.

Pavel Alekseevich knew that Ganichev, the head of the military hospital, had several bottles of American penicillin. A thief and a crook, he nonetheless was obligated to Pavel Alekseevich . . . But would he give it to him?

3

THE FIRST FEW DAYS—WHEN ELENA WAS NO LONGER dying but also not entirely alive—Pavel Alekseevich looked in on her in her screened-off corner of the ward and himself administered the injections of penicillin intended for wounded soldiers and twice stolen from them. She had not yet regained consciousness. She was in a place inhabited by talking half-people, half-plants engaged in an involved plot in which she figured as a, if not the, central character. Carefully laid out on a huge white cloth, she felt as if she herself were part of the cloth, with careful hands doing something to the cloth that felt like embroidering; whatever was going on, she felt the prick of tiny needles, and those pricks were pleasant.

Besides these caring embroiderers, there were others—villains, Germans even, it seemed, in Gestapo uniforms—who wanted not just for her to die, but something larger and worse than death. At the same time, something suggested to Elena that all this was a bit illusory, a kind of half-deception—that soon someone would come and reveal the truth to her. Over all, she surmised, everything going on around her had some relation to her life and death, yet beyond that there was something else awaiting her, something much more important and connected with the revelation of that ultimate truth, which was more important than life itself.

Once she overheard a conversation. A deep male voice addressed someone and asked for the biochemistry. An elderly female voice refused. Elena imagined the biochemistry as a big glass box with little clinking colored tubes that were somehow mysteriously connected to the mountainous landscape where everything was taking place . . .

Then the landscape and the little colored tubes and the illusory beings suddenly disappeared, and she felt someone tapping her on the wrist. She opened her eyes. The light was so crude and harsh it made her squint. A man with a face that seemed familiar smiled at her.

"That's good, Elena Georgievna."

Pavel Alekseevich was stunned: it was one of those cases where the part was larger than the whole; her eyes were so much larger than her face.

"Was it you I saw there?" she asked Pavel Alekseevich.

Her voice was weak, as thin as paper.

"That's entirely possible."

"And where's Tanechka?" she asked, but did not hear the answer as she once again floated into colored spots and talking plants.

"Tanechka, Tanechka, Tanechka," the voices sang, and Elena calmed down. Everything was as it should be.

After a while she regained consciousness for good. Everything came together: her illness, the operation, the ward. The attentive doctor who had not let her die.

Vasilisa Gavrilovna visited her. A white film covering one eye, her dark headscarf tied low over her brow, she brought Elena cranberry juice and dark-colored cookies. Twice she brought Elena's little daughter.

The doctor at first came by twice a day, then, later, as for the others, only during morning rounds. The screen was removed. Elena now began to get up, like the other patients, and to make her way to the washroom at the end of the corridor.

Pavel Alekseevich kept her in the ward for three months.

At the time, Elena was renting a corner of a room behind a calico curtain in a rotting little wooden house on the outskirts of town. The landlady, who also appeared to be rotting, was exceptionally quarrelsome. She had already evicted four tenants before Elena. The Siberian city that before the war had boasted barely fifty thousand inhabitants now burst at the seams with evacuees: the employees of a munitions factory and of the design office where Elena worked, the staff and students of a medical school and its clinics, and two theater companies. Except for the prisoners' barracks in an immediate suburb, no housing had been built in the town since the Soviets had come to power. People were packed like sardines in every crack and corner.

On the eve of Elena's release the doctor arrived at her apartment in an official automobile, with a chauffeur. Frightened by the car, the landlady hid in the pantry. Vasilisa Gavrilovna responded to the knock at the door. Pavel Alekseevich said hello and was struck by the smell of slops and sewage. Not removing his sheepskin coat, he took three steps inside, pulled back the calico curtain, and glanced inside at their beggarly nest. Tanya sat in the corner of a big bed with a big white kitten and looked at him in fright, and with curiosity.

"Quickly collect all your things, Vasilisa Gavrilovna. We're moving to different quarters," he said, surprising himself.

Moving a high-risk patient who had miraculously survived to this garbage heap was out of the question.

Fifteen minutes later their entire household had been packed into a large suitcase and cloth bundle, Tanya was dressed, and three maidens, kitten included, sat in the back seat of the car.

Pavel Alekseevich took them to his place. The clinic occupied an old mansion, and Pavel Alekseevich's quarters were in an annex in the courtyard. It had once been the mansion's kitchen and the servants' quarters. The large stove had been repaired and was used to cook food for the patients, the space had been partitioned, and Pavel Alekseevich had been allocated two tiny rooms with a separate entrance. In one of those rooms he now settled this family. His future family.

The first evening, left alone with Tanechka—Elena would be released only the next day—Vasilisa, having said her prayers as usual, lay down

13

alongside the sleeping girl on the rigid medical examining couch and was the first to figure out where all this was headed . . . Ah, Elena, Elena, with a husband who's still alive.

Vasilisa Gavrilovna confirmed her suspicions the next day when, after crossing the courtyard, Elena first entered Pavel Alekseevich's house. Weak and pale as a ghost, she smiled somewhat vaguely and perplexedly, even a bit guiltily. But that day Vasilisa Gavrilovna had no grounds for suspicions or reproaches—those would come several days later. Amazing how this old spinster with not the least experience of relations with the male sex could be so attuned to the stirrings of love still in the bud.

All February it was bitterly cold. Pavel Alekseevich's quarters were well heated, and for the first time in several months the women knew warmth. Possibly, it was the dry heat of wood the women had so missed that warmed Elena's feelings. Whatever the reason, the love she felt for Pavel Alekseevich attained degrees she had never known before. From the summits of a new realization of love and of herself, her marriage to Anton Ivanovich now seemed flawed, artificial. She drove from her mind the tiny, dim thought of her husband, and day after day put off the minute when she would have to tell herself the sad truth, all of which was exacerbated by the fact that no letters had arrived from Anton for almost six months, and she herself had not written to him for a month so as not to write the truth or lie to him.

At half past five every morning Pavel Alekseevich brought a bucket of warm water from the hospital kitchen—a luxury as inconceivable then as a bathtub full of champagne in other times—and waited behind the door while Elena bathed. Then he bathed, brought a second bucket for Vasilisa Gavrilovna and Tanechka, and tossed more firewood into the stove, which they stoked almost incessantly. Vasilisa sat in the other room until both of them left for work, pretending to be asleep. Elena knew that Vasilisa was an early bird who began her devotional muttering still in the middle of the night.

She doesn't come out because she doesn't want to witness my disgrace, Elena surmised. And smiled.

In the morning she felt especially happy and free. She knew that on the way to the plant everything would slowly begin to fade and that by day's end not a trace of her morning happiness would remain: as evening approached, her sense of guilt and shame mounted and did not pass until Pavel Alekseevich took her into his strong nighttime embrace . . .

Pavel Alekseevich was forty-three years old. Elena was twenty-eight. She was the first and only woman in his life who did not drive away his gift. The first night she spent in his room, he woke up in the darkness before dawn with her tickly braid spread along his forearm and said to himself: "Enough! So what if I never again see what other doctors can't see. I don't want to let her go . . ."

Although a misogynist, for Elena, odd as that was, his gift had made an exception. In any case, Pavel Alekseevich continued to see the colored glimmer of life hidden inside the body just as he had before.

Probably IT had fallen in love with her too, Pavel Alekseevich concluded.

NOTIFICATION OF THE DEATH OF ELENA'S HUSBAND, Anton Ivanovich Flotov, arrived a month and a half after she had spent her first night in Pavel Alekseevich's room. The notice came in the morning, after Elena had already left for the plant. Vasilisa cried herself dry over the course of the day; she had never liked Anton and now she reproached herself particularly for her dislike.

That evening she placed the notice in front of Elena. Elena turned to stone. For a long time she just held the flimsy yellowish piece of paper in her hand.

"My God! How can I live with this?" Elena pointed a finger to the large, clumsily printed numbers of the date of death. "Do you see what date it was?"

It was the same day she had spent her first night with Pavel Alekseevich.

By this time Pavel Alekseevich's broad back in neat surgical dressing gown with ties at the base of his powerful neck had come to shield her from the rest of the world as well as from the perished Anton with his cool eyes and rigid mouth set against a thin face entirely deprived of any Slavic fleshiness.

From that moment on her love for Pavel Alekseevich would be forever tinged with a feeling of incorrigible guilt before Anton, killed the same day she had betrayed him . . .

Vasilisa saw something else in the numbers—forty days had already passed.

"Too late for me to offer prayers or for you to be a widow." Vasilisa began to cry.

SEVERAL DAYS LATER VASILISA ASKED FOR TIME OFF FOR one of her mysterious absences that she more announced than requested. Having spent many years living with Vasilisa, Elena was well aware of her peculiar habit of suddenly disappearing for a week, two or three, and then returning just as unexpectedly. This time, though, she could not let her go: all days off had been cancelled in the drafting office where with easy hand she drafted production plans for the transmission gearbox of an improved tank. The rules of war did not allow for excursions about the country, and there also was no one to babysit Tanya . . .

4

ALTHOUGH THOROUGHLY IMMERSED IN HIS PROFES-sional, medical affairs, Pavel Alekseevich was perceptive in many respects and took a sober view of life happening around him. Certainly he enjoyed the privileges of a professor and director of a major clinic, but the disastrous situation of his medical staff, insufficient food supplies even in the obstetrics ward, the cold, and the shortages of firewood, of medicines, and of dressings did not escape his notice . . . Although he had observed all this before the war, somehow, from somewhere, the idea had crept into his head that after the war everything would change, improve, be more just . . .

Possibly, his very profession, his constant, almost mundane-seeming contact with fiery lightning—at that critical moment when a human being is born from a hemorrhaging canal, from the uterine darkness of nonexistence—and his professional participation in this natural drama were affecting him both outwardly and inwardly, as well as influencing his opinions: he knew both the fragility of human beings and their supernatural endurance, which far exceeded that of other living organisms. Years of experience had shown him that the abilities of humans to adapt far exceeded those of animals. Had physicians and zoologists ever investigated this phenomenon together?

"I'm thoroughly convinced that no dog could ever withstand what humans do." He chuckled to himself.

Pavel Alekseevich possessed a most important quality for a scholar: the ability to ask the right questions . . . He kept a close eye on current research in the fields of physiology and embryology and never ceased to be amazed by the unfailing and even somewhat punctilious law that determined the life of a human being while it was still in its mother's womb and dictated that every observable event occurred with great accuracy—not to the week or day, but to the hour and minute. This timing mechanism worked so precisely that exactly on the seventh day of gestation every embryo—a spherical accumulation of undifferentiated cells—split into two cell masses, inner and outer, with which amazing things began to happen: they bent, unlatched from each other, and turned outward, forming sacs and nodes—part of the surface migrating inward, and all of this recurring with incomprehensible accuracy, millions and millions of times over. Who or what provided the directions for how this invisible performance played itself out?

Through an unnamed higher wisdom, a single cell formed by an immobile and slightly nebulous ovum, surrounded by a radiant wreath of follicle cells, and a long-nosed spermatozoa, with its fusiform head and a spiraled jittery tail, inevitably grew into a bellowing, twenty-inch, seven-pound, thoroughly senseless human creature, which—as dictated by the same law—developed into a genius, or a dolt, or a beauty, or a criminal, or a saint . . .

Precisely because he knew so much—in fact everything there was to know—about the subject at the time, he could picture for himself better than anyone else the cosmic soup from which every little Katenka and Valerik emerged.

His father's library had contained a multitude of books on the history of medicine, and he had always enjoyed retracing the path of this quaint antiquity: he delighted in, marveled at, and sometimes chuckled over the fantastic opinions of his long-deceased colleagues—the ancient Egyptian high priest, the world's first professional anatomist, or the medieval jack-of-all-trades who let blood, performed Cesarean sections, and removed corns, all for the same fee.

He would never forget the text of a letter, which he had found as a youngster, written by the Babylonian priest and physician Berossus to a pupil explaining that thirty years ago the star Tishla had entered the constellation of Sippara, and since that time boys were being born larger, more aggressive, and with their little hands positioned as if holding a spear . . .

"Little wonder," the ancient physician continued, "that the last ten years have seen incessant war: these boy-warriors have grown up and are incapable of becoming plowmen. It must be that the goddess-protectress Lamassu is rewriting the table of fates."

Pavel Alekseevich had consulted German reference books to determine who this Lamassu was who was rewriting the destinies of generations. She turned out to be the goddess of the placenta. This idolization of separate organs and sense of a cosmic link between earth, sky, and the human body—entirely lost by modern science—amazed him. All these touching superstitions notwithstanding, could it be that an entire generation might share a common personality, a single identity? Was it only social factors that defined generations? Might it not in fact be the influence of stars, diet, or water chemistry? After all, Pavel Alekseevich's teacher, Professor Kalintsev, had spoken about the hypotonic children of the beginning of the century . . . He had described them as languid, slightly sleepy babies, with puffy bags under their eyes, half-open mouths, angelically relaxed little hands . . . How unlike today's children, with their tightly clenched little fists, tucked toes, and tensed muscles. Hypertonic. With a boxer's stance—fists clenched to protect the head. Children of fear. Better equipped to survive. Only what are they protecting themselves from? Whom are they waiting to be struck by? What would the Babylonian scientist Berossus, priest of the goddess Lamassu, have said about these children?

Thoughts of these frightened children led Pavel Alekseevich in another direction: contemplating the fates of those close to him, he realized that almost all of them also had been crippled by fear. The majority concealed some unsavory fact about their family's origin or background or, if unable to hide it, lived in constant anticipation of being punished for crimes they had not committed. His assistant, Valentina Ivanovna, was descended from one of the wealthiest merchant families; another colleague bore like the plague his half-German blood; the clinic receptionist's brother had emigrated in 1918; and Elena, who had just entered his life, had admitted that her parents had perished in the camps while she herself had been spared a similar fate thanks to her grandmother, who had adopted her on the eve of her parents' move to Altai. Even Vasilisa Gavrilovna, an absolutely common person, turned out to have her own tangled little secret. Each had something to keep quiet, and each lived in expectation of being exposed.

With the beginning of the war, this amorphous, almost mystical fear had abated somewhat, replaced by another, more immediate fear for the lives of the men who had gone to the front. They were being killed by real, age-old enemies—the Germans. Yet in fighting and dying at the front, these men defended not only the country, but, to a certain extent, their families from their earlier, prewar terror: the agents of vigilance seemed to have forgotten about rich grandmothers, overeducated grandfathers, and relatives abroad. The death notices that arrived made everyone equal in grief. Orphanhood, hunger, and cold did not discriminate between the children of perished soldiers and the children of perished prisoners. Now everyone's future was tied to victory; no one's dreams lay beyond it. The virtually unspoken love that had arisen between Pavel Alekseevich and Elena in whispers and to the crackle of smoldering logs so fully absorbed them that they both put off all inevitable thoughts about the future: they were not terrified, yet.

5

PAVEL ALEKSEEVICH ADOPTED TANYA IMMEDIATELY AFTER the wedding and, as Vasilisa would say, "took her into his heart." This "his own" little girl embodied all the thousands of newborns he had helped come into the world: pulled out, cut out, and saved from asphyxiation, cranial trauma, and other injuries that not rarely accompany childbirth.

Other people's children were momentary, though. You spent great energy and work on them, and then they disappeared, and Pavel Alekseevich almost never saw these boys and girls at the age when they started to smile, to study their fingers, to delight at recognizing the face of a loved one, a pacifier, or a rattle.

Already during the first hours of a newborn's life Pavel Alekseevich could discern manifestations of temperament: a strong will or passivity, obstinacy or laziness. But more subtle personality traits do not usually appear in the first days after birth, when the child is recovering from the herculean effort of being born and transitioning to its new existence. He knew a great deal about other people's babies, but nothing about the child living in his house. The discovery turned out to be astonishing.

Tanya was barely two years old, and Pavel Alekseevich was old enough to be her grandfather. The sincere delight he took in her had the patina of an old man's affection for all the new things that occur in children and no longer occur in adults. He noticed the fold on her wrist, the dimple on her waist; he discovered that her dark hair was not one single dark-brown color, but was lighter and softer, as though of a different sort, at her hairline, on her neck, behind her ears.

New words, new movements, everything about the intellectual development taking place in this two-year-old person elicited Pavel Alekseevich's keen and loving interest. He never allowed his thoughts to consider that another woman could have borne him a different child, his own, perhaps even a boy, who would inherit not someone else's brown hair but his, Pavel Alekseevich's, light hair and tendency to early baldness as well as the strange shape of his hands with their huge, wide palms and triangular fingers that narrowed radically at the nail, and who would inherit, eventually, his profession.

No, no, even if Elena could give birth again, he was not entirely sure that he would want to put the love he felt for Tanechka to test or comparison. He said this to Elena as well: I can't imagine another child; our little girl is a genuine miracle.

It is hard to tell what derives from what: is a child's good character the result of the boundless and unconditional love its parents lavish on it, or, just the reverse, does a good child bring out all the best in the parents? Either way, Tanya grew up loved, and they three were especially happy when together. Vasilisa, though she was a member of the family, was an auxiliary member of this triangle who merely lent additional stability to their existence.

Sometimes, when Tanya woke up before the adults, she trundled over to her parents' room and dove between them like a calico fish, demanding with a sleepy, happy voice "bugs and quiches." She had started talking very early and without error even from the outset, and for her these "quiches" were the play of a grown-up person capable of poking fun at herself, the child.

"Here, and here, and here." She pointed her finger at her forehead, her cheek, and her chin and, on receiving her parents' kisses as lawful tribute, she searched with amusing gravity for a place on Pavel Alekseevich's scruffy cheek to give a smacking kiss in return.

After Tanya started school, this kissing ritual turned into a farewell kiss before walking out the door. These fleeting moments of contact, seemingly quite insignificant, were the tiny nails that held their daily life together.

Generally reserved, even with his beloved wife, and strictly observing the bounds of propriety in both gesture and word, with Tanya Pavel Alekseevich would degenerate to senile baby talk. He smothered the child with a lovey-dovey collection of flora and fauna: "my sweet little cherry," "daddy's baby sparrow," "my black-eyed little squirrel," "chubby little apple." Tanechka ate it all up and had her own collection of tender nicknames for her father: "my favorite dog," "Hippopotamus Hippopotamusovich," "Mr. Catfish Whiskers."

Pavel Alekseevich spoiled Tanya with a passion. Now and then Elena would have to put a chill on his ardor. He could walk into a toy store and buy up its sparse stock. But his mad indulgences seemed to do Tanya no harm, and she had none of the greediness or imperious possessiveness of the child who knows no limitations.

To Pavel Alekseevich all fabrics seemed too rough for his child's skin, all boots would give her blisters, and all scarves would scratch her neck. He would shift his gaze to his wife, and his heart ached with amazement at how fragile and tender she was; he wanted to swaddle them both in batiste, down, and fur . . . There was a strange disconnect between Pavel Alekseevich's ascetic inclinations, as well as the harsh and brutal realities of his life as a surgeon, Elena's automatic habit of taking the lesser and the worst so easily and naturally that no one noticed, and Vasilisa's parsimoniousness and strictness with the little girl, on the one hand, and, on the other, Pavel Alekseevich's burning desire to put his daughter and wife under a bell jar so as to protect them from drafts, crudeness, and all the vulgarity of life around them.

By September 1944, Pavel Alekseevich's clinic had returned to Moscow. Elena's apartment in Trekhprudny Lane, which she had been counting on, was now occupied by two low-level NKVD officers, and the young family found itself in the same dormitory where Pavel Alekseevich had led his lonely, humble life before the war. It was a half-basement, which was spacious enough, but damp, and hardly suitable for a child. As if especially to assure them that their concern for her health was not for naught, Tanya often caught colds and coughed for long periods on end.

Pavel Alekseevich and Elena Georgievna's family life was so happy that even Tanya's illnesses lent a particular note of closeness between the spouses. For a long time Pavel Alekseevich's first words on returning from work were a concerned "Did she cough?"

Vasilisa would shrug her bony shoulders: big deal, the kid coughs . . .

"Unfeeling old woman," Pavel Alekseevich thought to himself as he pulled off his huge overcoat filled with cold from outside, shooing Tanya away from the cold air when she stuck her head out into the hallway . . .

6

LIKE HIS LATE FATHER, PAVEL ALEKSEEVICH HAD, BEYOND doubt, the qualities of a man of state. Although his father's rank as an officer in tsarist times had cast a long shadow over Pavel Alekseevich's career, the second war seemed to have eradicated this unpleasant spot in his biography: his father, though an officer, had been a doctor and perished in a war with Germany. Now, when the country again was waging war with the sons of those same Germans, Pavel Alekseevich was retroactively pardoned his dubious heritage. Soon after returning from evacuation he was summoned to the ministry, where it was proposed that he author a plan for the organization of peacetime health care in his own areas of specialization, obstetrics and pediatrics. The war was coming to an end, and while a commission had not yet been created, the assumption was that he would head it. Pavel Alekseevich was supplied with statistics that had been compiled incompetently, frequently with errors and incomplete data, but to a certain degree revealing nonetheless the horrible demographic situation. It was not just a question of the irreversible loss of an enormous part of the male population and, with that, a drop in the birth rate. Child mortality was enormous, particularly among infants. And there was one more factor, one not quantified in official statistics, but all too well known to any practicing physician: a large number of women of reproductive age died as a result of illegal abortions. Officially, abortions had been made illegal in 1936, at practically the same time that Stalin's Constitution had been adopted.

This prohibition was a sore spot in Pavel Alekseevich's work: nearly half of all emergency operations were the consequences of underground abortions. Contraceptives were practically nonexistent. Physicians were obliged under pain of criminal penalty to examine each woman brought in by ambulance "to inspect for evidence of an underground abortion." Pavel Alekseevich avoided such veiled denunciations and entered the condemning words *criminal abortion* in his patient's medical history only when the patient was dying. If the life of the woman were spared, such a medical opinion would have put the victim as well as the person who had performed this age-old procedure in the dock. Several hundred thousand women were in labor camps precisely because of this law.

The extensive program Pavel Alekseevich was charged with developing encompassed social as well as medical aspects.

The project reminded him of any one of those papers submitted to his reigning Highness by the best sons of the fatherland, among them both romantics and dimwits, a broad spectrum of interesting characters, from Prince Kurbsky to Chaadaev. His own father, Aleksei Gavrilovich Kukotsky, had been among them.

Pavel Alekseevich foresaw that after the war major changes would shake the very institution of the family; he expected a large number of single mothers and viewed this phenomenon as socially inevitable and even advantageous. He considered it imperative to introduce various benefits for single mothers, yet at the same time believed that the first step had to be the repeal of the resolution of July 1936 prohibiting abortions.

As work progressed, the project expanded and turned into a veritable utopia between the lines of whose fantastic constructions shone serious and very constructive ideas that were far ahead of their time. For example, it presupposed the establishment of social services for parents, sex education for young people, and the creation of a network of children's homes and sanatoria where the care and upbringing of both physically and mentally healthy children would be practiced based on scientific principles. This in part echoed pedagogical methods forbidden in the 1930s and even smacked slightly of Chernyshevsky. The need for medical genetic consulting also had not been overlooked: Pavel Alekseevich intended to charge his school friend, Ilya Goldberg, doctor of genetics, with organizing this aspect.

The Minister of Health at the time was a woman beyond her prime, an experienced bureaucrat and a party member from the salt-and-pepper top of her head to the stubborn calluses on her feet; she also happened to be the only woman in the government. For years she had been known as Workhorse, partly because it sounded like her surname, and partly owing to her indefatigability and rare ability to plug on, never swerving from the assigned path. She even liked the nickname, and not infrequently, having allowed herself a good bit to drink with close company, was wont to boast: "Yes, it's true, the Russian woman is a steed with balls. She can tackle anything!"

She was incontestably the number-one woman in the country, a symbol of women's equality, and International Women's Day incarnate, after, of course, the mythological Rosa Luxemburg, Clara Zetkin, Zoya Kosmodemianskaya, and the eternally youthful Liubov Orlova. All of them, Workhorse included, resembled each other in one way: they were all childless . . .

Initially, when the project of reorganizing health care was only just getting under way, Workhorse was a major supporter, but as Pavel Alekseevich's work increasingly gained scope, her enthusiasm cooled. In fact, she got scared. The project looked too radical, demanded enormous financing and—and this was the main thing—risk. In many respects blind, deaf, and dumb, Workhorse possessed superhuman acuity for the fluctuating moods of those higher up, which she regarded as the interests of the state. Intuition told her that at the moment the state's interest hardly lay in the field of obstetrics and gynecology, or in maternal care or pediatrics, but in other loftier endeavors.

Academician Oparin, for example, had already explained how organic matter had evolved from inorganic matter through the introduction of electric currents blasted—with a boost from the doctrines of Marx and Engels—into a primary broth of ideologically trustworthy protein molecules. Another academician, Trofim Lysenko, had almost succeeded in subordinating Mother Nature to the wave of his magic wand, and she had already made a firm promise to him to behave as required by the carrot-and-stick method. A third academician, that world-famous woman Olga Lepeshinskaya, was within inches of conquering old age, and a foot from conquering death itself. The atom had already agreed to become peaceful, and rivers were ready to flow wherever needed, instead of where they so desired. Soviet science—medical science, in particular— was in full bloom even without the repeal of that infamous resolution on abortions, while the great leader of all times and peoples, paralyzed left arm stuck in his jacket, used his working right arm to accept an immortal bouquet from the hands of a little blond girl (who subsequently on investigation turned out to be Jewish) and smiled wisely . . .

Still, that bald gynecologist came to the ministry every week to badger the minister with one and the same question: had she sent the project upstairs? No, no, and no! At the present moment there was no way she could take it upstairs. What if they suddenly took it the wrong way? Besides, ideas usually travelled in the opposite direction: not upward from below, but downward from above. For the moment they had forgotten about reorganizing health care, and she was not about to remind them of it. Workhorse stalled the best she could: not a single resolution went any further without first being discussed in the party's Central Committee, and her acute inner sense said to wait. Pavel Alekseevich insisted. After more than a year of fruitless negotiations with the minister, he committed, ultimately, an act thoroughly unethical by bureaucratic and military standards: he penned a missive over the head of the Minister of Health to the Central Committee, addressed to Politburo member N who oversaw social issues. As required by standard protocol, the letter began with the magical formula "Under the leadership of . . . ," but it was written in impeccable old-fashioned language, with precise argumentation and devastating—both literally and figuratively— statistics.

THIS TIME PAVEL ALEKSEEVICH LOCALIZED THE PROBLEM: he submitted not the entire project, but only a fragment related to what he saw as the most pressing issues, those concerning the legalization of abortion.

Several months passed, and Pavel Alekseevich had already stopped waiting for an answer when at 9:00 A.M., during a staff briefing, a phone call came in from the Central Committee offices on Staraya Square. Pavel Alekseevich excused himself and walked out of the staff room with a scowl. Someone had violated the rule: no phone calls during briefings. But this was an invitation to an audience at the Central Committee, an urgent one at that.

Ten minutes later the official car was already pulling away from the clinic. Alongside the driver sat a gloomy Pavel Alekseevich. The call had been unexpected—the most ominous kind. He was particularly unhappy about the urgency. Before leaving he managed to do only two things of primary necessity: he drank down a full glass of diluted spirit alcohol and picked up the briefcase he had long ago prepared for this occasion. Still, on the way to Staraya Square he thought that he had been wrong not to drop by the house to say good-bye to his family . . .

At the security post at entrance number six he was stopped and told to leave his briefcase. Inside the briefcase was a flat-sided anatomy jar with a sealed wax top; the jar was to play a decisive role in the forthcoming conversation. After protracted explanations and objections, the briefcase was allowed to proceed to the meeting together with its owner. Pavel Alekseevich was led down long carpeted corridors. This far from pleasant journey felt like a nightmare. Pavel Alekseevich once again regretted that he had not stopped at the house. The two guards assigned to him—one to his right, the other to his left—stopped at the door.

"This way."

He went in. The Renoir-esque secretary, shimmering pearly pink, asked him to wait. He sat down on an austere wooden bench, spreading his knees far apart and placing between them the old briefcase with which his father had once delivered reports to a government buried long ago. Pavel Alekseevich prepared himself for a long wait, but he was summoned two minutes later. By this time the alcohol had reached all the ganglia of his nervous system and released its serene warmth and calm.

In a long inelegant office behind an enormous desk sat a little man with a puffy face sculpted from dry soap—one of those faces seen ruffling on May Day posters in the spring.

"His kidneys are shot to hell, especially the left one," Pavel Alekseevich automatically noted to himself.

"We familiarized ourselves with the contents of your letter," the important party personage pronounced monarchically.

Both the sound of his voice and the barely evident disdain on his face communicated that the cause had been lost.

"Nothing to lose now then," Pavel Alekseevich thought, and slowly undid the briefcase buckles. The important personage fell silent, creating an icy pause. Pavel Alekseevich extracted the flat jar, slightly covered with condensation, brushed his palm across the front glass, and placed it on the table. The important personage leaned back in his chair in fright, pointing to the specimen with his puffy finger, and asking with disgust: "What have you dragged in here?"

It was a resected uterus, the most powerful and complexly structured muscle of the female body. Bisected lengthways and opened outward, and not yet having lost all its color in the formaldehyde, it resembled a boiled yellow fodder beet. Inside the uterus was a sprouted bulb. The monstrous battle that had taken place between the fetus, enmeshed in dense colorless fibers, and the translucent predatory sack that more resembled some sort of sea creature than an ordinary onion, such as one might use in a salad, was already over.

"I ask that you note: this is a pregnant uterus with a sprouted onion inside. The onion is inserted into the uterus and then begins to sprout. The root system penetrates the fetus, after which it is extracted together with it. When nothing goes wrong, that is. When something goes wrong, they wind up on my operating table or go directly to the Vagankovo cemetery . . . More often the latter . . ."

"You're joking . . ." The party functionary recoiled.

"I could bring you pounds of these onions," Pavel Alekseevich politely answered the paled functionary. "Official statistics—and I cannot conceal this—do not at all correspond to the reality."

The party boss stiffened.

"What gives you the right . . . ? How dare you?"

"I dare, I dare. Whenever I manage to rescue a woman after a criminal abortion, I have to enter 'spontaneous miscarriage' in her chart. Because if I don't, I'll put her in prison. Or her neighbor, who also has small children, while half the children in our country are already fatherless. Believe me, this onion is the cleverest, but not the only, method of aborting a pregnancy. Metal knitting needles, catheters, scissors, intrauterine injections of take your pick: iodine, soda, soapy water . . ."

"Stop, Pavel Alekseevich," implored the by now white bureaucrat, who had remembered how before the war his wife also had resorted to something of the sort. "Enough. What do you want from me?"

"We need a decree legalizing abortion."

"You're out of your mind! Don't you understand that there are the interests of the state, the interests of the nation? We lost millions of men during the war. There's the issue of replenishing the population. What you're saying is childish babble." The official was truly upset.

"Not a bad idea bringing that jar," Pavel Alekseevich thought. The conversation, it seemed, had swung to his advantage. He had begun it correctly, and now he had to end it correctly.

"We lost millions of men, but now we're losing thousands of women. A legal medical abortion does not involve mortal risk." Pavel Alekseevich frowned. "You see, improved general health in and of itself will lead to an increase in the birth rate . . ." Pavel Alekseevich's eyes met the bureaucrat's. "How many orphans are left behind? Orphanages also are fed out of the state budget, by the way . . . This has to be resolved. It will rest on our conscience . . ."

The party boss grimaced, deep folds forming beneath his chin.

"Take that away . . . , the talk happens there." He pointed at the sky.

"I'll leave you this specimen. Maybe it will come in handy."

The official threw up his hands. "You've lost your mind! Take that away immediately . . ."

"Based on incomplete statistics—highly incomplete—twenty thousand a year. In Russia alone." Pavel Alekseevich scowled. "You're responsible for them."

"You're going too far," the party boss bellowed, no longer resembling his May Day portrait at all.

"That's because you're not going far enough," Pavel Alekseevich cut him short.

That was how they parted. The specimen remained on the grandee's desk near the pen-and-ink set embellished with the iron head of a proletarian writer.

THOSE FIRST YEARS AFTER THE WAR WERE VERY SUC-cessful for Pavel Alekseevich: his department, suspended during war, regained its right to full-scale operations. Two of Pavel Alekseevich's best pupils who at the outset of the war had retrained and left obstetrics and gynecology for several years returned. The number of positions in the clinic doubled. New research slots were still not being granted, but even in the worst of times Pavel Alekseevich had managed to conduct research and save up certain ideas that awaited their moment. He was contemplating cures for a certain type of female infertility, had done deep research into female oncology, and had come upon interesting links between pregnancy and the malignant processes that arose in women's bodies during this period. His thinking brought him very close to the idea of treating cancer with the aid of hormonal growth inhibitors. His gift of intravision provided no answers to his questions, but it helped him to see more clearly certain general pictures of the life of the body. His vision of the life of society and state was, on the contrary, completely unclear. It seemed to him, as it did to many in the initial postwar years, that former prewar errors would dissipate on their own and that life would acquire some reason. The project he was developing would insure the accelerated dawning of the bright future, at least in his area of competence.

Despite his successful—as it had seemed to him—visit to the high-ranking boss, his project was not moving forward, the commission still had yet to convene itself, and he continued persistently and methodically pounding the threshold of the now even more guarded Workhorse to make his case that the time had come to modernize existing health care. She politely heard him out (rumors of his escapade had reached her immediately), but insofar as she had not been given any direct orders, she continued to be extremely careful with Pavel Alekseevich. She even thought it advantageous to treat him kindly. Owing precisely to her initiative, at the end of 1947 Pavel Alekseevich was awarded the rank of corresponding member of the Academy of Medical Sciences and, at about the same time, assigned an apartment in a newly constructed building for the medical elite. It was like advance payment for future state achievements. The advance was splendid: a three-room apartment with a walk-in pantry off the kitchen. Vasilisa was the happiest of all. For the first time in her life she had her own room. Seeing the pantry, she burst into tears.

"There it is, my little monastic cell! God grant I die here."

No matter how hard Elena attempted to persuade her to live in the main room, together with Tanechka, Vasilisa refused.

By standards of the time they were rich beyond measure. Only Pavel Alekseevich's generosity was equal to their wealth, thanks to which there was never any spare cash in the house. Twice a month, on payday, after their late dinner, Pavel Alekseevich would announce: "Lenochka, the list!"

Elena would bring him the list of those to whom they sent monetary aid. Since before the war Pavel Alekseevich had sent money to his cousin's daughter, a half-aunt, an old surgical nurse with whom he had begun his career, and his friend from university, Ilya Goldberg, who since 1932 had been either in a camp, or in exile, or in some provincial hole.

Before Pavel Alekseevich's marriage there had been no list as such: he just remembered and sent the money. But now, when his wife compiled the list, adding to her husband's her own distant relations, her girlfriend from school stranded in Tashkent, and several of Vasilisa's old lady friends, Pavel Alekseevich even acquired a certain respect for his big salary. Since the circle of people was rather extensive and could change from month to month, Pavel Alekseevich would look at the list and sometimes inquire about a name.

"Musya? Who's that?" Hearing out the explanation, he would nod.

Then Elena would announce the grand total, after which Vasilisa would scurry into his office and solemnly bring out the old leather briefcase. Pavel Alekseevich opened the briefcase and divvied up the banknotes. The next morning Vasilisa wrapped each amount separately in newspaper, then, for some reason, wrapped all the newspaper bundles into an old towel, then, one hand clutching her change purse and the other Elena's arm, she went to the post office, and only there, at the window, handed the money over to Elena, who sent off the money orders.

Vasilisa moved her lips. Elena thought that she was counting the money. Vasilisa was saying her favorite prayers. She had few words of her own, and she was accustomed to conversing with her God in fragments of the psalms and prayer formulas. When she experienced an urge to add something from herself, she invoked the Immaculate Virgin as "darling, dear, please do this and that, so that everything will be all right ..."

Vasilisa's world was simple: on high sat the Lord God, the Holy Mother of God with all the angels, all the saints, and mother superior among them; then came Pavel Alekseevich; and then they, the family, and everyone else—evil people to one side, good people to the other. In her eyes Pavel Alekseevich was almost a saint: at that hospital of his he helped everyone, good and evil, just like the Lord God. Even mortal sinners who had taken the lives of others. That Pavel Alekseevich's chief concern was to legalize that sin had not yet occurred to her.

7

AFTER TURNING FIVE TANECHKA SPROUTED AND LOST her baby fat: her face acquired angles, and moist blue shadows appeared under her eyes. Her cough would go away, then come back again. They called Isaac Veniaminovich Ketsler, a friend and classmate of Pavel Alekseevich's late father. He was more than eighty; he had worked at the former St. Vladimir's children's hospital since 1904, and after retiring he continued to make the daily trip to his clinic, where he was allowed to keep his office.

Isaac Veniaminovich was renowned for his divine ears. They even looked unusual, enlarged with age, flabby and dry, like an elephant's. A fountain of gray hairs spurted out of his ear canals, while his elongated lobes hung in long wrinkled folds. For all this, Isaac Veniaminovich was hard of hearing until he put his short black tube in his ear and placed the wide end against a child's back. His hearing improved especially if he pressed his old ears directly against the ticklish tiny patient's squirming body.

"We have a primary infection right here," Isaac Veniaminovich said, pointing a finger just below Tanya's clavicle.

"In the upper right lobe. You need to go the Institute of Pediatrics and have Dr. Khotimsky do an X-ray for you . . . On the Solyanka, Solyanka Street . . ."

Pavel Alekseevich nodded. He knew the place well: an old structure near the Ustinsky Bridge built at the beginning of the nineteenth century as a foundling house for abandoned infants, the children of wayward village girls, maids, and seamstresses to Moscow's Babylon who had not managed to keep their transgressions from becoming newborns . . .

Pavel Alekseevich looked at his daughter, undressed to the waist, with his special vision, focusing it several inches just below the surface of her milk-white skin, but he sensed nothing except his own restless concern.

"Unfortunately, it's a widespread phenomenon," Isaac Veniaminovich mumbled, walking his fingers around Tanya's ear and down her neck, stopping below her chin and then entering the depths of her armpits.

"She is lymphatic, lymphatic. Likely, her thyroid is slightly enlarged as well. How is her appetite? Bad, naturally. How could it be good? And vomiting? Does she vomit frequently? *Heraus*? From the stomach?"

"Very frequently." Elena nodded.

"A spoonful too much and she starts to vomit. We never try to talk her into eating more."

"As I thought," the old man responded with satisfaction. "She's spasmatic." He put an ear to her stomach. "Does your tummy hurt? Here?" He poked his finger at a certain spot. "It aches right here, does it?"

"Yes, yes," Tanechka was delighted. "Right there."

"That's what it is," Pavel Alekseevich brightened to himself. "The old man's ears are clairvoyant. Not his eyes, not his fingers . . ."

Strain as he might, he could not see anything this time. The picture he had grown accustomed to seeing—of a person from the inside, the mysterious landscape of organs, the turns of rivers, foggy caves, hollows, and the labyrinth of the intestine—would not open up before him . . .

Not turning off his discouraged vision, he looked at Isaac Veniaminovich. The crimson light of a cancerous tumor enveloped his stomach. The locus was in the pylorus, and a cluster of metastases crept along the mediastinum. Pavel Alekseevich closed his eyes . . .

Tanya got an X-ray. They found something. Blood tests confirmed the diagnosis. The old pediatrician's recommendations turned out to be amazingly old school. The child was prescribed Switzerland, within means, naturally—that is, suburban Moscow Switzerland. Many hours outside, sleep in the fresh air—much to Vasilisa's horror, for as a simple person who had grown up in a village, she did not believe in fresh air. And, of course, good nutrition and cod-liver oil. In a word, Thomas Mann's *Magic Mountain*, although Isaac Veniaminovich had never heard of it. And no medicines like that newfangled PAS: why strain the liver or overload the kidneys?

Pavel Alekseevich nodded, and nodded, and then asked pointedly whether the old pediatrician wanted to have his own stomach examined.

"My dear colleague, at my age all natural processes have slowed down to the point that I have a good chance of dying of pneumonia or heart failure."

"He knows everything. He's right," Pavel Alekseevich agreed in his heart.

THEY RENTED A BIG WINTRIFIED DACHA NEAR ZVENI-gorod that belonged to a career admiral banished for the minor infraction of grand larceny to an honorable exile as chief military attaché at the embassy in Canada. That same autumn the Academy of Sciences was distributing dachas, and Pavel Alekseevich was invited to submit an application. For some reason he refused. He could not have explained to himself why, but he had an inkling: they were offering him an awful lot these days. Would it later cost him the skin off his back? He did not even tell Elena about the offer of a dacha.

Tanya and Vasilisa were settled at the rented house. No matter how hard Pavel Alekseevich attempted to persuade Elena to quit that worthless job of hers and remain at the dacha, she refused flat out. She did not want to quit her job or leave Pavel Alekseevich by himself in the city all week.

The dacha was huge, two-storied, with pseudo-Gothic china cupboards and sideboards filled with porcelain and useless knickknacks. A piano stood in each of the two main rooms, upstairs and downstairs, among a herd of rock-hard wooden armchairs and chairs with carved backs. The piano upstairs was a black concert grand; the one down-stairs—an upright with a cracked soundboard, made of rosewood with bronze detail. It could not be tuned, but they figured that out only later, after Pavel Alekseevich and the watchman had carried it into one of the two rooms they would live in—for Tanya. A teacher from Zvenigorod was hired, and she came to the house three times a week.

Within a few weeks, on Sunday evenings, after heating the house toasty warm, Pavel Alekseevich and Elena would sit down in the carved German chairs that smelled of theft, as did everything else in the house, and Tanya played them bashful tunes learned that week . . .

Thus passed two years. Tanya remembered the winters much better than the summers. Perhaps because winter in Russia is twice as long as summer. She would later recollect her childhood as a time of whiteness, not illness: morning portions of sweet goat's milk in a white porcelain mug; outside the window thick, wavy snowdrifts along the ground and small round pillows of snow festively embellishing the fir-tree branches above; the white gleam of the keys of the piano she would sit down to after breakfast while Vasilisa washed the dishes. Later Vasilisa would give her a wooden shovel and order her to clear paths. Tanya moved snow around with her shovel until Vasilisa would offer her a new task—feeding the birds.

The lot surrounding the house was enormous, and Pavel Aleksee-vich had set up four feeders, and Tanya watched for hours on end as red-breasted bullfinches and yellow-cheeked titmice fed from the little wooden table under the slanting canopy. Sometimes she and Vasilisa, each with a covered canister—one small, the other large—walked to a spring about a third of a mile away to gather tasty water. A spring flowed nearer the house, at the edge of the enormous lot, but sometimes it got buried during snowstorms and the water could not break through to the surface. Every day they went to the village for goat's milk, visiting their old woman friend, her goat, and her dog that lived in the front entrance-way with her black puppies.

Tanya was constantly busy. She did not know the difference between work and fun. There was nothing forced in her life. Even cod-liver oil, which she had not liked before, became tolerable after Vasilisa treated the black puppies to pieces of bread sprinkled with cod-liver oil and they snatched them up as if they were undreamed of delicacies.

Living her happy life in the countryside, Tanya missed first grade. She completed the first-grade program at home. She could read well and had mastered counting. Penmanship was more difficult. Tanya would get upset because her letters were not as beautiful as those in the practice books. Her recuperation was complete. Isaac Veniaminovich, who could have testified to the fact, was no longer among the living.

TOWARD AUTUMN TANYA WAS BROUGHT BACK TO THE Moscow apartment and started school, going straight into the second grade. Preparations for her first day at school were made with great labor and care. They had a school uniform sewn for her—a brown dress with a stand-up collar, attachable white collars and cuffs for dress occasions, black sleeve protectors, two black aprons, and a white apron with pleated ruffles on the shoulders, also for special occasions.

"Just like an angel." Vasilisa sighed devoutly.

And in her childlike soul she began to look up to Tanya. She herself had never attended school, and that uniform had not been pieced together from some old dress, but cut from a whole piece of new wool cloth, which seemed to her a sign of particular distinction. She even thought to herself: "Beautiful enough to bury . . ." She did not mean anything bad.

They also bought her a stack of light-bluish notebooks with porous pink blotting paper inside, an aromatic wooden pencil box with precious contents: new pencils, erasers, pens . . . They even ordered new high shoes for Tanya at a special shoe atelier that no one in the family had ever been to.

Tanya had been dreaming about school for a long time: she had been promised that at school she would find all the girlfriends she so missed having during her happy tubercular childhood in Zvenigorod.

On the first of September, Elena brought her daughter to school. She found the teacher and left Tanya in the classroom, alone and confused, with a heavy schoolbag and a thick-stemmed bouquet of plump asters. There turned out to be too many girls to be friends with. They were noisy, but one could deal with that. What was most unpleasant was that they all touched Tanya, her braids, the ruffle of her apron. One even managed to grab her by her white sock . . .

35

The classroom turned out to be exactly as Tanya had pictured it. The teacher pointed to her seat next to a fat little girl with braids wound in little donuts around her ears. In the middle of the lesson Tanya's neighbor bumped her elbow, and Tanya made a huge blot on the first page of her notebook. She froze. This had happened to her before when she filled out her lonely writing books in Zvenigorod, but now she was horrified. She had not yet recovered from her shock when her deskmate leaned over and pinched her painfully on the leg. That was when Tanya understood that the bump on the elbow had been on purpose, and she started to cry. The teacher walked up to her and asked what the matter was.

"May I go home?" Tanya whispered.

"You may go home after the fourth period," the teacher said firmly.

For the first time in her life Tanya had bumped up against someone else's will, against force in its mildest form. Until that moment the wishes of those around her had fortuitously coincided with her own; it had never occurred to her that life could be any other way . . . It turned out that's what adult life was—submitting to someone else's will . . . From that point on, it turned out, in order to be happy as before, you had to make sure that you yourself wanted exactly what adults expected of you . . . She, of course, did not think that; the idea, rather, had come upon her from above and begun to press itself on her . . .

Until the end of the fourth period she sat at her desk as if in a stupor, not getting up even for breaks. The girls whom she had expected to be her friends turned out to be malicious monkeys: they skipped round her, pulled her braids, pointed their fingers at her, and laughed meanly. Tanya tried to understand why they disliked her and could not imagine that they were just expressing their interest in her. She could not fathom that a few months later these same little girls would fight tooth and nail for the privilege of being her partner in line, doing class duty, or just walking down the corridor with her.

Tanya, as it turned out, possessed a rare quality difficult to define: no matter what she did—tied a bow, wrapped a notebook, shook drops of water from her hands with that distinctive upward sweeping gesture of hers, wrinkled her nose in a smile—each of her movements was immediately noticed and attracted the girls' attention, and she became a model for emulation. Even the way she chewed on the fluffy end of her braid

36

when she was lost in thought was imitated by all of the girls who had braids . . .

Despite the girls' adulation, Tanya never took a liking to school. Surrounded by dozens of little girls competing for her attention and friendship, she felt more alone than she had been in Zvenigorod. The only person who felt more left out was Toma Polosukhina, a downtrodden D-student with a raspberry ring of peeling dry skin around her mouth who sat in the last row. A withdrawn, slouching little girl no one wanted to sit with . . .

Toma did not belong to the ranks of Tanya's admirers: interstellar distances lay between them . . .

8

ELENA HAD CHOSEN A MODEST, VERY MODEST, PROFESsion. But she never regretted the choice. She liked everything about her work: the special illuminated desk, the drafting board, and the various sorts of paper with which she worked: cloudy, icelike tracing paper, fragile vellum, and slippery gray-blue blueprint paper. She liked both the smell of ink and the scrape of pencils. Even insignificant but necessary and skill-intensive tasks like sharpening pencils . . .

All these basic things she had come to understand while still an apprentice. Then, having worked a year or two, she fell in love with the more essential, very calming aspect of the draftsman's wonderful trade: in displaying itself, every object turned about in three views, which was entirely sufficient for it to be described in its totality, leaving no secrets and no hidden spaces inside. Everything as it was . . .

At times it seemed to Elena that all phenomena, like all objects, could be described from three vantages: front, side, and top. Not just a part in a tank motor, but the wind, and stomach pain, and any uttered word.

Her teacher had been her first husband, Anton Ivanovich Flotov, a great master—of the art, one might say—of technical drawing. They met in an obscure, insignificant place where Elena was a student and he an instructor of drafting. He appeared old, well-kempt, and dull, although he was only twenty-nine. She had just turned seventeen and had recently escaped the Moscow region agricultural commune—an amazing and extremely strange place—where she had spent her childhood. This community was Tolstoyan and directed by her father, Georgy Ivanovich Miakotin.

This girl who had grown up in special, entirely unique circumstances—taught to read with Tolstoy's children's books, milking cows while still a child, working (not playing at working) in the fields and in the communal kitchen, silent witness to dinner-table discussions of Vivekananda and Karl Marx and of folk and folk-liberation songs sung in monophonic style—felt lonely in Moscow, surrounded by an alien and dangerous world. Her grandmother Evgenia Fedorovna was the only person Elena was not afraid of.

More than love, what united Elena with Anton Ivanovich, her future husband, was an underlying sense of irrational guilt for "standing apart" from, "not blending in" with, the merry and amicable company of innocent people. Both of them sensed their social inadequacy but made no attempt to disguise it with political activism, breast-beating, or damning their unfortunate parents. They belonged to another, meek breed of human beings who preferred to retreat unobtrusively to life's sidelines, into the bushes, under a stone, into the shadows, not to be noticed.

Anton Ivanovich descended from a family of architects and builders—some of whom had emigrated, some of whom had been exterminated—and the entirety of his inheritance was his profession as a draftsman. Because of the revolution he did not manage to receive the German engineering training given to boys in their family. He was a first-class draftsman, worked at a large plant as a technical designer, and conducted courses in draftsmanship at the plant's school for workers.

Cautious and attentive, Anton Ivanovich studied Elena for a year before approaching her, then met with her on Sundays for another year, and married her only in the third year of their acquaintance—not out of ardent love, but with serious intent and after careful consideration, as with everything he did.

Elena's parents did not attend the wedding: her father was busy planting and would not allow her mother to go. Georgy Ivanovich invited his daughter and son-in-law to join them in Altai. Things at the commune were not bad, and while there was a lot of friction with the authorities, the members of the commune could not have imagined that in a year or so they would all be arrested, put in prisons and camps, and sent to places where you couldn't break the soil with a pickax.

Anton and Elena led a peaceful, quiet existence in Elena's grandmother's apartment. Their salaries sufficed for a modest life, and Elena had never known any other. In any case, after her childhood in the commune, life in Moscow seemed free and easy. The most interesting part of it was, perhaps, mechanical drawing.

Elena's bosses praised her as a diligent and capable young woman. It was written in her papers that she was from a commune—which looked good only because of a misunderstanding: the fact that it was a Tolstoyan commune was not mentioned; for this reason it was even suggested to Elena that she continue her studies at the plant's workers' school, but she had no desire to do so. She was happy just to sit at her drawing table, and even Anton Ivanovich was surprised by her eagerness to work.

Once she dreamed that Anton Ivanovich had spoken some ordinary phrase to her and that she could see the phrase not in the usual way, frontally, but from the side, in profile: like a thin fish face, wavy and drawn-out towards the top in a pointed triangle. What a pity, though, that on waking she could not remember the phrase. But the dream itself remained and did not fade. Afterward she surmised that every phrase must have its own geometry and that one need only concentrate in order to see it.

There is something draftable to words, she reflected. There is "construable space" in everything that exists; it's simply impossible to express.

She tried to talk to Anton Ivanovich about this, but he just shook his head.

"What fantasies you have, Elena . . ."

These dreams, however, occasionally recurred. They were perfectly senseless, containing nothing that could be retold, yet afterward she was always left with the vaguely pleasant sense of something new.

And now, when so many years had passed and Anton Ivanovich was no longer on this earth and Elena had even hidden away his photographs—so that her growing daughter would not accidentally discover that Pavel Alekseevich was not her natural father but her stepfather—every time she would sit down at her work table, she would open the antique German case of drawing instruments, a Flotov heirloom, and let out a sigh for the deceased Anton Ivanovich. She never forgot her guilt before him. And from time to time she still had those mechanical drawing dreams—why, what did they mean . . . ?

PAVEL ALEKSEEVICH DID NOT LIKE ELENA'S JOB: WHAT was the point of tiresome hours sitting at the design office? He was perplexed. Elena would defend herself.

"It's a good job. It makes sense to me."

"What's so good about it?" Pavel Alekseevich asked with sincere surprise.

"I can't explain it to you. It's beautiful."

"Whatever," Pavel Alekseevich granted craftily. "It's just very, very mindless," he teased.

"Oh, Pasha, what are you saying?" Elena took offense. "There's nothing mindless about it. Sometimes it's even very complex."

Pavel Alekseevich awaited this moment when her usually meek expression would change. She shook her head lightly, the fluffy curls at her temples that always resisted being pulled back into a bun fluttered, and her lips tightened into wrinkles at their corners.

"I mean that it's all so mechanical, no mystery." He raised a forefinger in front of her. "There is more mystery in a single human finger than in all of your drawings."

She gathered his finger in her hand.

"Perhaps there's mystery in your finger, but not in anyone else's. Perhaps there isn't any mystery in a drawing, but there is truth. The most indispensable truth. Maybe not the entire truth, just a part. One-tenth, or one one-thousandth. I know that everything has other content, not just the draftable . . . I can't explain," she said and put down his hand.

"It's been said before you." Pavel Alekseevich chuckled. "Plato said it. It's called *eidos*. The idea of the thing. Its divine content. A divine template that gives form to all worldly things . . ."

"That's not for me. That's too intellectual." Elena waved him off.

But she did not forget Pavel Alekseevich's words. That was it, philosophy. They used to talk about similar things at the commune, but at the time she had been too little for such conversations and fell asleep during them.

Pavel Alekseevich looked at her with a tender pride. Such a wife he had: soft-spoken, prone to silence, talked only when she had to, but if you could get her to say what she thought, her ideas were intelligent and subtle, her understanding profound . . .

Elena frequently had the urge to tell her husband her ideas about the "draftableness" of the world, about the dreams she had from time to time with technical drawings of all sorts of things—words, illnesses, even music. But no, no, it was impossible to describe.

Two seers of the hidden lived side by side. For him all living matter was transparent; she perceived the transparency of some other, immaterial world. But both of them hid from the other, not for lack of trust, but out of pudicity and the protective interdiction placed on all secret knowledge, regardless of how acquired.

9

THE RESEARCH TOPICS THAT INTERESTED PAVEL ALEK-seevich had always been connected to concrete medical issues, whether it be the fight against early miscarriages, treatments for infertility, or new surgical techniques for resecting the uterus or performing Cesarean sections in cases of incorrect presentation of the fetus.

The phrase "bourgeois science," which appeared in the newspapers with increasing frequency, made him smirk with disgust. From his point of view, the field of science to which he had given so many years of his life had no class subtext.

Irreproachably honest in the everyday sense of the word, Pavel Alekseevich had lived his entire professional life under the Soviets and long ago had grown accustomed to using formulaic language in his articles and monographs, opening sentences with fixed turns of phrase like "in scientific circles of the Stalin era . . ." or "owing to the untiring concern of the party, the government, and Comrade Stalin personally . . ." He knew how to express his own practical observations within the limitations of this cant. For him it was the formula for politeness in the present era, like "Your Grace" in the past, and had no bearing on the content of his work.

At the beginning of 1949 the campaign against cosmopolitanism began, and with the very first newspaper publication Pavel Alekseevich woke up. This was a new assault against common sense, and the attack on genetics and eugenics at last year's session at VASKhNIL no longer seemed to him just an ominous coincidence. As a member of the academy and director of an institute, Pavel Alekseevich found himself now at a level of service that required assurances of loyalty. He was supposed to speak out publicly and at least verbally demonstrate his support for the new campaign. The upper echelons were hinting insistently that now was the time. They also made highly suggestive reference to his project, which had been on hold for several years now . . .

A public speech of this sort was out of the question. For Pavel Alekseevich it would mean stripping himself of his self-respect, overstepping the bounds of ordinary, albeit bourgeois, decency.

For all his relatively free thinking Pavel Alekseevich had, after all, received a traditional education that copied the German model; his thought processes had been formed to fit a German mold. Historically, humanistic thought in Russia had been influenced principally by the French, but in the fields of science and technology German influence had dominated since the time of Peter the Great. The very concept of universalism, in the Latin sense of the word, appealed to Pavel Alekseevich, so he saw no global evil in "cosmopolitanism" per se.

On the eve of the general assembly of the Academy of Sciences, on one of the last Sundays of spring, he set out for Malakhovka to see his friend Ilya Iosifovich Goldberg, a physician and geneticist, to seek his advice. A less suitable adviser would have been hard to find.

A JEWISH DON QUIXOTE WHO ALWAYS MANAGED TO GET sentenced for something other than what he was guilty of just before the campaign against what he was guilty of began, Goldberg by this time had managed to sit out two insignificant (by standards of the time) prison terms and was gearing up for his third. Between terms he got several unusual (for him) lucky breaks when he by chance happened not to be in the right place at the right time, and disaster passed him by.

He had done his first stint in 1932 for a presentation he had made three years prior, in 1929, at an in-house seminar, all that remained of the long-defunct Society of Free Philosophers. The subject of his presentation had nothing to do with genetics. Goldberg, who made a hobby of rummaging through Western journals, had dug out of *Nature* or *Science* an article by Albert Einstein on the relationship between space and time. The article's mathematical austerity appealed to him enormously—before that he had never encountered works in which philosophical concepts were interpreted by mathematicians—and he did a presentation on it.

The affair was small change, and he got only three years. How many would he have got if they had had any inkling of what he was working on in those days—human population genetics?

After getting out, he worked for a while at the Medical Biological Institute, where he succeeded in publishing several articles on population genetics and gene drift. This time it was his unbearable personality that helped him avoid major unpleasantness: just before the institute was shut down he got into a verbal brawl with one of its leading researchers over, it goes without saying, some deeply fundamental scientific issues. Their quarrel was so heated that it ended in a fistfight. Witnesses to the incident said that a more comical sight than their fisticuffs would have been hard to imagine. In the heat of this scientific polemic Ilya Iosifovich knocked out his opponent's tooth, and the latter—insulted and injured—took him to court. As a result, Goldberg got one year for petty hooliganism.

Two weeks later the director of the institute, Solomon Levit, a foremost specialist in genetics, and several leading members of the institute were arrested, among them Goldberg's sparring partner with the knocked-out tooth. Both Levit and Goldberg's enemy were shot in 1937, while Goldberg—one more example of the ridiculous absurdity of Soviet life!—was released exactly one year later . . . Soviet power had a soft spot for hooliganism . . .

In the same lucky way Ilya Iosifovich dodged his next inevitable arrest. Released from prison, he left for Central Asia, where he took up an entirely new field of study—genetics and cotton selection. Although the witch hunt in the sciences was already in full swing—genetics laboratories had been closed down and many scientists arrested, but it was still unknown how many of them were shot—cotton production stood apart, because cotton was raw material for the war industry. The laboratory Ilya joined turned out to be semiclassified, and either out of negligence or error or as a result of the administration's dimwittedness, Ilya went unscathed … During this short, relatively calm period of his life, Ilya succeeded in marrying his lab assistant, pretty Valya Popkova, and in 1939—through an ironic joke of the heavens!—they gave birth to identical twins, the classic object of genetic research, to whom Ilya gave the significant names Vitaly and Gennady.

The family resided several years in the secure zone of the classified laboratory, until the war began. Then, the impassioned Goldberg—who had graduated from medical school in the early 1920s together with Pavel Alekseevich but unlike his friend had never practiced—registered for accelerated retraining and wound up in a military hospital as the head of a clinical laboratory. As a military doctor he made it through the whole war, from start to finish, without a scratch and was even awarded the Red Star (no trifle) for evacuating a medical transport carrying the wounded from a town captured by the Germans. What was most comical, but typical for Goldberg, was that owing to an altercation with the head of the hospital, he had loaded the laboratory inventory last, when the city was already captured, which he did not know, and the only wounded he evacuated was a staff colonel for whom a car had been ordered but which had not arrived because the road was already cut off.

When Goldberg finished loading, he saw a column of German tanks and, waiting till twilight, got behind the wheel of the covered truck with the inventory and the colonel and drove out of the town unobstructed, demonstrating not his customary garrulous heroism, but, on the contrary, exceptional composure totally out of character for frenzied, hotheaded Ilya …

Through the mercy of fate he was not arrested even when, at the very end of the war, he wrote an enraged letter to a member of the Supreme High Command about marauding and mass rapes of German women— behavior unbefitting Soviet soldiers, officers even, who bore the lofty title of soldier-liberators … On learning about the letter from its ingenuous, fuming author himself, the head of the hospital had a captain acquaintance in the SMERSH fish the letter from the mail stream and, once he had it in hand, destroy it immediately, after which he processed Goldberg for expedited demobilization and ordered him to go wherever he damn well pleased, preferably as far away as possible. Conscientious Goldberg, knowing nothing of his commander's noble maneuver, sent an inquiry to the Supreme High Command demanding an answer to the expropriated letter.

Goldberg, however, did not intend to bury himself in some backwater. He went to Moscow, extricated his family from Fergana, and began looking for a job in his area of specialization. After a while he discovered that the field of science that so fascinated him was almost nonexistent. He knocked about for a while without a job, then found shelter under the wing of a great woman, Margarita Ivanovna Rudomino, who hired the unemployed geneticist as senior bibliographer at the Library of Foreign Literature, where he spent almost three years among reference books and card catalogues in German, English, Polish, Lithuanian, and Latin, the last language having been acquired by him at the Peter-Paul Schule, the Lutheran school he had graduated from. Miraculously the school survived in Moscow until the middle of the 1920s.

Ilya Iosifovich's tenure at the library's staff offices on Razin Street, five minutes from the Kremlin, in the bowels of a collection almost untouched by censorship, modified somewhat his research aspirations. He reread tons of books on history: what now interested him was genius as a phenomenon and its inheritability. Genius itself, however, lent itself poorly to definition or formularization, while genetics was a strict science that studied qualitative phenomena, not quantitative. Where along the spectrum did one draw the line between good abilities, brilliant abilities, and genius? Goldberg scoured the encyclopedias of all epochs and nations and, as a starting point, compiled a verifiable list of geniuses based on the frequency with which they appeared in encyclopedias. Applying some clever statistical formula, he demonstrated the validity of this method of selection. Next, he worked on his selectees, which totaled about one hundred per century. He had cast his nets wide enough to encompass the Golden Age of Athens, the Italian Renaissance, and the period of the nobility in Russian literature.

The next stage of his work involved finding some sort of characteristic or marker connected with genius. He was absolutely confident that such markers existed, and the question he faced was how to find them. He searched for something like farsightedness in combination with a birthmark on the right shoulder, or left-handedness combined with diabetes ... He painstakingly combed the biographies of great people, searching meticulously for mention of the diseases that had afflicted geniuses, their parents; their physical features, defects, and deviations ...

He could have finished this unusually crackpot book ten years earlier if he had not, of his own bizarre will, lashed out in an unintelligible roar against Comrade Stalin's favorite, Trofim Denisovich Lysenko, at the VASKhNIL assembly. After growling out his accusations—replete with serviceman obscenities he never used before or after—he was carted straight from the historic assembly to Kashchenko Psychiatric Hospital ... It was there, his geniuses temporarily left to their own devices, that he wrote his denunciation—with detailed justifications, clear and precise argumentation, and absolutely devastating criticism of Academician Lysenko—to be sent to the science division of the Central Committee with a separate copy for Comrade Stalin personally ...

Once again, luck was with him: the director of the ward they had delivered him to by ambulance, an old psychiatrist named Shubnikov, took an interest in and sympathized with this unlikely hero, issued him the life-saving diagnosis of "schizophrenic," and released him with group III disability status.

Several months had already passed since Ilya Iosifovich had sent his three-hundred-page masterpiece to its addressees in the upper echelons; he had returned to his geniuses and their hereditary diseases and was awaiting an answer to his missive. Or arrest. This was the comrade that Pavel Alekseevich had chosen to advise him on "the current situation."

GOLDBERG AND HIS FAMILY LIVED IN A TWO-STORY wooden barracks-like structure. At one time it had been a factory dormitory, then the factory was closed, the workers were evicted, and the building sold as apartments. One of the apartments had been purchased by Goldberg after he returned from the front. In fact, Pavel Alekseevich had bought it. Ilya Iosifovich, who was incredibly punctilious when it came to money, made an exception for his friend, permitting him this philanthropic act, because unlike everyone else, Pavel Alekseevich had to understand that helping him, Ilya, he was helping all humankind—Goldberg attributed enormous significance to his research. It was his profound belief that science was charged with saving the world.

"The great materialist idealist," Pavel Alekseevich teased him in the rare hours of their peaceful conversations. But those hours of peace were sufficiently rare. Ilya Iosifovich did not tolerate objections and defended his most crackpot ideas with great passion, quickly overstepping the bounds of proper scientific argument. He was capable of infuriating even Pavel Alekseevich, and their meetings usually ended in quarrels, shouting, and door-slamming. Ilya Iosifovich reproached Pavel Alekseevich for knuckling under, while the latter attempted to justify himself: he was trying to save not the world, but just a few dozen, at best, hundred, pregnant broads and their spawn, which, in his opinion, was worth the effort.

For Ilya Iosifovich this was not enough: his ideas were so lofty they squeaked, and he prophesied that with the help of sound genetic theory the world order could be restructured entirely. In twenty years genes could be used as the building blocks for a new world of plants and animals with their beneficial qualities multiplied, and man himself could be redesigned by introducing new genes and endowing him with new qualities.

"What qualities?" Pavel Alekseevich inquired stiffly.

"You name it!" Ilya Iosifovich flung out his arms, and the thin vestiges of hair on his head stood on end. "We will learn to isolate from the genome individual genes responsible for genius, which will make it possible to create mathematicians, musicians, and artists in quantities unknown even during the Renaissance!"

"Hold on," Pavel Alekseevich stopped him. "That's called eugenics. We don't need large quantities of geniuses. They'll just wind up arrested and shot."

"Pasha, we're living the Inquisition right now. This has to pass, just like the Spanish Inquisition passed. The future belongs to us, to science. There is no other force capable of saving the world!" His long thin hands thrashed the air, and his bulging gray eyes shone with a sickly fire. With his yellowed hawkish nose, the enormous Adam's apple on his wrinkled neck, and his slouched, bony figure he was going to save the world!

Pavel Alekseevich shook his head, blinked, and tried to hold his tongue: he's mad, a holy madman! All that's missing is the helmet of Mambrino . . .

THIS TIME THERE WAS NO NEED FOR A LONG DISCUSSION. Ilya was gloomy. After the first bottle of vodka he fell into a monologue.

"We're losing time. We're losing our advantage! In the last few years several works of paramount importance have been published in the United States. Alfred Sturtevant is on the path to explaining the emergence of new genes! Where is Koltsov? Chetverikov? Zavadovsky? Vavilov! The genius Lev Ferri? Don't you understand that this is sabotage by enemies from within? The entire Lysenko campaign is sabotage! This campaign against cosmopolitanism is playing into the hands of imperialism, Pasha! It's their clever way of destroying Soviet science . . . Science should serve mankind, but the imperialists would have it serve bare profit, the golden calf . . ."

His voice first rumbled, then lowered, as if it had dried up. Moisture filled his light, red-vein-streaked eyes, then trickled from under his glasses . . .

This silly pathos made Pavel Alekseevich feel terribly awkward, and he twirled his empty glass, unable to get a word in edgewise. Finally, when Ilya Iosifovich fell silent for a moment as he rummaged in his pockets for a handkerchief, Pavel quietly spoke.

"Ilyusha, I think you're exaggerating, as always. Cosmopolitanism doesn't interest them. I think it's all a lot simpler: our Master simply wants to wring the Jews' necks."

Valya—once a skinny girl, then a fat matron, now having lost a lot of weight again—from time to time poked her curly head into her husband's narrow little study, which resembled a prison cell, where the friendly conversation was taking place, and whispered imploringly, "Ilyusha, the children . . . ," or "Ilyusha, the neighbors . . . ," or simply "I'm begging you: keep it down . . ." They drank one more bottle and, as always, had a complete falling-out before parting. Ilya Iosifovich stood one hundred percent for global justice, beginning with science, and was ready to lay down his life for it. Pavel Alekseevich did not believe one iota in justice; what interested him were trifles—pregnant dishwashers and the vile operations about which Cicero had once addressed the Senate. Ilya Iosifovich brought up that last point. Pavel Alekseevich perked up—he had always valued his friend's inexhaustible erudition.

"And what did Cicero say?"

"That," Ilya Iosifovich shouted, "these women should be executed, because they were stealing soldiers from the state! He was right a thousand times over!"

At this point Pavel Alekseevich paled and got up, pulling on his coat angrily.

"You've got a good head on your shoulders, Ilya. Too bad it wound up on a fool. So, in your opinion, women are supposed to give birth so that the bastards can send them into the meat grinder?"

He slammed the door on his way out. "Devil take him, the fool!" But he remembered about Cicero, even though he was pretty well sloshed.

THE NEXT DAY THEY SEARCHED GOLDBERG'S APARTMENT and arrested him. His denunciation of Lysenko had reached its destination.

Pavel Alekseevich learned of the arrest only a week later, when Valya, after much hesitation, decided to call him.

THAT LAST EVENING IN MALAKHOVKA A DRUNKEN PAVEL Alekseevich searched a long time for the train station, arrived home after midnight, and barely remembered what had happened. The next morning he felt so miserable that he diluted a half-glass of spirit alcohol and chased the hair of the dog. That brought some relief; in fact, it gave rise to a certain—for him atypical—devil-may-care attitude, like that of the sun, uninformed of the bloodthirsty nonsense of newspaper articles and of the people who wrote and read them.

In the entranceway, Elena, unnerved by the late-night return of her drunk husband and not having slept half the night, was pulling felt boots over her old shoes, getting ready to leave for work. Pavel Alekseevich, dressed in the military long johns he had worn since the war, came out into the corridor, flung open his arms, and shouted.

"My little girl! Let's go to the stables! To see the horses!"

Realizing that her husband was drunk, Elena was at a loss. She had never seen him in such dissolute condition, in the morning no less.

"Pashenka, what's with you?"

Tanya, who had already put on her school uniform and brushed her hair, squealed happily, "Hurrah for Daddy!"

And flung herself on his arm. He picked her up.

"We're playing hooky today!" he winked at his daughter.

"Call work, Lenochka, and tell them you're not coming in today. That you're sick. Leave without pay. Whatever!"

Something out of the ordinary was going on, something new. He was so reliable, there was never an ounce of doubt about his constant and invariable probity, and it was a joyous pleasure to comply with his wishes . . . With a perplexed smile Elena objected weakly.

"What stable . . . ? What horses . . . ? That's an unauthorized leave . . ." But she was already reaching for the telephone to call a colleague and warn that she was not coming to work today . . .

Pavel Alekseevich pulled off her gray goat-fur coat and explained, "We're going to the Institute of Horse Breeding. Prokudin has been calling me for ages to come and look at the horses. Let's go! Let's go! Tanya, put on your ski suit!"

"Really, Daddy?" Tanya still could not believe it. Vasilisa, on hearing the tumult in the corridor, peeked out of the kitchen doorway.

"Gavrilovna! Fried eggs! King-style!" Pavel Alekseevich ordered in a loud cheerful voice. Thoroughly perplexed, she went to carry out orders. King-style fried eggs were in fact country-style fried eggs, with fried onion and potatoes, which he ate only on Sundays; on weekdays, as in the past, he went without breakfast . . .

"And king-style for me too," Tanya piped in, thrilled by the new adventure.

They sat down and ate breakfast Sunday-style even though it was just an ordinary Monday. Pavel Alekseevich also drank a shot of vodka, and Elena looked at him in bewilderment: this had never happened before, drinking in the morning . . .

Something disturbing loomed in this morning adventure, she sensed, and following her intuition, without giving it a second thought, she asked: "Pash, you've got that meeting at the Academy today . . . You're obligated to . . ."

"I'm not obligated to!" Pavel Alekseevich bellowed. "I'm not obligated to anyone! Let them all get . . . !"

The vulgarism that had dropped from his large lips was forceful and weighty, like everything about him. The cloth covering the aluminum buttons of his shirt was washed out, exposing dull metal; gray chest hair like lamb's wool issued from his open collar, and the enlarged veins on his bull neck darkened . . .

Elena embraced his neck.

"Calm down, darling . . ."

And he calmed down, pressing her to his chest.

"Forgive me."

When they were all warmly dressed and already standing in the doorway with a sled for Tanya, Pavel Alekseevich issued instructions to Vasilisa Gavrilovna.

"If they call, say he's gone on a drinking binge."

She looked at him with an uncomprehending eye.

"Say it just like that: 'He's gone off on a binge.'"

Vasilisa was clueless, but fulfilled her assignment to the letter.

The impromptu tactic was ingenious. Pavel Alekseevich was not the only one who affected illness that day. But he was the only one who got away with it. He did not go to his clinic for two weeks and did not appear at the Academy for four months, not until he had established his reputation as a habitual binge drinker.

Whereas before he had drunk readily only at dissertation defense parties, family celebrations, or funeral banquets, now he began to drink on yet another occasion: every time passions started to run high and he was required to issue assurances, or sign something, or make a public address. He would conscientiously drink himself under the table, and Elena, who had figured out the real cause of his sudden alcoholism, would call the Presidium herself and in a sweet little voice inform them that Pavel Alekseevich could not attend because he had another one of his attacks, you understand . . .

At particularly vile times Pavel Alekseevich stayed at home, drank a glass of vodka in the morning, played with Tanya, taught Vasilisa how to make meat dumplings, or just slouched around the apartment, where he constantly found the little notes his wife Elena wrote to herself. Touching little notes that began with one and the same words, "don't forget . . . ," followed by: "buy apples," "take linen to the laundry," "take your purse to the repair shop . . ." What was funny was that there were so many of these notes, all of them with one and the same list: apples, laundry, repair shop . . .

He knew that Elena was not good at household chores, and her efforts not to forget anything, to get everything done on time, touched Pavel Alekseevich. His wife's virtues delighted him and her short-comings endeared her to him. That's what's called marriage. Their marriage was happy both night and day, and their mutual understanding seemed especially full because, being reserved and silent by nature as well as by upbringing, neither of them required the kinds of verbal confirmations that get worn out so quickly by people who like to talk.

Pavel Alekseevich's drinking binges, despite their initially diplomatic character, were hardly staged. But Elena, although worried about the health of her not-so-young husband, made no attempt to put an end to them. Women's intuition, not reason, as always, guided her. She knew nothing about the nature of alcoholism, especially Russian alcoholism, when the soul, finding no other outlet, finds easy and available consolation without lies or shame.

When binges occurred, Elena sometimes took vacation time, and she and Pavel Alekseevich would head out to the dacha. One of these short holidays occurred in the autumn, two others in the winter. There were no better days in her life than these drunken holidays when he cast off all of his numerous cares and belonged entirely to her. It was the fever of youth that they had both missed, the uncomplicated revelations of seeming bottomlessness, where everything climaxed—about this Pavel Alekseevich longed to forget, and sometimes he managed to—with a few milligrams of a secret and measured dose of a mysterious substance inside the tunica albuginea . . . And when he no longer had the strength to extend his arm for a glass of water, everything at the bottom went cold: all of it was in vain, in vain, for there remained that insurmountable boundary they were unable to cross together . . . The only medicine was to try again and again . . .

By his third binge Elena knew that the ensuing period of sobriety would be an ordeal for her. She both feared and deep in her heart awaited the morning when Pavel Alekseevich, having drunk his first liberating glass, would say to her:

"Get your things, dear, we're going to the countryside . . ."

AT THE ACADEMY IN THE MEANTIME THEY HAD STOPPED bothering him. The reputation of a drunkard was a peculiar sort of reprieve. No single other vice elicits nearly as much compassion in our country as alcoholism. Everybody drinks: tsars, archbishops, academicians, even trained parrots . . .

10

IN THE THIRD WEEK OF MAY A PREMATURE HEAT WAVE set in, making everyone a little bit sick. A few more days remained until the end of classes, but the curriculum had been covered in its entirety, and grades, both quarterly and final, had been given. It was already known who the honor students were and who would have to repeat a grade. The girls and the teachers at the school languished from the emptiness of time and its sluggishness.

Galina Ivanovna, an elderly schoolteacher, a worn-out nag with a flabby croup, came to class in a new summer dress, dirty beige with broken black lines that lost each other, then found each other, and emitted little sprouts.

Galina Ivanovna had worked with this group of girls for four years and had taught them everything she knew: writing, arithmetic, and drawing. Over these same years the girls had memorized both of her woolen winter dresses—one gray, the other burgundy—as well as her dark-blue suit covered with a layer of gray cat fur.

Since their first class that day the future fifth graders had been heatedly debating the teacher's new acquisition: the belt was a bit plain, without a buckle, and it had Japanese sleeves. Most of the girls were eleven-year-olds, the age when they were most unalike in terms of development, when some of them had already developed curves and growths of curly hair in the hidden regions of their bodies, while others were still thin, sexless children with gnawed nails and scratched knees. But the teacher's new dress intrigued both the former and the latter.

It intrigued Galina Ivanovna herself no less. She had sewn this dress not simply because her old one had worn out, but also because today, after classes were over, there would be a festive tea party to mark her fortieth anniversary as a teacher. During the class change Galina Ivanovna had even gone to the lavatory to look at herself in the mirror and straighten her collar. She had already achieved the rank of honored teacher, and now deep in her heart she dreamed that she would be given a real award—a medal or ribbon.

She devoted the fourth period to extracurricular reading. At first the girls read aloud in turn, every one of them poorly. Those who did not trip over their words rattled them out so senselessly that it was impossible to catch the contents. When she tired of correcting them, Galina Ivanovna took the book and began reading herself. Her voice, a bit high for such a large and stout person, was slightly nasal, but expressive. She read the part about freezing Kashtanka suffering on the shelterless street with particular depth and feeling.

Only a few minutes remained until the end of the lesson, and the most impatient were already silently collecting their satchels. The sun scorched at full capacity through the windows, and the girls to a one sweated in their woolen dresses that stuck to their wet armpits.

"A freezing dog gets no sympathy in this heat," Tanya thought to herself, and at that same moment heard first one, then another, sniffle of someone crying into her sleeve.

Galina Ivanovna stopped reading. The entire class turned to look back at the far corner of the last row where for the last four years Toma Polosukhina had sat, insensible and indifferent to everything. She was crying over the bitter fate of frozen, lost Kashtanka.

Desks slammed shut, and the girls jumped from their seats.

"Class is not over yet," Galina Ivanovna reminded them and, smiling professionally from the corners of her faded mouth, she said to Toma, "Why are you so upset, Toma? Didn't you finish reading to the end?" She tried to calm the girl. "Everything will turn out all right at the end."

"No it won't, no it won't!" Toma sniffled, tearing her cheek from the sticky school desk and wiping her nose with her apron.

She was one of the smallest, one of the least developed girls, plain and ordinary, like a sparrow or longspur . . .

The bell finally rang. Galina Ivanovna decisively closed her book. As if by magic everyone's drowsiness dissipated; the languid, intolerable heat outside the windows instantaneously metamorphosed into fine weather—excellent weather—as they all trembled with impatience and dashed to get out into the street to hop on chalked asphalt; skip rope by themselves, in pairs, or in whole groups; or just jump and kick about, like young foals or kid goats, somersaulting, pushing and shoving, and senselessly tearing about . . .

Toma was still sniffling as she collected her dirty textbooks when Tanya went up to her. Why she went up to her she herself did not know.

"What's wrong?" Tanya asked.

Tanya was no sparrow and no longspur; she was something rare, like a royal lily or a big transparent dragonfly. And both of them knew perfectly well who was who . . .

But that day Toma was going through something huge and awful that Tanya could never go through, and that made them equal, and even, perhaps, elevated Toma above the rest of the world, and for that reason, this little girl who had never said anything about herself and who would never be of interest to anyone said: "My mom's dying. I'm afraid to go home . . ."

"I'll go with you," Tanya offered fearlessly.

Were it yesterday, Toma would have been proud and rejoiced that Tanya was going home with her, but today she almost did not care . . .

They passed through the schoolyard, which rang with girlish shouts and shimmered with greenish gold, slipped through two courtyards, squeezed through a fence, and stopped at the entrance to the "partment." That's what Toma's mother called their housing, which had been assigned before the war to her husband, who had perished in 1944. It was a former garage, with a regular door cut through the garage door. Toma stopped in her tracks at the entrance; Tanya resolutely pushed the door.

It was the stench that hit first. The place reeked of sour dampness, urine, and kerosene, all of it rotten, decayed, and deathly . . . Two pieces of rope strung across the room were draped with wet linen. At the far end, under a wide low window that looked out onto a brick wall, stood the enormous bed on which the whole family—mother, Toma, and her two younger brothers—slept, as atop a Russian stove.

At first it seemed that the bed was empty, but when her eyes grew accustomed to the semidarkness, Tanya could make out a tiny head in a thick headscarf. Next to the bed stood a basin filled with brown linen. The girls approached the bed, the source of the horrible smells.

"Momma, Mom," Toma called.

A groan could be heard coming from the scarf.

"Maybe you want something to eat or to drink?" Toma asked, her voice full of tears.

There was no answer, not even a groan.

Toma pushed the smelly blanket to the side: the woman was lying on a red sheet. Tanya did not realize immediately that this was blood. The brown linen in the basin also was bloodied, but it had darkened with exposure to the air.

"She needs an ambulance," Tanya said firmly.

"She won't let me call an ambulance," Toma whispered.

"But there's a lot of blood; she's hemorrhaging . . ." Tanya was surprised.

"Yeah, she's hemorrhaging. She scraped herself out," explained Toma. Not sure that Tanya would understand, she explained: "She brings guys here, then she scrapes herself out. She scraped too far this time."

Toma sniffled. Tanya winced: bang, screech, crash . . . The walls started to float, her depth perception inverted, and a stinking abyss gaped before her . . . Life was caving in on her, and Tanya understood that from this moment she had left her former life behind her, forever . . .

"I'll call my dad, that's what . . ."

"That's what you say. He won't come here."

"Wait . . . I'll be back soon."

Within five minutes Tanya had reached the apartment. Her mother was not at home, and Vasilisa opened the door.

"You gone berserk?"

Not answering, Tanya rushed to the phone to call Pavel Alekseevich. No one picked up for a long time, then a voice told her that he was in surgery.

"What happened?" Vasilisa Gavrilovna tried to get her to answer.

"Ah, you wouldn't understand." Tanya waved her off.

It seemed to her that she must not reveal this awful knowledge to anyone, because no matter whom she told, their life also would collapse and fall apart, as hers had. The secret had to be kept safe . . .

"I'll be back soon," she shouted from the threshold and, slamming the door, dashed down the staircase.

Tanya remembered only vaguely how, not waiting for the trolleybus, she ran to the metro station, rode to the Park Kultury station, then ran once again down long Pirogov Street. It seemed like her running was infinite and went on for many hours. At the security desk of her father's clinic they stopped her.

"I'm going to see my dad, Pavel Alekseevich . . ."

They let her through immediately. She tore up the stairs to the second floor, pushed open the glass door, and there was her father, walking toward her, in a white surgical gown and round cap. A whole brood of doctors and students milled around him, but he walked ahead of them—taller and broader than them all, with a deep-rosy face and gray-tufted bushy eyebrows. He caught sight of Tanya. It seemed as if the air parted in front of him.

"What happened?"

"Toma Polosukhina's mother is dying. She scraped herself out!" Tanya blurted.

"What? Who let you in here?" he roared. "Go downstairs, to the reception area! Wait for me there!"

Tanya flew downstairs, gulping down her tears.

For all his bravery, he had taken fright. One denunciation would be enough to turn his life to hell . . .

Three minutes later Pavel Alekseevich came downstairs to the reception area. Tanya rushed over to him.

"Daddy!"

He stopped her again with his gaze.

"Now explain calmly what happened to you."

"Toma Polosukhina, Dad . . . We have to hurry . . . Her mother is dying . . ."

"Whose mother? Who?" Pavel Alekseevich asked coldly.

"Our janitor, Aunt Liza. They live in the garage, behind our house. She scraped herself out, she did . . . Dad, it's terrible there . . . Dad, there's so much blood . . ."

He removed his glasses and rubbed the ridge of his nose. The phrase "scraped herself out" from Tanya's lips . . .

"Okay, listen . . . Go straight home."

"How?"

"The same way you got here."

Tanya could not believe her ears. It was as if her father had been replaced by someone else. He had never spoken to her with such an iron voice.

Slouched, she went outside . . .

Thirty minutes later Pavel walked into the Polosukhin garage. His assistant Vitya was with him. The driver of the ambulance they had arrived in did not get out.

As soon as he set eyes on her, Pavel Alekseevich sized up what had happened: there she was, his patient, the unfortunate object of his professional concern . . . A wartime widow or single mother, probably alcoholic, and probably slept around . . . He touched the little janitor's wide cold hand and opened an eyelid with his finger. There was nothing to be done here. Near the bed stood the three kids, two little boys and a girl, who stared at him with big eyes.

"Where's Toma?" Pavel Alekseevich asked.

"I'm Toma."

Pavel Alekseevich looked at her closely: he had taken her at first for a seven-year-old, but now, having got a better look at her, he understood that she was indeed Tanya's classmate.

"Toma, take the boys upstairs to apartment number twelve. In the big gray house. You know where?"

She nodded, but did not budge.

"Go, go. Vasilisa Gavrilovna will let you in. You tell her that Pavel Alekseevich sent you. Tell her to set the table. I'll be there in a second."

"Are you taking Mommy to the hospital?"

He used his mighty figure to block their view of the bed and the miserable woman who was no longer.

"Go, go. We'll do what needs to be done . . ."

The children left.

"Well, we've gotten ourselves into a mess . . . She has to be taken to the morgue . . . ," the assistant half-implored.

"No, Vitya. We can't take her to the morgue. I'm going to send Vasilisa Gavrilovna down here. She'll be the one to call the ambulance and the militia . . . We were never here . . ." Pavel frowned. "You know yourself I'd take her if she were still alive . . ."

Vitya knew it all too well. Actually, all doctors knew how close this came to the criminal code.

Liza the janitor's death sent shock waves up and down the baptized population of the odd-numbered side of Novoslobodskaya Street all the way down to Savelovsky Station, raising a storm of passions and arguments that shattered friendships forever. After Vasilisa Gavrilovna called the ambulance and the militia, and the dead woman's contorted body was taken to the forensics morgue for an autopsy, scandal arose on two fronts—one having to do with housing, the other with medicine.

There were three significant contenders for the "partment." The first—Kostikov, the house manager—dreamed of getting the place for his own sister and her daughter, who had been living in his quarters for more than two years while she waited to get an apartment through the factory where she worked, but with little hope. The day of the death Kostikov took advantage of the opportunity to sign his sister up for the late Liza's job, and now he was sure the living space would not get away from them. The second contender was the electrician from the house management office, Kostya Sichkin, who was tired of living in a seven-by-four-foot room with three children and a fourth already on the way. There was one more contender, also not an outsider, a militiaman from the local beat, Kurennoy, who had the largest room in the dormitory, but was planning to get married, and waited in combat readiness. Other minor folk from the nearby barracks also would not have objected to an upgrade, but they had no chances whatsoever.

On the medical front things were more serious. The autopsy showed that Liza the janitor had died of hemorrhaging induced when the wall of her uterus had been perforated and some arm of ill-fated underground medicine, using an unidentified instrument, had pulled half of her intestine through the unintended puncture . . .

According to the criminal code this unsuccessful intervention was worth three to ten years, depending on the qualifications of the person performing the abortion: in the case of a lethal outcome doctors were given ten years, twice as many as an amateur. Which had a certain justice.

The whole neighborhood knew the names of the two women who practiced this impious trade: Granny Shura Zudina and the Moldavian woman Dora Gergel. The former was simpler and cheaper. She gave an injection and inserted a catheter. Usually it worked. Sometimes, with particularly muscular women or those who had never given birth, it did not. In which case Granny Shura shrugged and did not take any money.

Dora was a trained medic, and did everything by the book, with no misfires. She had moved to Moscow from Kishinev after the war. A swarthy beauty with fiery eyes—her suspicious but undiscerning neighbors took her for a Jew. She had a knack for anything she tried: although already pregnant at the time, she managed to marry a major; she was a crafty housekeeper—in Moscow, a new place for her, she quickly figured out what was to be had where, even when food was still being rationed. She got a job as a nurse in a hospital, although her nursing diploma was counterfeit, not even written in Russian. She performed real abortions at the patient's home, with painkillers even, but she was expensive. Richer people went to her, and Liza could hardly have afforded her. So the neighborhood concluded with no uncertainty that the whole mess was Zudina's doing.

The next day, an investigator showed up in the courtyard. The "partment" was searched, but no instruments or medications were found.

"Yeah, right, like the idiots are going to leave a trail of evidence," the yard joked. The inspector, a young kid with a thin neck, interrogated the neighbor women and blushed. No one said anything. But, as always, an informer turned up. Zudina's neighbor from the other side of the partition, Nastya-the-Rake, did not hold out, because she was a born champion of the truth.

"I won't say what I don't know. In Liza's case I didn't myself see her do it, but she's stuck it in others, and it works real good," she whispered directly in the investigator's ear.

"Did you yourself ever use her?" the inspector inquired.

"God forbid, I haven't had the need for a long time," the Rake pleaded.

"So how do you know?"

Here the Rake led him over to the plywood partition, tapped it with her nail, and immediately heard a reply.

"Whattcha need, Nastya?"

"Nothin'," the Rake answered zestily, then whispered directly into the investigator's ear: "You can hear everything, down to the last kopeck. Around here you can't sigh or fart without your neighbors knowing . . ."

The inspector wrote it all down in his notebook and left: now he had a lead.

The atmosphere of investigation, bickering, and hostility was so strong it penetrated even Pavel Alekseevich's peaceful abode. It all started the evening of the day Lizaveta was taken away. The Polosukhin children were put to bed in Tanya's room, and she moved to her parents' bedroom.

Only the adults gathered for a late dinner—Pavel Alekseevich, Elena, and Vasilisa Gavrilovna, who, though reluctantly, occasionally sat down at the table with them. For this to happen the occasion had to be special—a holiday or some event, like today's. She preferred to eat in her room, in peace and with her prayers.

Having finished his food, Pavel Alekseevich pushed aside his plate, turned to Elena, and said: "Now do you understand why I've spent so many years trying to legalize this?"

"Legalize what?" Elena, sunk in her own thoughts, asked. Polosukhina's children gave her no peace.

"Legalize abortions."

Vasilisa almost dropped the teapot: her world was shattered. Pavel Alekseevich, whom she so esteemed, was, it turns out, on the side of criminals and murderers, working on their behalf, on behalf of their shameless freedom. And he was a murderer himself . . . But that was impossible to imagine . . . How could it be?

Pavel Alekseevich confirmed it and started to explain. He was good at that.

Vasilisa clenched her dark lips and said nothing. She did not drink her tea, and pushed her cup aside, but she did not go to her room. She just sat there, silent, not raising her eyes.

"It's horrible, horrible!" Elena lowered her head to her hands.

"What's horrible?" Pavel Alekseevich was irritated.

"It's all horrible. That Lizaveta died. And what you're saying. No, no, I'll never go along with it. It's legalized infanticide. It's a crime worse than murdering an adult. A defenseless little . . . How can they make that legal?"

"Here we go: Tolstoyism, vegetarianism, temperance . . ."

She unexpectedly took offense on behalf of Tolstoyism.

"What does vegetarianism have to do with it? That's not what Tolstoy meant. Three of those creatures are sleeping in Tanya's room. If abortions were legal, they too would have been murdered. Lizaveta didn't have much need for them."

"Are you feeble minded, Elena? Perhaps they wouldn't exist. Then there wouldn't be three unfortunate orphans doomed to poverty, hunger, and prison."

For the first time in ten years a serious quarrel was setting in between them.

"Pasha, what are you saying?" Elena was horrified. "How can you say such things? Maybe I am feeble minded, but the mind has nothing to do with this. They're killing their own children. How can that be allowed?"

"And how can it not be allowed? They're also killing themselves! And what do we do with them?" He pointed in the direction of the wall behind which the pitiful, sickly children slept, children their mother had not succeeded in getting rid of in time. "What would you have done with them?"

"I don't know. I only know that you cannot kill them." This was the first time her husband's words had ever elicited in her a sense of disagreement, and he himself—a sense of protest and irritation.

"Think about the women!" Pavel Alekseevich shouted.

"Why should we think about them? They're criminals, they kill their own children." Elena pursed her lips.

Pavel Alekseevich's face turned to stone, and Elena understood why his subordinates feared him. She had never seen him like this.

"You don't have the right to a vote. You don't have that organ. You're not a woman. If you can't get pregnant, then you can't judge," he said to her morosely.

Their family happiness—easy and unstrained, their chosenness and their closeness, their unlimited trust for each other, all of it came crashing down in an instant. But he seemed not to understand. Vasilisa directed her single eye at Pavel Alekseevich.

Elena got up. With a trembling hand she lowered her teacup into the sink. The cup was old, with a long crack running through it. Coming in contact with the bottom of the sink, it shattered. Leaving the shards, Elena left the kitchen. Slouching, Vasilisa scurried into her pantry.

Pavel Alekseevich was about to go after his wife, but he stopped in his tracks. No, so it was cruel. How could she pick up stray cats and not feel any compassion for unfortunate Lizaveta? Who was she to judge . . . ? Let her think . . .

Elena thought all night long. She cried, and thought, and cried again. Alongside her, in her husband's usual place, lay warm little Tanya. Pavel Alekseevich went to his study.

Vasilisa Gavrilovna also did not sleep. She did not think. She prayed and cried. Now Pavel Alekseevich was the villain.

Pavel Alekseevich woke up several times, troubled by vaguely dark dreams. He tossed and turned, dragging the slippery sheet off the leather sofa.

Morning began very early. Vasilisa came out of her pantry as soon as she heard Pavel Alekseevich put on the teapot. She announced that she was leaving them. It was not the first time. It happened that Vasilisa would take offense at who knew what and ask for her separation pay. Usually, having stored up her discontent in her soul, she would disappear for several days, but return soon after.

"Do whatever you want," Pavel Alekseevich blurted, not yet recovered from yesterday.

HE FELT MISERABLE AND EVEN OPENED THE CUPBOARD and looked inside. There was no bottle. He did not want to send Vasilisa and, besides, it was still too early. He poured a glass of tea and went to his study. Elena did not come out of the bedroom. Vasilisa gathered her things. In Tanya's room Lizaveta's children were waiting for breakfast and tussling over toys they had never seen before and that belonged to someone else. Toma was trying to get them to argue more quietly.

When Elena came out to the kitchen to cook morning porridge for the pack of children, Vasilisa Gavrilovna appeared at the stove dressed in a new sweater and new scarf and with a mournful and solemn look on her face.

"Elena, I'm leaving you."

"What are you doing to me?" Elena gasped. "How can you leave me?"

They stood there, looking at each other, both tall, thin, and severe. One an old woman who looked older than she in fact was, the other close to forty, also getting up in age, but still looking twenty-eight.

"You do as you wish, but I'm not living with him anymore. I'm leaving," the old woman snapped.

"What about me?" Elena implored.

"He's your husband." Vasilisa darkened.

"Husband . . . shmusband," was all Elena said.

She could not imagine life without Vasilisa, especially in this unexpected situation, with someone else's orphaned children in the house. Elena persuaded Vasilisa Gavrilovna to postpone her departure at least until the fate of the Polosukhin children was decided.

"All right," Vasilisa said gloomily. "As soon as we bury Lizaveta, I'm leaving. Start looking for another housekeeper, Elena. I'm not living with him anymore."

THE FUNERAL TOOK PLACE ONLY ON THE SIXTH DAY, after the autopsy had been completed and they had established scientifically what had been clear without it. The relatives showed up, nearly all of them women: her mother, two sisters, and several old women of various degrees of kinship from sister-in-law to godmother. The one crooked little man called himself a brother-in-law. When she and Toma once dropped in at the "partment," Tanya marveled at these people and quietly asked Toma to explain who was related to whom.

The entire Polosukhin clan came from the region around Tver, but from different villages—the father's village and the mother's village. Toma's birth father had perished during the war, her younger brothers were not his—no one knew whose they were—but had inherited his name for free, and his family did not look favorably upon Lizaveta.

You might even say that her relatives were feuding. These people quarreled noisily and concurrently, crying and accusing each other of some prewar insults and injuries, kept bringing up something mysterious called a "carucate" and a "half-carcass" . . . It all sounded like they were speaking another language. Tanya got the impression that they were playing some adult game, divvying up things for fun . . . But they were divvying for real . . .

service and the burial, but Pavel Alekseevich would not allow it. Elena thought that Tanya should go because of Toma: "just to stand alongside her in this moment." This disagreement further deepened their silent enmity. He insisted, he grumbled, he demanded that Tanya be left at home.

"She's an impressionable child! Why are you dragging her into all this? It's a profanation! I can see Vasilisa! But what's Tanechka going to do there?"

"And what makes you think you have the right to a vote?" Although meek and not at all vindictive, she nonetheless delivered a shattering blow. She herself did not know how it came out. "You aren't Tanya's father, after all . . ."

It was mean revenge. The blow hit its target. It was one of those rare cases where both duelists lose. No one survived.

But Tanya did not go to the funeral: she had a temperature and stayed in bed.

The day after the funeral Lizaveta's elder sister Niura left, taking her two nephews with her. According to their agreement, Fenya, the younger sister, was supposed to take Toma. But something did not work out; Fenya had to swap some "furrings." Tanya, to whom Toma related all this, pictured a flower-bedecked village dance with grownup girls crowned with wreaths of cornflowers and daisies exchanging rings of fur. Tanya could not understand what sort of problem there could be with furrings. But soon Fenya herself showed up—a large, dark-haired woman who resembled her tiny fair sister only in her rare unattractiveness.

She sat for a long time in the kitchen with Vasilisa and Elena, first crying, then laughing at something, and drank two teapots of tea. They agreed that for the time being she would leave Toma here, in the city, and as soon as she was done with the furrings, she would come to fetch her. All through the conversation Toma stood hunched in the corridor with her bulging school satchel and her winter coat bunched in her arms, awaiting their decision.

Late in the evening, when everyone had dispersed, Toma crept into Vasilisa Gavrilovna's pantry—she felt more at ease with the help than with the other members of the family, including Tanya. Toma looked Vasilisa in her one live eye and fingered her hem.

"Aunt Vas, I can wash floors and do laundry. And stoke the stove . . . I don't want to live at Fenya's: she's got enough of her own . . ."

Vasilisa pressed the girl's head to her side.

"You silly bird. We don't have a wood-burning stove. And we don't wash the floors ourselves; the floor polisher comes and polishes them. But don't you worry: there's more than enough to do in this house . . ."

BUSY WITH THE FUNERAL ARRANGEMENTS, ELENA HAD forgotten Vasilisa's words about leaving. Over the past few days her quarrel with her husband had hardened, as if having grown a scab. They almost never spoke—only about household necessities. The first evening when the Polosukhin children had shown up in their house, before their quarrel, Elena had made her husband's bed in his study and taken Tanya into the room with her. At that point, it had not signified a quarrel, but was just a household necessity: there was no place for the three children to sleep . . . And so it remained the whole week, until Lizaveta's funeral.

Who knows: if the necessity had not arisen, might Pavel Alekseevich have found words and gestures to soften the insult, and would his wife, reassured of her husband's love, have had a good cry on his broad, hairy chest, and would everything have returned to usual . . . ?

The morning after the funeral Elena found Vasilisa Gavrilovna in the kitchen dressed in the new silk headscarf they had given her at Christmas and wearing new shoes . . . She sat up straight in her chair, a small fiberboard suitcase alongside her together with a large bundle with her linen and pillow.

Elena sat down next to her and started to cry. Vasilisa lowered her seeing eye, pursed her lips, pressed her hands to her breast in a cross, as if preparing to take communion. Silence.

"Where are you going to go, Vasenka?" Elena had not expected such resolve from Vasilisa.

"Wherever it was I came from that's where I'm going back to," Vasilisa answered sternly. "God be with you, Elena."

Vasilisa looked straight ahead, one eye white, the other blue. A hideous gaze.

"Does she really not love us at all?" Elena was horrified by the thought. She took from her purse all the money she had and silently handed it to Vasilisa.

Vasilisa bowed, picked up her belongings, and set off . . .

Just like that. As if she had not spent twenty years together with Elena. Disappeared, without saying good-bye to Tanya, or Pavel Alekseevich. Without looking back.

11

VASILISA KNEW EXACTLY WHERE SHE HAD COME FROM and where she was going: from the soil to the soil. Putting it in today's terms, she had the mindset of someone sent on a business trip to perform some assigned task and then return to her permanent place of employment.

The circumstances of her time on this earth since birth had been such that her own mother had used to say about her daughter, who was born late and unexpected: girl got no luck and no smarts.

Her older brother and the sister who had grown to maturity and not dissolved into the earth at infancy, as had the six or seven—Vasilisa's mother did not remember the precise number—babies buried at the rural cemetery, had long ago separated from their parents and left. Her older sister Dusya worked as a domestic in Moscow, and her brother Sergei was married in the neighboring administrative district.

The first misfortune to befall Vasilisa occurred very early. She was two years old when the only rooster in her parents' yard—an unsightly, voiceless creature—jumped up and pecked her in the eye. The little girl yelped, but no one noticed. A white spot began to develop on her eye, and by the time she was seven the eye was entirely clouded over by a white film.

Year by year Vasilisa's parents grew poorer, fell ill, and when Vasilisa was ten her father died. Her widowed mother knocked about for a year, then moved in with her oldest son, who had a prospering farm near Kozelsk. At her brother's place mother and daughter were treated like extra mouths to feed, told to live in the bathhouse, and not invited to the table. Vasilisa and her mother worked in the garden and lived off practically the garden alone. Sergei would bring them bread on holidays or when he was in a good mood, after he had drunk wine.

About thirty miles from those parts the renowned Optina Pustyn monastery prospered, although already on its way to decline. Spiritual life by that time had turned partly into a commercial commodity, of particular value to the owners of inns and taverns, not to mention the monastery's own hotels. People came there on foot from all over Russia, thousands of people of all social castes. One of the roads passed through the village where Vasilisa's brother lived. But he did not belong to that clever breed who knows how to extract profit from their conveniently located living quarters. Just the opposite—he was constantly annoyed by the poorer pilgrims who asked for lodging for the night, or panhandled, or walked off with anything that was not chained down. The majority of those streaming by on foot were beggars and half-beggars, monks and half-monks, and Vasilisa's brother hated all of them and considered them rabble and idlers. Sergei himself had never been to the renowned site: he attended services at the village church three times a year, and of all the church's dictums he observed only one: he never worked on major feast days.

Vasilisa was afraid of her brother: he never talked to her, and she knew only from her mother that when he was young he had sung and danced and been handsome, but that his temperament had changed after a girl he had fallen in love with rejected him. Their mother pitied him, but he took pity on no one—not on his wife, or his children, and even less on deformed little Vasilisa. That winter their mother caught cold and died. Vasilisa remained with the large family, for whom she was only a hindrance.

Soon after her mother's death a neighbor took Vasilisa to a celebration at the Optina Pustyn. Vasilisa was exhausted before she got there and barely managed to stand through the long monastery service, which brought her neither pleasure nor relief. But on the way back a miracle occurred, although it was almost impossible to describe because it was so small and insignificant, just Vasilisa's size. Her fellow travelers decided to have a rest, and she lay down about thirty feet from the road, in a dense hazel grove, and fell asleep. She had not slept long when she was awakened by voices beckoning her to move on. While she was asleep, the gloomy overcast day had brightened, and just as she opened her eyes the clouds parted and a wide ray of sunlight as thick—and just about as heavy—as a log broke a hole through the clouds and fell on the field right in front of her, illuminating a circle on the ground . . . Basically, that was the whole miracle. She knew that the circle was Jesus Christ, who was alive and loved her. In addition, she was completely convinced that she had seen this miraculous vision with both her eyes—the picture had been so three-dimensional and unlike anything that she had ever seen in her life.

The entire way back she sobbed softly, and her kindly neighbor decided that the little girl had worn one of her feet ragged. She removed the scarf from her head and told her to wrap her foot with it. Vasilisa did not object, wrapped her foot in the scarf, and limped the rest of the way back, because the headscarf made her bast shoe too tight and squeezed her foot.

Vasilisa somehow survived the winter at her brother's, and in the spring he sent her to their sister Dusya in Moscow. Dusya wanted to find her some sort of job. She arranged for her to be taken on as an apprentice at a tailoring shop on Malaya Nikitskaya Street owned by a compassionate woman of German origin named Lizelotta Mikhailovna Klotske. As soon as she saw Vasilisa's white eye, she realized that the little girl would never make a decent seamstress: even with two good eyes twenty years of work weakened the women's eyesight. But she did not let her go immediately, allowing her to stay on and try to acquire a skill. Although Vasilisa was only fourteen years old, rural life had so coarsened her fingers that they could not hold the small needles and thin threads. When they assigned her to ironing, that too turned out to be not entirely easy. With their little steam irons the other girls pressed pleats stiff and sharp as sword grass—you could cut your finger on them; Vasilisa's pleats were crooked and uneven, and they'd have to be soaked again and dried . . . Seeing that the newcomer, for all her diligence, had no talent for work with her hands, the kind owner charged her with cleaning the workshop.

Vasilisa herself did not see dirt; everything had to be pointed out to her. But once she saw what needed to be cleaned, she would scrub not just until it shined, but until she dropped . . . She did not know even the simplest things, such as that brooms need to be dampened and the floor sprinkled before sweeping. And how would she know, having lived her whole life on a dirt floor. When they told her, she sprinkled the floor so much that she needed a rag, not a broom, to soak up all the dirty water. At this trade, too, Vasilisa turned out to have "no smarts."

Lizelotta Mikhailovna Klotske could not keep Vasilisa on at the workshop, but she did not want to put her out on the street, so she decided to consult her old girlfriend from school days, Evgenia Fedorovna Nechaeva. She brought Vasilisa to Evgenia Fedorovna's place in Trekhprudny Lane. A certain helpless meekness in Vasilisa compelled these old friends to care for her.

Although she was rather tall and had long legs and a fine torso, Vasilisa's arms were short, and she constantly kept her large, coarse hands folded against her chest. Her face was long and ellipsoidal, her gaze mournful and severe, her nose thin and longish like her face, her skin a swarthy rose color, smooth, like enamel . . . In a word, not a pretty village face, but a Byzantine countenance.

"Not your typical look," Lizelotta said to Evgenia while the girl was being fed in the kitchen, "and not at all Russian. Interesting. Pity the poor thing has lost an eye . . . Think, Zhenechka, what use can she be put to? She's a very diligent girl, but entirely unfit for our business. She's also not suitable as domestic help, I think . . ."

OVER GENTEEL CUPS OF COFFEE THE TWO OLD FRIENDS decided that they would ask a third schoolmate for help—Anechka Tatarinova, who soon after graduation from school had lost her fiancé, entered a monastery, and for a number of years already had been abbess at a small monastery in the N administrative district . . .

Vasilisa remained at Evgenia Fedorovna's, and a week later transportation was found: a family of acquaintances was traveling to visit the abbess. They asked them to take Vasilisa along. Vasilisa carried a letter to Mother Anatolia, formerly Anechka, written by her old school friends. The letter contained a request to the abbess that she "take part" in deciding the fate of the poor orphan. "Take part" was already in its third iteration, but, amazingly, each of the petitioners was successful in her own way . . .

The family traveled by train and bought Vasilisa an expensive ticket in a car with compartments and sat her down on the velvet seat, which she stroked half the trip, feasting her fingers on the unusually soft feel. Then tea was served, but when they offered her some, she grabbed the glass so awkwardly that it fell out of the glass holder. The hot tea scalded her leg, but the pain of the burn was nothing by comparison with her horror at having broken the glass ... Her kind traveling companions tried to calm her down, but she was almost paralyzed by grief, as if she had destroyed not a glass but a living creature.

Toward evening they arrived in N, a beautifully snow-covered ancient city where they spent the night in a hotel on the same square as the train station, and poor Vasilisa once again reeled from magnificence she had never known. She was given a place to sleep with another girl, who, while obviously not of the same class as their benefactors, was also no country bumpkin. The beds where they slept had such white linen that Vasilisa feared soiling the pillow ... All this opulence gave Vasilisa no joy and only frightened her.

Early the next morning they set off in two wooden sleighs. Both the sleighs and the horses were handsome, entirely unlike her brother's in the village. Riding in the sleighs was more what she was accustomed to and more fun than on the train. The monastery was fifteen miles away, the weather was the best kind of winter weather—just below freezing with a springtime sun that blinded your eyes and tickled your nose ... It was the eve of Candlemas.

The horses sped gaily down the smooth road as if they too were gladdened by the sun. Vasilisa's scalded knee hurt a lot, but her embarrassment had been so great that the pain seemed to exist apart from her.

The monastery appeared behind a turn: it stood on a rise, like rice funeral porridge in a bowl, all white with glistening snow, with white walls and golden cupolas and an open bell tower that stood out artfully against the blue, rock-hard sky ... The sudden beauty of this sight melted Vasilisa's numbness, and she began to weep. Tears streamed from both her eyes. Her left eye could not see, but it could cry.

The sleighs stopped at the closed gates. The sister on guard came running out, waved her arms, and smiled: they were expected.

"The house has been prepared for you ... Reverend Mother has been waiting for you since yesterday evening."

OTHER GUESTS WERE ACCOMMODATED IN THE SMALL monastery hotel, but the abbess received those in her inner circle, this family and several others, relatives, in her small house next to the church.

The family's little girl, about seven years of age, demanded *kissel* as soon as she got out of the sleigh. The gatekeeper stroked the fur on her bonnet:

"Go to the refectory, my child. Reverend Mother said to leave some bread and *kissel* for you . . . Just then a small, lean woman in a tall, stiff black velvet headdress and wool habit came out. Vasilisa understood that this was the abbess . . .

The family that had brought Vasilisa with them lined up in single file along the narrow shoveled path and proceeded to the porch. Vasilisa was last in line. Greeting her distant relations, the abbess sensed an almost physical terror and awe coming from the stooped, poorly dressed little girl whose short arms with coarse red hands were folded across her chest.

They've brought their new domestic with them, the abbess decided, and beckoned the little girl to come closer. The little girl's clear, seeing eye closed from fear and the other one shone white as the abbess removed her fluffy black mittens and extended them to Vasilisa. Vasilisa was unable to take them and dropped them on the snow. The seven-year-old little girl who stood alongside her laughed into her fur collar . . .

And so it came to be that even before she had read the letter of recommendation, the abbess gave her heart's consent to accept Vasilisa.

Vasilisa began her monastery life at age fourteen: the first two years she was a worker, then she became a novice. Her novitiate was always connected to chores: in the kitchen, the cow barn, and the fields. They tried giving her other work, but she did not have a good enough voice for the choir, or any special womanly talent for gold embroidery. As before, she considered herself an insignificant, unimportant being, not worth the food she consumed. It was precisely this that so touched the abbess, and in the third year of Vasilisa's life in the monastery the abbess adopted as her own this novice dispossessed of any redeeming qualities in the eyes of the other residents of the monastery.

The abbess began to teach Vasilisa to read, at first Russian, then Church Slavonic. Learning came to Vasilisa with great difficulty. Mother Anatolia, aware all her life of her own lack of patience, practiced humility by teaching this sweet but exceptionally learning-disabled girl. Every day, immediately after morning services, Vasilisa spent an hour in the abbess's room. She placed her light-blue notebook on the edge of the table and looked at Mother Anatolia with a devoted and fearful gaze. Inclined toward intellectual pursuits—which she herself considered sinful games—and fluent since youth in multiple languages, the abbess marveled at the intricate variation in human abilities. There was no doubt that Vasilisa demonstrated the height of resistance to learning, not to say stupidity. Before Vasilisa the abbess could never have imagined that a person could repeat one and the same error so many times before learning how to write or pronounce a word correctly.

"Vasilisa, what does 'this day' mean?" Mother Anatolia would begin Vasilisa's lessons with this question.

Uncertain, Vasilisa rolled her only serviceable eye to the ceiling and for the fifteenth time replied.

"In the afternoon?"

The abbess shook her head.

"Yesterday?" The embarrassed pupil turned crimson.

"'This day' means 'now, at this time, today' . . ."

"This day the Maiden gives birth to the Transcendent One . . ." the teacher repeated innumerable times, warding off her irritation with a short prayer.

Vasilisa nodded happily, then, the very next day, she once again painfully searched the low whitewashed ceiling for an answer to the question, "What does 'this day' mean?"

Having observed the slowness and torpidity of Vasilisa's brains, the abbess now and again would conclude that she was dealing with a certain kind of mental retardation. And by this time, having spent nearly twenty years in monasteries, she knew that deficiencies of various sorts—intellectual, physical, or moral—were widespread phenomena and that a healthy person was sooner an exception to the rule of total global illness.

In addition to intellectual torpidity she noted her ward's insuperable ignorance and predilection for the wildest of superstitions, and guessed that the girl's rare obstinacy camouflaged a certain kind of preordination—like that of a plant that sends its roots downward and leaves upward and cannot be made to break this habit. But in Vasilisa's case all of these frustrating peculiarities were wrapped in a rare virtue, which the abbess also discovered in her ward. The soul of this backward girl harbored an inexhaustible well of gratitude, a rare ability to remember every kindness shown her, and a noble amnesia for all insults and injuries. Surprising as it might seem, it was precisely the injuries and various insults directed at her that she accepted as deserved.

Monastic life—the abbess had known for a long time—concealed unseen possibilities for oppression, violence, and sin. These were special, monastic sins of which secular people immersed in their pursuit of daily bread had no concept. Within the walls of a monastery human relations acquired much greater significance, and much more acute forms. Sympathies and antipathies, jealousy, envy, and hatred festered, sealed within the confines of strictly regulated behavior.

The abbess knew perfectly well that Vasilisa was sneered at, insulted, and mistreated, but she never heard a single word of complaint from her doltish little novice, who exuded only incessant gratitude. Having plumbed the girl's uncomplicated depths with her experienced vision, Mother Anatolia wondered: what sort of miracle was this deformed little girl with neither beauty nor talent, yet so richly blessed with the rare gift of gratitude? "A humble soul," the abbess decided, and made Vasilisa her cell-keeper . . .

Vasilisa now slept on a narrow bench in the entranceway, at the door to the abbess's room. At first she would wake up every ten minutes, like a nursing mother who constantly imagines that her child has begun to cry. When she woke up, she would rush to the locked door of the abbess's room, on the way overturning the slops bucket or knocking over the woodpile—the tiled stove in the abbess's room was stoked from the entranceway . . . She often woke the abbess, whose sleep since youth had been fragile and easily disrupted. For the longest time the abbess tried to impress on her that if she were awakened by a disturbing thought she should recite the Hail Mary three times before getting up. But Vasilisa emerged from her peasant's sleep usually only after she was already standing near the door, frightened by the noise she had made and only then remembering the Reverend Mother's instructions . . .

For all her dimwittedness and clumsiness, Vasilisa learned to sweep away the dust with a multicolored broom called a "chicken-wing" because of its shape, to wash windows to a brilliant shine, and even to steep tea "genteel-style."

In the fourth year of Vasilisa's residency the old priest and father confessor who had lived at the monastery for many years died. A new priest arrived, Hieromonk Varsonofy. He was young—barely more than thirty—but looked much older, with turtlelike skin, dry lips, and eyelids that folded over his dark Byzantine eyes . . . His education was decent, and he had been a monk since youth, precisely the type the church hierarchy itself came from.

Father Varsonofy taught church history and liturgics at the administrative district seminary and came to the monastery for brief visits, occasionally missing a week or two if he was having a difficult semester. The abbess treated him respectfully, even deferentially, and though usually reserved and of few words, he would often drink tea and engage in conversation with her. Despite the enormous differences in their backgrounds and upbringing, Mother Anatolia, an enlightened aristocrat, became close with Father Varsonofy, the son of a railroad worker and a peasant. She held the new priest in high regard: it was not often in monastic circles that one met a person who took an interest in life beyond the monastery's gates.

Mother Anatolia herself had retained her worldly habits: she read secular books, her girlfriends even sent her a literary magazine, and in church circles she had the reputation of a radical, because she admired Patriarch Philaret of Moscow and advocated translation of the Bible into vernacular Russian; that is, in the eyes of some church leaders she was not entirely trustworthy, with a certain disposition toward Lutheranism.

At the time, the young monk held entirely different, stricter views: he entertained no disposition toward Lutheranism, was irreconcilable with Catholicism, and as a meticulous reader of new writing in divinity studies he singled out Vladimir Soloviev, to whose work he strongly objected, as particularly pernicious.

Serving them at the table, Vasilisa was constant witness to their conversations. Removing the tea service, she would sit down on the bench outside the door and thrill at their clever words, and wonder why the Lord had brought her to such an enviable, rich, and divine place . . . She remembered well the backbreaking work of her childhood, the ache in her arms and back, the constant pain in her stomach from which she had suffered until she came to the monastery, the hunger, and most of all, the cold that for so many years had held her in its grip, abating only briefly in the fleeting warmth of July and August.

The last summer before the war Father Varsonofy left them for three months to make a pilgrimage to the Holy Land. During his stay in Palestine he learned that war had broken out and returned to the motherland on the very last steamship. He returned still very much under the impression of the sacred places, especially the Sea of Galilee, which he had circumambulated, offering prayers at each of the holy sites, which for the most part retained from antiquity only their geographical names ...

Vasilisa would sit near the door, petrified with astonishment: she was seeing with her own eyes someone who had seen the Sea of Galilee and the ruins of the synagogue at Capernaum, where the Lord himself had been. For her the abstract written word now acquired flesh and smell. The smell that came from the monk himself, though, was still the same—odors of a body rarely bathed mixed with the smell of dampness, the incense that had impregnated his clothes, and the tablets that he chewed to soothe his tormenting toothache. Vasilisa secretly pulled a putrid thread from his long overcoat, scraped the dirt from the soles of the galoshes in which he had made his journey, wrapped them both in silver paper, and preserved them as if they were relics. She even came to regard herself with a certain respect as someone who had seen someone who had seen the Holy Land ...

And so, over the next two years, sitting at the door like a bewitched mouse, Vasilisa learned of the course of Russian history—about unsuccessful military decisions and the abdication of the tsar ... There, on her bench, she also learned about preparations for the All-Russian Sobor and the possible election of the patriarch, and about the revolution ...

In the summer of 1917 Father Varsonofy was summoned to Moscow. But he did not forget the abbess and sent her letters from time to time. At the beginning of 1918 by way of a chance courier he sent the abbess a long letter in which he described autumn events in Moscow and Petersburg, the election of the patriarch, and his own concelebration of the Eucharist with Patriarch-elect Tikhon at the St. Nicholas Cathedral on Nikola-Vorobievsky Lane. He made fleeting mention of his own elevation to bishop the evening before. The abbess shared this last piece of news with Vasilisa.

"Is an apostle higher than a bishop?" Vasilisa asked, petrified by her own impudence.

"An apostle is more than a bishop, my child," the abbess answered wearily, once again marveling at the childish questions that preoccupied Vasilisa.

Several months later the abbess received from the bishop a large package containing, besides a letter, reports printed on poor-quality paper, with monstrous spelling, of changes brought on by the revolution. Even after studying them closely through her tiny eyeglasses on a black string, the abbess could make no sense of the contradictory nonsense of Soviet speech. In the letter, written with large cursive letters, she read, among other things: "Cruel persecutions have begun. It will come unto us to be witness to it as well. Rejoice!"

The next morning the abbess set out to the archbishop in N for an explanation. From him she learned the latest news—about the separation of church and state, about civil unrest in Petrograd, about the murders of Father Peter Skipetrov and Metropolitan Vladimir . . .

"They're closing all the monasteries," the archbishop whispered, blessing the abbess on her way out.

Reverend Mother was terrified and did not entirely believe what she had heard, but on returning to the monastery she began to scale down operations and prepare the monastery for the uncertain and, it went without saying, sorrowful changes she now awaited. But she could not possibly have envisioned the dimensions of the impending disaster. A few things she succeeded in doing: in keeping with the Gospels, she distributed the monastery's supplies to the peasants, very secretively and very discriminatingly, keeping only the bare minimum; she had a secret compartment constructed under the sanctuary altar and placed an iron-fettered chest containing the holy relics inside; the monastery's valuable archive was sent by courier to the eparchy library. She had already come to terms with the idea of closing the monastery, but could not imagine closing the ancient church.

She gathered the novices and the nuns and announced that they should think about leaving the monastery before the heinous persecutions commenced. Four novices returned to their parents' homes. But all the nuns decided to remain. The abbess announced to them that times had changed, that many would suffer for their sins and for the sins of their loved ones, and that the path for the majority of them should be to go out into the secular world and while living in that secular world nonetheless remain sisters to each other and brides of Christ.

That was all Mother Anatolia succeeded in accomplishing. Several days before the monastery was closed, they came for her. She was taken to the prison in N. Vasilisa asked to go with her, and the authorities benevolently agreed. The abbess prepared herself for the worst, but they sentenced her to three years exile in the Vologda administrative district. A week later, Vasilisa, demonstrating unexpected acumen, traveled to the monastery, gathered the vestiges of the abbess's things—two Gardner porcelain cups, a coffeepot with warmer, some of their mended and remended bedding, and a pillowcase with embroidered initials produced in Lizelotta Mikhailovna Klotske's workshop in times immemorial. With that they went.

Surprisingly, the trip was even pleasant, in a decent train car with four clerics—two village priests guilty of who knows what before the new regime, the eparchy's librarian, and the same archbishop who had just recently promised the abbess that the monastery would be closed. Their convoy was one solitary Red Army soldier, a village boy not yet thoroughly inculcated with revolutionary spirit. He treated his criminals with yet to be extirpated respect appropriate to their station . . .

For Vasilisa and the abbess three years turned into eleven. Eleven harsh years of suffering and heroism for the old abbess and of bliss for Vasilisa. Now in rural conditions she was accustomed to, she was for the abbess, who was hardly accustomed to this life, nurturer, protector, and guardian angel. Thrice they moved to new settlements, each time farther north, until they were banished to Kargopol, a nice little wooden town where Mother Anatolia died in the seventy-eighth year of her life.

Several days before her death Mother Anatolia instructed Vasilisa that after the funeral she should not remain there, but should travel to Moscow, to Trekhprudny Lane, to Evgenia Fedorovna Nechaeva. She blessed her and ordered her not to be afraid of anything. Vasilisa did everything her mentor told her: she buried her, waited around to mark the fortieth day, and left. She took with her the red velvet purse with two imperial ten-ruble pieces, her inheritance from Reverend Mother, and her silver piece of paper with the Palestinian relics.

She found her way to Trekhprudny Lane at the end of December. Evgenia Fedorovna took her in. In the housing committee there were people who still remembered old Nechaev, the builder. For the two ten-ruble pieces of gold one of those with a good memory entered one-eyed Vasilisa's name in the house registration roster. From that time on Vasilisa lived in Evgenia Fedorovna's household, with Elena, and later Anton Ivanovich. She served them as had become her custom from morning until night, never leaving an ounce of thought, time, or rest for herself: first Evgenia Fedorovna, then Elena, then Tanya, then everyone else she considered her benefactor ...

She had only one strange habit: twice a year—once usually in spring, right after Easter—she would abandon everything and disappear for a week, sometimes ten days. With no warning or explanation ...

"Vasilisa's got the itch for some freedom," Pavel Alekseevich chuckled.

It was indeed her only luxury—to travel, when her soul beckoned, to the wooden town of Kargopol, to visit the grave of Anna Tatarinova, the abbess Anatolia, to tidy up the grave, paint the fence, and talk to her, her only close relation. All the others were cousins ...

12

CLASSES AT SCHOOL ENDED, ALONG WITH THE PREMA-ture heat wave. Cold rain set in. They started packing for the dacha. Vasilisa had left, despite Elena's admonishments, and Elena felt completely lost: without Vasilisa, life—not to mention their move to the dacha—was all off-kilter. Usually all the packing was done quietly and well in advance by Vasilisa; Elena now had no way of estimating how much macaroni and kerosene or sugar and salt they should take or how to wrap and pack it all.

Toma did everything she could to be useful and to be liked, especially by Tanya. For her, Tanya had always been a creature of a higher order, and now, when they spent all their days together, she sensed Tanya's goodwill toward her, and put her on a pedestal.

Pavel Alekseevich moved to the dacha together with the whole family, but that summer he practically did not live there, coming only on Saturdays. His admonitory quarrel with his wife, which at first had seemed to him not that significant, had grown into full-fledged emotional dissonance. Pavel Alekseevich's words about her inadequacy as a woman wedged like a splinter in Elena's heart. The barrier turned out to be insuperable: Elena now spent the night on the sofa on the enclosed terrace. When Pavel Alekseevich visited, he would stay in his study upstairs. Their bedroom was vacant. He also had been inexpressibly offended: it was as if with her words Elena had deprived him of his paternity.

They both suffered and would have liked to talk it through, but there was nothing to apologize for: they both felt that they were right and had been unjustly insulted. They were not accustomed to talking things out, and they had never been able or wanted to discuss the intimate aspects of their life. Their alienation only mounted.

On Sundays Pavel Alekseevich rose early, woke the girls, and took them down to the small river. They would splash about until lunchtime, and he taught them to swim. Then they returned home and ate dinner. Toma tried not to scrape her spoon against her plate, to use her fork, and not to gorge herself on bread . . .

For all their emotional dissonance, their family life followed a well-trodden path: Pavel Alekseevich brought home enormous amounts of money, and Elena read through the lists and sent money-grams and packages. But without Vasilisa this festive and solemn ritual seemed to have lost its meaning. Two chance coincidental events—the family quarrel and Toma's appearance in their household—somehow merged into one, and with deep-seated hidden hostility Elena observed the mousy little girl barely as tall as Tanya's shoulder.

At the very end of summer Vasilisa returned, as if nothing had happened. Catching sight of her on the path that led to the terrace, Elena began to cry. Vasilisa too broke out into tears. She was black with suntan and thinner than usual. She explained nothing, and Elena did not ask any questions. Both of them were happy. The next day a letter came from Toma's aunt asking them to "keep the niece at least until Christmas." Elena read the letter while Vasilisa nodded her scraggly head to the rhythm of the words. They both fell silent. Then Vasilisa made coffee—it was her only gastronomical weakness and over the course of her wanderings she had missed coffee more than anything else. Vasilisa poured herself a big mug of watery brownish drink and was the first to resume the conversation left hanging long ago.

"Well, we got to decide what to do with little Toma . . . She's not a puppy or a kitten. Fenya doesn't want her. She either goes to a children's home or she stays here."

"I'm thinking." Elena scowled. Her heart was in no way inclined toward this little girl, but she already knew that her heart was irrelevant, because the child had already attached herself to their household and nothing could be done about it.

"I think we should keep her: she's really an ugly kid." Such was Vasilisa Gavrilovna's incomprehensible logic.

"Vasya, what are you saying?" Elena was shocked. "We should take her because she's ugly?"

"Who else is going to take her, Elena? No lips, no hips, and barely a brain. With us she'll have food on her plate, shoes on her feet, and clothes on her back. Look at all the clothes Tanya's grown out of. And then she'll be in God's hands . . . It's not up to us . . ."

"Which means we should adopt her," Elena nodded doomfully.

"So talk to him." Since returning Vasilisa had not once spoken Pavel Alekseevich's name, referring to him only as "he."

Strangely enough, Pavel Alekseevich was prepared with an answer. Apparently, he had thought about this earlier: apply for guardianship.

"Why, of course! Why hadn't I thought of that?" Elena, who in no way could picture herself in the role of mother to the unattractive little girl, beamed. Vasilisa Gavrilovna too was delighted, though she hardly understood the fine legal differences between guardianship and adoption.

And Tanya was pleased. Toma had come to occupy a special place in her life, something like a talking dog one had to take care of. She never put a morsel in her mouth without Toma and was always ready to give her the best of everything, but at times, tiring of Toma's silent and timid presence, she would slip out on her own to take a walk or visit neighbors . . . Toma never took offense, but tailed Tanya constantly for fear of losing her.

Just before they left the dacha, Pavel Alekseevich himself announced to Toma that he was inviting her to live in their house until she grew up and received her education.

"Okay, I agree." The little girl accepted the invitation with dignity.

Deep in her heart she was terribly disappointed. She would have liked Pavel Alekseevich to be her real father, as he was for Tanya.

By September they returned to Moscow. Tomochka had been fully accepted into the household, and life followed its usual course. Only Elena Georgievna and Pavel Alekseevich's family happiness had faded and withered. Pavel Alekseevich's clumsy attempts to restore spousal relations met with no success. Particularly the last time when on one of his binges in the middle of the night he had entered their bedroom, where Lenochka dreamed her lonely, illuminative dreams, and heeding neither her protestations nor her disgust, he committed loveless rape, coming to his senses only in the morning and horrified by the events of that night.

He tried to ask for forgiveness, but she just nodded, and, without raising her eyes said flatly, without any expression whatsoever, "There's nothing to discuss. I ask only that it never happen again."

He saw the bouncy lock of hair that, as always, had fallen out of her bun and hung in a loop from her forehead to her ear; he saw her cheekbones and the tip of her nose, and he burned with shame and desire, and at that moment he would not have hesitated to give the best thing he owned, his nameless gift, so as to restore the happy simplicity and ease with which until not long ago he had been able to place his index finger into the dimple beneath that soft lock of hair and slide it from there down along her narrow backbone in the even groove of her spine to the slightly elevated base of her tailbone—os sacrum, the sacred bone . . . Why, by the way, was it sacred?—and further downward, between her tight-pressed musculus gluteus maximus, past the delicately ridged button of her perineum, parting her slightly flaccid labia majora and shy labia minora to settle in her vestibulum vaginae and feel her satiny moist mucosa—he knew all this anatomy, morphology, histology—and caress with his finger the longish bead of her corpus clitoridis—ellipsis, space, heartbeat—further and further, through the thin forest of hair on the tangible round of her mons pubis, past her cosmetic, double-stitched scar (he hadn't realized then that the effort had been for himself), upward toward the tiny funnel of her navel, past the sharp nipples of her breasts spread in different directions, and stopping at her infraclavicular fossa so that the bowed arches of her clavicle spread beneath his palm . . .

He winced with his entire face and moaned: it was all over, gone. Silently he left their bedroom, went to his study, pulled an uncorked bottle from behind the curtain, and opened it . . . He drank. And smiled. That putrefied, sick uterus he had removed ten years ago had taken its revenge. The wretch.

How in the world had those idiotic words spoken in anger and aggravation been born in his head? What had made him say to her "You're not a woman"? To her, the epitome of femininity, perfection. Lost. Everything was lost. He drank another half-glass and realized that he would not be able to fall asleep. From the bottom drawer of his desk he pulled his favorite folder with the blue inscription: PROJECT. He opened it. He read the first page: Stalin's name was mentioned twice. He shuddered again.

"How have I managed to live so long with the happy delusion that I was a decent person?" Pavel Alekseevich put the cruel question to himself. He pulled out the first page of the manuscript, folded it in four, and ripped it apart twice. Then tidily placed the pieces in the wastepaper basket. He looked through the entire manuscript—the leader's name was not mentioned anywhere else. He yawned, shook his head, but could not fend off the disgusting gnashing of his heart and realized that there was nothing else left for him to do except fall asleep.

Pavel Alekseevich never bothered his wife again. Just as he never again attempted to discuss this new sad state of affairs with her.

That last nocturnal episode, which in no way coincided with Elena's sense of her husband, in fact changed little: her hurt was so profound that she could no longer do anything with herself. It was as if the phrase her husband had spoken in anger had killed all desire and poisoned the very soil from which the need for tender contact, for caresses, and for spousal intimacy grew.

Over time the hurt neither increased nor decreased. It penetrated her to her depths, and Elena lived with it the same way people live for years with a birthmark or a tumor.

Even outwardly Elena began gradually to change: she lost weight and acquired sharp corners. Her softly rounded movements, the soft angled turn of her head, her catlike manner of curling up in an upholstered chair or on the couch, lightly easing her body into every corner of the furniture—her natural, unique way of moving that had always attracted Pavel Alekseevich—was abandoning her.

The clothes that had once suited her, with the round collars, gathered sleeves, and innocent open necklines that revealed her slightly drooping, but long neck, had by then gone out of style, and she happily recut and resewed all her light dresses for the girls—the one with the tiny flowers, the one with the small wreaths, and the one with the little bouquets—and bought herself two suits (one summer, the other winter) and turned into a school marm.

Sitting next to his wife at family dinner one Sunday, Pavel Alekseevich sniffed the air. Through the crude aromas of Vasilisa's simple cooking came something new: instead of her former flowery scent, Elena smelled of widowhood, dust, and vegetable oil. Almost like Vasilisa, only Vasilisa's smell was mixed with either sweat or the stench of old greasy clothing . . . He moved his eyes from his wife to Tanya, and smiled to her: what a delightful little girl she was, her mother's image, all Lenochka . . . The former Lenochka . . .

The happy period of their marriage was over. Now all that was left was the marriage, like everyone else's, and even, perhaps, better than most people's. After all, lots of people survive somehow from day to day, year to year, never knowing joy or happiness, only mechanical habit.

Never, ever—they both understood—would they reenter the happy waters they had sailed for ten years . . .

TIME AND AGAIN ELENA'S GAZE WOULD STUMBLE UPON the puny little girl with the habits of a small rodent—benign, meek, and as pathetic as could be—the unintentional cause of their family's breakdown, which for Elena was more bitter than all the misfortunes she had endured, including the deaths of her parents, of her grandmother, of her husband, her own deadly illness, and even the war. Living with her was impossible, but so was getting rid of her, sending her back to her relatives, or placing her in a children's home.

Vasilisa mumbled, as if to the wall: "And you thought it would be simple? Nothing is simple . . . You're gonna have to work at it now . . . Yes, you are . . . You can't just pray that one away . . ."

What sins of Elena's did she have in mind? Vasilisa Gavrilovna had her own special, complicated way of adding things up, but underlying her method was a strange, even if somewhat silly, truth.

13

Elena's First Notebook

MY LIFE IN AND OF ITSELF IS SO INSIGNIFICANT AND I myself am so insignificant that it never would have occurred to me to write anything down, were it not for the fact that my memory is getting worse and worse. It needs some sort of external reinforcement: smells, sounds, objects, that elicit memories, pointers, references . . . So let there be at least this little notebook, and when my memory fails entirely, I will be able to look at it and remember. It's so strange how you grow up and acquire knowledge, and past events take on completely different meaning, depth, a sense of God's agency, and I want to excavate my own life, like an archeologist, uncovering layer after layer, so as to understand what is happening to me and to my life. Where is it taking me, and what is it trying to tell me? I can't understand; I don't know how. The most horrifying thing is that my brain has become like an old porcelain cup: it's filled with tiny cracks. My thoughts suddenly cut off, lose themselves, and it takes a long time to pick up their trail. Periods when I drop out. Sometimes the image of a person takes on a life separate from the name of its owner. A person you know well, have known for a long time, a loved one—suddenly you can't remember their name, no matter how hard you try. Or just the opposite: you remember a name, but not the person behind it.

I constantly write notes to myself: don't forget this, don't forget that. Then I lose the notes. Not too long ago I found one and had a real scare: it was written in my hand, but, my God, what spelling: a letter left out here, whole syllables out of place.

Deep in my heart I suspect that this is the beginning of some terrible disease. I just wrote that and now am entirely convinced of it. And it scares me. No one in our family had anything similar. Although Grandmother, it seems, had an older sister who reverted to her childhood when she got old. It's awful: your whole life then becomes senseless. If a person has forgotten her own life—her parents, and children, and loves, and joys, and losses—then what was the point of living? The other day I was thinking about Grandmother Evgenia. And I couldn't remember her patronymic. I'd totally forgotten it. It made me so upset. And then the next day it just came to me on its own: Evgenia Fedorovna.

I have to write everything down—everything. For myself. And maybe for Tanechka. She's going through this period of distancing herself. She's totally preoccupied by her studies, wants to become a biologist, and has grown unusually close to her father. But they've always adored each other. Only he doesn't have as good a sense of her as I do. When her head or her stomach hurts, I know exactly how it hurts . . . And the fact that Tanechka seems not to have any interest in my life and leans more toward her father doesn't really mean anything. I am sure that she will still need me. And she needs to know everything that I know. After all, it's not just the big, significant events that are important. Surprisingly, the more distant they become, the more important the small, insignificant events are. Especially dreams . . . I've always had dreams, and such powerful ones that now my earlier recollections and childhood dreams seem to be intertwined and I can't say for sure which image is from the real past and which from a dream. Tanechka needs to learn about all my petty trifles while they still haven't been lost by my faulty memory. For example, it seems to me that I remember how I first learned to walk: I'm alone in a very large room, propped up against a green velvet sofa. It tickles. Kitty-corner in front of me is a white tile stove, a Dutch stove, and I want to touch it. It is smooth and alluring. I collect my strength. It's very scary. I'm afraid to walk without anyone's hand, but it seems to me that I could run over to it. I screw up my face with effort, push off from the sofa, and run. Fly almost. And run palms first right into the tile. It is unexpectedly hot. I scream. A large, mustached woman with a swarthy face appears from nowhere and sweeps me up into her arms . . . Where was that? Probably in Moscow, in Grandmother's apartment. Mother said that I started to walk very early, before my first birthday. Can a child that age really remember anything? Or was it a dream after all? There's no one to ask.

My father, Georgy Ivanovich, was no ordinary person: he was a dreamer endowed with the rare ability to convince others of his ideas, a homegrown philosopher, from a young age an ardent revolutionary who even hung out with terrorists, but after the events of 1905 he turned to Tolstoyism. After he became a Tolstoyan he professed other ideals, and working the land became his religion. After that he never again lived in the city, but organized Tolstoyan farm collectives in various regions, all of them failures, except the last, the one in Troparevo.

When he was young, Father was very handsome. He had an aquiline nose and bright black eyes. Probably that was his Greek or South Caucasian blood. Mother, on the other hand, does not look very pretty in the photographs taken when she was young: a chubby face, tiny eyes, and a potato nose. When she was older, though, when I already began to understand things, Mama got prettier. She lost a lot of weight, her face acquired more distinct characteristics, became more memorable. Father was a man of unlimited passions. He liked to argue, took offense easily, and was quick-tempered, but incredibly kind. No, not kind, selfless. He was truly a man of the future, as I understand it. He had something in common with PA. He never thought about his own benefit, in fact, he didn't really understand what that might be. He was ready to give everything away. But except for his books he had nothing, and his library was always communal. His bookplate had a curlicue border with the words "From the Public Library of Georgy Miakotin."

He professed nonviolence as passionately and energetically as everything else. Now I'm able to judge him soberly: he supported nonviolence in public life, but was a terrible despot at home. He was gifted with the rare ability to instill his ideas in others; there was something infectious about him. Like Tolstoy he had many acolytes and followers. I think that Mama in fact was a victim of his rare, seductive personality. She followed him everywhere, trusted him in everything. He would change his convictions, and she couldn't keep up with him. For her everything was more superficial, though; for her the main thing was that she loved him immensely, and for his sake she gave up her life as a modest music teacher in the city for life in the countryside. In the countryside she didn't teach music, but cooked porridge for dozens of people, did laundry, and milked cows. She learned to do it all. All of it was beyond her capabilities, but she made the effort on Papa's behalf: in addition to everything else, she wanted to be his best student. She did everything he wanted. Except for one thing: she returned to her parents' house in Moscow to give birth. And left her tiny children with them to raise until we were old enough. I was the last, the third. Father was very angry with her for doing this. Because the other Tolstoyans all raised their children on the land. But this was the only issue that Mama did not concede to Father. Until I was four I was raised by my grandmother, then, at my father's insistence, taken to live with them in the commune.

After collectivization started, the authorities launched frightening attacks against the commune, although, you would think, it was that same ideal collective farm the Bolsheviks intended to organize throughout the entire country. In the first year of collectivization, they even proposed that my father, an experienced commune manager, join the administration and help organize collective farms. But he refused.

"Our communities are voluntary, and that's what keeps them alive, but you're proposing to organize people through the use of force, which does not coincide with my views," was how he explained it to the party bosses.

At first they left the members of the commune alone, but clearly not for long. Following deliberations and discussions it was decided that they look for new locations, farther away: the village of Troparevo was much too close to the capital. They began their search in 1930, but it was 1932 before they not only found a place but put up their first log houses in the foothills of Altai. Just before they moved, Mama begged Papa to leave me in Moscow. I was fifteen years old, and Grandmother was able to adopt me. I became a Nechaeva. Probably that's what saved me from arrest—my grandmother's surname.

In Altai, in Solonakcha, their life took a horrible turn. After that I never saw any of them. My brother Sergei was drafted, but refused on ethical grounds: he did not want to carry a gun. He was tried by military tribunal and sentenced to death by firing squad. He was like my father: unbending. But Vasya was a gentle, tender little boy: they called him shepherd boy. He was the only one of us who truly loved the soil and farming not abstractly, out of theoretical considerations, but from the heart. Animals listened to him.

Mishka the bull would follow him around like a puppy. Vasya drowned in the Ob River five days after he was handed a draft notice. The next day he was supposed to appear at the draft board in town. That was 1934. Soon after, my parents were arrested. They were given ten years without the right to send or receive letters. Grandmother tried to track them down: before the war she stood in all sorts of lines. But she never got an answer. She silently maintained that they had all perished because of my father. Basically, that's how all the Tolstoyans became extinct. I visited Maroseyka Street where there used to be a vegetarian cafeteria. But the place was unrecognizable. No publishing house, no cafeteria . . .

But I wanted to write about something else. Here's another image from my early childhood: I'm sitting at a large table with huge basins of raspberries in front of me. The berries are almost the size of eggs. I pull the fat white stems out of the centers of the berries and put them in a large cup and toss the berries into a bucket, as if they were no good, trash. It's the inedible white centers that are valuable. The smell of the raspberries is so strong that it seems as if the air itself is colored with a reddish-blue tint. Inside me churns this difficult, serious question about how what's most important to some can be trash and garbage for others. Was this a dream?

There are lots more just like this. I'm carrying a bowl of chopped greens for tiny baby rabbits. The stronger of them jump up first, while several little scrawny ones can't make their way to the food. I have to sort these weak ones out and put them in a separate cage. So the stronger ones wouldn't trample them. That seems not to have been a dream. But maybe it was a dream? It's difficult to imagine that such tender liberties were allowed at our commune. Life was very harsh . . .

All these colorful trifles somewhat confuse and, if you will, soften the images of my memories. The commune where I lived from the time I was four, in Troparevo, a not so distant suburb of Moscow, was small: only eighteen to twenty adults and about ten children, all different ages. But we had our own school. We were taught to read using Lev Tolstoy's primer. And our first books were, of course, Tolstoy's. The story of the plum pits: how it's bad to lie. About the wooden trough for the old grandfather: how one should treat one's parents well. There was almost never enough food, but it was divided equally. When there was a lot—that happened too—it was still shameful to take a lot.

The Teachings of Christ Presented for Children: I have memories of it from early childhood. I read the real Gospels only much later, when I was living with Grandmother . . . To say that the adults in the commune loved Tolstoy would be an understatement: they idolized him. As a small child I had my fill of him. It's even funny to admit, but they fed me such a steady diet of his articles and philosophy that I wouldn't go near *The Cossacks*, *Anna Karenina*, or even *War and Peace*. I read his novels only after the war.

But that's not what I want to talk about. There's something else. Since I was a little girl from time to time I've had moments when I seem to lose touch with the here and now. I think that many people have this experience, but because it's so enormously complicated to describe these occurrences—for which our impoverished language has neither the words nor the concepts—no one even tries to share their experience with others. I have noticed many times how a child will suddenly stop in the middle of playing, eyes empty, fogged over, and then a second later is once again rolling a truck or dressing a doll. The child just drops out for a while. I'm sure that everyone knows the feeling of stopping dead in your tracks and losing all sense of the passage of time. How can I describe this, especially since I'm not a writer? Yet for some reason it seems important to try to get all this out. Perhaps it's precisely for this reason that I've stopped trusting my own memory, which constantly fails me.

The most frightening experience I've ever had—and the most impossible to describe—is that of border crossings. I'm talking about the border between everyday life and various other conditions I'm acquainted with but that are as difficult to describe as death. What can a person who has never died say about dying? But it seems to me that each time you drop out of everyday life you die a little bit. I love my profession of drafting precisely because it has an exact set of rules that can be used to organize everything. There's a key to the transition from one projection to another. What I'm talking about, though, is when there's a transition, but from one time to the next you never know what laws govern it, which is what makes it so frightening.

Merciful Lord, all those journeys ... All of them different ... The most frightening thing that happened to me—for that matter the most frightening transition I ever underwent—happened just after my grandfather's death. In order for you to understand this, I need to say a bit more about my family.

Everyone feared my grandfather—my mother and my grandmother included. That I was afraid of him is perfectly understandable. I was a frightened little girl in general. When he died, I was seven years old. In 1922. He was a building contractor, and at one time he had been very wealthy, but had lost it all before the revolution. I know very little about the history of my family, especially this part of it. All that survived in Grandmother's version was that a train station pavilion he had built caved in, several people died, and he himself was hurt and his leg had to be amputated. There was a court trial, and that was his ruin. After the court case Grandfather never recovered. Usually he would sit in his deep armchair with its back to the bay window, and against the light background his face would seem dark, especially when it was sunny. Grandmother and Grandfather lived in Trekhprudny Lane, in the Volotsky buildings. My grandfather himself had built them, in 1911, I think. It was a garret apartment. The elevator never worked. Climbing up the tall staircase took a long time. Grandfather basically never left the house. He was always ill, breathed with a rasp, smoked smelly tobacco, and walked around the apartment with two canes. He never used a crutch. He just kept it near the couch.

In those years we—I mean the commune—kept cows and brought milk from Troparevo to City Hospital No. 1 on the Kaluga Highway. We had a cart and a communal horse. Mama sometimes took me with her, and after having delivered the milk, we would ride from the Kaluga Highway to the vegetarian cafeteria on Maroseyka Street. I remember carrot tea with saccharine, and soy cutlets ... In the same building there was a publishing house and the Tolstoy Society's offices. My father's relationship with the society's administration was not very good. It seems strange, but as far as I can judge now, the Tolstoyans were always fighting, arguing, and trying to prove something to each other. My father was an ardent debater. Between him and his father-in-law, my grandfather, there were deep hostilities, for political reasons. As for my grandmother,

Evgenia Fedorovna, my father somewhat despised her for her Orthodox Christian beliefs, and though he never argued with her to the point of breaking off relations, he was always instructing her how to practice her faith correctly, the Tolstoyan way . . . Like Tolstoy, he did not recognize miracles or other mystical phenomena; for him the main thing was moral content. And Christ was the epitome of morality. I look back on this all now with a smile, because I constantly have before my eyes our Vasilisa, who has not the least conception of morality. She says, "that's God's way" or "that's not God's way," and hasn't a thought about good and evil, and judges only by her silly heart. While Papa had a theory for everything.

My mother visited her parents almost secretively. In any case, I somehow realized that I was not supposed to tell my father about our trips to Trekhprudny. It was kind of Mama's and my secret. Like the several spoons of farmer's cheese Mama withheld from sale as a present for her parents. Dairy products were not for our consumption. Only the sick and little children were given milk.

Grandmother always received us in the kitchen, which was right next to the entrance. Grandfather never came out of the room at the far end of the apartment, and I did not realize that Grandmother kept our visits secret from him. He extended his dislike for my father to my mother and would get frightfully angry if word got to him that Mama had been at Trekhprudny. A very, very cruel and intolerant person Grandfather was. He barely tolerated his grandchildren.

Mama told me that he had a long and painful death, and cursed terribly until his last minute, damning everyone and blaspheming. They did not take me to his funeral: it was freezing cold. After some time had passed—I think not less than six weeks had passed—Mama brought me to Grandmother's during Holy Week and left me with her because I had just broken out with chicken pox. While I was sick, I slept in the room where Grandfather had lived. They put me on his couch, which stood rather strangely in the center of the room. Probably in the last months of his life, when he could no longer get out of bed, they had turned the couch in order to be able to approach him from both sides. He was very heavy, and it was very difficult for Grandmother to change his linen by herself . . .

I was very ill for about three days, and then the healing sores just itched. Grandmother gave me some sort of tranquilizer, and I remember that it made me sleep and sleep, so that I confused day and night. Once in the middle of the night I heard a knock that seemed to come from the neighbors'. I was surprised in my sleep. What were they pounding nails at night for? Harder and harder. Each strike hit me right on the bridge of my nose. That's because I'm sleeping, I explained to myself. I have to wake up. But I couldn't. Then the blows seemed to coalesce, as if an invisible jackhammer were boring with great pressure into my forehead . . . The drill gnawed deeper, the vibration was unbearable, and it seemed as if all of me were being dragged into a velvet-black, spinning abyss. This was no dream; it was something else. And it lasted long enough for me to figure out two things: first, that what was happening to me was stronger than pain, and the suffering was not physical, but some other kind. Second, the spinning blackness began in the middle of my forehead, formed a funnel, and carried me off beyond time. I was terribly nauseated in a strange way, but if I had been able to vomit, I would have vomited up myself . . . Pain encircled me from all sides; it was bigger than me; it existed before me. I was simply a grain of sand in an unending stream, and what was happening, I guessed, was what is called eternity . . .

All these explanations come to me now. Then, as a little girl, I could never have found the words. But since then, whenever I recollect this event, a vibrating nausea arises just beneath my heart.

But then the drill stopped. I was lying on Grandfather's couch, but the room with the striped wallpaper, with the darling little bay window, was not there. This was some unfamiliar place that resembled nothing else. It was a low-ceiling space illuminated with a dull brownish light that was so weak that the ceiling and the walls disappeared into the gloominess. Perhaps it was not a room at all, but some terribly closed-in space with what resembled a wretched sky overhead. There were a lot of unpleasant things there, but after all these years I don't want to strain my memory to resurrect the details, because when I think back to then I begin to feel sick.

A multitude of muddy shadow-people filled the space around me. Among them was Grandfather. They moved about painfully and aimlessly, squabbling slightly, and paying no attention to me. I didn't want them to see me. Especially Grandfather. He limped, as he had when he was alive, but he had no cane.

This state of powerlessness and sadness was so heavy, so contrary to life, that I guessed that this was death. As soon as I thought that, I saw myself behind our house in Troparevo on a bright summer afternoon with patches of sun and shadow. A large poplar toppled by a recent tornado lay across the path, and I walked along it, stepping over broken branches, slipping on the damp trunk, and inhaling the strong scent of withering foliage. Everything was slightly spongy: the tree trunk under my slight weight and the layers of decaying foliage. A dream inverted: from there to here.

Here, in the place where I was, there was no real light and no shadows. There, behind the Troparevo house, where the fallen tree lay, where the sole of my shoe slid along the velvety tree trunk, there were shadows, and spots of light, and an immeasurable wealth of shades of colors. Here everything was unfixed and brown, but real. There everything was unreal. Here there were no shadows. Darkness doesn't have shadows. Shadows are possible only where there is light . . .

I lay as if paralyzed, unable even to move my lips. I wanted to cross myself, as Grandmother had taught me, but I was sure that I could not even lift my hand. But my arm lifted easily, and I made the sign of the cross and recited "Our Father" . . .

A man in a clay mask resembling an ordinary oven pot approached me. Through the clay eye slits in his mask he stared at me with bright blue eyes. These eyes were the only thing that had any color. The man sneered.

My prayer hung tangibly over my head. Not that it was weak. It just did not go anywhere. It was cancelled. This dark place was located in some place far away from God's world, in a solitude so unimaginable that light did not penetrate it, and I realized that prayer without light is like fish without water—dead . . .

I could hear the buzz of a conversation—sad, decayed, and deprived of any sense. Nothing but lethargic irritation, a languid argument about nothing. And Grandfather's voice: I ORDERED, you ORDERED, I did not ORDER . . . This "ORDERED" was a being . . .

The one in the clay mask bent over me and started to speak. I don't remember what he said. But I remember that his speech was unexpectedly coarse and vulgar, ungrammatical; he chided me, even mocked me. His words, like the brownish clay on his face, also were a mask.

"He can speak using other words; he's deceiving me. Liar," I thought. And as soon as I said that to myself, he disappeared. It seems I had exposed him with my thought alone . . .

SHADOWS FLUTTERED HERE AND THERE, AND ALL OF this lasted timelessly long, until I saw that this place had no walls, that merely the thickened gloom created the appearance of a closed space, while in fact this cramped, dark place was enormous, infinite; it filled everything, and nothing existed besides it. It was a maze with no way out. I became terrified. Not for myself, but for Grandfather, and I began to shout.

"Grandfather!"

He seemed to look in my direction, but either he didn't recognize me, or didn't want to recognize me, but just continued mumbling, looking at me with his faded brown eyes: I ORDERED, he ORDERED . . .

Suddenly everything shifted and began to slip away. Like the shadow of a cloud across a field, the dark space began to move off, and I saw first a part of the wall in its striped wallpaper, then all of Grandfather's room in the gray predawn gloom.

I had not awoken, I simply was not asleep. The morning gloom, depressing and unpleasant on ordinary days, now seemed a live pearl color full of promise, because even the nighttime gloom of this, our world, is a shade of our earthly light. What had been shown to me there was the absence of light, a sad and unwelcoming place. That was it, the shadow of death . . . And when the last edge of the darkness floated out of the room and disappeared somewhere to the north, I heard a clear, youthful, indubitably male voice saying:

"The middle world."

TO THIS DAY I HAVE NO IDEA WHAT THAT WAS . . . OF ONLY one thing am I almost certain: all of that was shown to me because my crippled grandfather with his gloomy face slipped among the crowd of shadows.

Later, when I grew up and read the Gospels and the Epistles of Saint Paul, I returned to this event, to this otherworldly encounter, and thought, Does the apostle know that not all of us change, that some do not change at all and preserve forever their lameness and gloominess, and that what's behind all this is sin? I do not condemn Grandfather, by no means—who in our family can judge whom? But Mama once let slip that when Grandfather's case with the train station pavilion that had collapsed was under investigation, his guilt had not been proven, but that the accusation had been that he had used poor-quality materials, which caused the ill-fated pavilion to collapse and the workers to die ... Theft or bribery ... The usual Russian story. And so, is it going to be this way forever, with no forgiveness whatsoever? Did the apostle promise deliverance from sin only for those without sin? No, I don't understand ...

And what about my memory lapses? What if I forget? I forget so much these days, I probably also forget my sins. So then what's the point of repentance and forgiveness? If there's no guilt, then there can be no forgiveness.

Tiny pieces of my life seem to have been washed away as if by water. In their place a blank space has formed, as when you wake up after you've dreamed that you had a really important discussion with someone inhumanly intelligent but you can't pull, can't drag any of it out into your waking life, and everything important stays in the dream. You get this horrible feeling that there are valuables stored in some sealed room that you can't get into. Although sometimes you manage to return to an old dream, to the same person you were having the conversation with, and continue the conversation where it broke off. And he answers, and everything is clear as day. But then you wake up and once again, there's just blankness.

I had one of those blank spots appear where I committed a betrayal. I still remember it, but just the fact. For a long time I haven't felt any repentance or shame. Apparently, I forgave myself. And the way I committed the betrayal: easily, with no pangs of anything, not even hesitation, or thought. I am talking about my dead Anton. There was a poem that was very popular during the war, Konstantin Simonov's "Wait for me, and I'll return"... At the end it goes: "Only you and I will know how among flames and fire your waiting saved my life ..." Instead I caused his death by not waiting.

I fell in love with PA not even at first sight, but as if I had loved him even before I was born and merely remembered anew my old love for him. I forgot Anton as if he were just a neighbor, or a classmate, or a colleague from work. Not even a relative. Though I'd lived with him for five years. He's the father of my only daughter. Your father, Tanechka. I see nothing of Anton or his family in you. You really do resemble PA. Your forehead, your mouth, your hands. I won't even mention your facial expressions, your gestures, and your habits. But I can't tell you that PA is not your natural father. So, it turns out that first I betrayed Anton, and then I robbed him, deprived him of his daughter. Can you ever forgive me?

Overall, I'm certain that PA means more for Tanya than I do. He's meant more for me than I have for myself. Even now when everything is so hopelessly ruined between us, fairness demands I admit that I have never met a more noble, more intelligent, or kinder person. And no one in God's world can explain to me why this best-of-the-best person has for so many years served the greatest evil there is on this earth. How can these two things coexist in one person? In my heart I sensed it all, knew it all back then when we were in evacuation and he took the Romashkins' kittens away. At first I couldn't believe that he had drowned them. Now I believe everything. After all, with just one phrase he crossed out our love, all ten years of our happiness. Destroyed everything. Destroyed me. Cruelty? I don't understand. But that's exactly what I don't want to remember now. For me right now it's important to restore everything that's slipping away from me, that always, before PA appeared in my life, played such a large role. My dreams and early memories.

What I see—what's told to me and shown to me in my dreams—is much richer and more significant than what I can put to paper. I have a wonderful spatial imagination, professional in a certain sense. Probably I am particularly sensitive to space, and for that reason have found myself in its mysterious back alleys, like that "middle world." On the other hand, nothing comforts me more than my dear mechanical drawing, where each structure is strictly and completely transparent.

The dreams I see exist in some sort of dependency on the everyday waking world, but I won't even try to describe the nature of that dependency. There is doubtless logic to the transition, only it remains on the other side and never emerges into waking reality. It's perfectly clear to me that even though my hyperphysical journeys to various strange places violate all possible laws, my presence in those places is no less real than everything that surrounds us here, where I write with a pen in a school notebook Tanya started and abandoned at the very beginning because the school year had ended. No less real than the houses, streets, trees, and teacups here.

But again, the key to it all is sealed in a room, in a room without doors. In general, a lot of different things in my dreams are connected with doors and windows. The first, probably most important, door I saw was a very long time ago, not as a child, but when I was a teenager. I can't say for sure when, because this vision is always accompanied by a sense of having encountered something already seen before. As if it were possible first to commit something to memory and then to be born into the world with the memory.

This door was in a cliff, but at first I saw the cliff, which was of dazzling fresh limestone so totally and abundantly flooded with sunlight that all the details of its coarse texture, all its uneven surface—a memorial incarnate to a hardworking civilization of small shelled animals long ago extinct—were as visible as if under a magnifying glass. Then my gaze shifted, a screw turned, and a slight swell swept over the surface, and I saw a door with a bas-relief surface cut into the side of the cliff. The relief was very distinct but it didn't add up to an intelligible image. The smooth lines intersected, weaved, and flowed into each other, until finally my eyes adapted, and then the meaning of the image revealed itself to me. I made out a high pallet containing a smoothly curved body that flowed downward from the top, delicate hands folded in meekness, Jewish heads with tall brows bent low, and, above them all, the lone figure of the Son with the Theotokos as child in his arms . . .

The door was ready to open; a shadow even seemed to flit across a crack in the aperture in the cliff, and I was invited to enter. But I took fright, and the door, sensing my fright, once again reverted into the bas-relief on the white cliff, becoming flatter and flatter as I watched, gradually being covered over by the white meat of the limestone until it disappeared entirely.

I was not ready to enter. But there was nothing irreversible or irrevocably lost in this. I simply wasn't ready. I'm still not ready.

Then it was as if I were told: Leave. Let your fear expend itself in life's travails. And when your pain, your longing, and your thirst for understanding exceed your fear, come back again.

That's approximately what I heard at the door. It was said tenderly. By the way, people always speak tenderly to me.

There was another thing about the door. It led from one space to another. But there weren't any walls or anything else resembling a barrier between these two spaces. Just a door. Not even a door, a doorway. But everything visible through that doorway was different: the air, the water, and the people inhabiting it. I desperately wanted to go inside, but the space of the doorway was hostile and would not let me through. Its hostility was so great that it wasn't worth trying. I stepped away. And then it occurred to me: you should try, make an attempt . . . I turned around. But the doorway was no longer there. And the space wasn't there. Only ripples in the air left by a vanished opportunity.

I also remember how Grandmother died. As happens with the righteous, she knew in advance of the day of her death. Not long before Grandmother's death Vasilisa had left for who knows where—she suddenly got the urge, you know how even now that still happens with her. But on the eve of Grandmother's death she returned. By that time Grandmother had not got out of bed for a week, had not taken any food, and had drunk only small amounts of water. She was not in pain, at least, so it seemed to me. Her whole life no one had ever heard her complain. She did not speak, answering questions only by shaking her head to say no. No to everything. Vasilisa sat alongside Grandmother and read something devout. I think now that it must have been the "Office of the Parting of the Soul from the Body." But maybe something else. Grandmother was well over eighty years old and looked like antiquity itself, an Egyptian mummy. Despite her horrifying thinness, though, she was very beautiful. Those last days she did not open her eyes. But her face was not unconscious. Just the opposite, it was the attentive face of a person concentrating on some important and weighty question.

On the eve of her death her young neighbor dropped by to borrow wineglasses: it was her birthday. I opened the cupboard and took out several different wineglasses, among which there was one real beauty, an antique with a worn gold pattern. The neighbor started looking it over and began to gush. She spoke rather loudly, and her squeals of delight over this beautiful glass were very inappropriate: Grandmother lay dying in the same room.

"My, they knew how to make things then. They don't make things that way now. It must cost . . ."

And just then, in a clear and rather sonorous voice, Grandmother—without opening her eyes—fully conscious, and even severely, made a pronouncement.

"My child, you're disturbing me . . ."

FOR TWO WEEKS SHE HAD SAID NOTHING, AND THE LAST three days it had seemed to us that she was unconscious . . . I don't know how we disturbed her, what important business we tore her from . . .

A day later, at sunset, when we—Anton Ivanovich, Vasilisa, and I—were sitting at the table, her clear, loud voice suddenly rang out from its weeklong oblivion.

"The doors! The doors!"

Vasilisa flew down the long corridor—clattering with her old shoes that fell from her heels—to open the front door. She switched the latch, and the door flung open. Just then a stream of air rushed through the open window leaf in the direction of the front door, the light, cold draft touching Vasilisa as it blew past . . .

I turned toward Grandmother. She exhaled, and never inhaled again. The draft seemed to dart back. The front door slammed shut of its own, and the window leaf jerked on its hinge. A sunbeam darted from Grandmother's face to the shifting glass. The sunbeam, a little golden clot, was solid, and as it flashed on the scoured pane we heard the faint sound of shattering glass.

Anton Ivanovich stared at the window leaf and shook his head. Vasilisa, who had sensed everything instantly, crossed herself. I went over to Grandmother, not yet quite believing that everything was over.

Her death had been as serene as it could be. It was "a Christian death, peaceful, painless, and without shame." But at the time I didn't know that's what it was called. Vasilisa knew.

Grandmother's face turned solemn and joyous. The pale-pink skin of her head peeked through her bluish-gray hair; her forehead and nose hardened and froze like fine porcelain clay, and her wrinkles smoothed out. Her eyebrows were sable, with tiny brushes at the bridge of her nose. It was precisely at that moment that I distinctly realized how much I resembled her . . . Our white cat, Motya, who had lain at Grandmother's feet since she had taken to her bed, got up, went over to the edge of the bed, and jumped to the floor.

Anton went to see what had happened to the window leaf. He still hadn't realized that Grandmother had died.

"The draft shattered the glass," he mused in wonderment, picking off a piece of dried putty. "There's a big piece of glass in the back stairwell; I can cut a piece of it for the window leaf . . . Good thing that it's a rectangle; any of the other window panes could be real trouble . . ."

The window, indeed, was semicircular at the top, with small asymmetrical pieces of stained glass, and almost all the pieces were irregularly shaped. The house was in the moderne style, built by Grandfather in better times . . .

Windows and doors . . . Windows and doors . . . Even a child knows the difference. A door is a boundary. Behind a door lies another space. You enter it, and you yourself change. It's impossible not to change. While a window merely lends its knowledge for a time. You look, and then you forget. But that's already concerning my dreams.

That day, the day of Grandmother's death, Vasilisa's hour arrived. She knew everything about death. How it's done. How to bathe, dress, and mourn the dead. What clothes to dress them in, what prayers to read, what to eat and what not to eat. I submitted to her completely, without the least hesitation. And not only I, but Anton too. She took everything in stride, issued instructions, and we did as we were told.

By evening Grandmother lay stretched out on the expanded dining room table, her hands crossed in meek submission across her chest and bound together with an old stocking, her chin propped with a headscarf folded over four times into a halter, and her eyes covered with two large worn five-kopeck coins. Where had Vasilisa dug them up? Had she brought them with her?

An icon lamp burned at the head of the table, and Vasilisa read slowly in Church Slavonic before the icon. I sat on a stool next to the table, saying farewell to Grandmother. I was twenty-four years old. Neither my brothers nor my parents were alive at that point, but I learned of my parents' deaths only many years later: at that time we still didn't know what "ten years without the right to send or receive letters" really meant . . .

It was the first death I ever witnessed. I can't say that I was frightened. I stood in profound respect before this incomprehensible event and tried with all my powers to understand what was taking place: the chasm impervious to reason or emotion that separates living and dead, and especially that instant itself when live and warm Grandmother had metamorphosed into a strange, unneeded thing that had to be removed from sight as quickly as possible and tucked away deep in the earth. Everything Vasilisa did—solemnly and unhurriedly—was soothing, precisely because without all her incomprehensible actions it would have been impossible to remove this cold object. The white shirt, the shroud, and the new leather slippers that Vasilisa had examined so nitpickingly, as if Grandmother really needed this light pair of new shoes with blunt toes and metal-lined holes for laces in order to journey the easy roads that lay beyond the grave . . .

Anton Ivanovich requested that the coffin not be taken to church, but that the priest be invited to the apartment. Everyone was under observation and frightened. Pursing her lips, Vasilisa nodded, and late in the evening on the eve of the funeral she brought to the apartment a wee old man to whom she could entrust the departure of her benefactress. Anton Ivanovich left to spend the night at his relatives' because he didn't want to know anything about the whole business: he had a good job at the plant and a blemished family history.

The old man who showed up looked like an ordinary beggar. But when he took his vestments and an epitrachilion from his bundle and donned his Iberian cross, he turned into a priest. With greatest piety he spread a piece of embroidered fabric on the desk, which Vasilisa had washed clean. It was the antimension with pieces of relics: on it he consecrated the Eucharist. That was the first liturgy in my life. We had never been taken to church: that had been Father's condition when he had allowed the children to live at Grandmother's. The version of Tolstoyan Christianity in which we were raised after Grandmother returned us—three- and four-year-olds—to our parents totally rejected the ceremonial aspect of religion, recognizing neither church, nor the Theotokos, nor icons, nor saints . . . This time I really wanted to take communion, but wasn't able to say so. The priest then performed burial rites. After the secret prayer service was over, the little old man slipped away imperceptibly into the night. I never saw him again.

The night after the burial I woke up and went into the kitchen. I don't know why. Maybe to get something to drink. There in the kitchen in her usual place sat Grandmother in her blue dressy dress with starched lace collar. On the table in front of her there stood a tea glass in a metal holder. She was drinking tea. Everything looked so usual that I began to wonder whether I had dreamed that she had died.

"Tea?" she offered. I nodded. The teakettle was hot. The teapot had a fresh brew in it that was unusually fragrant. I poured myself some tea and sat down next to Grandmother.

"So you didn't die, did you?" I asked.

She smiled, and her white, even teeth gleamed. She has new false teeth, I thought, but said nothing so as not to embarrass her.

"Die? There is no death, Lenochka. There is no death. You'll soon learn this."

I finished my tea. We were silent, and it felt good.

"Go to sleep," she said, and I went without asking about anything.

I lay down in bed next to Anton, who was mumbling something in his sleep.

And fell asleep immediately. What had that been? A dream? Not a dream? Neither a dream nor not a dream. A third something. I don't know what to call it. A third state equidistant from the dream world and the waking world . . .

Now, after all these years, I suspect that in addition to this small conversation Grandmother said something else, but the rest of it has not been preserved in my memory. What was preserved for the rest of my life was just my firm knowledge that when you are inside a dream, all of your usual world turns into a dream. Waking reality and dreams: they're like the front and back sides of the same cloth. And what about that third state? Is it like a top view in mechanical drawing?

Over time, with increasing experience, I have learned how to distinguish one from the other almost infallibly. In the usual daytime world things are totally deprived of mystery and their real content. Although

103

expensive cups get broken and it can be very sad when a favorite thing is ruined, and in our family—out of poverty and family tradition—we used to glue cups back together, repair broken things, darn, and patch coats and pots, still when a thing becomes truly unusable, it gets thrown out.

In dreams, things are not entirely real: a cup might not always hold water—as if it still hasn't been trained to. Things in general come to exist not of their own, but only at the moment when they are needed, and as soon as the need disappears, they immediately disappear. They are abstract until you think, "What was the picture on that cup?" And then the picture appears. In and of themselves things don't get damaged and don't grow old: they are deprived of any independent existence. That's what I've figured out.

But the third realm is something else entirely. Precisely the way things behave makes it easiest to distinguish a real dream from what I call the third realm. For example, the tea glass Grandmother Evgenia Fedorovna was holding was not a glass at all. It was an identity, like Grandmother herself. Possibly, it had its own name, unknown to me. It was large, of a particular size in order to fit an unusually large tea-glass holder, and both of them were custom-made. The tea-glass holder, it seems, is a distinctively Russian object. Nowhere do they drink tea the way they do in Moscow. But this tea-glass holder was particularly Russian, made of thick silver in the shape of a little tree stump, the surface of the silver imitating wood bark and the holder's handle shaped like a little ax wedged into an upwardly slanted branch covered with tiny glued-on leaves and stalks of leaves blown away either by the peripeteia of kitchen life or the fantasy of an apprentice at the Fabergé factory where the tea-glass holder had been crafted. An ostentatious object designed for merchant tastes, of the kind intended as a gift, with a polished plaque for the inscription: "TO DEAR VASILY TIMOFEEVICH . . ."

Grandmother had smiled a fleeting smile as she drank her fragrant, dark-gold tea from Grandfather's glass, but the inscription had been missing. Where could it have gone, that piece of rhymed nonsense composed by his colleagues: "Timofeich, time for tea! Some like honey, some like jam, but Vasya is a cookie man!"

... On closer examination the tea-glass holder turned out to be more elegant than the original, which has survived to this day. There in the third realm it seemed to look nicer; at the very least it differed from its real-life self just as the fragrant, exotic tea differed from the ordinary yellowish slops that Grandmother Evgenia Fedorovna had drunk all her life, even when she had lived in her rich father's house ... She didn't like strong tea ...

Approximately the same thing happened with all the objects I happened to see while not in dreams or in memories, but in that third realm: they were, if not more refined, then enhanced to a certain degree of perfection. As if an invisible craftsman had worked on them in order to return to them their dignity and true character. In any case, that's what could be said with complete confidence about Grandmother's formerly dressy dress. The next morning, I woke up back in the completely ordinary world and first thing headed for Grandmother's armoire and pulled the dress out to look at it in the light: it was slightly faded in the shoulders and the drooping collar was mended in several spots. I swear: at night the dress had been new, and the collar solemnly stiff ...

And the teapot in the kitchen was still warm ...

The next time Grandmother invited me to tea was in the spring of 1941. You, Tanechka, were two months old; you were a weak, cranky child, and both Vasilisa and I were exhausted. That night Vasilisa had lain down with you in order to give me a chance to get a good night's sleep. I was awakened by the smell of tea, the same tea—I recognized it immediately. I went into the kitchen. Grandmother was sitting at the table. The teapot was hot, and the silver tea-glass holder stood on the table in front of her, but she was not drinking tea and did not offer me any. She was dressed strangely: in a beret draped over with a country-style headscarf and in an overcoat with large, neat patches, and buttonholes edged with new fabric. As soon as I walked in, Grandmother stood up: she had a big bundle in her arms. She opened it up and shook her head.

"No, it's too big."

And the big bundle immediately became smaller. The bundle's metamorphosis did not surprise me in the least: one word had been enough for everything to become as it was supposed to be. Grandmother began to gather kitchenware in the contracted bag, meticulously examining each object. Three spoons, three cups, three plates. A small pot, a frying pan, and a metal mug for cooking children's porridge. Then she added salt and dry cereal to it.

Her demeanor was stern and sad. Then she took the tea-glass holder, pulled out the glass, and poured the tea into the sink. Fresh, strong-brewed, fragrant tea. Then she unbuttoned her overcoat, unfastened from the collar a small golden brooch in the shape of an arrow with emerald gemstones, placed it in the tea-glass holder, and put them in the bundle as well. It seemed as if she wanted to say something to me. But she didn't say anything, and just pointed to the stuffed little bundle.

I told Vasilisa about it. Vasilisa crossed herself, nodding her head up and down.

"Oh, Elena, they're coming for us. They're coming for us . . ."

But they didn't come for us. I remembered all this when three months later evacuation of the plant began. The little bundle, and the brooch. Vasilisa had everything prepared. She knew what the vital necessities were. The only thing that didn't make sense was why Grandmother had chosen to appear to me and not to Vasilisa. Vasilisa was much more practical, and she had a lot of experience, although at the time Vasilisa had told me nothing of her secret, heroic, and implausible life.

Anton was certain that he would not be called to the front. He was an engineer, and practically all engineers had deferrals. But owing to confusion and stupidity he was mobilized, while people who knew less than he did remained at the plant. It's possible this was somehow connected to his unsociable personality. He never was friends with anyone, never trusted anyone. To be honest, I see absolutely nothing in common between the two of you . . .

We didn't even say good-bye to each other properly. There was terrible panic at the plant: at the end of June rumors were already circulating about the plant being evacuated, and we had to archive part of our work in progress, and the entire section was piled with papers and drawings, while there was already half as many employees, and everything was upside down and hopelessly confused. On top of all that, you were ill, Tanechka, and twice a day Vasilisa brought you to the checkpoint. I would go out to nurse you, but I did not have much milk, and I was nervous and afraid it would disappear entirely.

And so, preoccupied with childhood illness, Anton and I said goodbye, and it was only after he left—the gathering point was on Mytnaya Street for some reason and he had forbidden me to go there, so Vasilisa went—that I realized what had happened.

Having cried the night through, you fell asleep, and I collapsed alongside you. It was very hot. Our apartment was directly under the roof, and in the summer it was intolerable there. So it was hot in reality, and I also dreamed that it was hot.

Whether it was on earth or not, the place was completely unrecognizable. The soil was reddish and dry, dusty, and filled with stones. Strange plants grew—resembling cactuses, but as huge as trees. The thorns on them were sharp and retractable, as if made of blue iron. The trees breathed through these thorns, and they would extend out and then fold back in, like a cat's claws when it's asleep. Up ahead, Anton Ivanovich wandered among the prickly trees, not looking back. He wore a military uniform, but the uniform was old-fashioned: tight-fitting leggings, a short jacket, and Anton Ivanovich himself thin and with the build of a young boy. If you two have anything in common, it's body type. The narrowness in your hips, and that upward stretch of neck and chin. Yes, that's it. It had never occurred to me before.

So, there he was, walking off, while I rushed after him, wondering why he wouldn't stop and wait for me. Especially since those cactuses, though they stood in place like plants are supposed to, kept snagging me and scratching me with their claws, no matter how hard I tried to stay as far away from them as possible . . . The distance between us kept increasing, although I was walking fast and he was walking very slowly. But I couldn't shout. I don't know why; all I know is that it was impossible, forbidden. He kept moving farther and farther away, and at the last minute I saw him not on foot, but on horseback. He galloped quite skillfully among the trees until he finally disappeared entirely. At that point it was as if I was allowed to return, and the cactuses withdrew their steely claws and grew smaller and smaller, until they were the usual size, like the aloe and kalanchoe plants on windowsills, and the soil was no longer red, but ordinary, with grass that was ordinary but very soft and tender . . .

Vasilisa sometimes does good interpretations of dreams, but that time she said little.

"Each of us travels the preordained . . ."

BUT I KNEW THAT WITHOUT HER. OF COURSE, THE FIRST thing that came into my head was that he would perish at the front. But why that black uniform, those cactuses, those thorns . . . Why was it forbidden to shout? The main point is buried. But the most surprising thing is that ultimately it will all become clear. I am absolutely sure that nothing is shown to us by chance, that nothing is superfluous . . .

But still, lots and lots of things are unclear. For example, in the waking world it's clear as can be to everyone that life is logically and irreversibly divided into past, present, and future, and all our feelings and all our thoughts are well adapted to this. Even our language and its grammar. At the same time there is a completely amazing unity to each given moment when two people are together, even if just in the same room, and each of them has a different past and—when one of them leaves the room—a different future, too, while for that single instant their present is one and the same. And moments like that occur not all that infrequently. And they leave very strong impressions. And when you remember them, it's as if they were restored, but in some sort of new grammatical category that doesn't exist in our language . . . So it's difficult to explain. I can't explain . . .

Many things have been shown to me that I can neither understand nor explain. For example, back in Siberia when I was lying in the hospital after my operation, and it wasn't clear whether I was alive or not, my consciousness just sort of floated somewhere, in some mist, but not in water. Then someone pulled me out of it, and I found myself in a white-painted bed, and PA appeared. And it immediately became apparent that the accumulation of water I had been floating in was the past, and that I had always been acquainted with this man with the round forehead and wide-set eyes. Both in the past and in the future. But he himself belonged to the present. And even now, as I remember back, I sense myself in the present more strongly than ever before. Because PA possesses a special power for residing in the present.

But what variabilities we undergo in the present! A lot slips by without a trace, leaving no impression whatsoever, fleeting by as if it never happened, while other things move slowly, distinctly, meaningfully—as if for a poor student forced to learn everything by rote, without forgetting anything, to the very last letter. Of late, I often feel frightened that I could forget the most important things. And so I'm writing things down, convulsively, understanding well that I'll forget all the same, but the main thing is that what I write down is only a shadow of what I see and feel . . .

Another experience—or vision?—I had also relates to that realm of the most important which in no way belongs to the present. To what I tentatively call the third realm. "The Great Waters"—I'll call it that because this condition or event—they're hardly distinguishable—has to be designated with words of some kind . . . In any event PA wasn't around then; it happened before him . . . Basically, before he appeared I had been in many places, including the Great Waters . . . But my "I" was somewhat different then than it is now: blurred, small—like a child's or just undeveloped. And blind, it seems. Because no pictures, no images from those occurrences have been preserved in my memory. There was nothing firm, rigid, or angular, just moisture—encompassing or flowing—and I sensed myself to be more moisture than a hard body. But moisture that doesn't spread, condensed moisture like a piece of undissolved starch in watery *kissel* or a jellyfish in the foam along the shoreline. The wealth of impressions I perceived in my blindness was immense, but all of them occurred on the surface of my not entirely delimited body, while my "I" was hidden deep below, in the middle . . . Impressions that were sooner those of food—tasty, not tasty, tender, rough, thick and sticky, sometimes sweet and so sharp they made me shiver and feel feverish, and sometimes simply sweet, or particularly sweet—from which I couldn't tear myself away, and they seemed to suck in my entire being and lead me off somewhere. I also experienced various kinds of motion, like swimming, but more chaotic and requiring great effort, and while moving I encountered various streams that washed over me sometimes tenderly, and sometimes vigorously, like a massage. They stroked me, made me ticklish, tenderly sucking me in, then letting me go . . .

The main thing was the satisfaction. Of hunger, thirst, the need to be touched, and of the mutual interaction of liquids. Probably this was some primal sexual satisfaction, but not connected with any other particular being. It was a caressing, fertile environment that consisted entirely of turgescence, effusion, and partial dissolution of me in another, and another in me . . .

A blissful state. But long, rare threads of pain would creep into this bliss and induce me to move, and the new movement led to new bliss . . .

That's it approximately . . .

Then something new and horrible set in. Were it not so absolutely dark, you might say that Gloom had set in. It was greater than any form of consciousness, all-penetrating, like water or air, and uncontrollable, like the elements. And at the core of my tenuous body my little "I" writhed with the anguish of fear.

It was not a human pain, which has its dimensions—beginning, end, rise, fall. The anguish I experienced had no dimensions. It was absolute, like a geometric point. Aimed entirely at me. I experienced something similar in childhood when I wound up in the place once inhabited by my dead grandfather.

I felt a particular kind of nausea. But it wasn't my stomach or its contents, but my own "I" that was ripping itself from inside my body and, unable to find a way out, shaking me with spasms. My inviolable, secret, and precious core—protected by the mass of my fluid body from external streams of cold, warmth, acidic sourness, and excessive sweetness—trembled harder and harder, more and more agonizingly, while my body with all its jellylike blood vessels, sensitive, tender pores that absorbed thick sour streams, and fingerlike protrusions of various types capable of excreting their own liquid, which had been created anew within my flesh—my entire complexly organized body yearned to contract, to leave, and to hide from the moist horror that like an ocean covered the surfaces of all bodies . . . My body seemed to know that the horror was penetrating it through and through and not just flowing over its surface . . .

These two desires met each other halfway: my core impregnated with horror from within, pushed outward, while my corporeal part, attempting to escape an external horror, pushed inward. At the moment when it all grew entirely unbearable, my whole being contracted, collapsed, and almost ceased to be . . .

Although the spasms and cramps rent me apart, there was a shade of pleasure in this hellish pain.

A slight vibration—which at first I hardly felt and which formed a kind of weak background—intensified, taking the form of a funnel-shaped shell, and began to suck me in, intensifying the gloom—which had seemed to have reached its limits—by yet another degree. At that point my being could no longer withstand, something inside me snapped and shifted, and I turned myself inside out and immediately realized that the whole world was turning inside out together with me . . .

It was agonizing, but reassuring. I was participating in this inside-out movement, almost like a woman in labor who physically and spiritually facilitates a process that would take place even without her participation . . . it would just take longer and be more difficult. Like a woman in labor, I too tried to push myself out better, hiding all my elongated organs that used to be suspended freely in water, and pushing out the innermost part of myself. I felt it working. My strength was ebbing, the horror had almost receded, when a new feeling arose, one I had never experienced before: I had to hurry. In this new and not yet entirely evolved incarnation, a new dimension—that of time—was already ticking, already marking out invisible boundaries. I tried to hurry—and an invisible film snapped with a deafening ring. I turned myself outward. I had pulled myself out.

Bliss is the state of non-pain. Until I knew pain, I was unable to imagine bliss. There was no more horror and no more pain (a variation of horror). The whole world had become different; I had become different. Only a small part of my "I" remained unchanged, but it was so small that it barely contained itself and was entirely on the verge of dissolution, on the verge of disappearing.

The great novelty was that my body, accustomed to locating itself around its own undefined center, now was entirely inside, and my innermost core was now on the outside and experienced a weak current, a light sensation of movement along its newly constituted surface. Probably my body, accustomed to deriving everything it had needed for its composition and movement from the external world, had not gone entirely inside: at the very least, one large protrusion remained on the surface and opened itself up. Not moisture, not water, but air filled my inner body. It expanded slightly, then fell again. My breathing engaged. But I had not even succeeded in thinking through my new thought about how every imaginable form of bliss, like pain, always has yet another degree, when something on my surface broke and new apertures opened up, and I saw Light. Had my "I" acquired vision? Or had something happened in the world that had not happened before? I don't know. Light had formed. And Eyes had formed. And I closed them, because at the pinnacle of bliss there was pain ...

For whom and for what am I writing this *Diary of a Madman*? Who will believe me if I don't entirely believe myself? Will you read all this to the end? Will anyone read this at all? And why? Perhaps you shouldn't bother ... I'm talking to you, Tanechka, but at times I forget and write whatever comes into my head so that it won't dissolve into nothing.

Yesterday I came home from work, and Vasilisa said, "Someone called for you ..." Five minutes later I couldn't remember the name of the person she said had called. I asked her again. Once again Vasilisa said who. But this morning I again couldn't remember. What's more, it seems to me that yesterday I had spoken with one of my friends on the phone, but I can't remember with whom ... It's a strange kind of absentmindedness, a total lack of attention. I do what I can so that no one notices. It seems to me that this unfortunate quality displays itself least at work. There I don't forget anything or mix anything up. Except I couldn't remember the name of the new draftswoman. I had to write it down on a piece of paper and put it in my pencil jar. "Valeria." To tell the truth I committed it to memory right away. There, now I finally remember who called yesterday: it was Valya, Ilya Goldberg's wife. She called from a phone booth, said something I couldn't quite understand. She asked that PA get involved in something. And I forgot to give him the message ...

It seems that PA has noticed that something's wrong with me. Sometimes I catch his "medical" gaze on me. Since the day Lizaveta the janitor died, more than half a year ago now, our relationship has fallen apart completely. He tried to explain himself to me several times, and I see that he's suffering because of our falling-out, but there's nothing I can do with myself. The words he spoke that night still stand between us, and I don't know whether I could ever forget them. "You are not a woman. You don't have that organ." It's true. But why is that so offensive?

Things at home are very bad. For everyone. The only one who feels great is our little foster child. She sprinkles sugar on buttered white bread. And eats a loaf of white bread a day. With a happy, self-forgetful look on her face. At the same time, though, she's always looking askance, as if she were guilty or had stolen something. She's gained weight. Tanechka has helped her catch up with her schoolwork. In the end it's simply mind-boggling: I lost PA because of her.

Tanechka, why am I writing about this to you? You're only twelve years old. But one day you'll grow up and fall in love with someone, and then you'll forgive me all this nonsense.

He drinks a lot. He always smells of vodka—either just consumed or the reek of yesterday's. He's very gloomy, but I am certain that it's not just because of me.

For Old New Year's—Vasilisa observes only the old calendar—she prepared a table, baked her clumsy cabbage pie, thick as your foot, and made potato salad with bologna sausage. She boiled up beef-hoof aspic. The house reeked all day from it. Her eternal fasting has ceased tempo-rarily. In the evening PA came out to the table and put a newspaper in front of me. One of the articles was circled—about doctor-murderers. I looked at the list: half of them were his friends. The majority—Jews. He poured a glass of vodka, and chased it with a piece of cabbage pie. Then he winked at Tanechka, petted Toma on the head—she beamed—and returned to his study ... I really wanted to talk to him, but it was impossible.

I went to bed and before falling asleep asked: Tell me what's happen-ing, what will happen to all of us? But nothing was shown to me.

14

ON JANUARY 13 OF THE NEW 1953, PAVEL ALEKSEEVICH went on another drinking binge. But this time there was no cheerful revelry, and no dacha. He was morose, silent, and would not come to the phone. He went to the clinic no more often than three times a week, and by two in the afternoon he was already home. Tanechka, with whom he had always spent much of his time at home, was now in the constant company of Toma.

Both Pavel Alekseevich and Tanya hesitated to offend Toma by leav-ing her alone, so only in the early morning would Tanya peek into her father's study for a few minutes—to joke, giggle, and whisper in his ear one of her baby nicknames for him.

Two other children often came to the apartment, Ilya Iosifovich Goldberg's sons, Gennady and Vitaly—thin, awkward, with breaking voices and violent acne. They came almost every day to eat dinner. Elena invited them, knowing the family's difficult straits: Goldberg had been in prison since 1949, and Valya, who had worked in the laboratory of a Jewish doctor just arrested, was fired the day after. Left without a job, she fell ill, living from one heart attack to the next with respites only to take another trip to deliver a care package to her husband. She herself never ceased to be amazed that she was so sickly . . .

Vasilisa, whose clumsy and charitable hands passed on hundreds of money transfers and parcels, was unhappy about these dinnertime visits: as she saw it, alms were supposed to be handed out as small change or bread, not in the form of expensive meat patties. Elena guessed the reason for Vasilisa's discontent, but said nothing . . .

Throughout the entire country, meetings of indignant citizens were held, and within the health system these events were conducted with particular inspiration. Anyone with any reputation was obliged to speak out and revile the criminals. Pavel Alekseevich realized from the outset that all doctors down to the very last one were being corralled into collaborating in these shameful accusations. He had not the least doubt that the doctors were completely innocent. Pavel Alekseevich was deeply depressed, and for the first time in his life he contemplated suicide. The thick volume, rebound in red leather, of Mommsen's *History of Rome* lay constantly on his desk and whispered to him: in the period of late antiquity Pavel Alekseevich so loved, suicide was considered not a sin, but a courageous way out of a hopeless situation taken for the sake of preserving both honor and dignity. Pavel Alekseevich tried this seductive thought out on himself.

The holes in his relationship with his wife, which refused to be darned and only grew wider, depressed him. His beloved daughter was too small to become his confidante. Their closest friends now were almost all under arrest: geneticist Ilya Goldberg, forensic pathologist Jacob Shapiro, ophthalmologist Petya Krivoshey . . . All except Sasha Maklakov, his old university buddy who had long ago left medical practice to become a bureaucrat and unexpectedly turned up among the more inspired Jew-hunters . . .

But the biggest surprise awaited Pavel Alekseevich in his own home— Vasilisa Gavrilovna, who sincerely and absolutely despised Soviet power, for the first time in her life had taken its bait: the idea of covert enemies, clever doctors, and Jewish sorcerers struck a chord in her medieval soul. All the pieces of the picture fit: the Jews had led the revolution, killed the tsar, and destroyed the church. What could you expect from the people who had crucified Christ?

Vasilisa quaked, gasped, and prayed. From the street and from lines in stores she brought back eye-popping stories of doctors infecting their patients with blood from cadavers, blinding newborn infants, and inoculating their gullible patients of Russian descent with cancer. An enormous number of eyewitnesses and victims emerged. People refused treatment from Jewish doctors, and a mass psychotic fear of poisoning and the evil eye set in . . . Staff reductions, purges, trial by rumor . . . Lydia Timashuk received the Lenin Prize for exposing an underground ring . . .

During these months Vasilisa had no choice but to remain Pavel Alekseevich's sole conversation partner, or, rather, listener. Elena went off to work, and the girls—to school. Following her morning grocery raids, Vasilisa came back to find Pavel Alekseevich waiting for her in the kitchen with a pot of coffee. He displayed an extreme degree of insensitivity and completely ignored Vasilisa's obvious lack of interest in, and complete inability to maintain, a conversation. While she unloaded her patched shopping bags, he would settle in with a cup of tea or something stronger and embark on an unrushed lecture . . .

In fact, the lecture was intended for a different audience, one more enlightened and more populous, but there was no other: he could not lecture students on his investigations—having nothing to do with questions of medicine—into the history of antisemitism and its religious and economic roots. Mommsen served as his primary source, after whom Pavel Alekseevich rummaged around in the works of Josephus Flavius and real authors from antiquity; he read Saint Augustine and some of the Church Fathers . . . He worked himself toward the Middle Ages . . . Antisemitism, to his amazement, had plagued all of Christian civilization.

Vasilisa gloomily peeled carrots, sorted millet and buckwheat, and chopped cabbage. You couldn't say that she did not hear Pavel Alekseevich, but for her his brilliant lectures were written in a foreign language. She was able to extract only the general idea that Pavel Alekseevich did not believe in the insidiousness of the Jews, just the opposite—he even condemned those who attacked the Jews. As he got more and more worked up, Pavel Alekseevich quoted something in Latin and then in German, which confused poor Vasilisa even more. Maybe he's a Jew? Until recently she had believed in Pavel Alekseevich as in the Lord God, but after his fatal revelation, after he himself admitted to doing everything in his power to legalize infanticide, she did not know how she should feel about him. How much had he given away without ever counting? How many people had he helped without even knowing their name? And he was cutting children out of their mothers' bellies, killing little babies ... Maybe he's the Anti-Christ? She seemed not to distinguish the various shades of gray between black and white, not to mention pink and green, and for that reason, lips pursed, she fried onions and maintained total and disapproving silence.

Once, having consumed a bottle of vodka over the course of a two-hour monologue, Pavel Alekseevich noticed that Vasilisa had not touched the coffee he himself had made for her.

"Vasilisa, sweetie, why didn't you drink your coffee? Don't tell me you're afraid it's poisoned?" he joked.

"So what if I am?" Vasilisa muttered.

Pavel Alekseevich wanted to laugh, but stifled his laughter. As happens with alcoholics, his mood suddenly changed. He was overwhelmed by repulsion for his life. He became morose and slumped.

"A great nation, damn it . . ."

Vasilisa crossed herself and whispered a prayer for protection: Pavel Alekseevich was now on her suspect list.

15

THE STALIN ERA ENDED ON MARCH 5, BUT A LONG TIME passed before anyone figured that out. Early in the morning that day the leader's death was announced over the radio. By this time he had been dead for several days, but those who were now supposed to steer the Soviet Union were so discombobulated that they decided first to inform the world that he was ill. These fallacious news flashes about a corpse's health communicated more than just the gradual decline of his already nonexistent wellness. Medical terminology and statistics were cited that said little to the average person, but in itself the very phrase "the urine test was normal" conveyed that those on high also unfastened their fly, took out their member with thumb and index finger, and produced a certain quantity of urine. Even if it was of the very best quality, it was still urine! That was the first, devastating blow to the cult of personality. The new leaders also needed time to get accustomed to the idea that ultimately even the most immortal die.

The country's population reacted stormily: they sobbed, fainted, and collapsed from shock-induced heart attacks. Others sighed with relief, secretly rejoiced, and gloated in their hearts. But even the deceased leader's covert enemies—he hadn't had any overt ones for a long time—were in a state of confusion: how could they live without him?

Pavel Alekseevich's family represented the full range of possible reactions. Toma, who had surprised everyone with her businesslike cool at the funeral of her own mother, was now absolutely choked with grief. For a full two days she sobbed, taking short breaks to eat and sleep. She literally, in the biblical sense, ate her bread with tears.

Tanya experienced great discomfort and awkwardness: she found nothing in her heart comparable to the torrid emotions Toma displayed. She felt ashamed of her own lack of sensitivity, and, to the extent it was possible, she appropriated Toma's grief. The latter wept so sweetly and selflessly that out of pity for her Tanya managed on someone else's account to drop a few tiny tears of her own.

Pavel Alekseevich experienced a great sense of relief: there would be changes, now there would be changes. The absurd case of the doctors, in his opinion, would have to be dropped now. He expected controls to be loosened, and even pulled the folder with the dark-blue inscription PROJECT from his bottom drawer . . .

For her part, though, Vasilisa, who had long despised the powers that be and who gloated on the day Stalin's death was announced, on the next day suddenly grew morose, fell into a stupor, and kept shaking her head and—making a fig with her small fist under her black rayon headscarf—repeating incessantly, "What's going to happen now?"

Pavel Alekseevich, seeing her consternation, chuckled.

"We'll survive, with God's help!"

Elena, hearing Pavel Alekseevich's remark, smiled: she found it very amusing that Pavel Alekseevich the nonbeliever was reminding Vasilisa of God's help.

"When things calm down a bit, I'll try looking for my family again," Elena resolved.

Since 1938 the fate of her parents had been cloaked in impenetrable mystery. Ten years without the right to write or send letters had ended a very long time ago, but in reply to the inquiry she had sent back in 1949 she received a response stating that because she was not a close relation of her parents she had no right to submit an inquiry. Elena's adoption by her grandmother, necessitated in order to save her from repression, now deprived her of the right to obtain information on the fate of her real parents lost somewhere in Altai . . .

"It's going to be worse now, even worse," Vasilisa muttered.

Elena, quiet as always, just shook her head.

"It won't be worse, it won't . . ."

ATTENDING CLASSES OR GOING TO WORK DURING THOSE days of national mourning seemed blasphemous. Workers came to work and were gathered at meetings. Upper-echelon, lower-echelon, and lowest-of-the-low-echelon bureaucrats, as well as average Soviet people, delivered incoherent words of grief—fantasy infused with make-believe—sobbed, and composed mournful telegrams to the supreme address: Moscow, Kremlin . . . Then, with a Lenten look, they drank tea, smoked themselves into a stupor, iterated the same gnarled, sincere words, and sobbed again, only now not on a grandstand, but in the smoking room . . . Certain people who felt otherwise discreetly looked the other way, finding neither compassion in their hearts, nor tears in their tear glands.

Children went to school, but classes were not held, replaced by a kind of exhausting nervous idleness. They read poems about Stalin and listened to Beethoven over the black loudspeaker . . . Tanya would remember well those quaggy, dragging hours filled with stuffiness and an infernal ennui that exceeded the usual schooltime boredom. The plaster bust strung with a garland of holly and artificial flowers was attended by an honor guard of blubbering Young Pioneer girls who stood almost as plasterlike as the deceased leader. Skinny little Sonya Kapitonova—the girl at the top of the gymnastics pyramid who, propped on the quivering shoulders of her heftier classmates, had not all that long ago shouted from her live tower "Thank you, Comrade Stalin, for our happy childhood!" fainted at the foot of the bust and struck her head against the massive pedestal.

Their gallant physical education teacher, practically the sole male teacher at the school, carried her off to the nurse's room in his arms, to the undisguised envy of the older girls. The teachers scurried about and called an ambulance, and a crowd of girls in a tizzy over the turn of events shoved and pushed each other near the nurse's room, while Tanya stood at the window in the lavatory watching the snowy blur outside the glass, saddened once again by her own hard-heartedness.

It was already known that the national farewell procession would begin at noon the next day in the Hall of Columns in the House of Trade Unions. Their principal had said that they would be taken there as a group, but not on the first day. The girls were worried that they would be deceived and not taken there. Toma was full of determination to scout out the situation in advance and go on her own, early in the morning, so as to get a good place in line. For some reason she was sure that only the senior girls and honor students would get to go.

A rather poor student—although with Tanya's help she had caught up—Toma had no shortage of practical ingenuity.

Toma found Tanya in the lavatory, drew her close, and pressing her mouth to her ear, whispered, "Nadezhda Ivanovna said that tomorrow everyone is going to the Hall of Columns to pay their respects. The coffin's put up so that anyone can go see. Wanna go?"

"They won't let us." Tanya shook her head. "No way Dad will let us go."

"We won't tell him. We'll just pretend we're going to school and not say anything . . ."

Tanya pondered: the proposition was tempting. She really wanted to have a look at dead Stalin. She also remembered how they hadn't taken her to Toma's mother's funeral. On the other hand, she had not learned to lie to her parents . . .

The girls left school together. On the last turn toward their building Toma stopped, like a little goat, and announced resolutely, "You do as you want, but I'm going to the Hall of Columns right this instant to find out what's going on . . ."

This was the first time in their almost yearlong life together that Toma had made an independent decision. Usually she followed Tanya's lead in everything. Tanya stamped about in place, and they headed off in opposite directions: Tanya, as usual, turned in the direction of Novoslobodskaya, where they lived, while Toma headed down Kaliaevskaya Street toward the center of town . . .

At home there was only Vasilisa, and she did not ask where Toma was. Toma returned only toward six. Her absence had passed unnoticed. Before falling asleep the girls whispered back and forth for a long time. As a result of her excursion Toma knew what most Muscovites still did not: the center of the city had been barricaded off, with trucks and soldiers blocking all passageways, and since yesterday evening people had been lining up in columns . . .

Tanya slept poorly: she dreamed an unending dream from which she longed to wake up, but could not. In her dream she was overcome by a sense of duty, and the idea lurked that if she were able to wake up, she would be able to shirk having to fulfill an important assignment . . . The assignment was to take something very important to some place. What exactly the important thing was she did not remember, but it was small, the size of a fist, totally amorphous and, moreover, invisible. All through the night poor Tanya walked up an empty staircase, looking for a passageway or an elevator. She was supposed to find a certain address, but there were no apartment numbers, and no doorways where the numbers might be written. In addition, she was in a hurry, because the conditions imposed by her dream included urgent delivery. Yet everyone she encountered was either afraid of her or just mean: no one wanted to talk to her . . .

Toma woke Tanya very early. A true villager, she always woke easily. The girls slipped into the kitchen. Vasilisa had not yet come out of her pantry. That meant it was not yet six thirty.

It was a plot, an escape, truancy, and an excursion to boot. Tanya prepared sandwiches and wrapped them in a worn piece of the carbon paper her mother brought from work in which they wrapped everything. Usually their father took a thermos with him on long walks, but Tanya did not know where he had hidden it. Toma boiled water, and they both drank a cup of tea with yesterday's tea leaves. Tanya listened: there was still the sound of mumbling coming from the pantry, but they had to hurry. Vasilisa ended her obeisances by seven.

"You write the note," Tanya said with an intonation of hidden imperative, handing Toma a piece of paper.

"What do I write?" Toma asked.

"That we had to leave for school early today."

"You write it yourself: you write better than me," Toma groused.

"If I write it, they'll know right away that I'm lying." Tanya shoved the pencil into Toma's hand. "Write it already."

They put on their winter coats. Toma—a new one, bought especially for her not long ago. Tanya—an old one with an extended hem of beaver lamb from another coat. Toma stuck her legs into felt boots with galoshes. Tanya laced up high boots with a fleecy trim. Proud red boots made to order at an atelier for not just anyone. No one had anything like them. Pavel Alekseevich had been displeased to see these new additions: it was not good to stand out. But on that day all the petty details would prove significant, even these ostentatious boots . . .

Five minutes later they headed downstairs, hid both their satchels behind a radiator, having first put the sandwiches in the pockets of their coats, and set off for the Novoslobodskaya metro station. On the metro they only got as far as Belorusskaya. The transfer to the radial line toward the center of town was closed, and when they emerged upstairs, they discovered that Gorky Street was cordoned off. They saw an enormous multitude of red-and-black flags, and the ever-practical Toma wondered when they had managed to sew so many of them. From there they returned to Novoslobodskaya on foot, turning down Kaliaevskaya Street onto Chekhov Street.

The closer they approached to Pushkin Square, the more people there were, and even though there was no public transportation and people walked in the street, everything bottlenecked at Pushkin Square, where passage to Gorky Street was blocked by trucks and a chain of soldiers.

Toma, who knew the city much better, pulled Tanya off to the left, and they found themselves on Pushkin Street in a tight crowd of silent people.

In this city accustomed to long lines no one had ever seen anything like this line before. For the moment it still preserved the shape and character of a line: it shifted, moved ahead slightly, rocked, squabbled, reeked, and ranked everyone fairly, giving each an equal ration of what they wanted—in this case, a piece of the spectacle about which each and every one of its participants would tell for the rest of their lives. But this line had one particular quality that made it singular and unique in all of Soviet history: people came here of their own free will and not out of some necessity—to grab a bread ration, a piece of soap, a quart of kerosene, or a forty-pound sack of grain . . . They had been standing in line all night to pay their civil respects, to bow, to grieve collectively, and to express their grief . . . and something elemental, deeply bestial—like a presentiment of an earthquake or the smell of a distant forest fire—had driven them from their homes and herded them into a single pack. Those who like Tanya were unable to find this invincible call deep in their hearts stayed home . . . But Tanya had been brought here by the ingenuous Toma, a child of the street, of communal apartments, and more susceptible to the laws of the herd.

No one had organized this funeral march, as all parades were usually organized. And the militia—in part paralyzed by the introduction of troops, in part thrown for a loop by all the various, mutually exclusive directives issued by the city's authorities—was thoroughly unable to deal with the patient lines that slowly and irreversibly closed in on each other.

The girls squeezed between people, passing the theater where not long ago they had been taken to see *Swan Lake*; now they were simply incapable of imagining that such an amazing inanity as ballet could even exist in this world . . . They bored their way to the corner of Stoleshnikov Lane and got stuck near the small flower shop on the corner. The window of the half-basement shop was set so low that a fat water pipe driven into the wall of the building blocked the windowpane, which extended about two feet below the level of the street. A wide-spaced iron grating covered the rectangular pit just beneath the window. Their slow, laborious movement seemed to have bottlenecked, and then suddenly from somewhere below, from Pushkin Street, a sound—midway between a roar and

122

a howl, a prolonged moan, and a muffled shout—swept over them like a strange tidal wave.

The sound came closer, crescendoed, and seemed like something entirely disconnected from the crowd, like the wind or rain. Holding each other by the hand, the girls now clasped each other even more tightly. The stalled crowd shifted and pushed them straight into the pipe protecting the shop window. A woman just in front of them with a big silver fox collar twisted around and let out a wild howl. The pipe seemed to have broken her in half. She hung from the pipe briefly, and the people pressing from behind trampled the lower part of her body into the window pit, and then with a loud thump her whole body toppled into it . . . When she fell, she was as dead as the silver fox on her shoulders.

The girls were swept past the pipe, then hauled toward the opposite side of the street right into one of the trucks lined up one after the other. They had just seen that woman crushed against the pipe and understood that there would be nothing they could do if they got pushed against the side of the truck.

"Get down," Toma shouted. It was the only direction they could go—down. They were swept under the truck. There, between the wheels, among orphaned galoshes, they lay on the street—jumbled feet and the hems of clothing blocking the light to the right and to the left. It was stuffy and terrifying. Toma began to cry.

"Don't cry," Tanya said. Toma turned her pale face toward her.

"I feel sorry for Stalin . . ."

"Then you're an idiot," Tanya said in a tired adult voice.

She did not feel a drop of pity for Stalin. Inside she felt disgusted, as if by some immoral act. Probably because they had played hooky from school. She was so ashamed and felt so bad for having lied . . . Especially to Dad . . . The family probably already knew that they were not in school, and Vasilisa was probably waiting for them with dinner, wondering where they were.

They lay underneath the truck for quite a long time. It reeked of a public toilet, grease, and gasoline. At one point the forest of shoes, tattered trousers, and coat bottoms shifted and parted and seemed to thin out a bit.

"Let's try getting out of here." Tanya pulled Toma out from under the truck.

Just at that instant a break in the crowd occurred, and they slipped out from their shelter. While they had been lying under the truck, they had forgotten how easy it was to get lost in the crowd: their grip weakened, their hands broke apart, and they were pulled in different directions . . . They shouted desperately, but even as they still heard each other's voices they floated, like two splints in a river, in the most uncertain of directions . . .

When they lost each other entirely, their powerful but nonetheless ordinary fear gave way to panicked terror. Toma was picked up and carried toward the wall of a building where the windows of the secondhand fur shop on the first floor had already been boarded up. The double doors onto the street also had been boarded up from within. Lower down, at the level of Toma's chest, a part of the wooden door had been pushed in and the boards were coming apart. When Toma was pressed against the boards she pushed one of the boards with her shoulder, and it caved in, and Toma tumbled into the dark space between the two doors and found herself inside, as if in a cabinet. She sat down on her haunches and froze.

Toma could not recall how many minutes or hours she sat, huddled, watching through the wide crack between the boards as one set of feet in trampled footwear slowly replaced the next . . . until she saw a familiar red boot. Something lifted her from the ground. She pulled apart the boards and grabbed the leg just above the fleecy fur trim and shouted with all her might, "Tanya! Tanechka!"

It felt to Tanya like a dog had seized her by the leg.

"Where would a dog have come from?" The thought was running through her head, when suddenly she heard Toma's voice.

"Tanechka! This way, down!"

Not letting go of Tanya's leg, Toma pressed her entire skinny body against the loose board, which obediently gave way, and Tanya, crouching, squeezed into the narrow space between the doors. This movement downward toward the ground that killed so many that day saved the girls.

They reached for each other like long lost lovers, hugged, and froze. At precisely that moment they became sisters. Everything else remained as it was: Tanya's uncontested superiority and indulgent patronage and Toma's groveling deference, servile gratitude, and inner imploring dependence, but their sisterhood—imposed by circumstance and until now dubious, even false—had become real. All their lives they would remember this minute; the memory never faded—their hours embracing in a doorway six inches from a stampeding crowd, from death itself, which from that time on both of them saw in their minds' eye as a closed, dark, malodorous place where unfortunate victims were trampled, their faces, extremities, and very souls crushed beyond recognition . . .

Suddenly Toma burst out, "Tanya, our satchels are behind the radiator in the entranceway!"

"The sandwiches, the sandwiches!" Tanya remembered and pulled the fatally crushed sandwiches out of her pocket.

They gushed with laughter—who knew why. Most likely because their terror-wracked childish hearts needed this . . .

In the meantime, Vasilisa Gavrilovna was running through the darkening yards of their neighborhood and howling like a conjurer, "Tanya! Toma! It's time to come home!"

Elena Georgievna stood in the corridor near the phone on the wall, spinning the black dial with a numb finger. Everywhere the line was busy: the militia, the morgue, the ambulance station . . . Pavel Alekseevich, who had set out after three in the afternoon in search of the girls, also was nowhere to be found. Having stuck an officer's flask of diluted alcohol in the pocket of his overcoat, he wandered along the edges of the city center, where he kept encountering militia and army barricades, and his mind boggled at the thought of how the funeral procession's organizers had managed to re-create the Khodynka massacre in the center of a city crisscrossed with streets, lanes, walk-through courtyards, and, after all, metro lines. He could not find a single spot where even a trickle of the cordoned-off crowd might have escaped. There was no hope of finding the girls, who he had no doubt had slipped out of the house to go to the funeral.

He stood on the corner of Kaliaevskaya and Oruzheinaya streets, leaning against the wall of the milk store. He remembered that there were still a few drops at the bottom of his flask, and he drew out this last gulp, stuck the empty flask into his pocket, and just at that moment felt someone pulling at his sleeve. A crafty goggle-eyed kid looked him in the eye from below.

"Hey, gramps, want me to take you?"

125

"Where?" Pavel Alekseevich did not understand right away.

"I know a way to get through." The boy gestured ambiguously in the direction of Karetny Lane.

Pavel Alekseevich waved him off and walked away. His mood could not have been gloomier. At Belorussky Station he saw a whole column of ambulances . . . They were stuck in the roadblock of trucks.

"A hecatomb, a hecatomb," Pavel Alekseevich suddenly said aloud, surprising himself. At the moment, he did not know how right he was.

16

PAVEL ALEKSEEVICH NEVER DID LEARN THE FATE OF THE monstrous sample he had brought to the high party office on Staraya Square. Though greatly impressed by his conversation with the mad doctor, the cautious bureaucrat decided not to raise the question of this delicate matter in the Politburo.

For several years the glass jar stood wrapped in paper on the lower shelf of his bookcase; on the eve of one May Day, in the fever of a general housekeeping in honor of the luminous holiday, a cleaning woman carried it out to the big garbage bin in the basement.

Strangely enough, "Soapface" turned out to be impressionable, and a few months after the great leader's death the project to legalize abortions was studied and discussed. The state—having murdered countless millions of its citizens over the thirty-five years of its existence—deigned to allow women to decide the fate of the anonymous life that had sprung in their wombs against their wishes. A few demiurges signed, the valve at the top opened, and medical institutions were sent the corresponding circular that legalized the artificial interruption of pregnancies.

The former high party official who accomplished this on his last ascent of Olympus—there was no going any higher—to the day of his death (which occurred not long after) considered himself the great benefactor of the human race, while Pavel Alekseevich never did find out what role the ill-fated jar he had brought to Staraya Square had played . . .

The fate of the unfortunate hostages of their sex never ceased to concern Pavel Alekseevich; as before, he spoke at all conferences connected to infant and maternal welfare. He did not feel that he had won a victory: the conditions at maternity hospitals were, in his opinion, catastrophic. He returned once again to his principal project, hopelessly attempting to convince the country's leaders of the necessity to reexamine the principles of health care financing, and delivering impassioned speeches about environmental concerns and a multitude of other factors that would adversely affect the next generation's health ... The word "ecology" had yet to enter the vernacular.

In the mid-1950s Pavel Alekseevich's research interests took him in an unanticipated direction. While investigating several types of female infertility, Pavel Alekseevich discovered previously unknown phases within the monthly cycle. He focused his attention on women who had given birth to children after long-term infertility. He called such children "Abraham's," and meticulously studied and surveyed the women who had given birth to their first child in their first pregnancy after many years of childless marriage.

At the same time, by way of the work of the renowned Chizhevsky, he embarked on the study of natural cosmic cycles and biorhythms. Embryological research had shown that cytokinesis in fact occurred with clockwork precision. Comparing the daily activity of a human being with the speed of processes occurring within a woman's body, he arrived at the theoretical conclusion that a certain percentage of women could not conceive at night.

His reasoning contained much that was intuitive and undocumentable by contemporary research standards, but it was based on conjecture about the existence of ova with unusually short phases of activity.

At the end of 1953 an amazingly handsome middle-aged Azerbaijani couple from Karabakh appeared during one of Pavel Alekseevich's office hours. He was an artist, from a well-known family of carpet-makers, thin, with fine features and swarthy gray hair. His wife resembled her husband, like a copy of him reduced in size, with the same fine features, the same Persian facial structure. The lilac-tinged red silk of her dress, the emerald green of her shawl, her antique dark-silver jewelry ...

Their tests showed that there was nothing wrong. Two healthy human beings who in twenty years of marriage had not given birth even to one little girl ... The grief and disgrace of the wife.

Pavel Alekseevich looked at them for an indecently long time and listened: his secret adviser insisted.

"You must lie with your wife when the sun is at its zenith," Pavel Alekseevich said in a strict tone of voice. "A year from now come to see me . . ."

The couple arrived not a year, but a year and a half later. And they brought with them a marvelous belly—taut, high, and with a beautiful little girl inside, whom Pavel Alekseevich himself delivered, and then, two years later, a boy . . .

Azerbaijan, Armenia, Central Asia—his first patients came from those areas. Then Russians began to come. Approximately half of them were hopeless, and Pavel Alekseevich always saw them and told them that there was nothing he could do to help. Some couples he recommended move to the East—to Vladivostok or Khabarovsk—for several years: this was a continuation and further development of his ideas having to do with natural rhythms and time zones . . . The table of his office was now covered with charts no one could make any sense of and that looked more like astrological tables than test results. The numbers of "Abraham's" children continued to grow. And of each Pavel Alekseevich would say deep down in his heart, "Today I gave birth to you . . ." A child of midday, a child of dawn, a child of sunset . . . Expensive gifts piled up in his austere apartment: precious carpets, Chinese vases, and French bronze . . . He never charged a fee, but he also never refused donations. From time immemorial healers and priests took only natural products as payment for their services. As a rule, his patients were people of means who lacked only a child to complete their happiness. The poor either were not childless or did not go to doctors . . .

Both classical and the most modern Western medical books ceased to interest him, and he spent many hours in the history and foreign-language libraries reading medieval treatises, antique rarities, and translations of the books of the ancient priests . . . He was searching for something in these Sibylline allegories . . . The secret of conception—that was what interested him. Nothing more and nothing less.

His own wife had securely locked the door of their bedroom to him for all times of the day. He had long ago given up on restoring their suspended marital relations. Following his memorable ignominy, she seemed indeed to have stopped feeling like a woman. But she was just over forty, and over the years her beauty had grown all the more expressive. Her face seemed as if drawn anew by a more demanding, more experienced artist. The maternal puffiness of her mouth and cheeks was gone, and a new expression had appeared in her eyes—one of keen attention directed not outwardly, but inwardly . . . At times it seemed to Pavel Alekseevich that while answering his infrequent questions she was thinking of something else.

Relations between husband and wife could not be called bad: as before, they guessed each other's desires, sometimes read each other's thoughts, and avoided having their eyes meet. She looked at his neck, and he at the bridge of her nose . . .

17

TANYA WAS HER PARENTS' JOY. CODDLING AND INDULGING his daughter, Pavel Alekseevich expressed his concealed love for his wife. Elena felt that and was grateful to him for it, but answered him in a strange way by giving Toma more attention and care. A certain emotional balance was therefore maintained, while Vasilisa implemented a general strict policy of fairness by placing equal portions on their plates. This had stopped making sense long ago: food was plentiful, and everyone except Vasilisa had forgotten about food rationing, ration cards, and ration stations.

Tanya grew into a beautiful young girl—very lively and very talented in all pursuits, be it music, drawing, or the sciences . . .

In school they were already approaching the end of the ninth grade, and it was time to choose a profession, but Tanya was torn in different directions. Before Toma had appeared in their household Tanya had planned to enroll in music school, but as soon as Toma came to live with them, Tanya, to Pavel Alekseevich's great chagrin, gave up music. For him there were no more pleasant moments at home than those spent watching her supple spine and fine shoulder blades as they moved under her sweater when she sat at the new instrument bought especially for her. Pavel Alekseevich kept wanting to get an answer as to why Tanya had absolutely refused to go to music school, but she would only clam up, then hug him around the neck, tickle him behind the ears, and mumble something about the Big-Eared Elephant, giggling and squealing, but uttering not a word in response.

Considerably later both Pavel Alekseevich and Elena understood what had happened to Tanya: apparently, she thought that her success in music would hurt Toma, who had never heard any music except what came out of the radio transmitter.

Tanya now found her father's library more and more alluring. As always, Pavel Alekseevich worked a great deal, spent long hours at the clinic, and after arriving home and eating a quick supper in the company of a silent Vasilisa or a reserved Elena, he ever more often found Tanya in his study settled in a cozy nest of two throw blankets and sofa cushions, cat and book in hand ... Near Tanya on the edge of a chair, with no comforts whatsoever, sat Toma, just as small as she had been at twelve, only fatter. One after the next she embroidered pillows, using a double Bulgarian cross-stitch on the lilac or exaggerated fruit patterns she clamped into her embroidery hoop. Her hunger—long ago forgotten and seemingly sated—had awakened in her a love for this luxury of the poor ...

The girls were very attached to each other, and their attachment contained a mutual amazement: just as Tanya could not understand what pleasure lay in pulling threads through a stiff pattern, so Toma wondered how anyone could sit half the day with their head stuck in a boring book.

Observing the very different girls—his adored Tanechka and the charmless Tomochka, the scrawny feral brought into their home by special circumstances, Pavel Alekseevich, with his habit of regarding all phenomena in the world exclusively from a scientific point of view, fell to theorizing, noticing here too the manifestations of some great laws of nature that while not yet formulated nonetheless objectively existed.

Just as from the moment of fertilization a human embryo completes all the stages of its development to the hour and minute, Pavel Alekseevich thought, so in the child more complex psychophysical functions engage at strictly regulated intervals in strictly determined sequence. The chewing reflex cannot precede the sucking reflex. Yet both are stimulated from without: the feel of a nipple or even of some chance object, be it the edge of a sheet or the child's own finger, arouses the instinct to suck within the first days of life; the placement of a piece of solid food on gums swollen from teething arouses the instinct to chew at the age of six months.

The functions of the higher nervous system are stimulated in exactly the same way, Pavel Alekseevich reflected as he observed the grown-up girls in his own family. Needs awakened at a certain age and unmet from without in the surrounding environment weaken and, possibly, die. Needs, therefore, precede necessities.

"They'll accuse me of Lamarckism." Pavel Alekseevich laughed to himself.

"It's possible the whisper was born before the lips, and leaves fluttered in treelessness"—these lines had been written long ago and their author had already perished in the camps, and they never did make their way to Pavel Alekseevich's consciousness. But there was no other person for whom this ingenious poetic epiphany was more comprehensible as a translation of a fundamental idea from the language of science to the language of poetry . . .

The child, tired of lying, that wants to sit up, will turn and fidget. Extend a finger toward it, and it will grab it and do what it so thirsts to do but still does not know it does. It will sit up. When it has matured enough to walk, give it the chance to take its first step. Otherwise it, like a child raised by animals, will never learn to walk on two legs but, like an animal, will move on all fours.

Give a child music when it feels the need to dance, a pencil when it gets the urge to draw, a book when it has matured to this level of obtaining information . . . How tragic it is when a new skill, a new need has ripened from within, but the moment has been lost and the world makes no effort to meet that need halfway . . .

Take Tomochka. Her mother had left her diapered in her little bed until she was two years old, because the poor woman had to go to work and there was no one to look after the little girl, and daycare was not even imaginable in blacked-out, evacuated Moscow. When Tomochka was set on the floor, she already had no urge to walk. She sat in a corner, on a pile of rags, and played with rags. She saw her first book only in school, when she was seven years old. Everything had been held back, everything slowed down. The poor little girl . . .

But Toma hardly thought of herself as unfortunate. Just the opposite, she was thoroughly convinced that she had drawn a winning ticket. A year after her introduction into the Kukotsky household, at the request of her Aunt Fenya, Toma had been sent to the village for the summer, and Toma, who had never spent a summer at Fenya's when her mother was alive, came to despise village life with all her heart. She was horrified by the poverty, the filth, and, most of all, by the difficulty of daily life where she could not relax, as she would have with Tanya at their dacha, but from morning till night fed pigs, babysat Fenya's three-month-old little daughter, and laundered filthy rags in cold water . . . Silently and unwillingly she did everything, never disobeying Fenya. Twice she traveled by bus to a distant village to visit her brothers. Her brothers horrified her: they had turned into villagers; dressed in rags, barefoot and dirty, they fought and cursed like adult peasants. Toma felt neither sympathy nor pity for them. Loving them was out of the question.

By the time she returned to the city Toma had firmly resolved that never again would she go to her aunt's and that she would do everything possible in order to remain forever in the Kukotsky family.

Toma was completely unconcerned about whether she was loved in her new family. In their household she had her own place, which more resembled the place of a house pet. There was absolutely nothing insulting about this: in some households the entire world order revolves around a little dog that has to be taken out every morning or a cat that eats only a certain type of fish.

Toma had her own bed in the room she shared with Tanya, her own place at the table between Tanya and Elena Georgievna, and many other things that she had never had before when she lived with her mother: her own comb and toothbrush, her own towels in the bathroom, and a nightshirt—the existence of which she could not even have imagined before. In return nothing was asked of her. Surprisingly, much larger demands were made of Tanya—for misbehaving, for returning home late from school, and for the untidiness Tanya was constantly guilty of. Toma would cover for Tanya. Sometimes she would wipe up the puddle she left in the bathroom or wash the teacup she had left on the table, and, sometimes, when they were late returning from school, she would take the blame for their tardiness.

"Aunt Vasya, they made me stay after to redo an assignment, and Tanya waited for me . . ."

And Vasilisa, who had already reheated the girls' dinners twice, would stop grumbling. She would even refrain from commenting on Toma's behavior more than necessary, although she was very observant and knew perfectly well the real reason for all these little deceptions . . .

As for their studies, there was nothing to be said. Tanya was practically an honor student. All she lacked was vanity to become a straight-A student. In the time she spent living in their household Toma had succeeded in becoming a solid C student. The complication lay in that everyone was dissatisfied with Tanya's Bs, but overjoyed by Toma's rare B. A certain sensitivity was required of everyone in the household, who must never forget that equality was an exclusively theoretical thing and could not be regarded as a serious principle even in so practical an area as a child's upbringing. Ideas of equality concerned Elena somewhat— memories of her Tolstoyan childhood were still keen. Vasilisa did not nibble at the bait.

"Tanechka is special, and Tomochka is something completely different."

For that reason she would say to Toma simply, "Let me teach you how to brine cabbage, fry fritters, and other things, otherwise when I die you won't know how to do anything . . ."

Tanya's lack of such skills did not worry Vasilisa, but she obviously considered Toma her successor in her amorphous household position, which she herself endured with patience and a certain pride. It was precisely with Toma that Vasilisa could suddenly start a conversation about the most important and protected part of her life, about what was sealed in her little pantry as a result of Pavel Alekseevich's longtime ban. In Tanya's early childhood he had adamantly forbidden Vasilisa to have any conversations of any sort with the child about the divine. For that reason Vasilisa taught not Tanya but Toma the two most important prayers and instructed her in any and all difficult situations to turn to the Mother of God.

"In mathematics too?" Tomochka inquired simply when Vasilisa was explaining to her that her protectress and intercessor was the Mother of God, who cared for all orphans.

"What about Holy Queen Tamara?" Toma reminded Vasilisa, who had earlier spoken to her about her patron saint, Queen Tamara, after whom she had been named in baptism.

Vasilisa became angry and explained inarticulately, but with conviction: "Don't you understand, they're completely different things . . ."

IN THE KUKOTSKY HOUSEHOLD TOMA BEHAVED EXACTLY as demanded by her role as adopted child. Placing great value on the practical amenities showered on her, she feared losing them and tried hard to make her presence in the household both pleasing and useful. While there was always a grain of solicitousness to her manners, it was compensated for entirely by the fact that she adored Pavel Alekseevich, sincerely admired Tanechka, and for reasons she could not explain deep down in her heart, feared only Elena Georgievna.

Her relationship with Vasilisa was much more complicated. On the one hand, Vasilisa was just like her—not an urban creature; on the other hand, Vasilisa saw right through her, and if Vasilisa merely glanced at her over her string-trussed eyeglasses it was not at all pleasant, as if she knew some secret and very unpleasant thing about Toma. While there was a special kind of bond between the old servant and the little foundling, Vasilisa miscalculated entirely when she attempted to mold from Toma a successor not only to her dishwashing-housekeeping realm, but to her spiritual realm as well. It did not work out. If Toma, at first obeisant, memorized all the basic prayers and with drowsy attention heard out all of Vasilisa's bumbling sermons, by the time she was fifteen, she began to slip away from Vasilisa—having figured out, likely, that she had no need for Vasilisa's underground valuables—and grazed exclusively alongside Tanya, while Tanya buried herself in her father's books, dragged her to the cinema, to the theater, and to concerts, and these outings were not just for culture's sake: boys were also involved, which made an immense difference to Toma.

In Tanya's presence she played an unenviable role, but she really did not need her own boyfriend, and the very atmosphere of an outing— wherever—in the company of young men suited her entirely. Just as she had once relished those innumerable sandwiches with butter and sugar, her toothbrush, and her nightshirt, she now took pleasure in the fact that boys bought their tickets, took them to the refreshment stand, and treated them to soft drinks and cake . . .

The boys did not think to conceal from Toma that she was an obligatory appendage to the holiday of an outing with Tanya to wherever, but this hardly distressed Toma: she had no need for any one of them in and of himself, but as a group they bore witness to the fact that Toma's social status in society was very good because she got to go to the Bolshoi Theater, the Maly Theater, and the Art Cinema, and was treated to free refreshments in addition.

Among the young men attracted to Tanya's simple gaiety, obvious good looks, and curly hair, were the Goldberg brothers, who had been enamored of Tanya since that horrible winter in 1953 when they went to Pavel Alekseevich's to be fed. The feeding had not really ever stopped: the boys' mother died soon after Ilya Iosifovich was released, and the old geneticist, who had courageously survived his last arrest without having to sign a single false statement, was totally destroyed by the death of his forty-year-old wife.

He fell apart physically too, losing as much weight as if he were in the camps. His only salvation was the work with which he loaded himself down beyond measure. He reviewed books for all the reference journals that would take him, and he kept writing his genius book about genius. Goldberg's home life also fell apart; housekeepers came and left, one after the next. One stole, the other drank. The third, an intellectual Jewish woman who came three times a week, he suspected of being an agent of the KGB. In a word, in the absence of the deceased Valya, the Goldbergs' favorite food—meat patties with fried potatoes—either did not taste right or was laced with the poison of suspicion, which was not life-threatening, but also not conducive to good digestion.

Once again, for the umpteenth time, Vasilisa demonstrated great insight and was the first to note that the meat patties were now in major competition with Tanya, and that it was time to figure out why those boys had taken to visiting every Sunday as well as on the occasional weekday . . .

The Goldberg brothers were identical to the point of being indistinguishable, but Tanya clearly favored the one who was studying to be a doctor. On Sundays they often lingered after lunch until supper, and Vitaly, the medical enthusiast, would pour fat in the fire when he talked about the complexity and fascination of studying at the medical institute, about the passions of anatomy and the mysteries of physiology . . .

The second brother, Gennady, who had chosen physics, contented himself with contemplation of this lively conversation, said nothing, and only occasionally answered the confused questions Toma, confident that Gena was her share of the package, put to him . . .

NINTH GRADE CAME TO AN END, AND IT WAS DECIDED that for their last summer vacation from school the girls would go to Yalta. Pavel Alekseevich at first planned to go with the family, but at the last minute was prevented from doing so by an unexpected prestigious trip to Switzerland to take part in a conference on infertility. Pavel Alekseevich laughed to himself: infertility interested Switzerland, the richest country in the world, but not China, Asia, or Africa . . . Pavel Alekseevich agreed to go to Zurich, and Vasilisa was offered the opportunity to travel to Yalta in his stead. She held out for a long time, and even argued slightly with Elena on this score, but in the end she agreed, on the condition, though, that first she would leave for three days to take care of her own affairs. And she left . . .

Owing to this unforeseen jaunt everyone arrived a day late for their reservation at the resort, because Vasilisa did not return on the appointed day. But the delay was compensated for by the notes of divine delight Vasilisa emitted all twenty-three remaining days she spent on the shore of the Black Sea.

All the women vacationers saw the sea for the first time. And each in her own way. Vasilisa found evidence of the might and wisdom of the great Lord God. The mountains made a greater impression on her than did the sea, but both evoked her delight in the Creator who had produced this grand inventory. Stoic and not inclined to cry, she frequently dabbed away incomprehensible tears with her crumpled handkerchief, and her usual occupation—in the absence of cooking, laundering, and cleaning—was to sit idly on their terrace looking out in the direction of the mountains, her face immobile, her gaze arrested, as if beyond those mountains there were still others visible to her alone . . . From time to time she would fall into ecstatic mumbling, and Elena—long familiar with her prayer repertoire—managed to catch bits of the psalms, of which Vasilisa knew only the fiftieth by heart, the rest only in bits and pieces, scraps, and separate phrases, from which she constructed her inspired babble ... "If I ascend up into heaven, thou art there: if I make my bed in hell, behold, thou art there. If I take the wings of the morning, and dwell in the uttermost parts of the sea, thou art there too ... Out of the mouths of babes and sucklings hast thou ordained strength ... The Lord is merciful and gracious, slow to anger and plenteous in mercy ... For he commandeth and raiseth the stormy wind ..."

Food at the resort was abundant, which was somewhat offensive for Vasilisa, so as soon as she caught her bearings, she refused to go to breakfast and came only to supper with everyone else, where she took her place at the table assigned them and enjoyed the service. The waitresses served her food, asked her why she had again not come for lunch and should they bring her anything else ... Her satisfaction was tinged with a certain uneasiness, because in her not-great but tenacious mind she knew well that if someone has more than she needs, then someone else does not have enough ... And her Christian soul, despite the luxury of their vacation, experienced a bit of shame. In the end she admitted to Elena that if it was going to be like this in heaven, then she would have to ask for the other place, because all this made her feel guilty.

Toma felt no guilt at all. She and Tanya exulted like puppies in the sun and the sea; they splashed, swam, and sunbathed with no thoughts for anything else. It became apparent in the process that Tanya enjoyed universal popularity among the young and not so young men, from the merchants at the market—where the family occasionally dropped in to make some exotic purchase like homemade cheese, that sticky South Caucasus sweet known as *churchkhela*, or a bunch of some unknown herb—to the young captains vacationing at the military sanatorium next door.

In the evenings the girls set off for the dances held in the cafeteria or on the embankment. Tanya danced, while Toma sat on a chair along the wall—or stood, if there were no chairs—in the company of two or three girls who were not popular. Toma went only for Tanya's sake; left to her own devices she would never have gone along only to put up with this shameful boredom. She was somewhat surprised that intelligent Tanya found anything good in a dance called "a fast foxtrot" or "a slow tango."

At 11:00 P.M. Elena Georgievna set out to look for them on the crowded dance floors and brought them home to sleep. Sometimes Tanya managed to make a date with an artful dancer and crawl out the window and disappear for half the night. Their family had been allotted two double rooms, and the girls occupied the one without a terrace.

Credulous Elena turned out to be unprepared for such craftiness on her daughter's part and never discovered Tanya's midnight adventures. Tanya's first kisses did not make much of an impression on her: they smelled of some particularly stinky shaving lather and the unforgettable scent of Chypre aftershave and gave off an odor of boot wax and military action. Tanya rolled with laughter, and the young men—already slightly intimidated by her youthful beauty—retreated, hurt. In a word, Tanya brought back not a single romantic tryst from her trip to the South. She had the best time of her life.

Toma, on the other hand, acquired a lifelong, profound love in Crimea. On an excursion to the Nikitsky Botanical Gardens grace descended upon her: she fell in love with botany like girls fall in love with princes. It happened at the very end of their stay in Crimea, two days before their departure. Overall, the excursion to the gardens fizzled: the bus broke down and took a long time to fix, then the weather deteriorated, and although it never rained, the midday sun darkened, and the elegant luster of the South Shore grew turbid.

At the entrance to the Botanical Gardens they had to wait for their guide, who had gone to attend to other matters as a result of their delay. They stood alongside a dark-bronze plaque engraved with: "The Botanical Gardens were established in 1812 by Kh. Kh. Steven, a graduate of the St. Petersburg Medical Academy..." There was no one there to tell them that Christian von Steven was no stranger, but a close friend of Nikita Avdeevich Kukotsky, Pavel Alekseevich's direct ancestor, and that the foundation for this state undertaking had been laid during the friends' first joint trip through the Caucasus Mountains in 1808, that Nikita Avdeevich had visited his friend here in Crimea on more than one occasion, and that among the seven thousand pages of the great herbarium of the Taurida administrative district there were not a few specimens collected by Kukotsky himself...

Finally the guide arrived—a fat man in an embroidered Ukrainian shirt and gold-framed glasses who distantly resembled Nikita Khrushchev in a good mood—and led them down the shaded footpaths. It was cool and mysterious. The guide talked about the abundance of Crimean flora, about rare endemic plants that lived exclusively in this region, and about ancient myths connected with the plants . . .

Toma was a city girl and despised the countryside—one could say—for personal reasons. When she had spent her summer months in the village during her childhood, she had never noticed nature of any sort; everything there seemed ordinary and insultingly poor. For her, forest, field, and pond were connected with hard work: she was sent to the woods to gather berries for sale, to the field to help with the harvest, and to the pond to rinse laundry. Here in Crimea in the Botanical Gardens nature was selfless: it demanded no laborious effort. Even the sea, the salty water that no one had to haul in buckets from under the hill, had been created exclusively for the joy of swimming and diving.

Toma surreptitiously stroked the leaves—some smooth and some furry, some dry as old paper, and the needlelike conifers—that lined the paths of the Botanical Gardens, filling her fingers with a joy they had never known before. Insufficiently caressed in infancy, not having known a loving touch in her childhood, now, though provided with everything she needed, she was still as deprived as ever of the loving touch without which a living thing suffers, falls ill, and withers . . . Perhaps her small size could be explained by the fact that growing up without love was as difficult as without some special unknown vitamin . . .

Their Khrushchev-look-alike guide turned out to have a completely magical voice, and what he said was a real fairy tale.

"Here we have an acacia," he said, pointing to a small tree covered with sweet yellow blossoms, "one of the greatest trees ever. According to ancient Egyptian beliefs, the Egyptian goddess Hathor, the Great Cow, who gave birth to the sun and the stars, also could assume the identity of an acacia tree, the tree of life and of death. Acacia was the oracle of one of the great goddesses of fertility in Western Asia, and even the ancient Jews, who rejected idolatry, were seduced by the acacia: they called it the 'shittim tree,' and in ancient times built the Ark of the Covenant from it . . ."

Of all the things he said Toma understood only one word: "cow." Everything else was incomprehensible, but cool. It turned out that every tree and every bush, and even the tiniest flower, all had a foreign name, a history, a geography, and—most amazing—a legend about its presence in the world. While she, Tamara Polosukhina, had nothing of the sort; even by comparison with a fir tree or a daisy she meant nothing . . .

She also got the feeling—Toma had no formed thoughts, only feelings garnished by thoughts—of a mutual sympathy between herself and the plants as well as an equality with them in their insignificance.

"Probably among all these plants there's one that's exactly like me . . . If I saw it, I would recognize it right away," Toma thought, stroking a rhododendron or boxwood as she walked.

Tanya and Toma almost never coincided in either their thoughts or their feelings, and if they did, it was exclusively thanks to Toma's ability to adjust herself to Tanya's thought waves. This time they were thinking about one and the same thing: if I were a plant, what kind would I be?

At the shop near the exit from the Botanical Gardens, with pocket money that Tanya spent immediately and recklessly and Toma scrimped, Toma bought two sets of postcards with local and Mediterranean types of plants and a boring book called *Flora of Crimea*.

That day the question of finding an appropriate profession for Toma, which Elena Georgievna and Pavel Alekseevich had been pondering and only Vasilisa considered completely decided—that Toma would follow in her footsteps—was resolved.

Still ahead was the tenth grade, a whole year to figure out details and prepare for exams. Tanya had set her sights on the biological faculty, to the amazement of Pavel Alekseevich, who could not imagine any other path for his daughter except medicine. But Tanya talked incessantly about higher nervous functions, about studying consciousness—the first American science fiction books had already been translated, and the Goldberg boys diligently supplied Tanya with the same. It was very romantic, much more romantic than a physician's everyday routine. As for Toma, Pavel Alekseevich took her to the Timiryazev Agricultural Academy. There they were greeted with circumstance appropriate to Pavel Alekseevich's rank, shown the experimental fields of corn and soybeans, and the laboratories. What impressed Toma was the artificial climate laboratory, the greenhouses with plants from the South; everything else reminded her of boring life on the collective farm with its crop rotations, cursing at the collective farm office, and village melancholy. On the way home she told Pavel Alekseevich she really did not take a hankering to the Timiryazev Academy and that she would prefer to go to a place where they worked with southern plants. Pavel Alekseevich attempted to explain to his foster daughter that once she received an education, she could work at the Botanical Gardens or at the Institute of Medicinal Plants, or anywhere else, but Toma would hear none of it: she did not understand why she needed an education if she could work at the Botanical Gardens without one. What she wanted most was to admire the beautiful plants, to care for them, to touch them occasionally, and to inhale their smells . . . In the meantime she set up a whole family of clay pots of all sizes on the windowsill and puttered with lemon and tangerine seeds . . .

18

AND SO IT CAME TO PASS THAT A YEAR LATER TANYA TOOK university entrance examinations, overcoming steep competition and her own—who knows from where—fear of tests, while Toma simply applied for gardener courses at the Moscow Executive Committee of the City Soviet of People's Deputies, from which, six months later, she would receive a white piece of paper testifying to her acquisition of a new profession.

Tanya did not make it into the day division, earning one less point than she needed, but she was accepted into the evening division. By September 1 she had to get a job in her field of specialization in order to be able to present proof of daytime employment. Pavel Alekseevich— who had not even considered helping Tanya matriculate by making a single phone call to one of the university's heavyweights equal in rank to himself—now picked up the phone and called his old colleague, Professor Gansovsky, a physician and researcher, who headed the clinic of pediatric brain defectology and a laboratory specializing in brain development. Pavel Alekseevich's request was modest: would they hire his daughter, a student in the evening division of the biology faculty, as a lab assistant? Professor Gansovsky chuckled and said that he could take her as soon as tomorrow.

Pavel Alekseevich delivered his pride and joy several days later. Tanya recognized this building alongside the Ustinsky bridge from childhood: they had brought her here for an X-ray or for an appointment with the pediatric cardiologist . . . But now she entered through the battered door of the yard entrance, through a corridor with a black board with numbered tags hanging from it. This was a completely different experience. She was coming to be hired for a job.

Professor Gansovsky lived almost year-round at his dacha and did not come to work every day, but he had made an appointment with Pavel Alekseevich and his daughter for that day because one of his leading researchers, MarLena Sergeevna Konysheva, had prepared the manuscript of her doctoral dissertation for him to read and was supposed to give him the weighty volume.

Old Professor Gansovsky's relationships with his female research staff were prolific. He was already over seventy, his bald spot shone merrily with shades of henna and silver, but the fringe of hair encircling his temples from ear to ear was dyed deep chestnut. His eyebrows he kept their natural black, and for that reason his entire henhouse debated constantly whether he dyed his eyebrows, and with what . . . Despite a coquettishness unworthy of his sex, he was so unconditionally masculine that his hair coloring—not quite war paint and not quite mating colors— sooner caused frustration than scorn. Not tall, but broad-chested, with large birthmarks on his cheeks, he resembled an old boxer, in the canine sense as well. In his laboratory full of women he was tsar, and his entire female staff—with the exception of janitor Maria Fokovna, practical nurse Raiska, and his two graduate students (one an Ossetian, the other Turkmen, both inclined to consider their boss's indifference a form of discrimination)—had passed through his powerful, disproportionately long arms and, if truth be told, had not been left dissatisfied. Pavel Alekseevich was unaware of all these piquant details of Gansovsky's biography. In order to know gossip you have to take a certain interest in it. Pavel Alekseevich was not even aware that Gansovsky's first wife had worked in the laboratory all her life, while his second, younger wife, had done her graduate work there and stayed on at the clinic for her residency, or that there was yet another woman, who had not achieved the rank of wife—Zina, the plump, sweet-looking, not very young woman whose son Gansovsky helped raise—plus Galya Rymnikova, tall as a bell tower with a head the size of a doll's, who had worked as his personal lab assistant for two years and then left in a huge scandal that barely fit under the rug, and a few more trifles, of interest, generally, only to the participants in this long-running performance. On the other hand, Pavel Alekseevich knew Gansovsky's superb publications on embryogenesis of the brain, and for this reason considered him a suitable mentor for Tanya.

Tanya was led into the professor's office. There were bookcases with pedigreed volumes, two bronze busts of who knows whom, and some large glass jars with brain specimens—stiffened spirals the color of children's soap ... In the space between the windows hung black-and-red-colored charts and photographs of tinted landscapes whose rivers were micron capillaries, and their banks—fibers of striated muscle, flowing through huge mountains with gaping hollows: all of this seemingly geological activity had been captured under a microscope lens of not even God knew what power ...

"I'm going to put you, Tatiana Pavlovna, in the hands of my student, MarLena Sergeevna. She will teach you how to perform the necessary histologic work. She's a great master of slide preparations. We'll start with that ... and take it from there ..."

Rising, he turned out to be short-legged and half-a-head shorter than Tanya, but he moved with the speed and deliberateness of a tennis ball. He gestured with his arm for them to follow.

The laboratory was located in an old building and occupied two floors as well as some recesses between floors with windows adjacent either to the floor or to the ceiling, as if the building's two former floors had been remodeled as three. The two honored academicians walked ahead of the slender, curly-headed girl whose heart skipped a beat with every smell—from the animal facility, of something chemical, boiled, stinging and nasty, and yet attractive. Probably a young girl with her sights set on the theater experiences the same sensations her first time backstage.

The corridor took its last turn near a fire hose curled like a snake behind a glass door, and they entered the inner sanctum ... It was all glass and crystal, transparent and splendid. There was an old laboratory table with a marble top suitable for a gravestone, a broad-shouldered cupboard with heavy sliding glass doors and transparent shelves with gleaming instruments laid out inside, and racks of laboratory glassware with sterilized insides. A wonderland of small glass tubules, of spherical and conic flasks ...

Ordinary wooden desks held microtomes on stocky iron object-stage platforms and monstrous triangular dissecting knives with razor-sharp edges. Microscopes—their little copper details and various screws gleaming—stood with horns raised. Torsion scales shone under glass covers that thickened unevenly toward the bottom ... And there was a great variety of still other, yet unfamiliar objects that attracted Tanya's enchanted gaze.

At the marble laboratory table stood a tall, unattractive woman with salt-and-pepper bangs, narrow eyes, and too short a distance between the tip of her nose and her upper lip. Her face expressed fastidiousness, cleanliness, care, and something else particularly attractive to Tanya— something between confidence and impeccability ... Her medical coat gleamed with the whiteness of mountain peaks, her hands were scrubbed for surgery, and she performed the most delicate movements with her fingers.

Glancing at them for an instant, she buried herself once again in her lapidarian operations, apologizing that she needed a few more minutes to finish.

"It's old German equipment," Pavel Alekseevich noted with surprise.

"Yes, all prewar. Brought from Germany. But so far we haven't figured out a way to make anything better yet. Jena optics, you know, Solingen steel ... ," Gansovsky smirked. "I brought it back myself. This equipment here is from Humboldt University ..."

But Tanya did not hear what they were talking about. She could not take her eyes off MarLena Sergeevna as the latter worked the satiny pink round bubble form on the preparation table with exquisite tiny scissors and thin tweezers. Nearby on the marble tabletop lay a whole string of identical glass containers with more pink bubble forms and a repulsive-looking dental surgery tray.

"MarLena Sergeevna, I've brought to you the daughter of our dear Doctor Kukotsky. A budding biologist," the professor heh-hehhed rather disgustingly, "for you to train. Why don't you have a chat with the girl while I show Pavel Alekseevich the laboratory . . ."

They left, leaving Tanya. MarLena Sergeevna nodded to her.

"Come closer and take a look at what I'm doing . . ."

And Tanya looked. The scholarly woman destined to become Tanya's idol for several years used manicure scissors to slit the surface of the pink bubble form, which turned out to be the tiny little head of a newborn rat, folded back the edges of the incision with tweezers, and meticulously, so as not to disturb the tender white substance—the most complex thing created by nature, the brain tissue—below, removed a cranial bone the thickness of a child's fingernail . . .

After slicing small disks from the stem, MarLena Sergeevna removed them with the light touch of her tweezers, laying bare two elongated hemispheres and the two olfactory bulbs that jutted forward. Not a scratch or cut could be seen on the mirror-form surface. The brain shone like mother-of-pearl. With her thin tweezers MarLena Sergeevna pinched the elongated brain where it connected to the spinal cord, lifted this flickering pearl with a special little spatula, and just as the brain rested on the spatula, Tanya noticed a faint network of blood vessels barely visible to the eye. A moment ago the brain had rested, as in a bowl, in its natural bed and had seemed like some sort of architectural construction; now it slid like a heavy drop from the chrome-plated spatula into a glass container filled with transparent liquid . . . The container held several other identical peas that had already managed to shrivel a bit . . .

"This requires great concentration and accuracy," MarLena Sergeevna said. "Actually, small cuts along the sides are admissible, because what interests us is not the surface, but the deeper layers of the brain . . ."

As she spoke, she raised a gauze napkin from the tray: several newborn baby rats scurried about inside together with the already decapitated trunks whose heads had been sacrificed to the lofty and bloodthirsty god of science . . . This dreadfully lawless combination of the living, blindly scurrying, warm and trusting, with the headless, "decapitated," as MarLena Sergeevna said, made nausea rise from Tanya's stomach to her throat. She gulped back saliva . . .

"My little rats," the learned lady said, picking up a little rat with two fingers, stroking it on its narrow spine, and then—with a different, larger, pair of scissors lying to the right of the tray—accurately and precisely cutting off its little head. She tossed the slightly shuddering little body into the tray and lovingly spread out the head on the object glass. After which she looked searchingly at Tanya and asked with a shade of strange pride: "Well, do you think you can do that?"

"I can," Tanya answered without hesitating for a moment. She was far from sure that she really could.

"I have to," she said to herself and, heroically stifling the urge to vomit, she picked up the tender satiny nastiness of a newborn—warm to the touch—baby rat with her left hand and the cold perfectly ergonomic scissors with her right hand, and clutching that silly immortal soul in the grasp of enlightened reason striving toward science, she pressed down on the upper ring of the scissors with her thumb. Crunch—and the little head fell onto the object glass.

"Good job," a soft female voice said approvingly.

The sacrifice had been accepted. Tanya had passed the test and was initiated as a junior priestess.

19

AS THE YEARS PASSED, PAVEL ALEKSEEVICH FOUND MORE and more sense in reading the ancient historians.

"It's the only thing that allows me to tolerate today's newspapers." He tapped his firm, iodine-framed fingernail on the leather cover of *The Twelve Caesars*.

As Vasilisa cleaned his study, he sat in the girls' room, awaiting the end of this monthly ritual. In surprise Tanya raised one thin brow with its hereditary brush in the corner.

"I don't see any connection, Dad."

"How should I put it? Julius Caesar was considerably more talented than Stalin as a commander; Augustus—one hundred times smarter; Nero—crueler; and Caligula much more inventive when it came to depravity. Yet everything, absolutely everything—the bloodiest and the most sublime—becomes the exclusive property of history."

Tanya sat up on her pillow.

"But it's sort of sad to think that everything is so senseless and all the victims have died in vain."

Pavel Alekseevich grinned and stroked his book's shagreen cover.

"What victims? There are no victims. There is only the instinct of self-justification, of justifying actions that are sometimes stupid, sometimes senseless, but more often malicious and mercenary . . . A thousand or so years from now, Tanechka, or perhaps five hundred, some old gynecologist like me—no matter what progress occurs our profession will always be around—will read the ancient history of Russia in the twentieth century, and there will be two pages about Stalin and two paragraphs about Khrushchev. And a bunch of anecdotes . . ."

Tanya smiled. "That's not so, Dad. They will know Akhmatova, Tsvetaeva, and Pasternak, while Stalin and Khrushchev will merit mention for the sole reason that they repressed them."

"That will happen when there's true communism," Toma inserted wistfully as she carefully bathed an ailing *Monstera deliciosa*.

Pavel Alekseevich was in a good mood and allowed himself to joke.

"No, Tomochka, it will be only after that . . ."

"I should ask Tanya later what he meant by that," Toma decided. No one had ever told her that anything could come after communism. Although, ultimately, what difference would it make, since we won't be around anyway . . . She had something serious to worry about: pale spots had appeared at the base of the plant's leaves, and their wax covering had somewhat softened in those spots. She stroked the leaves' surfaces with the soft tips of her fingers: yes, they really were softer. And there seemed to be a similar spot on her treasured *Yucca* plant.

"Oh, no, not a virus!" she thought in horror, forgetting about communism forever. She was already a rather experienced employee of MosUrbGreen and had dealt with plant viruses twice, but those had been state-owned plants—one in the square in front of the Bolshoi Theater, and the other in the greenhouse that sent them seedlings. In both cases the virus had proved incurable, and it had wiped out the marigolds and the gillyflower. But these were her plants, her favorites, and Toma stuck the thumb of her left hand in her mouth and chewed in concentration at the root of her nail . . . Having chewed off a microscopic bit, she set to inspecting her jungle—by the end of the 1950s the Kukotsky apartment had metamorphosed entirely through her efforts: there was not a single surface left without pots of plants and jars with evergreens.

At first the rigid green plants had been pleasing to Elena's eye, but then she embarked on a lame struggle against the tin cans and old pots and pans in which Toma potted her nurslings. Elena bought clay pots and planters, but the tin cans from the trash kept multiplying. Once the windowsills were thoroughly occupied, the vernicose army advanced to the dining room table and the desks, and then descended to the floor. The nursery, which had once been Tanya's room, looked like the storeroom of a florist shop.

The abundant vegetation did not disturb Tanya at all since she was practically never at home. In the early morning she ran off to work—to her rats and rabbits, operations and preparations—and from work she rushed straight to the university, returning home only at half past eleven, dead tired. On days when she had no classes she also disappeared for hours on end, either visiting friends or at various entertainments. Toma gradually stopped participating in Tanya's life after hours. Tanya had taken up with some new friends: the Goldberg boys had given way to other, more interesting young men who never came to the apartment.

Elena usually arrived home from work shortly after six o'clock to find not Tanya, but Toma—children's watering can in hand—whispering to her plants. Toma's workday ended early, and by four thirty she was already at home. Grumbling, Vasilisa fed them all separately.

Pavel Alekseevich labored like a worker at a steel plant, two shifts back-to-back. In addition to the institute and the clinic, he had begun teaching advanced qualification courses for doctors, which at once amazed and irritated everyone: it hardly befit an academician to spend three nights a week lecturing until the wee hours to provincial obstetricians and old midwives who, if they had received any medical training at all, had long ago forgotten what it had consisted of. He completely neglected his duties as a member of the Academy. Like a schoolboy playing hooky, he failed to appear at Presidium meetings and avoided his superiors. His reputation as an alcoholic was augmented by rumors of his eccentricity.

Long ago the upper echelons at the Ministry had changed: Workhorse was replaced first by an old KGB man trained in veterinary medicine, then by a famous surgeon who was also a ruthless careerist and a thief. With no regrets Pavel Alekseevich said good-bye to his great project of reforming health care, and the reforms took place without his participation, although the papers he himself had long ago forgotten still lay in the safe of the new minister, who occasionally skimmed them, to no avail.

Despite his frosty relations with his superiors, Pavel Alekseevich's influence in medical circles was unusually far-reaching. All those provincial ladies from the distant corners of the huge country were trained by him both in the old methods of assisting birth and in new approaches to sustaining pregnancy, in the treatment of inflammatory processes and of postnatal complications ... He wrote several textbooks for middle-level medical personnel—which category he considered unfairly neglected— and a monograph on questions of infertility.

But his principal concern always remained his large-bellied patients, who came to him with their damaged wombs, their malfunctions, and their fears. He saw them at consultations on varying levels: weekly office hours, by special request of acquaintances, and private consultations. Although the Kremlin Hospital had already been in existence for some time, the wives and daughters of the heads of state often appealed to him—for assistance giving birth, for an operation ...

In one section of the clinic with the euphemistic tag "Diagnostics," they performed dilatation and curettage, some of which was in fact diagnostic ... It was practically the only place in the city where anesthetics were administered; at other clinics sin was punished severely, the impudent decision to rid oneself of an unwanted child almost always included trial by pain ... In this section four surgeons and four registered nurses dilated and scraped nonstop all sixteen hands at a time. The most primitive of anesthetics—local administration of Novocain—twenty-five minutes of work, an ice bag to freeze the belly, and next in line ...

Pavel Alekseevich seldom came into this section. He considered the artificial interruption of pregnancy the gravest of operations in moral terms both for the woman and for the doctor ... Was it not here that the essential divide between humans and animals lay: the ability and right to step beyond the limits of biological law, to breed not at the will of natural rhythms, but of one's own desire? Was this not where human choice, the right to freedom, ultimately was realized?

Vasilisa represented the opposite—radically opposite—opinion. From the moment she replaced her adulation of Pavel Alekseevich with total rejection he even began to relate to her more seriously in a way. Her position was ludicrous, from a doctor's point of view, even ignorant and inhumane, but in its own way moral. What was sad was that her obscurantist abhorrence of abortion had influenced Elena, whom she had inculcated with Christian-church intolerance. Vasilisa's semiliteracy combined quite harmoniously with her views. But Elena? How could he explain to her that he was the servant not of Moloch, but of the miserable people of an invidious world ... Besides, he himself practically never performed artificial interruptions of pregnancy. Perhaps the only thing that theoretically interested him in the whole procedure was the issue of how best to utilize the valuable bio-products considered waste in these procedures. But that was being studied by hematologists, a whole laboratory of them, headed by a competent student of his ... No, there was another aspect that preoccupied Pavel Alekseevich, and he even recommended to one of his staff to give some thought to hormonal post-abortion protein folding, that is, the still completely unstudied process the female organism undergoes during artificial pregnancy termination, the hormonal consequences thereof, and how to assist the body in recovering from this condition with minimal damage ...

The dissonance between his reasoned professional activity and the stone wall of rejection he encountered at home—from his wife, that is, and not from brainless Vasilisa—aroused a certain reflectiveness in him, and, as if in self-justification, he constantly wrote comments and notes to himself in which he combined medical incidents with the most abstract considerations, a kind of homebrewed philosophy of medicine. He made absolutely no attempt to organize his scattered thoughts into something orderly or intelligible ... Ilya Iosifovich Goldberg, who was constantly producing innumerable sheets of paper filled with tiny script, each time announcing his latest grandiose plans to his friend, had cured Pavel Alekseevich of any desire to construct overarching theories or to erect planetary plans ...

Unlike Goldberg, who ignited like dry brushwood at each new turn of scientific thought, Pavel Alekseevich had spent decades observing one and the same object, spreading its pale shutters with his rubber-covered left hand, inserting his mirror with its bent handle, and peering fixedly into the bottomless breach of the world. From there came all that was living; these were the true gates of eternity to which all those girls, aunts, ladies, and grand dames who spread their thighs before him never gave a second thought.

Immortality, eternity, freedom—they were all linked to this hole that engulfed everything: including Marx, whom Pavel Alekseevich had never been able to read, and Freud with his ingenious and erroneous theories, and him himself, an old doctor who had accepted into his hands hundreds, thousands, an unending stream of wet, screaming creatures . . .

Whenever Ilya Iosifovich—long ago released from his penultimate (it later turned out) prison term, inspired by the recent revival of his beloved field, and captivated now by molecular genetics—waxed profusely about the secret code of life discovered in DNA by those lousy Englishmen, as he referred to Watson and Crick, and bristled at how we, the Soviets, that is, had been beaten to the draw, Pavel Alekseevich, his chin resting in his big knitted palms, would stop him in midflight.

"You, Ilyusha, are a hot-shit scientist, while I'm just a simple cunt-cutter, and I just can't figure what you're so worked up about. So those heathens invented that spiral of yours. They have good financing. The Swiss equipment in my clinic was made in what year? Nineteen hundred and four. And the centrifuge in your office, when was it made?"

"That's just the point, Pasha. If we had their money, we'd run rings around them. Our upcoming generation is super-talented, what potential!" For a moment his concern was replaced by a warm shadow. "You know my Vitaly turns out to have a terrific head on his shoulders. Just terrific! Too bad he's leaning toward biophysics. Blum seduced him . . . Don't you understand, Pavel, give us their money . . ."

"Where do they get their money from, Ilya?" Pavel Alekseevich tossed Goldberg some bait, and he bit instantaneously.

"The colonies, Pasha, the English colonies, imperialism and horrendous exploitation. You're like a child, Pavel. Amazing."

Pavel Alekseevich nodded.

"Child. Child. You're the child, Ilyusha. A case of gerontological chickenpox. I'm prescribing for you *spiritus vini*, one hundred and fifty grams three times daily. How, after eight years in the camps, can you even pronounce that awful word: *im-pe-ri-al-ism?*"

Pavel Alekseevich poured one hundred fifty grams of vodka exactly to the drop into a glass and slapped a slab of fatback on a heavy chunk of bread—the way Vasilisa liked to lay it on, thick . . . This time they were drinking in Pavel Alekseevich's study. Nowadays Goldberg frequently dropped in on the Kukotskys: the trip to Malakhovka was long, and he would sit in his laboratory until late at night and sometimes spend the night in the apartments of his Moscow friends.

Goldberg would jump up, overturn a chair, knock over a lamp, or at the very least sweep a plate off the desk.

"Because of types like you, types like me . . . ," the wounded Goldberg wailed. "My father had an account in a Swiss bank, he was a timber merchant! With a house on the Moika, and a house on Lubyanka Street. And a dacha in Yalta! Socially, I'm a dead man. I'm not the one to tell them that they're violating Lenin's principles. Who would listen to me? As far as this country's concerned, I'm guilty for life."

"Okay, so you're guilty. But what am I guilty of as far as this country's concerned?" Pavel Alekseevich asked, although he knew perfectly well what his best friend would accuse him of.

"What? Your father was a general! He had control of . . ."

Pavel Alekseevich yawned, shook his head, and asked Elena to give them a folding bed and linen. She had everything ready. She loved Ilya Iosifovich and felt sorry for him.

Ilya Iosifovich snored on his folding bed, defeated by fatigue and alcohol. Unable to fall asleep owing to this nasal trisyllabic music, Pavel Alekseevich reflected with the clarity of nighttime introspection. How much moral majesty and impassable nonsense could there be in one person! A Jewish dzhigit! Was it some kind of Jewish disease—Russian patriot syndrome? Like psoriasis or Gaucher's disease.

Pavel Alekseevich recalled a recent patient, a young Jew who had given birth to a second child with Gaucher's disease. A genetic ailment . . . Goldberg had said something about the accumulation of recessive genes in ancient peoples with high frequencies of consanguineous marriages. And blurted something about curing humankind through miscegenation. He practically raved about the creation of a new race of people . . .

In fact, when examined closely, everyone was sick. Everyone around was sick. His current assistant, Gorshkov, was sick with hate for his mother-in-law. Even the quality of his voice changed when he talked about her. But what's the point of talking about her: a cantankerous old woman with a bad heart and diabetes? His nurse, Vera Antonovna, was mad about microbes: she ran her own underwear through the sterilizer ... And Lenochka? With those dreams of hers ... ? Her eyes look inward, and what does she see there? You ask her something, and it's as if she's just woken up. Her face is filled with fright, tension. Toma whispers to her flowerpots; Vasilisa makes the sign of the cross over the stove before she turns on the gas ... It's one big madhouse. Tanechka is the only healthy person with normal reactions. But even she's been looking bad of late. Pale. With circles under her eyes. Either she's pushing herself too hard, or ... Maybe we should do an X-ray?

"I'll talk to her on Sunday," Pavel Alekseevich resolved.

Sunday mornings were usually their own, when they were absolutely alone. The evening before Vasilisa usually left town for services some-where. Of late, Elena, who had never gone to church before, had taken to attending services, as if to spite Pavel Alekseevich. True, she didn't go to the same place as Vasilisa. She had found a priest, a former architect, in some old church on the Ostozhenka, with whom she could also talk about her drafting dreams. Toma headed out to worship rhododendrons and oleanders at the Botanical Garden.

Sunday mornings belonged wholly to Tanya and Pavel Aleksee-vich. They had breakfast together and spent an hour or two discussing everything on earth—things at work, literature, politics. At night Pavel Alekseevich listened diligently on their ancient electron tube Telefunken to all the enemy "voices" that made their way through the clamorous jamming; Tanya took to reading the first samizdat to come out—the unknown verses of known poets as well as those of new, fresh-baked writers. Sometimes she handed her father something that had especially appealed to her. It was important for them to tell each other about every-thing. Politics occupied them to a certain extent, but both were much more interested in talking about blood vessels and capillaries.

Tanya had mastered the skills of a histology laboratory assistant as if it were child's play: the job demanded precision and dexterity, and she loved everything about it. She prepared stains, hematoxylins, using anti-quated, almost medieval formulas. She spent hours evaporating, settling, filtering, and redistilling. She told Pavel Alekseevich about her achievements, and he grinned: nothing had changed, everything was the same. When he had been a student they had studied slide preparations stained in the same way. With Erhlich's hematoxylin. Kulchitsky stain ...

Tanya enjoyed the entire procedure of preparing slides, which was governed by strict rules—from the moment the rat's brain slid smoothly into the fixing solution to using the heavy microtome knife to slice the opaque paraffin cube that contained the paraffined brain. A thin ribbon of micron cuts remained on the knife, and with a light brush Tanya would sweep them onto the slide, affix them, and stain them with the same hematoxylin she had spent three days processing ... Only Old Lady Vikkers's—Gansovsky's personal laboratory assistant's—slides were better than Tanya's. But Vikkers had not done anything else for the last fifty years. Besides, Karolina Ivanovna was incapable of mastering any technique on her own, while Tanya undertook each innovation with pleasure and a passion.

Tanya told her father in detail about the precise and rather tricky operation she had learned together with MarLena Sergeevna. They extracted a pregnant bicornate uterus from an anesthetized rat, spread the right and left horns of the uterus out on the shaved belly of the rat, and inserted a needle into the embryo's skull precisely at the vertex where the two hemispheres joined and where deep inside the brain there was a certain mysterious gland. When the insertion was successful, they were able to induce artificially an obstruction of the flow of cerebrospinal fluid and thereby induce experimental hydrocephalus, that is, water on the brain ... That is, of course, provided the operation was done well, and the rat did not miscarry or devour her defective young, and gave birth on time. Ultimately, all these delicate manipulations were supposed to lead to an understanding of the causes underlying this birth defect and, more-over, even more ultimately, to deliver humankind from this grave, but fortunately rather rare, affliction.

Tanya delighted in the sense of professionalism, entirely new for her, when eyes and hands work together, requiring neither commands nor oversight from above, performing their task independently and autonomously, while the task itself takes to one's hands as if rejoicing at the process under way . . . From Tanya's sighs of delight and the fervor of her stories focusing specifically on the details he recognized in her someone who was one with him by nature—a doer.

Pavel Alekseevich listened with sincerest attention—this kind of scientific enthusiasm was very familiar to him . . . Tanya had just completed her second year at the biology faculty, but she was already chin-deep in the game of science that Pavel Alekseevich understood so well. "Still, it's a pity she didn't go into medicine. She has good hands, but she'll spend her life gutting rats," the old doctor thought to himself.

In his treasured nocturnal jottings during those months he noted: "The windbags have achieved a stranglehold like never before. A preponderance of people has evolved whose profession consists solely of vapid and even malicious word-mongering. The entire nation has been divided into talkers and doers. Whole institutions and special appointments have been created—it's a terrible virus. What a relief that Tanya belongs to the species of doers. One's job, one's profession is the only thing one can stand on. Everything else is in flux."

The laboratory studied brain structure and development. Morphologists and histologists observed through the lenses of their primitive microscopes the developing microvascular trees of the brain, and tracked the mysterious process by which new networks in the brain were formed to replace those damaged or defective. Often they used the technique of experimentally infusing dye into the vascular system. The blood was gradually replaced by dye, and in specimens prepared afterward one could trace distinct dark branches filled with granular dark-gray caviar, which is precisely what the dye looked like under a microscope. This method was most effective when the infusion was performed on a live animal. Its heart would beat, not having figured out that instead of live blood it was pumping deadly ink, and only gradually, as it succumbed to oxygen deficiency, would the heart slow down and stop. More often, though, the injection was performed on a dead animal that had already been subjected to various scientific interventions. It was simpler, but the blood vessels did not fill as well with dye. The sets of instruments required for these two procedures differed somewhat, and it was at this relatively insignificant juncture that a decisive turn in fate awaited Tanya.

On one of their Sundays Tanechka proudly announced to her father that she had been placed in charge of the surgery room: she now kept the keys to the case that held all the laboratory's instruments. Now anyone who intended to enter the operating room in the space in the half-basement would have to come to Tanya for forceps, clamps, scalpels, and saws—the frightening and beautiful tools required for cutting and sawing bone tissue. There, downstairs in the operating room, they cut not just rats, but cats, and dogs, and rabbits ... But Tanya's principal responsibilities lay in preparing the thinnest of histological sections, and she was good at this work.

IN THE SPRING OF 1960 TANYA COMPLETED HER EXAMS with straight A's, and she was offered the opportunity to transfer to the day division. She refused, without even consulting her family. Although night school really was difficult, she had no intention of quitting the laboratory. Her real life was there, among the beakers, the rats, the slide sections, and in close communication with MarLena Sergeevna. Gansovsky himself had started paying attention to her. Old Lady Vikkers was planning to retire, and he was thinking about taking Tanya on in her place. MarLena Sergeevna guessed her boss's intention and, valuing Tanya as a laboratory assistant, told him just in case that Tanya was planning to transfer to the day division. A minor, but absolutely classical, intrigue developed out of a purely work-based situation. As usual in such intrigues, Tanya was clueless.

During the summer months the children's clinic attached to the laboratory usually closed down, except for the trauma section and the child development section that housed healthy children abandoned by their mothers while still in maternity hospital. Until these children turned three they were kept here under the watchful eyes of pediatricians and physiologists who observed the development of "normal" children, then sent them to orphanages. During these summer months when the clinic was virtually closed down, graduate students and researchers had the opportunity to focus on the "experimental" sections of their dissertations. Life at the laboratory became more intense, the operating room was in use every day and on a rigid schedule. Tanya's responsibilities also increased: she was responsible for sterilizing and issuing instruments.

The incident that would become the most significant in her entire life began very ordinarily and banally. Holding in her tenacious grip a tray covered with a cloth yellowed by multiple sterilizations, Raya, a cute laboratory assistant who limped on one polio-stricken leg, asked to be issued a set of instruments for ink injections.

"What are you injecting?" Tanya asked matter-of-factly.

"A human embryo," answered Raya.

Jangling her key, Tanya unlocked the glass case with its small metal treasures, pulled out tweezers, scalpels, and clamps from a broken sterilizing box, recounted all the antiquated metal piece by piece, and while selecting a clamp asked matter-of-factly, "Alive or dead?"

"Dead," cute Raya responded calmly, then signed for the instruments she had received, and set off lopsidedly along a steep staircase down into the half-basement . . .

She had already rumbled to the bottom of the stairs and was scraping the wall with her hand in search of the light switch when Tanya suddenly realized what exactly she had asked about . . . Realizing it, she put the key to the operating room in its place, took off her white lab coat and hung it on a hanger, and left the laboratory. She would never return there. Nor would she return to the university. Her romance with science had ended at that very moment, forever.

20

FOR A WEEK SHE SAID NOTHING. IN THE MORNING, AS usual, she left the apartment, set off on foot to wherever—downtown, to Maryina Roshcha, or the Timiryazev Academy. Never had she had so much free time. Summer had come late, and although it was already the end of June, the greenery in the parks was still new and untrampled, and the lindens had blossomed late, and Moscow's backstreets and courtyards held a special charm, the dilapidation of the old wooden houses—lovely and homey. Tanya wandered until she tired, then bought some bread, processed cheese, and a bottle of warm soda, and made herself comfortable in some secluded, cozy spot alongside some firewood sheds, or on the slope of an abandoned railroad track, or on a park bench . . .

She felt strange, torn. It seemed as if she thought about nothing, just walked and looked around, but deep inside her dwelt a thought that turned itself this way and that, from side to side, not a specific thought even, but the event that had struck her to the quick when she, Tanya Kukotskaya, had asked Raya Pashenkova if the embryo was alive, that is, if the child was alive, and if it had been, she would have given Raya the instruments necessary to inject dye into its veins, killing in the process not a baby rat or kitten or little rabbit, but a live child, a being with a name, a surname, and a birthday . . . Is every person that close to committing murder or was what had happened to her something exceptional?

Wandering the city from morning to night, she would return home, eat dinner, go to bed, and quickly fall asleep, only to wake up soon after to toss and turn, unable to fall asleep again. Once, in the middle of the night, driven by the emptiness of insomnia, she dressed and quietly slipped out into the street. She made her way through familiar neighboring courtyards that had metamorphosed into gigantic theater sets. The moon came out, quickly raced across the sky, and set just behind the Butyrsky prison. The wind then picked up, the sky lightened, and the new janitor hired to replace Lizaveta Polosukhina began sweeping the courtyard with a dry broom, raising a cloud of dust in the process . . .

By six thirty in the morning Tanya had returned home, lain down, and fallen asleep. When Toma began to rouse her, she muttered that she was not going anywhere today . . . Then Elena came and bent over her.

"Tanyush, what happened? You aren't sick, are you?"

Pulling the sheet over her head, Tanya answered in a clear voice, "I'm not sick. I'm sleeping. Leave me alone."

Elena was dumbfounded: what kind of an answer was that? Tanya was never rude . . .

Tanya woke in time for lunch. No one was at home; even Vasilisa had gone off somewhere. Tanya was delighted not having to explain anything to anybody, and set off once again to stroll about without purpose or sense . . . Palikha, Samoteka, Meshchanskie streets . . . Wooden houses, the last remnants of the old city . . .

Of course, she was prepared to talk about it all with her father and to hear what he—the main person in her life, the most intelligent and most learned—would have to say to her. But her father was not around; he had left on an urgent business trip, which made Tanya angry, and she even prepared a string of malicious words for him: whenever I need you, you're either operating, or at a consultation, or in Prague, or in Warsaw . . .

Another possibility was to talk to Vitalka Goldberg, but he was moonlighting at a collective farm in the Kostroma region . . . As for talking to her mother, Toma, or Vasilisa—she might as well ask the cat for advice . . .

When Tanya returned home, Toma had already tumbled into bed, her mother for some reason was not at home, and Vasilisa was sitting in the kitchen sorting buckwheat.

"Will you eat something?" Vasilisa asked.

Tanya did not feel like eating. She poured herself some tea, sat down opposite Vasilisa, and stunned her with a question.

"Vas, what do you think: when does a soul attach itself to a child, immediately upon conception or only at birth?"

Vasilisa bulged her one buttonlike good eye and answered without the slightest hesitation.

"Everyone knows: at conception. When else?"

"Is that church doctrine or what you think?"

Vasilisa ingenuously knotted her brow. She suffered from the persistent delusion that precisely what she thought was church doctrine, but now she suddenly had doubts: the second question seemed more complicated than the first.

"What are you torturing me for? Ask your father: he knows better." She suddenly became angry.

"I will ask, when he gets back." Tanya, leaving the dirty cup on the table, walked out of the kitchen.

Vasilisa closed her eye and wondered, "That's no accident . . . Why does she suddenly need to know about all that? Maybe I should whisper something to Elena?"

But, in fact, in Vasilisa's eyes, Elena herself was not entirely trustworthy.

21

PAVEL ALEKSEEVICH ARRIVED FROM POLAND WITH A SUIT-case full of presents. As usual, he had gone into the first shop he saw and bought everything there, including the suitcase. The shop turned out by chance to specialize in items for newlyweds; consequently, all his purchases were white, lacy, and in rather poor taste. Vasilisa and Toma oohed and aahed over the beautiful things, while Tanya and her mother only smiled at each other understandingly . . . Father had missed his target. However, the white shoes were just in time for both Elena and Tanya . . .

Three more days passed before Sunday morning, which Tanya so awaited. By this time over the course of her senseless walks she had arrived at a whole theory for rejecting the foolish, insane, rotten world, by whose laws she absolutely refused to live.

At breakfast she told her father about the main incident. Very restrainedly and precisely. He needed no time to mull things over; he instantly grasped the heart of the matter.

"You understand, what I want to talk about?" she concluded her story.

He sat silently, and Tanya waited also in silence for what he would say. He remembered her as a three-year-old, then as a five-year-old, and tried to apply to this grown-up young woman with the sad face all the silly nicknames of her childhood: Big-eyed Squirrel, Cherry, Kitten . . . Was there another defeat lying in wait for him?

"You want to talk about professionalism?" he asked his daughter.

"Precisely." She nodded.

"You see, a profession is a way of looking at things. The professional sees one piece of life extremely well but might not see other things not pertaining to his profession."

"Dad, I've read about the SS doctors. They conducted experiments on human beings to measure the impact of low temperatures and various chemical substances. They performed experiments using prisoners already sentenced to be executed. Exterminated, I mean."

"Yes, yes, I know. Terrible business. They were later tried at the Nuremberg Trials. You're right. This conflict essentially exists." He rubbed his eyes, which had immediately grown tired of this conversation. "Only don't forget that the sentence—both the doctors' and their patients'—in a certain sense had been signed in advance."

Tanya arched her brows.

"Are you trying to tell me that all people are mortal? If we take that into consideration, then it's even worse. Even more heinous. There's not a drop of sense in anything then. Right now we've got a child in the pathology ward, this tiny little body with a head three feet in diameter. A thin film of skin stretched over a huge bubble of water. And no rats are going to save him. Which means it's better to kill him and do a vivisection on him?"

"That is not even a possibility. That's idiotic reasoning." Pavel Alekseevich shrugged his shoulders. "She's picked up some of the family's prejudices," he thought with irritation, but decided that the conversation had to be played out to the end. "In our line of business, Tanya, the professional is the one who assumes responsibility, who chooses the most acceptable from available alternatives, and sometimes it is a choice between life and death. Medicine has its own code of ethics. Take Hippocrates and read him: he's already written about this. There are predetermined decisions: in my profession when it comes to a choice between the life of the child and the life of the mother, usually the choice is to save the life of the woman. It doesn't happen that rarely. As for your experience, the question here is absolutely speculative: for a minute it occurred to you that you could turn out to be a murderer ..."

Tanya interrupted her father.

"Dad, it didn't just occur to me. What have I been doing these two years? Murdering rats. I've slashed a whole mountain of rats. It seemed really easy. Snip, snip ... As a result ... Some barrier just sort of broke down ..."

"No, no, no. That's for your mother. I know nothing and don't want to know anything about those barriers. There is a certain hierarchy of values, and human life is at the top. And if in order to save the life of a single person, to learn how to treat only one human disease, hundreds of thousands—whatever number—of animals need to be destroyed, there is no question."

"Dad, you don't understand. I'm talking about something else. Lord take the rats. I'm talking about me. What's happened to me?" Tanya stretched out her amazingly thin arms.

"I don't see any tragedy here. It's a question of your state of mind as a professional. You hit a bump. That happens."

"One helluva bump! What's with you? Don't you understand? I'm cutting heads off of rats, piling up whole baskets of little corpses, in order to achieve some result. In order to discover something, to cure something, and along the way something happens to me that makes me lose my fundamental values: I lose sight of the difference between the life of a human being and a rat ... I don't want to be the good little girl who cuts rats anymore!" Tanya was almost shouting. Pavel Alekseevich frowned even more, and the wrinkles on his bare forehead ran almost all the way to the nape of his neck.

"I'm sorry, my child. And who do you want to be?"

Tears began to sprinkle from Tanya's eyes. Pavel Alekseevich could not bear this.

"I want to be the bad girl who doesn't cut anyone up!"

"Have a chat with Ilya Iosifovich. He's the philosopher. He'll prove to you that everything is material. You, and me, the rats, and drosophila: it's all one and the same. I'm not interested in philosophy. I work in applied science: breech births, double nuchal cords ... I refuse to try to solve problems of global significance. As it is, half the country is already busy doing that ... It's an irresponsible preoccupation. Anyone who does anything competent bears responsibility. The majority of people try to do nothing at all ..."

"I don't want that kind of responsibility!" Angry tears were now flowing down Tanya's face. She had expected sympathy and understanding from her father, but had found nothing of the sort in him. Pavel Alekseevich looked at her with an alien disapproving gaze.

"Then you should have stuck to playing the piano. Or replanting cactuses. Or, if you wish, do drafting ... and don't go into science ..."

"I'm not doing anything of the sort anymore. That's it. I quit." With slow, not entirely confident movements Tanya collected her cup from the table and placed it in the sink.

PAVEL ALEKSEEVICH WATCHED HER TENSED SPINE WITH the repugnant feeling that this had already happened to him before. Of course, he'd insulted, he'd hurt the girl, the old fool! Just as he'd done with Lenochka ... Insulted, Tanya had collected her cup from the table in the very same slow and uncertain way ...

He grabbed her by her pointed shoulders and hugged her.

"Tanya! Don't turn an experiment into a tragedy."

The slender young woman so resembled her mother at that moment that Pavel Alekseevich's heart wrenched. She turned her angry, tear-streamed face to him and said quietly, "You're just the same as the rest . . . You don't understand anything . . ."

She walked out of the kitchen, slamming the door loudly behind her and leaving Pavel Alekseevich in a state of profound dismay and bewilderment: what had he said that was so out of line, how had he offended his favorite little girl?

Pavel Alekseevich sat down at the head of the enormous table and sank his smoothly shaved head in his hands. He reflected . . . There was a multitude of factors that kept people from becoming close to each other: shamefulness, fear of interfering, indifference, and, ultimately, physical repulsion. But the stream flowed in the opposite direction as well, pulling and drawing people to the closest proximity possible. Where was the dividing line? How real was it? Having drawn around themselves their own magic circles—some wider, some narrower—people live in cages they have defined for themselves and relate to their self-designated psychic space each in their own way. Some cherish their imagined cage beyond measure, others suffer from its constraints, and still others seek to admit into their personal space only chosen favorites while excluding those who would impose themselves . . .

The majority of Pavel Alekseevich's many acquaintances could not tolerate self-isolation, fearing more than anything else that they might remain alone, face-to-face with themselves, and for that reason they were willing to drink tea, chat, and do all kinds of work just not to remain alone. Discomfort, pain, suffering—anything to be in the public eye, to be among people. There was even a proverb: misery loves company. But people who think, who seek to create, and are, in general, worth something, always fence themselves off with a protective band, an alienation zone . . . What a paradox! The most severe insults resulted precisely because people who are extremely close to each other draw the internal and external radii of their personalities in different ways. One man absolutely has to have his wife ask him five times a day why he's looking so pale. How is he feeling? Another regards even a slightly too attentive look as an infringement on his freedom . . .

"What a strange, singularly strange family we are," Pavel Alekseevich reflected. "Perhaps because only two of us—Elena and Tanya—are connected by real blood ties . . . The rest of us came together through the whims of fate. What inexplicable wind dropped gloomy Vasilisa at the door, or good-for-nothing Tomochka with her evergreen pleasures . . . Elena is melancholy, Tanechka is rebelling who knows why . . . Each in her impenetrable, separate cage, separate, and each with her own simple secret . . ."

In fact, Pavel Alekseevich had planned to do some work today: to skim through the American journals and write a commentary on a dissertation that had been lying around for two weeks already . . . But his mood was ruined, and he had no desire to read someone's son's dissertation. He opened the door of the cupboard—the bottle was where it should be—and peeled off the metal lid . . .

"And I'm to blame for it all, old fool. I've hurt everyone: Elena, Tanya, Vasilisa . . ."

22

TANYA FLEW OUT OF THE HOUSE AND RAN ALMOST AS FAR as the Savelovsky train station, then veered off to the right, then to the left, passing through a confusion of alleyways and courtyards, and stopping to look around only at the back entrance to the Minaevsky Market: a dilapidated wooden counter they'd not yet burned and mountains of market trash—everything from rotten vegetables to broken glass.

The sun blazed with its last presunset force. Both her tears and her rage had subsided. Tanya sat down alongside a shed. Nearby three boys of about age seven were playing cards. One of them had a cleft lip; the second—a stump instead of a right hand; and the third, more or less normal, had a face full of enormous pimples. They slammed their cards and cursed. Tanya felt awkward even looking in their direction. In the opposite direction sat a pair of drunks. These unimaginably filthy and strangely joyful beings were dressed too warmly for the summer, in sweat pants and winter shoes that were splitting into parts. Their gender was indeterminable. An empty bottle stood between them. They felt good. A gray loaf of bread and a piece of processed cheese lay on some cardboard, and their satisfaction veritably streamed above them in a pink cloud. They looked at Tanya and exchanged words.

One of the indeterminate beings beckoned to Tanya, and when she set off in their direction, extracted an unopened bottle of cheap wine from a scruffy bag and winked . . .

Their woolen ski hats of a color faded by dirt were pulled over their foreheads so that their hair was not visible, and only after peering at them more closely was Tanya able to determine from the unshaven face of the smaller one that he was a person of the male gender.

"Come on, I'll pour you some," one invited Tanya. Now it became clear that the second creature was a woman.

Her face was pitted, and the shadow of an old bruise lay beneath one eye.

Tanya stepped closer. The woman painstakingly wiped a glass with her black hand and poured almost to the top. Tanya took the glass and drank to the bottom. The woman chuckled with satisfaction.

"Ain't it the truth: he say you woun't, but I say nawbody don't say naw!"

Tanya felt like the object of an experiment and laughed joyfully in reply. The wine seemed very tasty, hit her immediately, and for the first time since she had walked out the door of the laboratory a week ago she experienced a sense of relief . . .

"Kind of you, it's very good wine." Tanya thanked them, returning the glass.

The drunken woman started. "Dawn't you drink naw wine, girl!"

She spoke a dialect not from Moscow, with strong "aw" instead of "o."

"I don't really drink," Tanya responded. The man, who had seemed good-natured at first, for some reason turned surly.

"Yah, we know how you don't drink. Chugged down the whole damn glass without chokin'."

"Pay naw 'tention to him, he a fool." The woman winked again, but her companion grew even surlier, slowly pulled out his bluish hand, tried to form it into a fist, but couldn't—his swollen fingers would not bend and just stuck out to the sides—and thrust it under the woman's nose . . .

With an unexpected coquettishness she slapped him on the hand.

"Aw, I'm scared now!"

"Watch out or I'll teach you a lesson . . . ," he threatened.

"Here," the woman pulled back in reconciliation and with nimble hand filled the dirty glass and handed it to the little man.

"That's more like it!" He took the glass with his gnarled hand and drank. Then with a pensive, slow movement he placed the empty glass alongside the untouched food and turned to Tanya.

"Whaddya sittin' there for: go get some more."

Tanya obediently got up.

"Of what?"

"Of what!" he teased. "Fine champagne! Get whatever you have enough money for . . . You know where to go? All the stores are closed; you need to go to the wooden house."

First Tanya bought a bottle of dry Gurdzhaani, but her choice turned out to be wrong, and the little man flayed his arms in indignation. They still drank it, though. Then, almost not making it, just before the kiosk closed, she went back and bought two more bottles of port wine, which turned out to be exactly right. Between the Gurdzhaani and the port a militiaman showed up and chased them all off. They settled down not far away in a cozy blind corner of the courtyard overgrown with burdock between three crumbling structures for which the word "building" would have been a misnomer . . .

Grace streamed down upon them. The couple no longer paid particular attention to Tanya. Over the entire time, except for interjections, the little man uttered only three articulate words: "Summer's good. Warm . . ."

A luminous bathhouse sweat poured over their filthy faces from under their wool ski caps, while the summer day lingered. This was neither laziness nor idleness, but repose.

For all of her almost twenty years Tanya had never found herself in so happy a place, where work, cares, duty, and haste had been annulled. This alcoholic couple possessed such a wealth of freedom that they could share it with Tanya.

The woman took off her shoes, egesting her filthy bare feet from the remains of her foot rags. Spreading her legs, she set her feet into the warm grass. It felt good . . . Then she took a couple of steps to the side and dropped her pants. Her backside gleamed with an unexpected whiteness. The man commented serenely on the event:

"Piss, bitch . . ."

Then he got the urge himself. He stood up, rolled back the elastic of multiple pairs of sweat pants, and pulled out his tiny tackle. The burdock shook under his healthy stream.

Tanya felt good, better and better as her inebriation increased, until she finally fell asleep right there in the shade of the soaked burdocks.

She was awakened after dark by an acute attack of nausea. She did not immediately realize where she was. She tried to move. She got up on her knees. She vomited violently. Then she wiped her mouth with a piece of rough burdock leaf. The couple was gone. She had to make her way out of there. She moved and was once again overcome by nausea. This time the vomiting spurted violently, and it seemed as if her stomach were ripping apart. Having emptied her stomach, she set out across dark courtyards illuminated only by the weak light of windows. She crossed one, then another, then a third. A tram clanged not far away, and she headed toward its recognizable music. The street was familiar. Tikvinskaya. Quite close to her house.

She felt better again, as if something wonderful had happened to her. Oh, the vagrants . . . Nice people free of all cares . . .

How wonderfully simple life is! I did something to myself . . . Snip! Snip! No more. No more pregnant rats, hydrocephalus, or developing capillaries!

A serene tranquility came over Tanya, the heavenly moment of contentedness and joy that had shone over the drunken pair of vagrants . . .

23

ELENA GEORGIEVNA SAT ON A NARROW WOODEN BENCH behind the collection box and awaited her priest acquaintance. The service was already over. The worshippers had dispersed. The cleaning woman clanged with her bucket. The metal scraping sound suited the church's hollow silence. In the refectory the priests, the church elder, and the choirmaster were eating dinner, and the smell of fried onions reached Elena. The lighting in the church was absolutely theatrical: the twilight was broken by thick columns of sunlight that fell from the high-set windows, and the scoured coverings of the icons caught in these streams of light shone, and the copper candlesticks burned, while in those places where the light did not reach there was only an enigmatic glimmer, patches of light, the quivering glow of candles about to expire ... Elena's soul was peaceful and quiet. She came here for moments like this: her worries now seemed mundane, her problems insignificant, and the conversation she had waited for so long—awkward and specious ... Perhaps she had asked Father Vladimir for a meeting for naught? Perhaps there was no need to tell anybody anything? And how would she put it? Yes, the world was falling apart. But she herself understood perfectly well that it wasn't the world that was falling apart, but her mind, which was losing precious splinters of knowledge, memory, and life skills ... She would have gone to a neurologist, to a psychiatrist, instead of to a priest, were the cracks of her consciousness not filled with something not of this world—more precisely, otherworldly—faces and voices, all of them unearthly, disturbing, but sometimes inexpressibly sublime as well ... Was this a charm? A deception? How could she put it?

The priest was already heading toward her, wiping his mouth, buried under his mustache and beard, with a checkered handkerchief ...

"Now, my dear, at your service," he said in an absolutely secular tone, as in the old days when he had worked at the Moscow Architectural Project office and Elena had occasionally done drafting work for him. "What problems are you having?"

ELENA DID NOT HAVE THE KIND OF PROBLEMS THAT COULD be discussed in such a vigorous, businesslike manner.

"I'm having difficulties with my daughter ...," she forced out of herself. She had not planned to talk to him about Tanya, but since the question of Tanya was concrete and readily comprehensible, she spoke about her. A feeling of betrayal clenched Elena. Tanya had not charged her to talk about her affairs with anyone, but there was no alternative, so she continued. "She's a very capable girl, good at her studies, but now she's suddenly left her job, does nothing, and spends her days and nights strolling about town, and she never says anything ..."

"How old is she, twenty?" Father Vladimir ruefully shook his crude thick nose, and his eyes looked out sympathetically from under his one long eyebrow joined at the bridge of his nose. "It's the same with mine . . . Kolya quit the institute, and Natochka left her husband . . . We raised our children without the church, and these are the pathetic results . . ."

Elena Georgievna felt excruciatingly bored, but leaving right away was impossible, so they spoke another twenty minutes about the harm of an atheistic upbringing, about the need to bring children to church beginning in early childhood, about the benefits of reading the Gospel, about prayer, and about other good and proper things. It was remarkably similar to what Vasilisa talked about in less sophisticated terms.

Shortly after three Elena walked out into the street. The sun shone, and it was still summer, but the place seemed entirely unfamiliar to her, and she experienced the kind of wild terror a child feels at having lost its mother at a crowded train station . . . She stood for a moment and waited: perhaps it would suddenly pass . . . This happened to her sometimes, but only for a moment, like an eclipse. This time her amnesia of the world lasted longer, and she would have to adapt to it.

"It's a city," she said to herself. "I'm in Moscow. I came here on the metro . . . Or was it a trolleybus . . . ? I'll have to ask where the nearest metro station is . . . There's a station near my building. I don't remember what it's called. It has colored stained-glass windows . . . I have a home. There's a phone in the apartment . . . The number is . . . I don't remember . . . I should ask the man I was just talking to . . ."

But she was unable to remember to whom she had just spoken and about what . . .

A tall woman in a light-colored suit, a silk scarf with grayish-blue streaks covering her graying hair, stood on the church stairs attempting to find some speck of texture on the empty mirror of the world that had just been filled with color and various details, each of which had a title or a name . . . She set off slowly down the lane. And walked, and walked, past places that were unfamiliar and more pleasant than not, but completely unrecognizable. She tried not to cross streets: that was too terrifying. When she tired, she sat down on a bench in some square. She wanted to ask the woman sitting alongside her what time it was, but she could not formulate the question: the words would not come together or be pronounced. Then someone familiar touched her shoulder.

"Elena Georgievna? Has something happened?"

The voice was a woman's, concerned. Elena never did remember who it was. This angel brought her home and helped her with the key. For some reason it was already late in the evening. She could not understand where the day had gone. Elena sat down in her armchair in the kitchen and remained there for a long, long time, until she fell asleep . . . Two other people were asleep at home—Pavel Alekseevich in his study, and Toma in the nursery. Alongside Pavel Alekseevich's couch lay an empty vodka bottle. Toma slept without having washed her earth-stained hands or turning out the light. That evening Vasilisa did not return home. Neither did Tanya . . . but Elena did not notice.

PART
TWO

1

THE SAND, PICKED UP BY A STREAM OF AIR, RANG LIGHTLY as it struck against the transparent stalks of the dry, brittle plants. A haze stretched across the horizon in every direction, and the sky held not a single suggestion of any light source. Tiny whirlwinds spun—dissipating, then rising up again—over barely formed, low-lying hills. The sand slowly rolled from place to place, flowing like dry water, but the outlines of this pale earth barely changed.

On one of the flat hills lay a woman, half-covered by the sand. Her eyes were closed, but her fingers sifted the sand, and gathering a handful, sprinkled it in fine streams.

"It's probably all right for me to open my eyes now," the woman thought. Hesitating a moment, she opened them. The soft semitwilight was pleasant. She lay for a little while longer, then rose up on one elbow. Then sat up. The sand tickled as it poured from her clothes. She examined the sleeve of her white nightshirt with the tiny green florets.

"Brand-new, made in Pakistan. A present: I didn't buy one like this," she observed to herself and sensed a certain discomfort from the knot of the white polka-dot kerchief tied village-style under her chin. She smiled and flung it off. Sitting straight up, she tucked her knees under her chin: that felt good . . . light and easy . . .

She stuck her hands under the hem of her nightshirt and felt the coarse scaliness of her legs. She ran her palms over her calves, and the sand fell off. The woman drew up her hem and was astonished by the sight of her legs: they were covered with rough cracks. Near the cracks the skin rippled with pink, scaly tubules. She rapped on them, and they fell off, exactly like paint off an old mannequin. She took a certain pleasure in scraping off this dried paint, releasing the dirty plaster dust underneath and exposing new young skin inside. Her big toes were particularly frightening: each of them was encrusted in a grayish-yellow layer from which the nail stuck out like an overgrown wooden mushroom.

"Yuck, how disgusting!" She rubbed the almost limy growths with a certain revulsion, and they unexpectedly detached themselves, falling off and instantly blending into the sand. They revealed new pink toes—like those of an infant. A pair of olive-colored canvas shoes with bone buttons appeared from somewhere. They were so familiar . . . Of course, Grandmother had bought them and a dark-blue wool sweater for her mother at the Torgsin store in exchange for a gold chain and ring: shoes for her . . .

Her hands, too, were covered with a dry, dusty crust. She rubbed them, releasing long, slender fingers, glove-smooth, without any knobs on the joints or dark raised veins . . .

"How wonderful," she thought. "I'm like new."

And none of this surprised her in the least. She stood up and felt that she had grown taller. Remnants of old skin dropped in sandy layers at her feet. She ran her hand over her face and hair: everything was her own, yet everything was changed. The sand crunched under her feet, and her heels sank into the sand. It was neither cold nor hot. It grew neither darker nor lighter: it was early dusk, and it seemed as if nothing here intended to change.

"I'm all alone." The thought ran through her head. Just then she felt a slight movement near her feet; a common household cat, gray with squiggly dark stripes on its sides, brushed against her bare legs. One of the innumerable Murkas that accompanied her everywhere. She bent over and stroked its arched spine. The cat purred in appreciation. Then suddenly everything changed: the air around her turned out to be inhabited. It moved with warmth, with waves of a certain quality that she could not put a proper name to: the air is alive, and it is not indifferent to me. In fact, it is rather well-disposed toward me . . .

She inhaled it. It smelled of something familiar and pleasant, but inedible. Where in the world had the memory of this smell crept into her head from?

She ascended a small hill and saw a multitude of similar tablelands.

"Rather monotonous." Then she set off forward, with no point of reference—there was none to be found in this place, really—with no intended direction, wherever her eyes would lead her. The cat walked alongside, its paws sinking lightly into the dry sand.

WALKING FELT GOOD. EFFORTLESS. SHE WAS YOUNG AND light. Everything was absolutely as it should be, although not at all like what she had prepared herself for so long. Nothing of what was happening corresponded to her now forgotten expectations; it all ran counter to the crude folk descriptions of the old women at church and the elaborate schemes of various mystics and visionaries, yet at the same time it conformed to her early childhood premonitions. All of the physical discomforts of her existence connected with her swollen, rusty joints, her sunken and stooped spine, her lack of teeth, her weakness of hearing and sight, and the slackness of her bowels had disappeared completely; she took pleasure in the lightness of her own step, in the enormity of her visual horizons, and in the marvelous harmony of her body with the world stretched out around her.

"How are they doing back there?" she thought, but "there" was bare and deserted. "Okay, so I don't need to know," she agreed with someone who did not want to show her any pictures. "They" also could not be made out as individuals . . .

She held something in her hand. She looked: it was a black lace headscarf, gathered along the seams and as rigid as if new. She spread it out: the pattern was familiar—not quite bells, not quite flowers, little bells braided together with sinuous whiskers. A memory seemed to break through from somewhere, as if through an invisible wall, and the woman smiled: at last she could orient herself . . . This was the headscarf she had searched for long ago when her grandmother had died. Grandmother had insisted on being buried in this headscarf, but she had hidden it so well that no one had been able to find it. So they buried her without it, covering her head with a white kerchief . . . She flung the headscarf on her head and with a familiar gesture tied it at the back of her neck.

She walked for a long time: nothing changed in the landscape or in time, and though she experienced no fatigue, she suddenly felt terribly bored. She noticed that the cat had disappeared. And then she saw some people—come from who knew where—sitting around a small campfire. Its transparent white-blue flame was barely visible, but streams of air flowed visibly around it.

She approached them. A tall, thin man with characteristic Semitic features rose up to greet her, his bald spot gleaming together with his smile, which was directed at her.

"We have a Newling," he said welcomingly. "Come here. Come. We've been expecting you."

175

The people around the fire stirred, making room for her. She stepped closer and sat down on the sand. The Judean stood alongside her, smiling like an old acquaintance. She felt awkward, because she could not remember where she had seen him before. He placed his hand on her head, chanting:

"That's good, that's good . . . Newling . . ."

And she understood that Newling was her name now. He was the Judean. The ten or so people sitting around the fire were men and women. Some also had familiar faces, but she had long ago grown accustomed to driving away those agonizing sensations of something once familiar and now fleeting; her efforts to remember, to excavate some scrap of memory and connect it to the fabric of existence had been so futile that she just waved them off as a function of habit. "They can't remember either," the Newling guessed, noticing with what breathless attention a smooth-shaven man sitting Asian-style slightly off to the side watched her. There were also two dogs and a strange animal the woman had never seen before.

"Just sit, sit and rest," said the Judean. Something she had never known before was taking place alongside the fire. More than anything else it seemed as if they were sunbathing . . . at twilight in the light of the small campfire . . . An enormous bulky woman wrapped head to foot in a crude flannel robe shifted, turning sideways toward the fire, while an old man with a gloomy face extended his arms, palms facing outward. A tall elderly woman in a black cowl that covered her face pressed toward the fire . . . Besides warmth the campfire exuded a radiating light that was very pleasant . . . One of the dogs rolled over on its back, exposing its stomach, covered with thin white fur. The mutt's mug had bliss written all over it. The second dog, a shaggy sheepdog, sat with its paws crossed in front of itself, exactly like a human being.

They sat for a while in silence. Then the Judean extended his hand over the campfire, making a gesture as if he were squeezing something in his hand, and the flame went out. In place of the burning fire the Newling saw neither ash nor charcoal, but a light-silver powder that blended with the sand before her very eyes.

The people stood up and shook the sand from their clothes. The Judean walked ahead, the others strung out in pairs or one by one behind him. The Newling remained sitting on the sand, studying them from behind:

176

though their movements were marked by total uncertainty, they seemed to share a strange singleness of purpose and concentration ... Last in line was the one-legged Limper leaning on a stick. Both his stick and his foot sank in the sand, yet although he was last, he did not lag behind ...

They had already moved rather far off into the distance when the Newling realized that she did not want to be left on her own, and she easily caught up with the chain, overtaking Limper, the Old Woman in a cowl, the Warrior in his strange jacket that seemed to have been taken from someone else, the strange creature—more likely human than animal, but absolutely not a monkey—and pulling up alongside Skinhead.

"That's good," he said.

2

TIME HERE WAS MARKED, AS THE NEWLING SUBSEQUENTLY noted, not by the alternation of days and nights, not by the changing of seasons, but solely by stops at the campfire and a sequence of events that struck the Newling as one stranger than the other. But nobody required that she express her opinion of what was taking place, and gradually she ceased to have any opinion at all of these various strange events, merely observing and occasionally participating in them. She did not always understand the essence of the events, but she never was forced to do anything against her will. Sometimes situations would arise requiring a certain effort on her part, but the general rhythm of their movement was such that their stops would occur just when she would begin to think that it would not be a bad idea to have a rest.

She long ago had come to realize that in these environs fatigue resulted not from their movement over the flat sand hills—movement that was really quite sluggish, although not enfeebled—but from the lack of that certain warmth emitted by the pale fire.

The locale was monotonous, gradually creating the impression that their seeming orientation toward some goal merely masked the fact that they were moving in a circle.

Yes, something was not right with the system of coordinates here, the Newling surmised at one point, and rejoiced, as she always rejoiced whenever her current existence was pierced by some thread from the past, which constantly loomed somewhere nearby but as if under lock and key, sooner an article of faith than a reality, like the dry plants in this place or the quite tangible tiny grains of sand that sometimes got in her eyes and irritated her tear glands.

One time the Judean sat down beside her and laid his hand on her shoulder. He had a habit, she noted, of touching his fellow travelers—on the head, the shoulder, or on the forehead sometimes ...

"Do you want to ask me a question?"

"I do ... Is there some other system of coordinates in this place?"

He looked at her with surprise.

"It's completely different."

"Not three-dimensional, that is?"

"It's multidimensional: everyone has their own set." He smiled with his thin lips, the wind stirring what remained of the gray hairs that grew just above his ears and on the back of his head beneath his bare crown.

"Does that mean that each of us is located in our own personal space with its own set of coordinates?"

"Not everyone. I know where you are and that fellow over there ..." The Judean pointed to Skinhead. "But you two do not yet fall within my space ... But that's not final. In these parts nothing is final. Everything is very mutable and changes with great speed ..."

"Ah-ha, that means time exists ..."

"And what did you think? Time exists, but not just one. There are several time systems, and they're all different: hot time, cold time, historical, metahistorical, personal, abstract, accentuated, reverse, and many, many others ..." He stood up. "Nice talking to you ..."

And walked off. The Newling sat, absorbing the rays of light with her body and filling with strength. That sickly fire nourished them all ... The deserted place, so infertile and poor, was becoming more interesting than one could have supposed at the very beginning. What the Judean had said about time was rather enigmatic, but she nonetheless had the sense that she had known about this but had forgotten. That thought almost burned her it was so unpleasant.

The Newling looked about: the fine sand, the silent people, and the boring landscape ... "Once I knew many other things—other places, other people—but I've forgotten it all; I can't remember anything. Perhaps I've fallen out of the realm of time where everything, everything in the past, took place?" She closed her eyes, because all that remained to her was the pleasure of the warmth and their eternal march through the fine sand . . .

Some of the travelers were so locked inside themselves and incommunicative that they reminded the Newling of patients at a psychiatric clinic. They fulfilled the Judean's infrequent orders lethargically at best, while he treated them like children—tenderly and with a firm hand. The majority of them recognized each other by sight, although they interacted little and only reluctantly. But there were some who were mutually disposed toward each other, and they would sit around the fire talking quietly among themselves.

New faces occasionally appeared, and some would disappear. Usually they disappeared unnoticed. Only one woman—gray and distinctively bandy-legged, weighed down with two sacks and a knapsack—left in everyone's presence. Once in what seemed relatively like morning, when they were just about ready to set out and even the fire had been extinguished, the woman approached the Judean, removed her cloth knapsack, placed the two stuffed bags at his feet, bowed, and kissed his hand.

He withdrew his hand, patted her comradely and roughly on the shoulder, and, extinguishing his smile, growled, "Well, go, go . . . They're waiting for you . . . You're a clever girl, go, and don't be afraid of anything . . ."

Those who bothered to raise their heads saw two festive green streams floating above her as a semblance of music sounded—something halfway between the short signals of some unknown radio station and études for a musician just beginning to learn some instrument still unknown to the world—and the woman disappeared, and all that remained in her place was the messy heap of discarded bags and a slowly diminishing smooth funnel of fading movement in the air. The mongrel grew agitated, began to bark, rushed over to the still fluttering spot, yipped inquisitively, its light head lifted upward . . . The second dog—the big shaggy one— sighed and covered its eyes with its paw . . .

Soon they were all walking down an indeterminate path, while the wind, full of fine sand, poured down on them a burden none of them needed . . .

Shortly thereafter, at their next rest, a newcomer appeared—a long-haired young man. Up to this moment, he had been wandering for a rather long time through the scraggy, blanched desert, his rust-colored cowboy boots sinking deep into the sand. He carried a bizarre little suitcase, and with the cold curiosity of someone who had just consumed some exotic drug he pondered where he had managed to wind up. His memory was completely blank. There were at least three things he did not know about himself: where he was; why he was hauling the ridiculous burden of that heavy little suitcase so ill-formed it was impossible to make it stand upright and it could only be placed on its side; and, third and most unpleasant, what was that dark vortex that kept flying over him now and again . . . The animated stream of air rumpled his hair and blew under his clothes—first too hot then too cold—nastily and annoyingly demanding, begging, whining . . . Besides these more or less distinct sensations, of which he was consciously aware, he also had the vague feeling of some enormous loss. The loss by far surpassed everything that he possessed, and in general everything that he had was, so to speak, absolutely insignificant in comparison with what he had lost. But what exactly he had lost he did not know.

He grew tired of walking, and he dropped onto the sand, shook his head, and white sand fell from his hair. He placed the little suitcase under his head. The sand crunched between his teeth and pricked him under his clothes. From somewhere off to the right the dark little vortex twisted upward, wobbled in the distance, and started to move toward him. Long-hair felt a fatigued irritation and said under his breath, "Get lost, will you!"

The vortex shuddered and stopped. Then the fellow decided that the vortex was sensitive to his moods and could be driven away by invoking his own inner powers. This was, perhaps, the first positive impression he had had of late. With the palm of his hand he swept a layer of sand off the suitcase and closed his eyes. You couldn't say he had fallen asleep: rather, he had fallen into a kind of catalepsy. While he was still conscious, he admonished himself: I do not want to come here anymore, no more coming back here . . . Sometimes such self-injunctions helped. He had experience with this sort of thing.

When he opened his eyes, however, nothing had changed except that his neck was stiff from the rigid corner of the bizarre object underneath his head. He wiped his neck and lay there a bit longer, and when he finally opened his eyes, he was encircled by people who sat in silence: they struck him as gloomy and poorly drawn. One of them was a bit more perceptible: he was bald, tall, and stood in profile, bent over a pile of dry stalks. He extended his hand over the tinder, and a thin flame rose up. The fire ignited of its own, without matches or a lighter. This somewhat calmed the young man: he had already visited places like this where water, fire, and wind merely laughed at the ambitions of small creatures who thought that with the flimsy reins of cause and effect they had tamed everything on earth . . .

That Jew playing with fire is the leader here, Longhair guessed.

The Judean approached him, rapped on the little black suitcase, and immediately revealed his perceptiveness:

"You'll hardly need that thing in these parts."

"I can't just throw it out!" Longhair shrugged.

"Naturally . . ."

"What's inside it?" The question had occurred to Longhair for the first time. "What's so important inside it that I'm hauling it around?"

"Open it and look," the Judean advised.

Longhair stared in amazement at his interlocutor: why hadn't that occurred to him earlier? But it hadn't . . . In part this too was consoling and reminded him of that stereotypical dream, familiar even to cats, where you want to move, to run, to save yourself, even simply just to get a glass of water, but your body won't obey you, and you can't budge a single muscle . . .

The little suitcase was locked with two clasps, and Longhair could not figure out at first how they worked. As he pondered the mechanisms of the intricate locking latches, his hands of their own pressed a bracket along the side and the suitcase opened. It was not a suitcase, but a case for an object of inconceivable beauty. The very sight of it took Longhair's breath away: it was a metal tube with a flared bell of yellow precious metal—neither warm gold nor cold silver, but soft and luminiferous. The elongated letters engraved in the oval stamp read SELMER, and Longhair deciphered the small letters immediately. He whispered the word, and it was sweet in his mouth . . . Then he touched the wooden mouthpiece with his fingers. The wood was matte and tender as a maiden's skin. Its curve was so acutely feminine that Longhair was abashed, as if he had inadvertently caught sight of a naked woman.

"What a wonderful . . ." He faltered, looking for a word: *toy, machine, thing*? Rejecting the inappropriate words, he repeated with a declarative intonation: "How wonderful!"

He had the urge to do something with it, but he did not know what . . . He tore off the tails of his plaid wool shirt, and, breathing warm air on the flared golden surface, he gently stroked it with the red-and-green rag.

Now he was walking with all the others, and the circling that seemed to some senseless or monotonous had acquired sense for him: in his black case he carried a wondrous object whose flowing, lithe outlines the case reiterated; he guarded it from all possible danger, particularly from the impudent black vortex that stretched out behind him in the distance awaiting the moment to attack him with its pathetic yowling and unpleasant touch . . . It seemed as though this vortex was somehow interested in the black case, because it kept trying to touch it. Longhair frowned. "Shoo," he said to himself, and the vortex leaped to the side in fright. At rest stops Longhair would extract the plaid rag from the back pocket of his jeans and lovingly rub the metal tube all the while they sat.

Sometimes he caught the gaze of the tall lean woman with the black headscarf over her voluminous hair. He would smile to her as he was accustomed to smiling at nice women, his gaze able to convey total happiness, love until the grave, and generally everything you would ever want . . . But her face, for all its loveliness, seemed to him much too distracted . . .

3

THEY MOUNTED THE NEXT LITTLE HILL. THE JUDEAN stopped, looked for a long time at the earth beneath his feet, then sat down and began to rake the sand with his hands. There in the sand lay a human doll, a gray manikin, crudely fashioned and damaged in places. From its punctured chest hung some sort of dark-blue string. The Judean pressed his finger against the doll's chest, palpated its neck, placed his fingers on its barely distinguishable eyes, then scattered a handful of sand over the doll's face. All the others also threw handfuls of sand, then silently crowded together in a cluster.

"Perhaps we should try anyway?" Skinhead asked the Judean.

"A waste of time. There's no way," the Judean objected.

"We should at least try. There are a lot of us. Maybe we'll manage," Skinhead insisted.

"What do you say, Sister?" He addressed the thin old woman hopefully. Sister, not lifting her cowl, shook her head with regret: "It's not ready yet, I think."

The Newling wanted very much to take another look at this human manikin, but the sand had already covered its clumsy figure.

"What do you say?" the Judean unexpectedly addressed the Newling.

"I would dig it out," she said, having remembered how she herself had lain just that way on the top of a cold hill.

"Are you willing to carry it?" He laughed, but his laughter was friendly and not malicious.

"You ought to be ashamed," Skinhead reproached him. "Your jokes, as always, are idiotic . . ."

"All right, all right. Here, aim your flashlight and take a look." The Judean sat down and quickly, almost like a dog, began to dig away the dry sand . . . "But keep in mind, if it doesn't work, it will hang on you."

Skinhead looked aside aloofly and grumbled: "And what's the volvox for then? Ultimately, it's entirely possible . . . Just a bit."

Sister pressed her hands to her breast and almost wept. The Newling sat down alongside the Judean and began to dig the earth near Manikin's feet. Skinhead dug the sand near the head . . .

The legs, which soon appeared out of the sand, were cracked with tubules of rolled-up paint exactly like those the Newling had had not long ago . . .

She scraped away the paint. Under it was a layer of dense material, but it was damp, claylike, not at all resembling the new pink skin the Newling had discovered under her worn shell. Skinhead worked on the head, removing some tattered patches of skin or paper.

"Let me warm it up a bit." The Judean gently moved Skinhead to the side.

"That's a good idea," Skinhead nodded. "Warrior, gather some tinder . . ."

The man in the military jacket nodded, and then appeared with several dry branches, which he fashioned into a vertical stack. The Judean approached, extended his arm, barely bent his finger, moved his thin lips, and the branches ignited with a bluish-white flame. They dug out the manikin. It was crude, its face poorly outlined, its arms and legs clumsily fashioned. Its sex was very distinct, and its entire configuration was expressly male, with wide shoulders, and with fingers, feet, and a penis that were disproportionately large. The figure emitted not the slightest signs of life.

"Volvox," Skinhead said into the air, addressing no one in particular.

The Judean, having anxiously palpated the manikin's neck and touched its stomach, frowned: "The material hasn't set. It's hopeless ... We'll all lose a stage and achieve nothing."

Skinhead was silent for a moment, thought, and said quietly so that the Newling would not hear: "You and your Jewish caution are keeping me from doing my job. I'm a doctor, after all ... I'm supposed to do everything possible to save the patient."

The Judean laughed and brusquely pushed aside Skinhead with a fist to his stomach: "Fool! I told you: doctors are fallen priests. You spent your whole life practicing secular medicine and now you want to foist it on us here."

"You're the fool," Skinhead snapped without malice and completely pro forma. "You believers have no sense of professional duty. You've dumped all your problems on the shoulders of your Lord God ... When it comes down to it, volvox is nothing more than an exercise in energy ..."

"Okay, okay, I don't object," agreed the Judean with a smile, and the Newling guessed that they were very close friends and that the connection between them was somewhat different from that among the others present here ...

The Newling felt with the skin on her face that the usually weak wind had picked up, and grains of sand were striking her lightly in the cheeks and forehead and burying themselves in her hair. The wind bore not just sand but thin stalks of grass, weblike clumps of prickly leaves, fragile vegetative threads, and dry moss. The fire burned, inclining slightly toward the ground, but with no intention of dying out.

The human manikin lay on the ground alongside the fire, and everyone stood around, waiting for something to happen. Skinhead pulled a ball of rather coarse thread out of his pocket and passed it to Warrior standing nearby. Having gone full circle, the ball returned to Skinhead. Everyone held the thread with two hands. To the right of the Newling stood Sister; to her left—Limper. The wind intensified, its direction impossible to determine as it blew from all sides and carried more and more vegetative rubbish. They all stood motionless, and dry stalks of grass, weblike fibers, and flying seeds of unknown plants stuck to their hair and their clothes; they clung to the thread stretched between them, and after a while they formed a circular fence of vegetative rubbish, open only at the top, while at their feet, alongside the fluttering flame, the crude manikin lay motionless. The Judean raised his arm over his head toward the very center of the opening, and the opening was covered over, forming the semblance of an ancient hut. The Newling sensed that her breathing was inconsonant with that of all the others, and she held her breath in order to join their common rhythm. Having done so, she discovered that besides their common breathing, they shared a common heartbeat and a common will directed at the insensible log, which seemed even to be resisting them, at least it displayed a certain discernable resistance to their common effort, to what might even have been called work. A very strong pulsation came from Sister on one side of her, while Limper merely designated his presence. The two strongest engines were Skinhead's and the Judean's.

The wind continued to rise, and standing was difficult, but the thread, which had seemed to be so flimsy, was durable, and it too conducted a flow of energy. The thread began to glow slightly, with the same pale-blue light as the fire, and the Newling felt their sphere lifting off the ground and suspended in the air. The manikin lying on the ground trembled, shuddered, and rose slightly off the ground.

"There, it's working." She heard Skinhead's satisfied voice. "Now we just need to breathe on it real hard."

They blew with all their might, and from the force of their breathing their sphere even expanded and contracted slightly, as if it too were breathing, and although the wind was carrying them off in some indeterminable direction, the Newling had the happy feeling of a child doing everything well and correctly and worthy of praise . . .

185

The stuffed manikin down below showed yet another sign of revival: its chest rose in a deep breath, and its penis became obviously erect. The manikin began to breathe, the wind immediately began to die down, the sphere started to settle, and soon they touched down on the earth. The vegetative walls of their air hut collapsed, and they all stood in a circle, still clenching the thread, around the reviving manikin, which moved its arm, ran its fingers across its chest, as if scratching itself, touched its flat—as had now become apparent—head, and coughed.

"Well? Is anything happening?" the Judean asked.

"The lungs are breathing, there's a grasp reflex, and an erection," Skinhead responded.

"Not a lot, but better than nothing," smirked the Judean.

Together the Judean and Skinhead dragged Manikin closer to the flame. It had become softer and now more resembled a human being in a deep sleep than a tailor's dummy.

The Newling felt that her strength was abandoning her, and she dropped to the ground. Looking about, she noticed that all of the people looked exhausted and half-asleep. The Judean threw powdered fuel from a matchbox into the fire, which made the flame glow dark blue and emit its nourishing light even more mightily . . .

4

THE QUALITY OF THE AIR VARIED: SOMETIMES IT WAS LIGHT, dry, and "well-disposed," as the Newling referred to it, and sometimes it grew heavy, dense, and seemingly filled with a dark moisture. When that happened, they would all move more slowly and tire more quickly. The wind, which never for a moment abandoned their caravan, also could shift: it might beat at your face, or cleverly peck at you from the side, or breathe down your neck. The light, however, always remained the same, and this more than anything else created the sensation of tiresome monotony.

"Tired of the local landscape?" the Judean quietly asked Skinhead. The Newling, who at rest stops tried to keep close to these men whose proximity made her feel more self-assured and protected, did not turn her head, although she overheard the quiet remark.

"Got anything more cheerful to propose?" Skinhead responded offhandedly.

"A small detour off the main route? Any objections?"

"That's news to me: you mean there's a route? And I thought that we were stomping around in a circle for some higher purpose." Skinhead smirked. He had long ago tired of the monotonous dim transitory light that deceptively promised the approach of either total darkness or sunrise . . . "I can tolerate the landscape: a desert like any other . . . If only there were sun . . ."

"Let's go then." The Judean examined the cohort dozing near the fire and searched with his eyes for the Newling. She was alongside them. "We'll take the Newling with us."

The Newling smiled with gratitude.

"And the others?" Skinhead spoke up, moved by a noble urge for fairness, or at least equality . . .

The Judean laughed: "What do they . . . We're not handing out vacation packages at the union office . . . Trust me, dragging the rest of them along is senseless."

Skinhead shrugged his shoulders.

"Whatever you say . . ."

"Let's go for a walk . . . ," he beckoned to the Newling with a tenderly assertive voice, and she stood up and shook out her clothes.

THE THREE OF THEM WALKED THROUGH CRUNCHING SAND. Distances in this place were relative and incalculable, measured solely in terms of fatigue and events along the way; for that reason one could say that their excursion began the moment Skinhead, and the Newling after him, noticed on the horizon a sort of flickering column of light that was moving in their direction or that they were quickly approaching . . .

The column glowed and filled with a metallic sheen. Then, there they were, standing at its base, which gradually metamorphosed into a rounded wall of translucent light metal . . .

"There," said the Judean, making an indeterminate gesture in the air, and a rectangular depression appeared in the surface of the wall, a doorframe, and a door appeared inside it. He pressed with the tips of his fingers.

"I know, I know how it's done; I've already seen this somewhere before," the Newling rejoiced inwardly.

There, beyond the door, the light was solid as a column, strong and dense, almost like water. They entered. The door, of course, disappeared, as if it had dissolved behind their backs.

Inside it was a bright, sunny day. Morning, but not early. The beginning of summer. A wall of huge subtropical trees stood not any which way, but arranged in order. The Newling understood that there was some simple formula underlying their arrangement, and if you could figure it out, you would understand the message they contained in themselves and for themselves, but which held meaning for others as well. The message was also encoded in the shades of green—from a pale green tone barely short of yellow to a rich green, triumphal as a choir—with all conceivable modulations in between: from the color of newborn grass to the pale silver of willow leaves to the shrill, the dangerous color of duckweed, opaque reed-green, plain Muslim-green, and even that machine-green you find only in hardware and building supply stores . . .

The Newling squinted with pleasure.

"How happy her eyes are now," thought Skinhead, who sometimes experienced the sensations of other people's individual organs . . . Now his own eyes exulted, transmitting their joy to the rest of his body.

A young woman sitting on her haunches between two cryptomeria stood up, and catching sight of the Judean, approached him, and they kissed each other heartily.

"He knows absolutely everybody," mused Skinhead. He and the Newling stood at a short distance so as not to interfere with their meeting.

"Landscape architecture was what I dreamed of . . . I wasn't able to finish the last year: I had only two exams and my diploma thesis left to write. But, see, I learned to do it all here." The woman stroked the cryptomeria, and it nuzzled against the palm of her hand as if the plant were a good pussycat. "These two are constantly arguing with each other; they just can't learn to get along. I keep having to mediate."

Her face was attractive, although a bit coarse: the bridge of her upturned nose was wide and indented, her mouth large; her eyes were enormous, gray, each of them double-outlined with black—once around the iris, and a second time by thick black eyelashes under broad, masculine brows.

188

"Let me show you, let me show you," she said, addressing Skinhead and the Newling. "My name is Katya."

The Newling noticed that Katya wore a man's sleeveless undershirt, the kind boxers wear in the ring, and the undershirt stretched over large young breasts. A multistring coral necklace covered her entire neck . . . Skinhead could see just what precisely was hidden under those cheerful corals—a slipshod pathologist's seam from the supraclavicular fossa down . . .

"I get the best results with trees: we speak the same language." Katya pointed to the two trees turned away from each other. "And these cryptomeria are my favorites . . . Maybe you remember that silly game called floriography? A yellow narcissus means unfaithfulness; a red rose—passionate love; a forget-me-not—fidelity to the grave . . ." She smiled, displaying teeth with spaces in between. "Well, the funniest thing is that it's all more or less true . . . So you need to plant them so as not to mix the messages they carry . . . This garden is for nameless children."

Skinhead and the Newling exchanged glances: what nameless children?

The Judean, who walked slightly off to the side, mumbled under his breath, "You could have figured that out yourself, without any hints . . . Yours are here too . . ."

The path of cryptomeria led downward toward the water. No water was visible, but there was a smell that promised water, the same smell that animals can sense dozens of miles away, the smell that leads them to watering holes . . .

The lake was quite small, round, and seemed slightly convex. Its blue water rippled and sparkled.

"Hard to look at?" Katya surmised. "At first my eyes hurt too, until they got accustomed to it. You need to look a little bit off to the side, not straight on. Shall we take a closer look?" The last question was addressed to the Judean.

He nodded. Katya ascended an airy little footbridge that hung in an arc over the lake. She lay down on her stomach and lowered both her arms into the water. Flapping her hands a bit, she uttered something quietly, then stood up, holding something in her hands that at first appeared to be made of glass. It sparkled. Katya slid the ingot of light, water, and blueness into Skinhead's hands. He took it into his cupped palms and whispered: "A child . . ."

The Newling did not see any child. The Judean crouched down on the footbridge and began to speak solemnly, as if at a meeting.

"It was born completely healthy, of healthy and handsome parents, and died a week later of an infection. The little boy cried and suffered. His father ran from their house, the best house in their city of stone, the only house made of wood, and for a whole week he lay on the ground, neither eating nor drinking, and prayed to the Almighty to spare his child's life. But that time the Almighty turned away from his favorite: he should not have taken carnal pleasure with another man's wife, even if her breasts were like two lambs and her hair like a herd of goats descending from the Mount of Gilead . . . And so on . . . He had even sent the beauty's husband to his certain death in order to possess yet one more woman, when he had more than enough of his own . . . Well?"

"No, I don't know," Skinhead shook his head.

"Hello! . . . This baby died—to put it in your terms—unbaptized. Then the couple had another baby. That one survived. They named him Solomon."

Skinhead chuckled: "How do you know? You've never read the Bible in your life."

"I have. Only at that time I didn't get the point. But I'm a Jew, you see. And Jews were given the Bible sort of by default. It's a part of us, and we're a part of it. Even if we don't want it that way. And even if you don't want it that way . . . Therefore, when it was presented to me at one critical moment, it turned out that it and I were one. Regardless of the fact that the world has never known anyone more idiotic, egoistical, or insignificant." The Judean smiled over the scintillating sphere. It was Skinhead's turn to mumble.

"My friend, what are you saying? That this is the elder brother of King Solomon, the one who erected the First Temple of Jerusalem? That it's two thousand seven hundred years old?"

"But it knows no time, only being," noted Katya, about whom they had forgotten.

"Okay, assume that's true. But what about the others? Who are the others?" Skinhead placed the scintillating sphere in Katya's hands. She walked to the middle of the footbridge, got down on her knees, arched catlike, and lowered the mysterious creature into the infant hatchery. Then she waved with her hand, beckoning them all onto the bridge.

The lake was full of—veritably swarming with—transparent, bluish spheres. The Newling remembered the long cardboard box where they had kept the Christmas ornaments in her childhood, and of them all, each wrapped in its own paper, her favorites had been the spheres . . .

"Of course, that's how it's supposed to be." The Newling grew excited. She could not have explained just what was as it was supposed to be.

"The unborn children, the aborted ones, are here too . . . Sometimes they ripen and reemerge," Katya explained matter-of-factly. "Speaking of which, that one over there, it's completely ripened." She stuck her arm in the water, attempting to fish out something that obviously did not want to be fished out.

"You and I used to be good at philosophy," the Judean began, but Skinhead interrupted him.

"No, no. I was more interested in history."

"Never mind. Remember Leibnitz's monads? It's very similar, you have to admit. And Saint Augustine was on the right track . . . Well, I won't even mention the Cabalists. For all the intolerableness of their method, they figured out a lot . . ." He suddenly smirked. "What was that your Fedor Mikhailovich Dostoevsky used to say about a child's tears? That comment he made to the Almighty about not having enough humanity . . ."

The Newling could not take her eyes off Katya, who had extracted a completely transparent sphere the size of a large orange, breathed on it, placed it on her palm, and stopped still. The sphere rocked slightly, then pulled lightly, and was about to begin its unsteady movement upward when suddenly, as if frightened by something, it once again sank into Katya's palm.

"He's afraid, the little one," said Katya with a happy smile. "It's very frightening for them at this point . . . They're going to do work. Some to commit great deeds, some—vileness . . . But this one here is very good . . ."

"Are there bad ones?" the Newling wondered.

Katya sighed.

"Yes, they're all different. There are frightened ones, and traumatized ones . . . And the more terror they've endured, the more evil they do . . ."

That sounded convincing, especially since the Newling once again got the sense that she herself knew something about all this.

"Take it," said the Judean to Skinhead.

Skinhead felt that he too wanted to hold the creature in his hands. With his palm he covered the sphere pressed against Katya's hand. Katya turned her palm so that the sphere lay firmly in Skinhead's hand. Judging by its weight and the sensation of warmth, disquiet, and trustfulness, this was a child. Undoubtedly a boy.

"Give it your blessing," said the Judean.

"That's up your Jewish line, not mine. I don't know anything about that." Skinhead smiled, not at the Judean, but at the being sealed in its sphere that promised to become an infant.

"It's no stranger to you. Give it to me . . . If you don't want to give it your blessing, don't. Just wish that it becomes a good doctor."

"Now you're talking," agreed Skinhead. "So be it."

The sphere lightly disconnected itself from his palm and, like a bubble of air in water, floated upward . . . until it reached a certain invisible barrier, where it slowed, then pushed against it with enough force to break through, and disappeared, leaving behind only the sound of the burst film and carrying away in the core of its essence the recollection of having overcome the boundary between two environments . . .

5

SKINHEAD WAS HAVING A DIFFICULT TIME NOW. MANIKIN barely moved, stopping dead in its tracks at times, falling asleep on its feet, and then Skinhead would have to fling it over his shoulder like a sack and haul it on his back, which cost him no small effort. The Judean offered to help several times, but Skinhead shook his spherical head with its few short bristles and harrumphed him off.

"It seems to me that you did your share of hauling back then." And he lugged on. Their rests became more frequent, apparently because of Manikin. After bathing in the sun for a while, it revived a bit and even walked on its own for a time. Once, when they were alongside each other during a rest, the Newling, taking a closer look at it, realized that its mouth was not cut properly and had only the folds of lips, its ears also were not drawn properly, its rudimentary eyebrows were barely traced on, and the eyes beneath them were weak-sighted. The Judean caught her gaze and said, as if offering advice: "Well, it looks like we're not going to be able to make it presentable on our own. We'll have to get help from above."

Skinhead, who stood nearby—at this juncture the Newling understood that the Judean had been talking to him, not to her—kneeled in front of Manikin, touched the back of its wrist, put two thick fingers to its neck, and attempted to raise one of its eyelids, which were stuck shut, but could not.

"Yes, probably," Skinhead agreed thoroughly morosely.

"We'll have to take a detour." The Judean drew a sweeping sign in the air.

They set off, as always, in their boring line through the boring sand, and they walked, as always, for a long time, always in the same—it seemed—uncertain direction; only the air seemed fresher, and it grew cooler, and the hills became higher, and the sand at first was harder and then replaced entirely by brown earth where here and there green plants poked through—like wormwood, nothing special, but the travelers were happy to see even this sickly greenery. The hills grew into foothills.

When it had become quite cold, a structure resembling a large shed suddenly appeared over one of the rises. In their amazement they all stopped in their tracks. It had been so long since they had last seen a human dwelling that a marble palace could not have impressed them more.

The Judean walked confidently ahead, while Skinhead had long ago fallen behind, lugging the heavy Manikin for the larger part of their journey. Even Limper had overtaken him.

Closer up, the shed more resembled some antiquated structure. The doors were high and hinged at both sides, like a gate, with timber-framing along the top. Entering, they were surprised once again: the enormous space resembled a dormitory, a sleeping area for schoolchildren, or a well-appointed barracks, with dozens of beds instead of barracks' bunks, standing headboard to the wall and covered with something white—either coarse sheets or thin blankets. The left wall was occupied by a huge stove with bluish-white ceramic tiles, obviously of Dutch origin, while the middle of the room was entirely taken up by a wooden table. In the left wall were two doors: one with a sign that read 00, while the other displayed a showerhead dripping dotted-line streams of water . . .

With amazement Newling studied the universally understood door signs. Only now it dawned on her that it had been a long time since she had washed or visited a toilet, even to urinate. How could it be that she had completely forgotten about these basic human needs? She immediately felt that her bladder was full and pushed the door of the WC. There was a white toilet, a sink, and a terry-cloth towel hanging on a metal hook. It also smelled strongly of soap.

"How many things have I forgotten!" she thought with horror and sat down on the toilet. The whole procedure went off without a hitch, and there was even an unopened roll of toilet paper at her service. She flushed, went over to the sink, and searched with her eyes for a mirror. There was none. But there should be one. She turned the old-fashioned brass handle, and water flowed out. She splashed her hands in the hard stream. The water was so strong and so heavy, and the sensation of the water was so powerful that tears trickled from Newling's eyes.

"How could I have gone all this time and never thought of water or of the fact that I'm a human being, who requires a toilet from time to time? Or about water, which is absolutely essential, yet, it turns out, one can do without? It never even occurred to me!"

She scooped a handful of water. It seemed heavy. She lowered her face into it: bliss . . . She splashed herself again and again. How good it would be to take a shower . . .

Newling left the lavatory. Skinhead had already laid out Manikin on one of the beds, and it moved its hands slightly. The others stood at the table, obviously confused. The Judean said something to them that she did not hear at first.

". . . we'll spend the night. We haven't slept for a long time, and today we're going to sleep here."

Newling looked around: now she wanted to go to the shower room. But there was no shower room anymore. In addition, the WC was gone too. Now in the place where there had been two doors there was nothing at all. An empty wall. She sat down in confusion on the nearest bed.

"I have to ask. I will definitely ask." Before she managed to think this strange incident through, the Judean approached and whispered in her ear.

"I'll explain later. It was an oversight on the part of the administration. There's not supposed to be a shower or a toilet in here. A slight mess-up." He smiled his thin-lipped smile.

Why is his face so familiar? Maybe because we've been walking together for so long . . . She felt that she was falling asleep. No sooner had she stretched out on the firm white bed than everything disappeared. "How nice" was the last thing she managed to think . . .

In the place where she was there were talking half-plants, half-people, and a fascinating plot was unraveling, of which she seemed to be the star. Carefully laid out on a large white canvas, she felt as if she herself were part of that canvas, and light hands were doing something with her, as if embroidering her—whatever it was, she felt the pricks of tiny needles, and the pricking was pleasant. She figured out in her sleep that what was happening with her had some connection to her life and death, but that there was something much more important behind it all, and it was connected with an incipient revelation of some ultimate truth more important than life itself.

She opened her eyes. Her back, legs, arms, and the back of her head felt hard and white. Her body felt good: it delighted in the bones of her arms hidden deep inside their muscles, in the bare heels of her feet touching against the sheet. Her heart delighted on its own, as did her lungs, and the happiest point in her entire body was the spot just above her stomach. She felt even better than she had near the campfire. But she did not want to open her eyes. Familiar male voices were carrying on an unhurried conversation that had begun long ago, at some point beyond the reaches of her memory.

"I'm completely unprepared," said one. That was Skinhead. "I don't know anything. What's more, something unpredictable keeps happening all the time."

"Nothing is predictable here. It's always an improvisation," answered the Judean. "When we dragged Manikin here, I didn't know that everyone was going to get worked on. Everyone's moved to the next level. Each to his own."

"Are you sure you have to leave?"

"Yes, I've finished everything here."

"Right away?" Skinhead was disappointed.

"In a little bit." There was the sound of glass ringing, as if glasses had been clinked.

"All right. So as the curtain drops tell me everything about Ilya Iosifovich," Skinhead asked.

The Judean chuckled.

"Doctor, you're a smart man and you made the diagnosis yourself long ago: 'a good head on a fool's shoulders.'"

"I've never been interested in climbing administrative ladders. You know that's not my sin. But why are so many things open to you? I say that without malice or envy."

"I know that. You see, great strength can accumulate through honest errors. And when released, the effect is meteoric. That's how I took off. Although the explosion itself was rather painful, even if instantaneous. You've always stood closer to intrinsic truths. What did they used to say: 'the truth is concrete'?" They both laughed. "Your path is slow, but true. Do you think being a saint is easy?"

Skinhead smirked: "Who here is a saint?"

"What do you mean who?" the Judean answered in complete seriousness. "You and I, and all the others . . ."

"What are you saying? I, a nonbeliever, and Manikin, and the monstrous Fat Lady? I don't understand."

"You're too much in a hurry. Don't rush. Remember how Ilya Iosifovich used to work like a madman, how it always seemed to him that just a bit more, just try a little harder, and he'd get the Nobel Prize for saving humankind? Now, as you see, I'm not rushing anywhere. You'll figure it out eventually . . . The amazing thing is that I had read everything. I knew everything. The necessary and the sufficient . . . Through a glass darkly. Never to the bottom, always in a hurry."

Something tinkled again.

"They're definitely drinking," guessed the Newling, who listened to their conversation with inexplicable excitement and a certain awkwardness. She even wanted to contribute, to make her presence known, but could not. Her body was as if switched off—she could not move a finger or use her voice . . .

"Yes," sighed Skinhead. "There's no reason for me to hurry. Especially now when she's here . . . Everything is so incredible."

"And unpredictable?" his interlocutor remarked with a certain acrimony.

"And that too . . . What strange medicine . . . Methodologically it's very much like ours . . . They even do sutures the way we do: double surgical knots . . . Even the needle, I thought, looked round . . ."

"And what did you think? The Spasokukotsky method of surgical scrubbing, Boehm trepanation, Bekhterev mixture . . . All our techniques came from there . . ."

"What's amazing is that they worked separately with the bone tissue, the blood vessels, and the nerves . . . I'm not sure I took it all in."

"You can be sure you didn't. Not all at once. All right, it's time. One more, and we're off. You'll see me off."

They distinctly clinked glasses.

"And what about them? Are we going to leave them here like this?" Skinhead was concerned.

"Doctor, Doctor," laughed the Judean. "Let them rest. Get their post-operative sleep."

The Newling was delighted even: she did not have to open her eyes and could sleep a bit. She immediately fell into a pure, transparent sleep in which the air fluttered not as usual, but musically, with a light radiance that coincided with the music. The vision nurtured and quenched her like food and water . . .

6

THE ROAD LED DOWNWARD, WINDING AMONG THE HILLS. They walked with a brisk step down the road and experienced that special inner force that pulls hikers along farther and farther, that is so strong that it requires some effort to stop, as if at the imaginary end of the path some breezy trail siren sang some imploring song.

They did not stop. The usual breeze blew, but instead of prickly, hostile sand, it carried scraps of smells, among them nauseating cinnamon and dangerous almond together with the delightful aroma of an old library—old leather, dry paper, and sweet glue . . .

The Judean walked slightly ahead with a mountaineer's gait, stepping with his bandy legs on the outer side of his foot. Skinhead followed, his shoulders lowered and his relaxed hands in loose fists, like those of an old boxer. Both of them felt that this locale was completely different, and this differentness—for the moment still unqualifiable—continued to mount. They both understood simultaneously that they were headed toward the East, whereas in that earlier place where they had traveled with other people there was no distinguishing direction. Here, though, the East soon made itself known by its pale and light-filled edge of the sky.

The road somehow accelerated on its own, leading down into a hollow, which kept growing deeper. The place gradually acquired the character of an inhabited space, although they encountered no people. The road was lined on both sides with large deciduous trees that resembled lindens, but with very tiny leaves. The trees, which had been planted at regular intervals, lent the place its quality of being inhabited. On the right, the hollow widened, and the road branched off along a cozy path. A board with a blue, sun-faded arrow was nailed to a post. They turned to the right.

The path quickly brought them to a long wooden structure with a high porch. The porch had recently been remodeled with white wood that had not yet managed to darken, while the structure itself was rather dilapidated. Curly low grass grew along both sides of the path, and even in the dim morning light it was apparent that the grass was light green, vernal, and not quite yet fully emerged. "Knotgrass," thought Skinhead, "just like the kind that grew in the field in Zvenigorod alongside the creek at the edge of our plot . . ." He bent down and ran his open palm along the grass and smiled: his eyes had not deceived him; it felt exactly the same . . .

"I think we're here," said the Judean, and they ascended the porch. They wiped their feet on a striped rug. They found themselves in a large entranceway where two earthy peasants sat—watchmen, to judge by their appearance—one wearing an old hat with earflaps, and the other in a cap.

An old man dressed in full monastic vestments stood before the watchmen, holding a paper ribbon with a poorly printed text and explaining something quietly to the gatekeepers.

"That's right. Nothing is allowed. Whatever you have on you is all right, but no unauthorized items are allowed," the watchman harped.

"That's not an unauthorized item; it's a prayer of absolution," the monk insisted.

"Sh . . . How many times do I have to repeat myself!" The watchman in the earflap hat grew angry. "Look at this, old man!" The watchman opened the rickety cabinet at his side and began extracting item after item: personal hygiene products in a plastic packet, an artificial leg, a wad of money from some unknown country and time, a stack of string-bound letters with a medallion in the shape of a crooked heart, followed, finally, by books, one after the next. They were all New Testaments—from antiquated ones dog-eared from hundreds of years of reading to new trilingual ones, the kind they have in hotels . . .

"You see, these are all unauthorized items . . . People keep bringing them, and bringing them . . . So, you see, give me that ribbon of yours and go on through . . ."

The monk placed his paper ribbon atop a black New Testament and walked dejectedly through the entrance.

The Judean and Skinhead approached the Cerberuses. The one in the cap mumbled something about passes. The Judean flung out his arms.

"Are you guys kidding? Passes were done away with long ago . . ."

"Maybe where you live they were done away with, but not here. Our administration demands we check. All kinds show up around here . . ."

Skinhead looked at them with tenderness: they were obviously locals, provincial peasants, and one of them had a very familiar face. He looked at him closely and recognized him: it was Kuroedov, the son of a bitch. He had worked as a guard at the clinic for many years. A cantankerous former KGB watchdog . . .

"Don't bother, Ilya. Let's go. What are you staring at, Kuroedov?" Skinhead walked resolutely past the men through the door.

Kuroedov looked at Skinhead, dumbstruck, then gasped and started waving his arms gleefully. "Holy Fathers! It's him! It's him!"

"You fool!" barked Skinhead, and the door on its stiff springs slammed behind them with a resounding boom . . .

There was no structure behind the door. It was a huge amphitheater with a round arena barely visible down below. The two wayfarers stood at the outside edge alongside the aisle that sloped stairless downward to the arena at the bottom. At first it seemed to Skinhead that there were no people there, but then he made out some people in the arena: they sat by themselves, spread far apart, at a great distance from each other.

"We need to go down," uttered the Judean, not quite confidently. They had descended quite deep, almost half the depth of the amphitheater, when the Judean stopped Skinhead. "I think this is good enough."

They turned into a side aisle and discovered that instead of the long bleachers they thought they had seen at first there were massive stone benches set rather far apart from each other.

"Sit here," the Judean offered.

Skinhead sat down.

"Can you see?"

In the center of the arena Skinhead could see a slight mound with a large opaque sphere on a separate podium. "Yes, I see a glass sphere."

"Try sitting over there," the Judean requested, and Skinhead moved down a row and made himself comfortable on the stone bench. He could see the same thing, only it was like looking through someone else's glasses: everything was hazy and had lost its sharpness.

"It's worse from here." Skinhead blinked.

The Judean nodded in satisfaction and proposed that he climb several rows higher. But from there all he could see was a whitish fog.

"You see, Doctor, I wasn't wrong: this is where you're supposed to sit." He seated Skinhead in his original place. "Just what the doctor ordered."

"Your jokes are idiotic," Skinhead sniffed. "Can you explain to me just what kind of a show this is . . ."

The Judean did not sit down, but stood alongside him, his hands on Skinhead's shoulders.

"This is where you belong. For now."

"And those sitting further down can see better?" Skinhead inquired.

"They don't see better, they see more. It's a particular kind of accommodation. What you see depends on your place, while the place depends on you. But don't let that get to you. They've spent more time studying." The remark sounded consolatory.

"Studying what?" Skinhead shot back.

"It. Being yourself." He looked at the sky. Even from here, from the depths of the amphitheater, it was apparent that the eastern side of the sky was filling with light.

"Sometimes you say intolerably banal things," Skinhead said, frowning. "Better you should tell me how not to be oneself."

"Everyone has to be born again. To give birth to himself again . . . Enough. You'll figure it out." He sighed bitterly. "So, now you and I will say good-bye."

"Forever?"

"I don't know. I think not . . ."

"Listen," said Skinhead, quashing the amicably romantic tone. "So what am I supposed to do with all those . . . with Manikin, and Limper, and Fat Lady . . . I have a hard time imagining what I can do for them . . ."

"You know, you've got the right approach. I think you'll manage. Put your faith in the Supreme Intelligence. It won't let you down." The Judean smirked, and his smirk suddenly wounded Skinhead.

"Are you laughing, Ilya?"

"That part of Ilya that still remains, Doctor, weeps. After all, it seems, you once believed in a Supreme Intelligence just as I did. So follow it."

Skinhead wanted to object, but there came a sound, at first not very loud, but alarming. It was the sound of a road. It reached his inner depths, and Skinhead felt a hole in his solar plexus, as if the sound had penetrated him and gone out his back, piercing his entire being. The sound contained a voice that announced very distinctly: "Are you ready? Are you ready?"

At the same time it was clear that someone else, not he, needed to ready himself. The sound was the sound of a trumpet . . .

The Judean leaned over and kissed Skinhead awkwardly and ran down to the arena, and it became clear that the voice of the trumpet had been calling precisely him . . . Suddenly he stopped, returned, and rummaged hastily in his pockets. He pulled out something that looked either like a small box or a large bug and stuck it in Skinhead's hand.

"I almost forgot. It's a lighter. That sticks to the palm of your hand. Take it easy! Everything will be okay! Very okay!"

He ran back down, skipping slightly, rather quickly, and the light locks of his poor hair flew behind him. An instant later he was alongside the platform, and two radiant indeterminate beings that could barely be made out piled into his outstretched arms a stack of books, papers, packages, and bags—the usual travel gear for a scholarly business trip . . .

The sphere split into two hemispheres. The Judean with his baggage stepped inside, and the sphere shut with a metallic click.

The sound of the trumpet—piercing, and resembling reveille at a Pioneer camp amplified multiple times over—mounted until the moment the metallic click was heard. Then the trumpet abated, and a weak electric-tinted buzz could be heard as the base of the sphere lit up slightly. The illumination increased, and the entire sphere filled with a cold bluish-white light that, despite its brilliance, did not light the arena; rather, it seemed, all its powerful incandescence was concentrated deep inside the sphere.

"He'll burn up . . . It's the end." Skinhead was horrified.

The buzzing ceased, the light inside the sphere was extinguished, and the sphere became cloudy and translucent. As if it were cooling down . . . It opened.

Out of the sphere emerged the Judean. His arms were stretched out in front of him, as they had been, as if they still held the pile of books. But there were no books. It seemed as if there was nothing at all.

"It burned up. It all burned up." Skinhead deduced what exactly it had been that his best, idiotic friend had been holding in his arms: all his thoughts, his work, his plans, his books, his reports, and all his silly accomplishments, his prison work, as well as all his noble deeds, which had always caused those around him so much suffering . . .

The Judean raised the palm of his right hand so that Skinhead could see perfectly clearly the thin light metallic plate on it. The plate bore a word that Skinhead was able to make out despite the distance between them.

INTENTIONS read the word on the plate.

"Lord, God," Skinhead implored, "but what about hell being paved with them? . . . Can our intentions really acquit us?"

The arena swayed, and the cooling sphere, and the edge of the brightening sky—all of it shifted to the side, like the shadow of a cloud . . . Once again they were walking single file through the gray sandy desert, and their legs sank into the sand, and the weak breeze carried bits of sand that it cast in their faces ... Up ahead marched Skinhead, while Limper brought up the rear, no longer limping ...

7

AFTER THEIR NIGHT IN THE SHED EVERYONE HAD CHANGED slightly. Most appreciably—Manikin. It was no longer stiff as oak, had become more flexible, and had acquired certain details: even its ear helixes had come to life and formed a primitive pattern, and while its eyes still looked out blankly, they no longer seemed blind.

"Likely our nighttime visitors worked him over particularly thoroughly," Skinhead noted to himself. "They're good at plastic surgery, no denying it ... And they made a leg for Limper: what's not clear only is whether it's a prosthesis or a transplant. It looks like they formed new bone tissue and fashioned the fibula and the tibia, then grafted the nerves and muscle tissue ... Fat Lady has become even fatter. Sister has become transparent; the light shines through her fingers ... Actually, everybody has changed except the Newling ..."

He watched surreptitiously from afar as she sat down on a hump, removed her shoes, poured the sand from them, then ran her marvelous hands (with a slight scar on the left one, between the middle and ring finger where a fishhook had lodged itself in her childhood) along her narrow long feet (she'd always been embarrassed by her large shoe size), and brushed off the grains of sand. Then she pulled off the black lace headscarf and loosened her thick chestnut hair, and it fell in three separate, springy locks—like hair accustomed to long years of tight braiding; she shook out the sand ...

Manikin, despite its improvement, worried Skinhead, while at the same time Skinhead was angry with himself: How had it happened that all of a sudden he had been put in charge of them? ... Who was he, anyway? Just like them, brought there from who knew where or why, confused and lonely ...

Skinhead had noticed Manikin's strange behavior even before its first seizure: it started to display signs of alarm, which was out of character for it. It would look over its shoulder, or squat down and cover its head with haphazardly fashioned paws. At one point Manikin stopped dead in its tracks and listened: from somewhere far away in the distance it was struck by a subtle terrifying sound aimed like a thin, sharp needle at its face.

The first time the wait was quite short: the needle pierced Manikin's forehead, and it fell to the ground with a loud scream. The seizure resembled epilepsy, and Skinhead immediately stuck the bowl of a spoon—where had it come from?—in its mouth, elevating its head on his knees so that its stone-hard skull did not beat against the ground. They had no medicine. If only he had about five tablets of phenobarbital . . .

Following this first seizure Manikin's life changed, becoming horrible and considerably more conscious. It was now constantly in one of two states—before "that" and after "that." But it knew that there was yet a third state—"that," which was horrid. "That" was followed by "after that." Manikin would get up, light as an empty sack, having completely forgotten what it had just undergone. Usually at that moment it saw Skinhead alongside it. If he was not there, Manikin would catch up with the rest, who sometimes had managed to go quite far. It experienced intense hunger and approach Skinhead, who without uttering a word stuck a small square cookie in its hand. Manikin ate the funny cookie and within a few minutes forgot about its hunger. It walked on and on once again, then suddenly recall how once when it had been walking just that way it had heard a subtle, terrifying sound. It anxiously attuned its hearing, and soon the sound arose: "before that" was approaching. The malicious needles, or bees, or bullets, that flew at it from some unknown distance multiplied. It seemed as if each of them was aimed at some particularly tender and painful part of Manikin's body: at its eyes, throat, stomach, gut . . . Each target would turn into a kind of independent organ and experience a woeful expectation, an ever-intensifying horror, and all these independent sensations of individual organs multiplied geometrically and expanded cosmically and uncontrollably so that Manikin's terror by far came to exceed its own dimensions, and in order to contain this uncontrollably expanding fear within itself it became enormous, much larger than itself, much larger than any largeness a human being could imagine. And all of this went on and on and on . . . At that moment Manikin would get the desperate urge to shrink, to become little, tiny, the most insignificant grain of sand.

It attempted to shrink into nothingness, but instead only grew more enormous, becoming an open target for all the arrows rushing toward it. The greater this insane expansion, this ballooning of its body, the more urgent was its desire to shrink into a grain of sand, into nothingness ... And then the blows struck. The first, to the head, was crushing and burned its way through. The blow was sharp, sabrelike, and gleaming black in color. Then another, and another. They came one after the next, striking the ever-diminishing bounds of Manikin's body, whipping, like lightning, the already charred but still shuddering tree of its body ...

Skinhead held its jerking head, not allowing its clamped jaws to lock shut. Sometimes Longhair helped him: clamping between his rust-colored cowboy boots the fragile case he never put down for a moment, he grasped the wildly arching body with both arms, softening the blows that the madman dealt to himself ...

Then Manikin would get up, and all of it repeated over and over ... Skinhead looked inside its skull and saw that the two small hemispheres were covered with a dark brilliant membrane of not entirely determinable localization: either under the thick meninges of the dura mater or directly below on the soft arachnoid mater or pia mater. After each seizure this membrane would be covered with a new network of fissures, and small pieces of the membrane had fallen away, shrunk, and allowed healthy pale-gray portions of the brain, networked with pink blood vessels, to emerge ...

"More analogues," Skinhead noted. "We also have an electroshock method for treating schizophrenia ..."

He would stroke the calmed half-wit on the head as the latter, like a child, rotated its head under the doctor's hand so that not a place was left untouched ...

Sister in the meantime had grown even more transparent, and when the journeyers sat down at the campfire, Skinhead noticed once how she pulled back her monastic cowl for an instant, and the face that peeked out from behind amazed him with its rare asymmetry—not one eye or eyebrow was where it belonged; there were only pale folds of limp skin with no eyelashes, and a scab on her forehead shaped like an eye, which bled at the center of the wound. With her almost invisible hand she replaced the cowl, and the location of her transparent hand against the background of her dark vestments was evident only because of her string of black woolen rosary beads.

Her departure passed unnoticed. Once after their usual rest her vestments lay alongside the campfire: her white blouse folded into her black inner rason; her cowl, the headdress of Eastern Orthodox Christian women monastics; and a red velvet purse. Skinhead opened the purse. Inside, wrapped in foil, lay a decayed woolen thread and a handful of ashes ... Her vestments smelled of cinnamon, which since childhood he had not been able to tolerate, bitter almonds, and incense ...

Sister had disappeared considerably, troubling no one, while the new person who just arrived caused everyone a mass of headaches. At first when he discovered himself next to the campfire, this middle-aged citizen of average height imagined that he was dreaming. And insofar as he could fathom no other state except consciousness and sleep, these woeful, somewhat constrained people sitting around the campfire seemed suspicious to him. The campfire itself, which burned at his feet, also seemed strange—too pale, and not hot.

"It's all stage props," the man in the sports jacket guessed. "Of course, this is a dream, a very entertaining dream."

He began to peer diligently into this rather strange dream so as not to forget it when he woke up and to tell his wife, Nadya, about it. Her dreams were always unusually stupid: either she was taking his sports jacket to the cleaners, or her soup was boiling over in the pot. He dreamed only rarely, and never had he dreamed anything as intricate as this one with the campfire. He tried recounting the people sitting around the fire, but could not. Either they kept moving around slightly or their numbers changed. On closer examination it turned out that these people were not quite real, but shadows of some sort. Only one of them stood out among the others: a large, thickset fellow with his head shaved clean, a patch of light from the fire reflected on his forehead, his head half bald. A Lenin forehead. He chose Skinhead as the most respectable of the bunch to be his conversation partner.

"I have to ask him ..." And then he stopped. He suddenly began to fear that this was no dream. And if it was not a dream, then the first thing he needed to ask was what this place was and how he had wound up here . . . If you ask that, they'll decide you're insane. What's more, he could not remember what exactly had preceded his arrival at this place, which was obviously in the countryside, in some unfamiliar locale, and not even in Central Russia . . .

He peered once again at the faces of the people, decidedly strangers and somewhat bizarre: next to him was a thuglike half-wit, indifferent as a rock; next to him a long-haired fellow sat in a lotus pose with an unnaturally straight spine and a saxophone case clasped to his chest. His son had once carried around just such a case before he left home . . . There was a mangy dog, a fat woman of simple origins, and—he even perked up and calmed down a bit—to his left a very beautiful woman with a good Russian face lay right on the bare ground, supporting her chin in the palm of her hand.

"That one's my type," he thought with pleasure. "She looks like Nadya when she was young . . ." The others sank into the twilight, the fire illuminating first someone's hand, then someone's back . . .

"Need to collect my thoughts and figure out what caused this lapse," he decided. The situation was unpleasant, but he felt no particular fear. He turned his thoughts toward home, the most secure place of his existence. So what did he remember? Nadya had served him a breakfast of fried potatoes and two meat patties. He distinctly remembered the patties lying on the plate angled toward each other. A piece of bread with sausage. Tea. It was Tuesday. He had a convenient class schedule: two more ninety-minute lectures on Wednesday and then free until Monday.

"Ever since I got promoted to full professor I've had a convenient schedule," he mused. "True, I have extracurricular obligations, the party organization, and meetings at the rector's office, which, by the way, I must not forget, are this week . . ." He drifted off on a tangent. "Right, next: I ate breakfast and took Kashtan out for a walk. In the distance I noticed that repulsive gray mastiff from the other entranceway . . . Then I went upstairs and changed . . ."

Just then he noticed that he was wearing his dark-gray dress suit with the lapels, not his dark-blue striped suit . . . He looked at the toes of his shoes: they were his black dress shoes. At that time of the morning he usually put on his old Romanian sandals with the slits . . .

"So, let's think this out logically," he told himself. "When I walked out of the house I had my briefcase. Today I'm lecturing first period to the fifth-year students on 'Contemporary Issues in Gnosiology'; second period—'Fundamentals of Scientific Atheism' to the entire first-year class ... I don't have my briefcase. I don't remember at all having delivered those lectures. I'm wearing different clothes. Consequently, between leaving the house and now, some event occurred that I do not remember ... It happened between 8:25 A.M. and ..." He wanted to look at his watch, but he was not wearing one ... "It's evening. But there's no being assured that only ten hours have passed between the morning I imagine to have been today and now. Any amount of time could have passed since the moment I stopped keeping track ... Consequently, I've had a lapse of memory. A cerebral vasospasm. So how do I reconstruct what happened next? Probably the Fourth Department Hospital, with a sanatorium or something similar after ... But how could Nadya leave me on my own? A sick person requires ... No, that's not like her ... Strange, strange ..."

The Professor politely addressed Longhair: "Excuse me, what time is it?"

Longhair looked at him with a blank stare and said, it seemed to the Professor, with contempt, "The same as it was ..."

"Typical hippie," the Professor summed him up in a moment and turned away. Skinhead looked distinctly more decent than the rest; he got up to go over to him. Once on his feet, he noticed that something was wrong with his sense of space: either the horizon was too close, or the sky was too low ...

"What a tight place this is ... Devil knows where I've wound up," the Professor thought, irritated. Skinhead stood up respectfully and walked over to him. "Sort of looks like Mayakovsky. The Professor liked Mayakovsky and often quoted him both in and outside the lecture hall ..."

Skinhead came right up to him and unexpectedly placed his hand on the Professor's shoulder, amazing him with this breach of formality. Skinhead spoke first.

"Professor, I ask you not to worry. And for the time being do not ask any questions. The situation you are in is highly unusual, and you will be required to spend a certain amount of time here. Then everything will be explained to you ..."

The Professor nodded guardedly. He was beginning to surmise what had happened to him . . . Of course, only the all-powerful services could do this: put a person to sleep, move him somewhere, and then do what they wanted with him . . . Of course, this was not 1937, but they were very powerful: the Professor knew this firsthand. He gazed intently at Skinhead. Who was this Skinhead guy anyway?

Skinhead was dressed in a white cotton shirt with a button at the collar . . . He was wearing a military shirt . . . Military underwear . . . Not quite clarity, but something was beginning to come together . . .

And the Professor was gladdened by his own powers of observation . . .

8

ONLY NOW THAT THE JUDEAN WAS NO LONGER AROUND did Skinhead begin to understand how many various responsibilities had fallen to him. At first it had seemed to him that his chief concern was Manikin with its constant seizures. But gradually it emerged that in that gray crowd there were no supernumeraries; each character had his or her own storyline. In fact, less a storyline than a task formulated in keeping with the famous fairy-tale maxim: "Go thither—unknown whither; and fetch that—unknown what . . ." It appeared that they all were welded to some task, like prisoners to a ball and chain, and that they could not leave this place until they fulfilled it. He also was getting the impression, however, that not all of them had even an inkling of what exactly the stage director of this entire production wanted from them. Even Skinhead himself did not know for sure why he was here.

Essentially, to the extent he could, he continued to do here what he had done all his life at the institute, the clinic, and the hospitals . . . Something not quite a physician's or a pedagogue's role . . . An auxiliary role . . . A midwife's . . .

When he had first seen the Newling here, she had been so familiar, with all the precious features of her face and her figure, with all her gestures, that he had realized immediately that she was separated from him by some impenetrable and insurmountable wall. She did not recognize him. His first and most urgent desire had been to take her by the hand, to stroke her hair and her face . . . But the Judean had warned him back then: "Careful. What we have here is a case of total amnesia. Let her get used to you, then approach her . . ."

"Will this ever pass?" Skinhead had asked, suppressing the desire to press her immediately to his body, to run his fingers from her neck to the crown of her head, to pull all those hairpins out so that her long chestnut hair would fall about her shoulders . . . This was his only woman, the one predestined for him, and he was prepared to start anew, to approach her as any man first approaches a woman he likes but has not been introduced to yet.

"Perhaps. In part . . . You can tell someone took care that you would recognize her, but that she would not recognize you . . . It seems to me," he concluded softly, "that in this case it's better not to resist, but to be accepting . . . To meet her on her own terms, so to speak . . ."

Since that time Skinhead had tried not to let the Newling out of his sight, and whenever a question or alarm appeared in her eyes, he turned up alongside her. Her presence, incidentally, created no particular difficulties for him; just the sore spot in his heart, that old scar, throbbed . . .

He had difficulties with the others. There were those two women, beyond doubt a couple—a rather comical one, owing to the enormous difference in their sizes, one petite with a large curly head and short arms and legs, and the other tall, long-legged, with a bent, rounded spine and a tiny head that sat snakelike on her long neck—who on closer examination turned out not to be girlfriends at all, but each other's captives. A small chain, like that on a bicycle, connected the tall one's right leg to the little one's left leg. It encircled their ankles in a figure eight. Skinhead saw that the chain's connecting clasp had been replaced by a shining ball of either glass or metal. When they walked, they inflicted pain on each other with each step, and when they sat down at rest stops, instead of the respite they might enjoy by not moving, they began slowly pulling at the ball, each movement causing the chain to dig deeper into their wounds . . .

"They're trying to divvy something up and can't do it," Skinhead figured out at a certain moment.

Shortly after, he discovered what could provide each of them some relief from their mutual torture: when he placed his huge hands, slightly inclined toward each other on their heads, they would calm down. Before his eyes their wounds stopped bleeding, dried up, and scabbed over . . .

The initial sense of disorientation Skinhead experienced after the Judean left soon passed. His lifelong assistant—what he called either his intravision or simply intuition—now awakened in him not at those moments when he was examining patients or performing operations, but in those situations when Skinhead experienced uncertainty or perplexity.

After one of their rest stops, when Skinhead waved his hand over the flame and turned off the lighter glued firmly to his palm, which made the fire lull, the heat ceased to be emitted, and only its remnant continued to warm his palm for quite some time, at which point he sensed clearly which direction they needed to go. What used to show him those "inner pictures" now suggested which direction to move in . . . They set off in their usual order: single, maximum double file—Longhair with his case, Fat Lady with her enormous stomach, and Tiny and Longlegs with their chain . . . Skinhead had prepared himself for a long trek, but rather quickly a dark structure resembling an outbuilding came into sight in the distance. Closer up, they discovered that it was not a structure at all, but a section of forest densely bound with leafless branches. Like a nursery. Strange low-standing trees. Their trunks and branches were almost identical in girth, grayish brown, without the slightest hint of leaves. From a short distance it seemed as if the branches moved slightly. There was something invidious about their movement.

"Let's go closer," said Skinhead, and all of them, like children, obediently moved closer. The branches really were moving. They were covered over entirely with strange creatures the size of large rats, with old, completely hairless, loose, baggy, wrinkled skin and just as gray-brown as the trunks of the trees. They gnawed at the bark hungrily, ravenously, emitting an almost machinelike buzz.

Skinhead took one of these creatures by the scruff of its neck and pulled it off the trunk. It grumbled with discontent: "Let me go, let me go . . ." He straightened out the fat but scrawny little animal, and his fellow travelers saw that this repellent creature was a human being. Its tiny legs and arms were atrophied, its head was oversized like an embryo's with barely perceptible slits for closed eyes, its nose undeveloped, and its mouth large and protruding, with bright-white rodentlike teeth. The muscles around its mouth automatically tensed, and its jaws continued to make their gnawing movement.

Skinhead petted the humanoid rodent and placed it back on the branch he had just removed it from.

"My Lord, who is that?" asked Newling in horror.

"The thirsty seeking to be filled," Skinhead said derisively, then hesitated immediately: What am I doing? Why am I teasing her again? What inveterate madness . . .

Some wall cracked or curtain tore, and a huge piece of former knowledge surfaced in her memory: her parents, her grandmother, their house in Trekhprudny Lane, the commune in Troparevo . . . Lev Tolstoy and the Gospel, not the Gospel of Tolstoy, but the original one that she had received from her grandmother . . . Immediately she choked on his derisive tone: she recognized the words from the Gospels that he had obviously and deliberately distorted: "Blessed are they which do hunger and thirst after righteousness: for they shall be filled . . ."

"No, no, I am not making a mockery. I'm sorry. That's just my way . . . I only wanted to say that that is their truth . . . All passion ultimately dies, does it not?" he continued, but her heart beat painfully from his words. "Just not everyone manages to find peace in the time allotted."

He bent over and picked up off the ground a startled creature that had just fallen off a tree trunk. Now it was not a human rodent, but resembled more a human worm. The creature was motionless, its teeth had disappeared, and its mouth had acquired a size proportional to its head, while its tiny face seemed completely childlike.

"That's it. It's been filled. Now it most resembles a five-month-old human embryo."

The Professor glanced over the Newling's shoulder. Something terrifying came into his head, and he asked hoarsely: "Is it dead?"

"What are you saying! There is no death, Professor. And this one, I think, is considerably closer to the beginning than to the end," Skinhead answered mysteriously.

At this point the Professor exploded: "I hate riddles! I demand a clear and concise answer to the question of what is going on here. If you consider it obligatory to show me all these so-called miracles, then could you at least explain your parables and allegories so that they make some sense . . . ?"

"What parables!" Skinhead laughed sincerely. "You and I haven't even got to the alphabet yet!"

"Mind you, I'm going to complain! I have important connections in the most serious of organizations too!" the Professor chirred, and Skinhead seemed to retreat at his shouting and started to reason with him.

"Do pardon me. I in no way wanted to offend you or anything like that . . . You and I can discuss all this, just not right now. A little bit later. Now's not the time. It's not appropriate . . ."

The Professor calmed down: that it was not appropriate was something he could understand; it sounded convincing. And it was also pleasing that at the mention of his connections Skinhead had changed his tone of voice . . .

The beautiful woman stood alongside, tears flowing down her cheeks. It was apparent to the Professor that Skinhead had his eyes set on her.

"The poor, poor things," she whispered. And unexpectedly quickly she asked Skinhead: "Is the tree bitter?"

He looked at her and responded very quietly, but the Professor heard it all down to the last word.

"Bitter? Of course, it's bitter . . ." He motioned with his hand that it was all right to keep going in the indicated direction.

9

IT WAS A LONG, LOW MOAN THAT DESCENDED INTO A uterine growl. Skinhead searched with his eyes for Manikin, but the latter kept stomping along on its sluggish feet. The source of the groan turned out to be Fat Lady, who was dropping to the ground. With a professional's hand Skinhead caught her up from behind. He helped her fall into a more comfortable pose. Fat Lady lay there, her legs bent at the knees as she attempted to clasp her enormous stomach. A puddle spread underneath her back . . .

"Is she giving birth?" Skinhead was astonished. "How strange that someone can give birth in this place . . . On the other hand, why not?"

The woman wore a flannel robe with large terry-cloth flowers, and a few of the buttons had managed to detach themselves under the pressure of her writing body. With skilled fingers he undid the rest. He pulled the hem of her nightshirt back toward her enormous floppy breasts, and what he saw took his breath away. At first it seemed to him that her body was bound with a multitude of thick pink and lilac-crimson plaits with large sea mollusks, similar to those of the genus *Tonicella* or *Neopilina*, growing on them, each of them the size of a tea saucer. He touched one of the shells: it was not separable from her body, but some sort of parasitical growth. All these plaits and shells were attached with cords that had sprouted in her stomach. There was even a sort of monstrously attractive artistry to this living network.

Never in his long years of medical practice had Skinhead seen anything like this. He had no instruments with him, only the silver spoon he stuck between Manikin's clenching jaws whenever its seizures began. Nothing but his bare hands ...

He began to examine her, at least visually, and attempted to shift one of the shell-like growths and to palpate her stomach. On first palpation he thought he felt the fetus's hand. High, very high up, right under her diaphragm.

"A breach presentation," he uttered, dismayed, anticipating additional complications with the turn of the legs. He wanted to continue his manual examination, but something monstrous occurred: the little fist he had just felt punched through the taut wall of the belly and came through to the surface. Fat Lady howled.

"Hold on, hold on, my dear," he calmed the woman.

What is this? Perforation of the uterus wall, the wall of the abdominal prelum, and the surface of the skin? That's unimaginable! How macerated must the tissues be for them to perforate under pressure from a fetus's hand? He pressed her stomach once again: it was hard and dense.

Just then his intravision clicked on, and an image appeared. The woman's entire womb was packed solid with infants, like a fish with caviar. The little fist he held in his hand belonged to a completely formed ninemonth-old fetus, as apparent from the dense little nails on its fingers—a significant indicator of maturation ...

With two fingers he expanded the opening from which the little hand had emerged. The woman moaned.

"Hold on just a bit, just a bit: you're giving birth to a little champion," he bolstered the woman with his automatically vigorous tone of voice.

The opening gave way easily, and, taking the child's hand into his own, his arm disappeared into the hole almost to the elbow: he was hoping to turn the child by the head. It turned very easily, but face-first, not neck-first. The doctor made it dive downward and placed his hand under the back of its head.

The woman moaned, but she was no longer shouting, and Skinhead continued mumbling his usual, calming somethings, without giving it a second thought.

"That's good, Mommy. Your first child? Second? You know what you're doing then . . . Breathe deeper, deeper . . . And not so fast, count to ten . . ."

Everything went quite quickly, quite wonderfully, and the little boy popped out. A normal, live infant lay in the doctor's hand covered in thick vernix caseosa . . . With no umbilical cord. A child could be born without arms, without legs, and without a head. But without an umbilical cord? The umbilical depression was deep, and clean, completely healed . . .

Despite his surprise, Skinhead did what needed to be done at that moment: he cleaned out the nose and the oral cavity, and, turning the infant upside down, smacked it on its moist buttocks. It emitted a deep insulted cry: "wah-wah . . ."

How long had it been since Skinhead had last heard this plaintive sound of new life? . . . The pathetic music, the hoarse song of lungs just opened, the first attempt at musical articulation from the cartilaginous flute of the vocal cords that frightens the performer himself . . . The infant cries out of fright at the new sound.

But this time everything was different, contrary to all rules, habits, and expectations. The infant easily detached itself from the doctor's palm—just as a bubble of air rises from an underwater plant to the surface, and still articulating the same two notes, it floated smoothly upward about three feet, then disappeared, leaving behind the sound of a burst rubber ball and a swift whirlpool in the air . . .

Skinhead barely managed to follow it with his eyes, when the woman in labor let out another howl, and he dropped down to his knees along-side her. Among the rainbow network of growths there were two gaping tears: out of one stuck a little foot, and from the other a gray little head was pushing its way outward. The place from which the first infant had just been extracted had closed into a folded navel, so there was no need to suture it. Skinhead attempted to feel with his hand whether the head and the foot belonged to one child or two.

The woman screamed. Skinhead, while pushing the leg back inside, pressed on the woman's stomach so that it was easier for the head to come through. A shell-like growth impeded the opening from widening, and Skinhead pulled the growth back with the silver spoon, using the fingers of his left hand to open up a path. The second boy was also without an umbilical cord, but Skinhead now thought only about how not to let this child float off into the sky. However, the phenomenon repeated itself exactly as before: the infant began to scream and to move its little hands, and although Skinhead held on to it tightly this time, covering it with his second hand, the infant slipped out from under his hand and, like a soap bubble, with the very same smacking sound, floated off, leaving one more quickly dissipating vortex.

With the third infant Skinhead struggled a lot longer because it came feet first—to turn it over had proved impossible—and to make matters worse, it pulled a section of the cord that had grown into the woman's stomach in its tightly clenched fist. This time, though, Skinhead was already not surprised when the back of the light, hairless little girl detached itself from his moist palm and floated into the air.

The difficulty with the set of twins lay in that they turned out to be in a single amniotic sack and could not emerge from the opening, so that Skinhead was forced to bite through not the umbilical cord, as do animals and women giving birth without help, but the elastic dark-blue rope around the woman's stomach, which, although it had emptied considerably, continued to be enormous.

The next child surprised Skinhead by emerging the most natural way, through the birth canal, but it also did not gladden him with an umbilical cord. That was the sixth. The seventh was born right after, also the old-fashioned way, but it was very premature and floated off the doctor's hand so reluctantly that Skinhead even regretted slightly that he had not attempted to restrain it. Strictly speaking, the last two were hetero-ovular twins, but developmentally one lagged behind the other by about seven weeks. That just doesn't happen ... True, with twins it frequently happens that one overwhelms the other in prenatal development ... But there was no time to intellectualize, because out of the woman's stomach poked the little hand of the next client waiting to emerge ...

When the multiple births finally ended, the woman asked where her children were. Skinhead stroked her face: it was she, his primary patient, the one for whose sake he had waged his battle with medical bureaucrats, with his colleagues, with his friends, and even with his family ... She was exhausted by work beyond her strength, hunger, birthing, loneliness, responsibility, and lack of money, and he explained as best he could that her children must be in heaven. She sobbed bitterly.

"But what about me, not a single little child for me, not one?"

She lay there as he kneeled before her. The tangle of growths and cords had slackened and now hung around her hips, which were covered with stretch marks and abrasions. He pulled at one of the shells, and it remained in his hand. Dense and alive as worms just moments ago, the cords crumbled in his hands, and the entire confused network fell from her body like a dry hull. Some sort of leathery membrane that reminded him of a shed snakeskin fell from the woman's hips. Her body recovered its human dignity. And her eyes, ringed by dark circles of suffering, looked at the doctor with gratitude. He knew well that exhausted, somewhat vacant look of a woman who had just given birth ...

"Can you walk?" Skinhead asked.

"I'll stay here," she answered.

Skinhead then buried the remainder of the monstrous growths in the sand, gathered several dry plants off the ground, and lit a fire.

"You rest, my child, just rest. Everything will be all right ..."

She began to move, and rose up on one arm. "What do you mean—all right ... ?"

Skinhead looked back: they were waiting for him. For the first time in their entire journey, he did not put out the fire as he left.

They set off further in their usual fashion, in single or double file, and Skinhead, looking back, could still see the bluish flame in the distance. Then he heard a hollow smacking sound, and when he turned around for the last time he saw nothing except the sand hills and his own tracks quickly swept over by light drifts of sand ...

FOR A WHILE THE PROFESSOR DISPLAYED A CERTAIN acquiescence and stopped battering Skinhead with questions. He tried talking with Newling: she just looked at him wide-eyed and benevolent, incapable of giving an intelligible answer to any of his questions. He deliberated at length how best to approach Skinhead so as not to lose face yet achieve some degree of clarity. This strange journey was dragging on, yet at the same time—the Professor sensed—his desire to find an explanation for it all was waning: an inkling had crept into his head, but he kept driving it away. What was more, a strange apathy had overcome him. The campfire had a twofold effect on him: it calmed him, but also dulled his mind . . .

One time the Professor sat down next to Skinhead at the campfire and addressed him with respectful courtesy.

"Could you tell me, please, whether you have any means of contacting my family, my wife, that is? I am certain that she is very worried . . ."

"In principle, I do. What exactly would you like me to communicate to her?"

"Well, first of all, that I'm alive and well. You see, we've been married almost forty-two years and have never been separated for any length of time. If for some reason I cannot be returned to my former position," here the Professor inserted a pregnant pause so that Skinhead would appreciate the full extent of his, the Professor's, discretion, "might she be sent to join me?"

Skinhead scratched behind his ear with his thick finger. "Hmm . . . Could you tell me whether or not your wife believes in God?"

The Professor was indignant: "Excuse me! Well, we're atheists, of course. I am a philosopher, a Marxist, and I teach Marxist-Leninist aesthetics. My wife is a party member . . ."

"I see, I see," Skinhead interjected. "Are there any people of faith in your family at all?"

"No, of course not. My mother-in-law was an ignorant village woman, but she died—rest her soul—in 1951 . . ."

"Well that's of no significance whatsoever." Skinhead seemed to want to calm him.

"I'm sorry. What's of no significance?"

"That she's dead . . . In principle, we can get in touch with her. Only, you know, I would advise you to limit yourself to a brief message, on the order of, say, 'Everything is all right. Don't worry . . .' How can you invite her here if you yourself don't have a very good idea of where it is you are?"

"Clever bastard. He's hinting that the place is classified," the Professor seethed, but his position was so tenuous that he could hardly make demands or insist. And clashing with this Skinhead was dangerous: he was obviously not high up on the pecking order, but how to get to someone higher up? There was no one to complain to . . . For that reason the Professor merely affirmed: "Yes. I really don't have a very good idea what this place is, and for a long time I've been wanting to obtain some information from you . . ."

Skinhead chuckled.

"I'm not too sure myself . . ."

"Well, fine, but maybe you know at least approximately how long I'm going to be held here and when I can go back home?"

Skinhead sighed—empathetically, it seemed to the Professor.

"I can't really say anything about your term either. As far as home goes . . . I'm afraid you won't be returning home ever again . . ."

The Professor gasped with indignation, but kept his calm and asked almost frigidly: "On what grounds?"

At this juncture Skinhead stood up and ran his hand over the fire. The flame went out, as if sucked up into this hand.

"We'll have occasion to return to that conversation. For the time being let's leave it at that your wife will be informed that you're all right, Professor . . ." The Professor imagined that there was a certain malice to the way Skinhead had pronounced his academic title . . .

11

THE NEWLING WANDERED THROUGH A MULTISTORIED building complex with long corridors and flowerbeds along the walls. An enormous number of doors led off from the corridor, each with a marker that was at once neither a number nor a letter but, as often occurs in dreams, very distinct. The Newling, skilled as she was in dreams, immediately guessed that these markers belonged to the category of things that exist only in dreams and never squeeze their way through to anywhere else when the dream is over. There existed a certain simple formula according to which some things, events, and impressions transformed themselves into another state just as they were, while others changed in strange ways in the process, and still others simply disintegrated. The Newling did not even attempt to impress the door markers in her memory: they were of the category that simply disintegrated. She walked past each of the doors and realized at first glance: the wrong one. The one she needed was connected to some elderly woman.

She had already rushed through miles of corridors and had a feeling that the marker she needed would appear at any moment. And, indeed, it did, and she opened the door. The room was bright, modest, and resembled a cheap room in some hotel off the beaten path somewhere in Vologda or Arkhangelsk. There was a sink in the corner, and an electric samovar stood on a table covered with a red-and-white checkered oilcloth. The bed was voluptuous, like the kind you find at home, with an abundance of pillows. There were flowers on the windowsills. Next to the door, on a bentwood chair, sat a chubby old woman, the bridge of her nose notched by her glasses and with a dog-eared book in her hands. On another chair slept a calico cat that was so fat it barely fit on the seat. It was around midmorning in the room. The old woman was waiting for her: they were either very good friends or distant relatives.

"Should we have our tea?" the old woman asked.

"With jam?" The Newling smiled.

"How else? I've made gooseberry, and strawberry, and forest berry." The old woman immediately opened the cupboard, where quart-size canning jars sparkled under paper lids.

"And wild strawberry?"

"How else? I gathered them myself . . . In the fields nearby . . ." From the bottom shelf she pulled a jar already opened, removed the paper lid, and lumped a large spoonful of thick, aromatic jam into the jam dish.

The Newling looked at the jam. "You didn't overcook it, did you, Marya Vasilievna? It's terribly thick."

The old woman waved her hand with annoyance: "I did overcook it just a bit. But it's better to overcook it than undercook it. It gels better."

"That's true," the Newling agreed.

The old woman plugged in the samovar and reached for teacups.

"It boils fast: I like it . . ."

The old woman set two cups on the table; the Newling asked for a third.

"Why three?" the old woman asked in surprise.

"For your Nadya," the Newling explained.

"Oh," the old woman seemed anxious. "I thought we were going there, but it turns out she's coming here?"

"What difference does it make? The main thing is that we get to see each other."

"That's true. She's having a very rough time these days," the old woman nodded.

"You should tell her that Misha gave instructions to say hello and to let her know that everything is all right."

The old woman continued to nod, while the Newling continued.

"And how are you doing, Marya Vasilievna?"

"Me? I'm good . . . I'm reading this book. There I was illiterate, but here I've learned to read."

"What are you reading?"

"This." The old woman slid the dog-eared book to the Newling. "*The Young Guard* by Fadeev. Nadya said a lot of good things about it . . . It's a good book. But it's so sad what happens to those kids. Only, is it all really true or did he make it up?"

"Something like that really happened." The Newling opened the volume. "To our dear Tanechka on the day of her acceptance into the Young Pioneers. Valya and Misha Remen. May 1, 1951."

The memory stabbed at her heart, and she woke up. The campfire barely burned. Everything was as usual. The wind had calmed down. People were relaxing. She herself sat a bit off in the distance, two dogs alongside her: a light-colored mutt with a tail that curled upward, and a large shepherd.

The mutt was the most ordinary, while the shepherd raised doubts: something about its canine essence was not right. There was something unusual about its faithful attentiveness toward both its human companion—you could hardly say *master*—as well as all the others. What was more, it did what no other dog could: it nodded and shook its head in response to questions: yes, no . . .

Dog Whisperer was a likeable man about thirty-five years old, with the posture of a professional soldier and a nondescript face. A reddish scar—like the trace of a hat band worn many years—crossed his forehead. He came up behind the Newling, and both the dogs turned toward him.

"You should go sit on the lee side . . . The wind is picking up," he advised the Newling.

"What?" she asked.

"So that it doesn't blow in your face . . ." He offered her his hand, and the dogs stood up, precisely as if making way for her to pass.

"How good it is that you and the dogs are here." The Newling petted the shepherd's dense fur. The shepherd smiled. "When I was a little girl I had dogs when we lived in the country . . . But in town I have only cats."

The man was pleased. "That makes a lot of sense. I also have only cats at home. I'm a professional dog handler, you know. Twenty years with dogs. Trained hundreds of them. I'm convinced: dogs should not be kept in apartments." His lips quivered and let drop sadly: "And in general . . ."

"What 'in general'?" the Newling wondered.

Dog Whisperer spoke heatedly and quickly. It was obvious that the idea had been brewing in him unspoken for a long time.

"You see, there's a lot of deep meaning in the expression 'they fight like cats and dogs.' Cats and dogs are two entirely opposite types in terms of their relationships with humans. A cat generally has no need for humans. What does it need? Warmth, food. That's true. But it has absolutely no need for humans. I would even say that cats despise humans. They're smarter than humans. Humans think that they're keeping cats, while in fact, cats keep humans. Cats can't be forced to do anything. They don't even like to be asked . . . I'm a trainer, I know: they don't want to submit for anything. They have their dignity. They need humans to serve them. And you know, I, for one, like their independence. Cats never grovel. For example, a cat may rub up against your leg and you might think that it's expressing tenderness . . . No, it's stretching its muscles and scratching itself against your legs. It's giving pleasure to itself, not its owner.

You, you serve the cat and not vice versa. With dogs everything is different." He placed his hand with two disfigured fingers on one dog's head. "Happy will confirm that."

The dog looked expectantly at Dog Whisperer: confirm what?

"A dog in an apartment is like a handicapped child. It needs your constant attention. Your help, your attention, your caring . . . Dogs, excuse my mentioning it, dogs even need to be taken out for walks because a trained dog will sooner die than do its business inside." He looked at Happy, who sadly nodded its head. "Who besides a human being will go to its death for the sake of an idea? Only a dog!"

The Newling was amazed: that had never occurred to her.

"Yes, yes . . . Search dogs, for example, will search for land mines . . . During the last war dogs attacked tanks! That is, I don't mean to say that they went wittingly to their deaths 'for the Motherland! for Stalin!' The dogs died for their own idea: in service to their masters . . ." Dog Whisperer turned polemically to Happy: "Tell me that's not so!"

The dog sighed a human sigh and nodded. Suddenly Dog Whisperer's vigor subsided, as he fell into silent thought for a bit, then, without raising his eyes from the ground, continued.

"That's my job nowadays: I work as a guide for dogs. They're all mine, my little dogs. I raised them in a kennel in Murom, trained them, and then they get sent wherever: some go abroad, to Afghanistan. Happy's an Afghan vet . . . I'm about to guide my twenty-fourth . . ."

"Where are you guiding it?" the Newling asked quietly.

"Where, where . . . Abroad . . . To the other shore . . ."

"Ah-ha," thought the Newling. "That means that some people here know where we're going . . . To the other shore."

12

THEY WALKED ON AND ON THROUGH THE MONOTONOUS, sad, and undulating desert space until they arrived. The sandy desert ended. They stopped at the edge of a gigantic fault filled with a gray fog. Somewhere off in the distance loomed the other shore, but it could also have been an optical illusion, so tenuous and imprecise was the jagged strip that could be either heavy clouds pressed to the ground or distant mountains or a forest closer in . . .

"We need to take a rest," Skinhead said, extending his fire-bearing hand over the dry branches. As always, the warmth and the light of the tiny children's campfire far surpassed the capabilities of the pathetic fuel.

Warrior—who had assigned himself the task of bringing several dry skeletons of former plants—looked into the fire and asked Skinhead: "Why does it require fuel? That fire of yours burns just fine on its own."

"Yes, I noticed that myself not long ago." Skinhead nodded, and then stretched his arm over an empty spot. Another campfire ignited. On its own, without any fuel . . . "You see how we've all grown a bit wiser of late . . ."

"Even too wise," the Warrior quipped morosely.

Skinhead pulled out of his pocket several dry square cookies with dotted symbols, just like ancient hieroglyphs, and gave each of them one. "Eat. You need to get your strength up."

The Newling long ago had ceased to be surprised. The taste of the cookies was indistinct, herbal, and reminded her of the flat cakes her mother had baked in lean years from dried goutweed seeds mixed with a handful of flour. They were pleasant to eat.

"We'll rest here for a bit, and then we'll make our way over in that direction."

They sat, absorbing the heat with their fatigued bodies.

Skinhead called Longhair over; the latter followed him unwillingly. Together they began digging at the top of a nearby hill. A while later they brought a bunch of whitish-yellow rags that seemed as if just removed from the linen sterilizer. They tossed them on the ground, and a multitude of tie-straps flew out in all different directions.

"Put on gloves and booties," Skinhead commanded.

Reluctantly they began to sort out the strange garments: the sleeves had long straps on the wrists, and the canvas leggings tied just beneath the knees. The garments were as cumbersome as they were uncomfortable, and it was particularly difficult to knot the strap on the right arm. The Newling helped Longhair cope with the dangling ties . . .

The Professor, who had begun digging through the pile trying to find a pair that matched, suddenly flung the rags aside and barked: "This is a mockery! You'll answer for this! You'll answer for this mockery! I'm not going anywhere! I've had enough . . ."

Skinhead walked right up to him.

"Quit your hysterics. There are children, women, and animals here, after all . . . If you don't want to come, you can stay here . . ."

The Professor regained his self-control and modulated his tone of voice.

"Listen! Would you just tell me why I'm here? What is going on here? What kind of a place is this?"

"The answer to that question lies on the other shore," Skinhead answered curtly. "But if you insist, you can stay here."

The Professor turned away, slumped over, and moved away from the campfire . . . He easily transitioned from overbearing bossiness to humble subordination.

Skinhead tied his own two booties and helped Longhair secure his case to his back.

Both campfires had burned down. Cold flowed from the fault, and it was incomprehensible how Skinhead intended to transport them all to the other side. He approached the edge of the fault. The others crowded like a herd of sheep behind him.

"We'll take the bridge. Come stand at the edge."

Cautiously, they approached the precipice. They craned their necks: there was no bridge.

"Look down, down there." People made out a metal construction looming in the unfathomable depths of the gray fog of the fault.

Skinhead jumped, and the entire monstrous construction swayed like a rowboat. His face, turned upward toward them, barely shone from below. He waved. Each of them standing up above shuddered, feeling trapped between necessity and impossibility.

"Manikin!" Skinhead called, and the latter obediently approached the edge. Its feet in their canvas bags sweated and felt heavy as stone. There seemed to be no force strong enough to make it follow Skinhead. But there was: far off in the distance a sound arose, barely audible to the ear, forewarning of an intolerable shower of black arrows. Manikin, doomed, did not jump—suicidal, it collapsed headfirst and disappeared in the fog.

The construction swayed again. At that same moment the Newling felt the sand under her feet move and shift. The sandy soil behind the crowded handful of confused people began to cave in and loosen, and an avalanche began behind their backs. It grew and widened, and a whole sandy Niagara whipped up behind them . . .

The next to plunge was Longhair. Then the pair of women chained together—Longlegs first, and Tiny screaming downward after her. With great dignity the former Limper approached the edge, sat down, and lowered himself, as if lowering himself into a swimming pool or bath. Warrior. The dog. One more woman in a running suit. A man with a briefcase. Strange Animal. A blindfolded little girl. The Newling stepped downward as one of the last . . .

None of them fell like a rock—they all descended slowly. Either the air streamed powerfully upward and supported them or the force of gravity in these parts was weaker. Down below the wind gusted. It carried them relatively far from each other in different directions. Some landed on the bridge's large crossing planks; others, like Longhair, were less fortunate. He stood on the intersection of thin pipes, and the closest vertical support was located at a decent distance and beyond reach. He rolled back and forth to maintain his balance. His case got in his way.

Worst off was Manikin. It lay horizontally, grasping a wide rail at the level of its chest, its arched soles pressed against an unsteady vertical support, and its entire enormous torso spread out in midair as if posed to do push-ups . . .

The uneven rocking of the entire construction caused by their fall slowly began to settle, but just at that moment they heard a hoarse howl: fear of being left alone in the sand overcame all else, and the Professor plunged into the gray fault. The bridge construction rocked violently, Manikin's soles slipped from the unsteady vertical support, and it now hung by its arms alone . . .

The wind would die down, then gust madly from the fault. The construction shuddered, shaking unevenly in response to each gust, and responded as if alive to each contact. The fog gradually began to dissipate, and the people could make out an artful steel labyrinth, constructed by some mad troll or insane artist. The Newling studied the construction with a professional's eye: she would never have agreed to draft a working design of this construction, which, she saw, contained strange gaps and inside-out turns, as if the façade and infrastructure had been reversed.

"It's fictive space, the thought occurred to her. It cannot exist in nature. And if it is fictive, does that mean that it's impossible to fall? The fall would be fictive then as well . . . But I'm not fictive . . ."

Skinhead demonstrated the agility of a circus performer as he jumped from pipe to pipe, changing levels. He went to each of them, lightly touched their hands, heads, and shoulders. And said something, explained something, inquired. He was tender and convincing.

"We have to keep moving. We have to make it to the other shore. Don't rush. We can go slowly. Even if we have to inch our way. None of you will be lost. We'll all make it there. Just don't be afraid. Fear impedes the ability to move . . ."

His words possessed a heightened effectiveness, and the people, who at first had frozen in the ridiculous poses the construction had caught them in, slowly began to maneuver.

Manikin tried to lift its legs and to rest its enormous body on the rail from which it hung by petrified fingers, but its strength failed it, and its hands, fatigued from the tension, were losing their grip, its chest was dropping lower, and it now hung solely by the tips of its tensed fingers. The stone weight of its body slowly pulled its fingers from the rail, and it waited indifferently for the moment when its fingers would pass over the rib of the rail and slip from the rail's side surface.

Within its murky consciousness a heavy thought turned like a lump of unrisen dough: I will fall, I will be dashed to pieces, everything will come to an end, and those arrows-bullets-wasps will no longer sting me in the head and stomach . . .

At the last moment it sought out Skinhead: he was nowhere to be seen; there was only Longhair rocking off in the distance, hugging some black object . . . Manikin unclenched its fingers and flew downward. Not like a stone, not like a bird, but like a crumpled piece of newsprint carried by wind blowing garbage . . .

Despite the lightness and slowness of its fall, the blow of its landing was shattering. Broken into pieces, it lay on the stony bed of a long-ago dried-up river among the remains of ancient boats, petrified shells, and two unmatched running shoes. Its body, shattered in all directions, was surrounded by small—larger than squirrels but smaller than rabbits—not entirely solid creatures, perhaps entities—the same kind that appear in dreams and then, on awakening, leave behind not a visual image, but only a kind of spiritual trace of warmth, tenderness, affinity . . .

The creatures gathered in a crowd, like inhabitants of a desert or tundra around airplane wreckage. Some, the most sensitive, sobbed, while the others shook their heads and lamented. Then one of them said: "We should call the Doctor."

Others objected: "There's no need for the Doctor. That's a corpse."

"No, no, he's not a corpse," said still others.

Someone with a young voice squeaked challengingly: "So what if he's a corpse! Corpses can be revivified!"

A kind of discordant meeting ensued.

Then the largest and eldest of them was wheeled in. He was so decrepit that you could see through him in places. He wheeled up close, accidentally running over Manikin's broken fingers with his front wheels. He sighed a bit and announced:

"He's a corpse. Condition zero."

The gathering stirred, burbled, and rustled.

"Can't anything be done for him?"

"There's nothing you can do." The Doctor shook his head flatly. "Except donate blood."

They all fell silent. Then one of them with round eyebrows and big eyes said, "There are a lot of us. We can do it."

One with a long nose interjected: "What about blood substitutes? There are substitutes for blood!"

But the Doctor did not even look in his direction.

"Six liters of live blood, minimum. Or there's no getting him on his feet."

"We'll do it, we'll do it," the gathering rustled. The Doctor in his wheelchair seemed angry.

"How are you going to do it? Each of you has six milliliters of blood. You can't donate more than half. You know that I gave five milliliters and my legs never returned to normal."

The squirrel-rabbits grew agitated and chattered again.

"If we bring him back to life, he will be . . . handsome . . . intelligent . . . They have children . . . and can build and draw things . . . Let him live . . ."

"Very well," the Doctor agreed. "But I have to remind you of the following: before you lie the remains of a criminal. A murderer. A very cruel and merciless one. And senseless."

They all took fright and fell silent. Then the curly-headed one with perky African hair quietly spoke.

"All the more reason. What's there to discuss? He needs to be given a chance."

"I don't disagree," smiled the Doctor. "I just want to remind you that according to the law of the Great Ladder, when you sacrifice your own blood you descend downward and lose part of your mobility, while he rises upward and acquires the qualities that you sacrificed for him . . ."

"Yes, yes . . . We know . . . We want to . . . We're agreed . . . agreed . . ."

They encircled the battered Manikin, and from out of nowhere there appeared a white sheet, and a mysterious medicine set to work . . .

THAT PART OF THE LABYRINTH WHERE THE NEWLING had landed held a chaotic accumulation of small landings a good jump apart, with the vertical supports underneath the landings, making it impossible to shimmy down them. The Newling successfully made her way across the landings until she reached one from which only a trained jumper could advance: all she could do was turn back.

She sat down in confusion. Looking down terrified her. She raised her head and looked upward. Up above ran a parallel chain of landings whose weight-bearing supports were relatively close, and she decided that after resting a bit she would try to modify her route. True, she got the impression that the upper path ran somewhat off to the side. But there seemed to be no other way out. Amazed by the lightness and responsiveness of her body, she hugged the scratchy metal pole and, pressing her entire body to it, shimmied up. Her canvas stockings and gloves protected her from the touch of the cold metal. But what was most surprising was that this exercise turned out to be quite fascinating, and her entire body rejoiced. What was there for it to rejoice about? Perhaps that it was so easily training itself to retract like a spring, push off, then recover in the air, and relax slightly before landing. Each ensuing shimmy was easier and freer, and she totally forgot any sense of constraint or danger . . .

That's probably what's so wonderful about sports, she guessed as she pulled herself to the landing above. Here there was more light, and from here the other shore seemed not so murky . . .

The Professor made his way along a crooked slippery pipe to an angled bollard and sat down on it. Two rusty rails hung in the air to the right, about six or seven feet away, but he decided not to attempt the jump. He sat morosely, intent on trying to comprehend how he had managed to wind up in this absurd, entirely fantastic situation. The wind blew from somewhere below, the bollard swayed, and everything was enveloped by a nasty, damp, oppressive cold.

"Maybe it's a dream, after all?" The Professor returned to this redeeming idea for the umpteenth time. He ran his fingertips across his face and head. He touched his gums with his tongue: his dentures were missing! How had he not noticed earlier? Where could those fine dentures made at the Fourth Department's dental clinic have gone?

He sat in a strange and uncomfortable pose, dressed in his best suit, wearing all his medals, but without a single document, and having lost his dentures. Or had someone pulled them out of his mouth? This is awful . . . Awful . . .

"Have I really died?" His fidgety brain, which had studiously avoided the word, suddenly slammed right into it . . .

In the dim fog to the Professor's left a familiar bald spot flashed by.

"Listen! Your Eminence!" shouted the Professor, and Skinhead immediately headed in his direction.

"Now, we need to gather our strength and, without rushing . . ." Skinhead began in his always low-key voice, but the Professor grabbed him by the sleeve of his white shirt and bawled.

"Will you just tell me finally, did I die?"

Skinhead stared with a lingering gaze at the cringing Professor and said exactly what the Professor did not want to hear from him.

"Yes, Professor. I can't keep it from you any longer. You died."

The Professor shuddered, and then he sensed a burning emptiness in his chest familiar from his heart attacks. His hands and feet grew cold. All these sensations were obviously signs of life, and this calmed him, and he began to laugh, placing his hand in the area of his heart.

"You're joking. But news like that really could kill me."

"I'm not joking. But if putting it another way makes you feel better, you can consider your worldly life over!"

"So am I in hell?" The Professor fidgeted on his bollard. "Keep in mind that I don't believe . . . in any of that!"

"Yes, I myself don't believe in hell. But for the time being you're going to have to reconcile yourself to the current state of affairs. It's very important right now that we make our way to the other shore . . ."

Skinhead took two large strides in the direction of the rusty rails, pushed them lightly with his foot, and they immediately fell in line with the bollard. After which Skinhead walked off.

The Professor sat in stunned silence. The fact was that Skinhead strode with his wide feet in their canvas surgical booties right through the air. His steps were sure and fast, and it seemed like the whitish fog yielded slightly beneath his feet, while he himself swayed like a circus performer walking a slack rope. Maybe there was a rope?

The Professor stepped cautiously onto the unsteady rails . . .

Longhair just rocked and swayed, and there was nowhere for him to move: the nearest landing was about ten yards away. The movement of the pipes he stood on had a certain complex rhythmic pattern to it, but he could not figure out what it was, despite his sensitive musical ear. For some reason he knew that as soon as he understood the numeric formula he would be able to direct his movement. He listened closely to his feet, to his tibia and femurs, to his thirty-two vertebrae-conductors—and the resonator of his skull . . . He was beginning to make something out . . . a kind of polytempo, one line superimposed on the other . . . Five thirds . . . That was it. His body responded and adjusted. Falling in step with the rhythm, he sensed that the swinging poles beneath his feet had become controllable to an extent. The amplitude of their motion around their axis increased. But this movement occurred parallel to the closest landing and did not bring him in any way closer to it. In addition, the second tempo got in the way and grew ever more recognizable . . . He had it: seven-eighths! The second axis of motion appeared immediately . . .

Something swung him violently, and he almost dropped his case. But he held on. He pressed it to his chest. He stroked it. His canvas glove kept him from feeling it, and he wanted to remove the glove. Swinging back and forth with a nervous, broken trajectory, he attempted to undo the ties on his left hand. The knot was tight and tangled; he bit at it with his teeth ... He felt unexpected help coming from the air itself. It was helping. The familiar vortex was spinning around him once again, but it seemed to have fingers and lips, even a woman's loosened hair curling under its own wind. This vortex of air turned out to have a woman inside.

The knot loosened and undid itself. Longhair dropped his left hand, tossed off the glove, and felt that the knot had loosened on his right hand as well.

"Quickly, open it up, open it up," sang the living plait of animated air. It was warm, even hot; it coaxed, caressed, nestled close, and hurried him ...

His movement corrected itself of its own, directed itself, and little by little brought him closer to the landing. Longhair pressed on the latch, the mechanism clicked, the vortex pulled the wonderful thing from its case, and placed it in Longhair's hands.

"Play ..."

His hands held an instrument. An instrument for ... With the help of which ... It was the most important thing for him, but he did not know how ... His right hand placed itself where it should go: his fingers fell in place and recognized the keys. His left hand searched ... It was followed by tormenting confusion.

Hot fingers ran along his neck, his chin, and touched his lips.

"Play already, please. It's still possible to go back."

The wooden mouthpiece nestled against his lips ... And the swinging pipes carried him back and forth, the rhythm of their motion penetrating his body and insistently demanding his complicity. His total complicity. He gathered air through his nose, relaxing his diaphragm to fill his lungs completely.

The vortex subsided and hung in the air. Longhair pressed his lips around the wooden mouthpiece: there was the promise of pleasure, of the most subtle part of it. His lower lip nestled against the wooden stem, his tongue touched the plastic reed. All together it was like a missing part of his body, an organ from which he had been separated. He was exploding from within: with his breath, with his whole self he needed to fill this queer creation of metal and wood that was as much a part of him as his lungs, his throat, and his lips ... He exhaled—carefully, so as not to frighten away the emerging miracle ... The sound was music, the intelligible word and living voice all rolled into one. The sound made the center of his bones ache sweetly, as if his bone marrow were responding with joy . . .

Poor humans—a head and two ears! Malleus and incus . . . Stapes and habenula . . . Three turns of the cochlea, the middle ear plugged with wax, and the Eustachian tube filled with scales of dead skin . . . Ten clumsy fingers and the crude air pump of the lungs . . . Music?! The shadow of a shadow . . . The approximation of an approximation . . . A suggestion suspended in the dark . . .

The most sensitive wipe away the tear spreading under their lower eyelid . . . A yearning for music . . . Suffering for music . . .

Lord God, come among us! He came. And stands behind the impenetrable wall of our earthly music . . .

The Professor heard and began to weep. His last hopes had dissipated: he truly had died, for such things did not occur on earth. He had always been proud of his musical ear, had sung in tune to the guitar, could pick out a tune on the accordion, although he had never taken lessons, and even his blockhead son had inherited his musical talent from him . . . But this was another kind of music. It spoke clearly and distinctly of the senselessness of and necessity for beauty. It itself was beauty— indisputable, heaven-sent, carefree, and with no practical application, like a bird's feather, a soap bubble, or the velvet violet face of pansy petals . . . It also spoke to him something that grievously shamed the Professor for those aimlessly lived years . . . No, that's not it, someone else had said that. The Professor was tormentingly ashamed of everything about himself, from birth to death, from toes to head, from morning till night . . .

All movement, all the clambering and grasping stopped. All fell quiet and still. Even the tiny creatures bustling about Manikin splayed at the bottom of the fault lifted their large-eyed little heads and listened . . .

But Longhair was almost not there. He was entirely dissolved in his music; he himself was music. Of his entire being there remained only a single crystal suitable only for recognizing that miracle in the making. There remained only a single point—of acute pleasure, before which all bright earthly pleasures were not even a prototype of perfect happiness, but a vulgar deception, like an inflatable woman with a hole that smelled of rubber . . .

He did not notice as the tender vortex lifted him upward, above the wobbly constructions, then higher, so high that there was nothing around

233

him except the whitish fog. The music continued to mount and to fill the world; it was the world, and the dot that remained somewhere on its edge grew smaller and smaller, until it disappeared entirely. And with that he pushed with all his being against the springy membrane, and exerting certain pressure he pushed through and emerged from it, preserving in himself the echo of the bursting film . . .

13

ON THE SHORE MORNING WAS BREAKING. THE DAWN WAS strong as undiluted alcohol, bare as a freshly laid egg, and irreproachable as the alphabet. Behind the Newling's back the fault smoked with fog, and she experienced it as a rough seam between two fabrics of different textures. What was more, it now was of absolutely no interest. The world unfolding before her eyes resembled the best of everything she had ever seen in her life. She remembered now all of her past—from early childhood, from the stove that had burned her childish hands, to the last page of that school exercise book whose last dozen pages were scribbled with lame tortured letters . . .

The light of two searchlights of a past and perfect morning resurrected in all its details illuminated the moment. The long torture of unanswerable questions—Where am I? Who am I? Why?—had ended in an instant. It was she, Elena Georgievna Kukotskaya, but completely new, yes, the Newling, but now she wanted to gather together all that she had known and at one time forgotten and all that she had never known, but seemed to have remembered.

She took several steps through the grass and was amazed by the wealth of impressions communicated by the touch of her bare feet to the ground: she felt every blade of grass, the mutual positioning of stalks, and even the vulvar connections between the thin blades. As if the blind soles of her feet had acquired sight. Something similar happened with her vision, her sense of hearing, and sense of smell. Elena sat down on a hillock between two bushes. One, just about to bloom, was a jasmine, with a simple and strong smell; the second was unfamiliar, with dense leaves highlighted with a light border along their edge. Its smell was sour and cold, peculiar. The earth emitted a multitude of smells—damp earthy mustiness, the juice of a crushed stalk of grass, strawberry leaf, wax, bitter chamomile . . . And even the scent of a person who had stepped there not long ago . . . She immediately recognized who.

Animal sense of smell, that's what it is, Elena noted. There were also too many sounds for such a quiet morning—the grasses rustled loudly, each with its own quality: the rigid grasses sounded more shaggy, while the softer ones emitted slithery sounds. The leaves of the shrubbery rubbed up against each other with a velvet swishing sound, and a bud exploded with the sound of a taut grunt. A titmouse flitting from a tree produced a chord with its wings and tail that left behind the light, bent whistle of air flowing over feathers spread out in flight. Moreover, Elena saw something she had never noticed before: as it flew by, the bird's tail feathers stood up almost vertically, while the pointed ends of its wings dropped downward, and its matchstick dark-gray legs pressed tightly to its gray belly . . . It slipped downward, and then, as if having changed its mind, turned its tail, dropped the tips of its wings, and soared upward . . . The geometry and aerodynamics of flight—study it as you would in school . . . How is it I never noticed that before, Elena wondered.

She sat atop the hillock, inhaled, watched, and listened, as she accustomed herself to the new earth and to her own self, also new. She hurried nowhere. Soon she felt that she had tired of the unaccustomed intensity of the sounds and smells, stretched herself full length on the grass, and closed her eyes.

It's silly to sleep when everything feels so good . . . But maybe I'll have a dream?

She fell asleep on the bare ground without even noticing that she herself was naked . . .

Skinhead, like a ship's captain, came onshore last. What was moving where was entirely unclear: was the fault moving away from the shore, or was the earth itself drifting in an unknown direction? It looked like the wind was pulling the structures up along the shore . . . Everyone he had helped by extending an aluminum, paint-spattered stepladder between the last landing and the edge of the bluff was disappearing somewhere. The last to come onshore had been the big shepherd dog, its paws slipping on the metal rungs. The dog was met by an entire brigade of tiny humanoid and at the same time slightly avian figures in white cocoons. They took it into their arms and hauled it toward a large tree scorched on one side. The landing on which Skinhead stood rocked and floated away from the shore. He almost dropped the stepladder. An unknown force pulled him forward with the flow of the wind, then rocked, overturned, and pounded his landing into the edge of the precipice.

Skinhead set foot on land. The first thing he noticed were the bones of his own foot, all twenty-nine of them, just as on an X-ray. Or twenty-eight? They shone unobtrusively through his skin. Skinhead noticed an unpleasant deformity: the joints between his os metatarsi and the bone of his big toe were enlarged. He addressed what he was accustomed to calling his intravision.

"Well, thanks for not having abandoned me."

IT WAS A WONDERFUL PLACE, IF FOR THE SOLE REASON that the sun was at its zenith, indicating noon, and Skinhead was delighted that he was once again in a place where there was west and east, north and south, and ultimately, up and down. He looked around and discovered that the fault had disappeared, had healed over, as if it had never existed. Skinhead smiled and shook his head: it wasn't much needed . . .

The world in which he existed evoked absolute trust, but it demanded he reject his former ways of thinking, and his long-standing ability to adjust to new circumstances prepared him to do this. Everything around him was green, peaceful, and warm. The wind brought the smell of a campfire and food. He set off to the East following the beck of the wind.

The half-scorched tree remained behind, and he did not see how they covered the dog lying on the earth with a big blanket and then drew lines and formulas over it.

"Everything all right? Did it come out correctly?" the smallest asked impatiently.

"I think so. As far as one can tell from the surface," the largest answered him.

"It will be a nice woman. Beautiful."

"And happy?" inquired the little one.

"Expect so . . . The potential is there . . . All its qualities are supposed to be transformed: fidelity, the ability to serve, ingenuousness . . . In this case an innate cheerfulness . . ."

"Then why can't we move to phase out and launch?" The little one bombarded its senior with questions, but the latter was patient.

"What are you saying? How could we do that? On the contrary: it needs to spend some more time here. So that the lower layers fill out. If we launch immediately, just imagine what she will dream of. It'll be awful! When those animal instincts start breaking through . . . This is *Canis lupus familiaris*, a predator after all . . . You should know what the results are when they're underprocessed . . . Well?" The older one awaited an answer.

The little one was at a loss: "We haven't studied that yet. I just started the third level . . ."

"All right, all right. If you haven't studied it yet, you will soon . . . But you'll also know from practical experience—werewolves, maniacs, and murderers of all sorts, from serial killers to those in the general staff . . . Got it?" He offered the clarification with pleasure.

"Oh!" The little one was amazed. "But making sure all the lower layers get filled out—that's quite a job!"

"And you thought our work was easy?" The older one raised the edge of the blanket. Under the blanket lay a large woman with an upturned nose and a receding forehead. "But if we do a good job now, it will be a very good woman, a loyal friend, and a devoted wife. Come on," he beckoned the younger one. He placed his sharp paws on the receding forehead and began massaging lightly . . .

14

THE FOOTPATH NOW WENT UPHILL. WHEN HE REACHED the top of the hill, he saw from above a small, narrow, winding river. In a sandy basin along the riverbank a campfire burned, almost invisible in the sun's rays, and a smoke-blackened kettle hung over the fire. Near the campfire, with his back turned toward Skinhead, sat a slumped old man with what remained of his gray hair surrounding a shining bald spot. Skinhead approached him and said hello.

"The tea's ready. The fish is done." The old man smiled and picked with his stick at the fish lying on a flat rock in the smoldering coals. "It's ready."

"Did you catch it in this stream?" Skinhead asked, as he sat down and accepted the hot fish arranged on leaves.

"Some fishermen brought it. I gave up all those pastimes—hunting, fishing—in my youth. To be honest, I also gave up animal-based food then. Out of moral considerations."

The baked fish was tasty, although bony. It resembled a large ruff or a marine goby, with a spiny dorsal fin. The old man then poured tea from the kettle into two aluminum mugs, pulled out a small package from his canvas bag, and opened it. Inside was a piece of comb honey.

The old man's face was familiar, but Skinhead could not put a name to it. He turned out to be rather chatty, and talked about his children, his grandchildren, and little Vanya, about whom he had worried so much and for absolutely no reason ... He lambasted someone named Nikolai Mikhailovich and bewailed his stupidity: "I used to think that stupidity was a misfortune, not a sin. Now I've changed my opinion. Stupidity is a great sin because what underlies it is overconfidence, that is, pride."

With pursed lips the old man sipped the murky but very tasty tea, then set his mug on the flat rock and sighed.

"Of course, I'm in no way exonerated by the vulgar rumors or even by the laudatory adulation we so seek in our youth. *The Sevastopol Stories* brought me that, went to my head, and fed my overconfidence. It was the basis for my own stupidity, which exceeded all the talents granted me for the taking by the Creator ... But the stupidity—the stupidity itself was mine alone ..."

"Why, of course, how didn't I figure it out right away! That's why the face is so familiar ... That face with Socrates's wrinkles, the little eyes under brushy eyebrows, the broad Russian duckbill nose, and that world-famous beard ..."

Skinhead egged the old man on, not without a certain craftiness.

"You're right, you're right. My wife was raised as a Tolstoyan and spent her entire life quoting you, while I kept kidding her and even teasing her: 'Lenochka,' I'd say, 'that genius of yours was rather stupid ...' She would take offense."

The old man knitted his brows and stroked his beard with his large, flat fingers.

"You said that to her? There weren't many who understood . . ."

"That was in your time . . . Nowadays a lot of people have figured it out . . ."

The old man coughed and grabbed his sack.

"Let's take a short walk: I'll show you my study . . . I, you know, have taken an interest in the natural sciences of late . . . I'm working on some theories . . ."

Skinhead stood up with regret. He was already being beckoned to the shore by that voice he had grown accustomed to minding, but Skinhead understood that he had insulted the old man and to refuse the invitation would have been thoroughly impolite . . .

The little house was hidden away in an old oak grove. It was small, the span of three windows, which were almost entirely hidden behind lilac bushes.

"The buds have already emerged and should blossom in about five days or so," Skinhead noted. The porch had three steps. There was a bucket in the entranceway. The old man opened the door into a rather large room with bookcases along the walls. There was a microscope on the table. A second table, near the wall, served as a kind of laboratory, with chemistry vessels and reactants of some sort . . . Amazing.

"You'll be more comfortable here in the armchair, please . . . I've been wanting to speak to a learned man, a contemporary scholar, for a long time now. My nobleman's education, you know . . . I didn't study the natural sciences in my youth. Goethe, I'll have you know, received a brilliant education. He knew mineralogy, devised his own theory of color, and had a profound understanding of the natural sciences . . . We, though, did our schooling at home . . . A half-baked education, in a way . . ."

Either the old man was playing the fool or pulling his, Skinhead's, leg . . . He couldn't tell . . . Then he pulled out his eyeglass case, extracted from it a pince-nez with a black ribbon, set the pince-nez on the bridge of his nose, and made a stern pronouncement, with even a certain suffering in his voice.

"For fifty years I've been pondering these questions. The local inhabitants are beings of a higher sort, of great simplicity of mind, and I am unable to discuss everything with them. What's more, it's very difficult—impossible almost—for them to make sense of our earthly tragedies because even though they are not entirely fleshless, their flesh differs from our worldly variety both in structure and chemical composition. Their skin is too thin . . . For me you are a conversation partner long overdue, the kind I have not had for many years . . ."

As the elder spoke, he unrolled some papers curled into a tube and flattened the ends with his hand, then pressed one side of the pile under two heavy tomes and the other under a marble paperweight.

"My discovery concerns love. At its cellular, so to speak, chemical, level. I'd like to share with you, Pavel Alekseevich, a few of my thoughts."

Skinhead had not heard his earthly name for quite some time, and he was amazed less by the content of the solemn speech of this majestic man with his slightly too fussy eyes, than by the sound of his name returned to him . . . A lost connection had been restored . . .

"Love, as I now understand, needs to be examined alongside other natural phenomena, like the force of gravity or the law of chemical affinity discovered by Dmitry Ivanovich Mendeleev. Or the law—I forgot, what was that Italian's name?—according to which liquids in various tubes all even out at one level . . ."

"He didn't attend school . . . Educated at Yasnaya Polyana, that's what . . ." Pavel Alekseevich chuckled to himself. "Apparently the sixth-grade middle school textbooks made a great impression on him . . ."

"*Haec ego fingebam*," proclaimed Lev Nikolaevich, "that carnal love is allowed for human beings! I erred along with all of our so-called Christianity. Everyone suffered, everyone burned in flames owing to a false understanding of love, owing to its division into the carnal and profane versus the intellectualized, philosophical, and lofty, owing to shame over one's own, innocent, God-given body for which joining with another is innocent, blissful, and good!"

"There's no doubt about that, Lev Nikolaevich," Pavel Alekseevich interjected quietly, looking over his shoulder at the graph drawn in red and blue pencil. It contained a crudely depicted ovum and spermatozoon.

"That inclination lies at the foundation of the universe, and the Greeks, and the Hindus, and the Chinese all understood that. We Russians, though, have understood nothing. Only Vasily Vasilievich Rozanov—an

essentially odious gentleman—saw the light to an extent. Our upbringing, the diseases of the time, the great lie that has come down to us from
the ancient monastic misanthropes have led to our not having achieved
love. And a person who has not achieved love of life cannot achieve love
of God." He fell silent and sulked. "Love occurs at the cellular level: that
is the essence of my discovery. All laws are concentrated in it—the law
of conservation of energy, and the law of conservation of matter. Chemistry, physics, and mathematics. Molecules gravitate toward each other as
a function of chemical affinity, which is determined by love. By passion
even, if you will. Metal in the presence of oxygen passionately desires to
be oxidized. And note the main thing: this chemical love goes as far as
self-renunciation! Giving themselves over to each other, each ceases to be
itself: metal becomes oxide, and oxygen entirely ceases to be a gas. That
is, it yields its natural essence out of love . . . And the elements? The way
water aspires to the earth, filling each and every crevice, dissolving into
each and every crack in the earth, the waves licking the seashore! Love, in
its most perfect form, also denotes denial of the self, of your own being,
in the name of that which is the object of your love . . ." The old man
wrinkled his dry lips. "I, Pavel Alekseevich, rejected everything that I had
written. It was misguided. All of it . . . Now I sit here, and I read, and I
think. And I weep, you know . . . I said so many stupid things, I stirred
up so many people's lives, but I never found the words of truth, no . . . I
never wrote what was most important about what was most important. I
failed to understand anything about love . . ."

"Pardon me, Lev Nikolaevich! What about the story about the young
peasant who fell off the roof and died? Wasn't that about love? Why
that's the best thing I ever read about love in my whole life," Pavel Alekseevich objected.

Lev Nikolaevich started. "Wait a minute, which story was that? I don't
remember."

"'Alyosha the Pot' it's called."

"Yes, yes . . . There was one called that," Lev Nikolaevich reflected.
"Maybe you're right. Maybe I did write one story."

"What about *The Cossacks*? Or *Hadji-Murat*? No, no, I can't agree with
you, Lev Nikolaevich. Isn't the word itself an element, and doesn't the
same process occur in it as the one you just described? And if our speech

is an element—even if not of the highest order, at least you'll agree, sufficiently highly organized—then you, Lev Nikolaevich, are the master of love and nothing less . . ."

The old man stood up. He was not very tall, bandy-legged, but broad in the shoulders and impressive. He went up to the bookcase: it held his first posthumous collected works in worn paper bindings. Lev Nikolaevich pulled out volume after volume, searching for the story. Then he opened it to the page he needed. Pavel Alekseevich looked tenderly over the old man's shoulder at the yellowed pages: the same edition had been rescued from Lenochka's apartment on Trekhprudny.

"So you propose that this is a good story?"

"A masterpiece." Pavel Alekseevich responded concisely.

"I'll be sure to reread it. I'd forgotten all about it. Maybe I really did write something worthwhile . . ." he mumbled, glancing through his pince-nez at the yellowed pages.

The sun was already setting. Pavel Alekseevich rose, said good-bye, and promised to come again, if he were able. Lev Nikolaevich, who had invited him for a conversation about the natural sciences, now seemed little interested in his opinion. He was in a rush to reread his old story. Like all elderly people, his own opinion was more important than anyone else's . . .

The old man walked out onto the porch with Pavel Alekseevich and even kissed him good-bye. Pavel Alekseevich rushed to return to the place where not long ago there had been a riverbank.

15

THE FOOTPATH WOUND ALTERNATELY UPHILL, THEN DOWNhill, and Pavel Alekseevich marveled that the view here—constructed of various planes—was layered, as in the theater, so that a tree in the distance was as visible as the grass alongside the path. At each turn new details of the local world order opened out before him: it turned out that the bed of the stream was raised, and that the water flowed thick and slow. A large pink fish was motionless in the water and looked at Pavel Alekseevich with an unpiscine gaze that was both benevolent and intrigued.

The next turn revealed a low-lying, curly garden. In the garden stood a bench nailed together from white planks. A tall woman got up from the bench and came out to meet him, tapping a striped cane ahead of herself. This could only be Vasilisa, no one else. Her eyes were covered by a white bandage like the blindfolds children use when playing blindman's bluff. But there was something else that was strange about her face. When she came closer, he saw that above the bandage, in the middle of her forehead, there was a large—more bovine than human in size—bright blue eye with thick girlish eyelashes.

"Pavel Alekseevich, I've been waiting for you. I've been sitting and sitting, and you never come." Vasilisa rejoiced. They were already next to each other, and he embraced her.

"Hello, Vasilisa, sweetie."

"We've met again, thank the Lord," she sniffled. Pavel Alekseevich nodded. The eye had two tear ducts, so it was neither left nor right and very symmetrically placed in the center of her forehead. "They took away the old eyes and gave her a new one?" he thought, but, it turned out, he said aloud. Vasilisa laughed. Pavel Alekseevich realized that he had never heard her laugh before.

"They didn't take them away. They operated on them. On these, the little ones. They said that only you could remove the bandage. After I told you something. But they're clever: they didn't tell me what to say. So I've been sitting here on this bench and thinking all the time about what to say to you."

"And?" he inquired. "And what is it?"

"Forgive me, Pavel Alekseevich," she said ingenuously. Pavel Alekseevich was astonished beyond words. What sort of child's play was this: planting her on that bench and punishing her, ordering her to ask for forgiveness . . .

"It's all silliness. It doesn't matter." He waved her off.

"What do you mean? I grouped you with the evildoers. Forgive me. And now take off the bandage. Please."

They returned to the bench. Vasilisa shuffled with her stick, and Pavel Alekseevich supported her by her elbow. How strange: didn't that beautiful bovine eye see anything?

The bandage had been applied competently, the cloth was high quality—imported, apparently. He removed the bandage and unfastened the protective cap from one eye. Under it there was yet a layer of gauze. Carefully he detached it. All the sutures were internal. The eye was swollen, and the eyelids slightly stuck together.

"Well, open your eye, Vasilisa."

She hesitated. Then opened it. She blocked the other with the palm of her hand. She looked at him with one eye.

"You haven't changed a bit, Pavel Alekseevich."

"And the second one?" he asked.

"No, I'll wait for a while with the second one. I'm more used to it that way. So, have you forgiven me then?"

"I was never mad at you, you fool."

She laughed again. Her laugh was a girl's, bashful. Resolutely, he turned her head in its carpet-design headscarf toward him and undid the second eye. She squealed, now entirely like a little child. Then she placed her hand over her mouth and said pleadingly: "All right. You go now. God willing, we'll see each other again. There are a lot of things to do . . ."

He rose from the bench, sighed, and asked after all the question that he had been wanting to ask from the very beginning.

"Listen, Vasilisa, why were you using a stick to walk? Doesn't that third eye see anything?"

"It's worthless. Doesn't see a thing."

"Nothing at all?"

"Not quite. I could see from afar what you were really like."

"And?"

"It's hard to put into words . . . In the image and likeness you are . . ."

He waved his hand and set off.

16

SHE HAD REALLY DREAMED IT. A VERY SIMPLE DREAM— water. It splashed at her ankles, and then rose higher. At first the water rose slowly, then it began to whip from the side and from above, and she was no longer standing on the bottom, but suspended. The water kept coming, poured over her head, filled her nose and mouth, and made breathing difficult. Impossible.

"Now I'll drown," she realized, when she was over her head in water. She held her breath, then slowly released the last remains of warm air through her nose and saw a cluster of bubbles float upward. "How stupid it is to drown, when everything has ended so well . . ."

When holding her breath was no longer possible, she opened her mouth and allowed the water to enter her. But either the water was not really water, or she was not quite herself, because nothing terrible happened; she didn't choke, although at first she sensed a cool stream filling her throat and lungs.

She dove and swam off. The water penetrated her body, and this was just as natural as if it were air. Floating islands of seaweed and schools of small varicolored fish engulfed her. The layers of water overhead were pale, the color of the northern sky; below—blue dark as ink, with no bottom to be seen. But, when her eyes accustomed themselves, she was able to make out the subtle twinkle of stars. Warmer streams mixed with cold ones, creating a sliding movement, like that of the wind.

Her body did what she wanted it to, but she could not remember having been taught to swim. It seemed that she had not known how to swim before. She pulled her arms above her head, cupped her fingers together, quickly rose to the top, and came up for air. That's when she woke up.

She exhaled: a small amount of water ran from her nostrils and mouth. A slippery garland of seaweed had tangled itself around her knee. Her hair dripped. Using both hands, as if wringing linen, she squeezed the water out of her hair and walked away from the shrubbery to a sunny place. Her hair dried quickly in the sun, but immediately began to curl above her forehead and along her temples, which she did not like. Straightening out the locks of hair, she pulled them between her fingers, as if through a giant comb.

"Elena." She heard her own name and turned around. Before her stood her husband, Pavel, neither young nor old, but exactly as he had been when she had met him—forty-three years old.

"Pashenka, finally," and she pressed her face into the most familiar part of his body, where his clavicles came together.

He sensed how the outlines of her moist, thin body corresponded with precise detail to the breach inside him, closing the lifelong wound that he had borne within him since birth, pained and suffering from melancholy and dissatisfaction without even realizing what hole they resided in.

Elena with all her being wanted only to hide herself entirely inside him, to enter him forever, to give him her defective memory and pale "I," secure in nothing and adrift in splintered dreams and constantly losing its uncertain bounds.

It was not he entering her like a spouse, filling that narrow aperture of hers that led to nowhere; it was she entering and filling his hollow core, the center he himself had been unaware he had and had suddenly discovered within himself.

"Soul of my soul," he whispered into the damp curls above her ear as he pressed her tightly to himself.

At the place where their skin met she melted with happiness. This was the attainment of the unattainable that brought people who love one another together in conjugal embraces, over and over again, for years and decades, in their unconscious aspiration to achieve liberation from physical dependency. But poor human copulation ends in inevitable orgasm, beyond which there's no greater corporeal proximity. Because the bounds are set by bodies themselves . . .

Between them the impossible was taking place. Of what remained within the confines of human comprehension there was still the sensation of their bodies—of one's own and another's—although what in earthly existence was known as interpenetration in this other existence expanded beyond all horizons. In this newly formed oneness, this mutual ascent into the orbit of a different world, they discovered a new stereoscopy, an ability to see many things at once and to think many thoughts simultaneously. All these pictures, thoughts, and sensations appeared to them now in a perspective that made Elena simply smile at her former fear of being lost, of losing herself in spaces stretched between unknown systems of coordinates, and of losing the axis she once really had lost—the axis of time . . .

A final surge of intravision showed that the two arciform branches of her fallopian tubes lay where they were supposed to be, the uterus that had been removed in 1943 was in its former place, and not a trace remained of the scar across her belly.

But that does not mean that what had been was no longer, they—man and woman—guessed. It means that everything—thoughts and feelings, bodies and souls—can be transformed. Even those tiny—nonentities, just about—transparent projections of bodies that had failed to transpire, whose journey on earth had been interrupted by the grim circumstances of disfigured, bloody life . . .

When they had settled into each other, free and happy, soul to soul, hand in hand, letter to letter, it turned out that between them there was a Third. The woman recognized him immediately. The man—an instant later.

"Was it You?" he asked.

"I," came the answer.

"Merciful God, what an idiot I was . . ." the man moaned.

"It's nothing to fear." A voice familiar to him since youth calmed him. There was nothing to fear . . .

PART THREE

1

ELENA AWOKE IN HER OWN BED, IN HER OWN ROOM, BUT in a somewhat strange, not-herself condition: her head was empty and hollow, and when she rose from her pillow, everything keeled over sideways ... Adjusting to the unpleasant sensation, she lowered her legs to the floor and attempted to collect her thoughts. The last thing that she remembered clearly was walking out of the church in Obydensky Lane and stopping on the portico. After that there was a gaping void. Then she set her thoughts in the reverse direction: the church portico on which she had stood, the oppressive conversation with the priest before that, and before that, the evening before—her conversation with Tanya. Tanya had informed her with an unexpectedly crude challenge in her voice that she had left her job and was planning to quit the university.

Before that, the evening before, Tanya had quarreled with her father, Vasilisa had reported. Vasilisa had also reported that she had found three empty bottles in Pavel Alekseevich's study. Everything in their household was upside down, and now her head was falling apart.

Elena once again attempted to get up, but everything again swam before her eyes. She asked Vasilisa to call a doctor.

The district doctor, a finicky and good-for-nothing matron, arrived toward evening. She measured her blood pressure. It was normal. But she indicated a tentative diagnosis—a transitory form of hypertension, wrote out a work-release form, and promised to send a neurologist to the house. She did not prescribe any medicine. She was afraid to. For her, house calls to this building filled with distinguished doctors were sheer punishment. Vasilisa cared for Elena all day as best she could: brought her tea with lemon and kept trying to feed her. But Elena did not feel like eating.

Rather late in the evening Pavel Alekseevich arrived. He was disturbed by the news. He dropped into Elena's bedroom and sat down on the bed, smelling of vodka.

"What happened?"

"Nothing in particular. My head is spinning." She did not want to mention her loss of memory. It was too terrible for words ...

He pressed his hard thumb to her wrist. He listened. Her pulse was normal, and the volume was good. There were no irregularities . . .

"You're tired. Upset. Maybe you just need to relax. Should I get you a reservation for the Academy of Science's sanatorium?" Pavel Alekseevich asked.

"No, Pasha. You see what's happening with Tanya. How can I leave her now?"

"In the past he would have said 'reservations,'" Elena noted to herself. "We haven't been anywhere together in eight years . . ."

They talked about Tanya. Pavel Alekseevich felt that it would all work itself out.

"A growing-up crisis. I think we should give her the opportunity to make some decisions on her own."

Elena lethargically agreed. In fact, she had hoped that her husband would be able to do something quickly and wisely that would clear up all of Tanya's troubles, and that everything would be all right again. But Pavel Alekseevich merely asked if he should arrange for a decent neurologist. Elena declined: one was coming from the local polyclinic tomorrow.

"Why didn't I offer to go to the sanatorium with her?" Pavel Alekseevich reproached himself as he walked out of the room.

Everything between them was just a hair off.

Each of them had an opinion about the abrupt turn in Tanya's life. Strangely enough, the sternest judge turned out to be Toma. The girls had lived together in one room for eight years. By now Toma understood—not merely in some wordless, malleable childish way, but with the logic of a maturing person—just what a lucky number she had drawn on the day of her mother's death . . .

The thoroughly bourgeois values she had been afforded, first in the form of clean sheets and decent food on her plate, and later more subtle things of a refined nature—such as gentility and reserve, cleanliness not only outward, but inward and known as decency, and a sense of humor among them that assuaged all situations in which other people Toma knew would begin to shout or even strike each other—all of these values, both physical and spiritual, Tanya was betraying, declaring with her behavior alone that she spat in the face of their world order.

That spit both stunned and outraged Toma. She had so internalized the lessons of family life that she expressed her opinion, as best she could, quaking at her own daring and fear of losing Tanya's goodwill as a result of her comment. Complex things connected with how life works or a person behaves, when translated into her impoverished language, read approximately as follows: "Your parents have done so much for you, while you, you ungrateful girl, just spit on all of this and, to top it off, you've dropped out of school!"

For Toma the last was the most sensitive point because now in her second year at the landscaping department, where she fawned over domestic asters and Holland tulips, she had experienced certain stirrings inside: for the first time in her life she wanted to go to school. She had not expressed this to anyone aloud yet, but in her head she had been calculating whether it would be better for her to go to technical school or to aim higher—for the forestry institute.

Vasilisa's take on Tanya's odd transformation was simpler: the girl was out for a good time.

Elena essentially shared Vasilisa's point of view, but in milder terms. She saw the reason for her daughter's changed behavior not in Tanya herself, not in her spiritual life, but in certain external events, in the bad influence of new people in her life whom Elena did not know.

Pavel Alekseevich postulated that Tanya was undergoing an overdue youth crisis. Likely he was closest of all to the truth. While attempting to analyze the mechanism of this breakdown, he nevertheless ruled out that the reason lay in that completely—from his point of view—insignificant episode with the stain and the dead fetus that Tanya had related to him with such emotion. It seemed to him that the reason lay somewhere deeper down. In addition, he was disturbed by that phone call from Professor Gansovsky, who first went on at great length about Pavel Alekseevich's exceptional scholarly reputation, then—with the help of the generalizing pronoun "we"—led him to understand that he included himself among the few researchers who were conscientious, and, at the end, gave Tanya an outstanding recommendation, offered to hand back her resignation, to give her time (two months even) to have a good rest, and then in September to leave behind all her silly whims and return to her work as his personal, not MarLena Sergeevna's, laboratory assistant.

He asked Pavel Alekseevich to pass on to Tanya that he expected to see her during his office hours that Tuesday, after twelve noon . . .

After hanging up the phone and thinking about the conversation, Pavel Alekseevich arrived at the conclusion that Tanya had got into some professional conflict with MarLena Sergeevna, whom Tanya had too quickly, from her first day on the job, set as her model.

Tanya's life no longer coincided with the family's schedule: by the time her father came home from work she was already gone and, showing up before dawn, she slept until noon, so it took no small effort for Pavel Alekseevich to intercept her and convey to her the contents of his phone conversation with Gansovsky. Tanya just shrugged.

"What's the point of going? I'm not going back there anyway."

"Tanyusha, that is certainly your right. But don't forget that I made that request on your behalf and brought you to the laboratory myself. Don't put me in an awkward position. Ultimately, one has to observe certain proprieties," he said, more than diplomatically.

Tanya vituperated: "How I hate all your proprieties!"

He took her by the head and stroked it.

"What do you want to do, little one, change the world? That's already been done . . ."

"Dad, you don't understand anything!" She bawled into his chest.

Then ran off, leaving Pavel Alekseevich dismayed: the girl was twenty years old, but acted liked a teenager . . .

2

THE LATE SLUGGISH SUMMER DREW TO ITS END WITH AN August heat wave. Tanya had been living her strange nocturnal life for two months and was increasingly more drawn into it. The geography of her lonely walks expanded. She traipsed the lanes of old Moscow and developed a particular fondness for the Zamoskvorechye region with its stocky merchant houses, enclosed gardens, and an unexpected chain of ancient trees that stood like guards before nests of gentle people demolished long ago. She often strolled along Patriarch Ponds, exploring the baffling confusion of its connected courtyards. She liked to go by way of

Trekhprudny Lane and the Volotsky buildings that her great-grandfather had built, approaching from the side of the Shekhtel building, then turning left and ending her tour at the ponds, just before dawn, dozing a bit on her favorite park bench on the side facing Bolshoy Patriarshy Lane.

The night people there, with whom she occasionally struck up conversations, were entirely unlike ordinary day people who filled the streets when it was light out. Morosely sobering drunks, unlucky prostitutes, the twelve-year-old boy who had run away from home, homeless couples who for the sake of their refugeless lovemaking nested in entranceways with wide windowsills and unlocked attics . . . Once, on the uppermost landing of a staircase that led to a locked door onto a roof she stumbled on a sleeping man and was horrified: was he dead . . . ?

The other thing about night people was that they came in shifts depending on the hour: before one in the morning, you could still encounter a lot of decent couples on their way home. In fact, these were not night people, but day people simply slightly delayed. After one, they were replaced by loners, inebriated for the most part. They were not dangerous, although sometimes they accosted her. They would ask for something: a cigarette, matches, a two-kopeck coin for the phone booth; or offer something: to have a drink, to make love . . . She sometimes had conversations with these inebriated loners . . . The most dangerous people, it seemed to Tanya, came out between three and four thirty. In any case, her most unpleasant meetings occurred at that particular time.

She spat out like a plum pit all her former knowledge from school and from books. What interested her now was a different kind of experience, the kind that privileged unexpected maneuvers and nimble moves: she delighted every time she found a new courtyard that connected two dead-end lanes or a building with entrances at both sides—the façade side and the servants' entrance side. She knew Moscow's last water pump, forgotten by the waterworks' authorities and still functioning in the area of the former Bozhedomka, and she discovered an apartment in a half-basement—a thieves' den?—where very criminal-looking types gathered at night. The miles she trekked at night were paved with reflection: until recently, life had seemed to her an even uphill journey, a gradual ascent, the goal of which was a scientific accomplishment combined with merited success and even, perhaps, fame. But now instead of this heroic picture she saw a trap, and science seemed as much an idol as that wretched imposed socialism which of late radio announcers had started to pronounce as "socialeezism," trucking up to the barely literate Khrushchev, who could hardly put two words together . . . When she had been little, the world had naturally divided itself into "grown-ups" and "children," "good people" and "bad people." Now she had discovered a new dimension: "the obedient" and "the disobedient." This was not about children, but about adults—intelligent, enlightened, and talented adults . . . Tanya decisively and happily crossed over to the second category. True, she was still not quite clear where her father stood: he did not fit in either category. He seemed to be socially useful, that is, obedient, but he always acted of his own accord, and forcing him to accept someone else's opinion or to submit was impossible . . .

Once in a dead-end courtyard in Sredne-Kislovsky Lane Tanya found a stern old man sitting very erect on a park bench, his back not touching the rolling back of the bench, his wooden hands leaning on a lordly wooden walking stick with a sturdy polished handle. Tanya sat down on the edge of the bench. Without turning his large head, which was illuminated at an angle by the weak streetlight, he said to her in a deep voice: "Tanya, I think it's time to put dinner on the table."

"How do you know who I am?" she wondered, at first not realizing it was pure coincidence.

"I'm telling you again: it's time to eat dinner."

"Where do you live?" Tanya asked.

The old man seemed a bit perplexed, then worried, then answered not entirely confidently.

"I live . . . here."

"Where here?" Tanya asked again, this time realizing that the old man had lost his memory.

"In the town of Gadyach, in the Poltava guberniya . . ." He answered with dignity.

"What is your name?"

"It's time to serve dinner." He shifted on the bench, attempting to raise himself from its depths, and leaning on his cane. "It's time to eat dinner." He sank back down, unable to liberate his rather unwieldy body.

Dawn was approaching. Tanya helped him free himself from the deep bench that was as awkward as a wooden hammock and said, "Let's go. It really is time for dinner. Tanya's waiting for you with dinner."

She led him off to a precinct station where they might help him find the cunning Tanya who had not put dinner on the table on time. At the precinct station, as she turned the majestic old man over to the petty powers-that-be, Tanya noticed the writing in white paint along the length of the cane: "Pechatnikov Lane, House 7, Apartment 2. Lepko, Alexander Ivanovich."

"Good-bye, Alexander Ivanovich." Tanya bid him farewell, regretting that she had not noticed earlier the calling card written along the stick.

"The penultimate stage of freedom." Earlier such a thought would not have occurred to her.

When she left the precinct station, dawn was already breaking. The night people had taken cover, while the day people had not yet emerged from their lairs. Tanya was in a wonderful mood, and she decided that after getting some sleep she would go to the laboratory around one in the afternoon, when all the lab assistants got together in the prep room for tea, and that she would buy a cake and some candy as a way of celebrating her liberation . . .

Her tea party did not go as planned. Of the six lab assistants three were on vacation, one was ill, and the remaining two were precisely the least pleasant—the elderly Tasya Kukharikova and thieving Galya Avdiushkina. They each ate two pieces of cake and put the rest in the refrigerator. There was no one in the laboratory: some people were on vacation, some at a conference, and others on their research day in the library. MarLena Sergeevna also was away.

Tanya dropped into her former room and with no regrets or sentimentality whatsoever recollected that first day when her father had brought her here. Everything stood in its former place: the microscopes, the microtomes, the torsion scales, the batteries of glass bottles of alcohol and xylol secured with slightly bent metal lids. What had once seemed to her the temple of science now looked poor and dilapidated. In the molecular biology building at the university they had been using an electron microscope for a long time already, they had modern equipment—not the stuff in this museum of the history of science, the nineteenth-century room.

She wanted to have nothing to do with any of this anymore. Only the smell—the heavy laboratory smell of alcohol and formaldehyde mixed with vivarium and chloroform—remained, after all, a bit thrilling.

Tanya pulled out the drawer of her desk and gathered her personal belongings: a long wooden cigarette holder, a compact for face powder, a typed collection of Mandelstam's verses, and—who knows for what purpose—her notebook . . . She tossed it all in her bag and headed for Gansovsky's office. She knocked on the antiquated door with its opaque glass inserts. She entered. Gansovsky—tanned, his hair freshly dyed brown, in his white coat—was sitting at his enormous desk, reading a journal.

"Come in, come in."

The only chair for visitors held a mountain of books. He indicated to Tanya that she sit on the folding wooden library stepladder. The bookcases ran to the very ceiling and could not be reached from the floor. In its folded state the staircase resembled a high chair.

"Take a seat."

Tanya plopped herself on the tiny upper platform, which turned out to be rather uncomfortable. Her legs did not reach the floor, so she rested them on the lower rung. Her orange skirt, which was very short, as dictated by the latest scandalous fashion, gathered almost at the level of her panties, and she noticed the tenacious male gaze with which the old academician surveyed her bare legs. Gansovsky removed his gold eyeglasses, neatly folded them temple to temple, and looked at Tanya most empathetically.

"Well, Tatiana Pavlovna, I hear you're planning on leaving us."

"Yes, I've already resigned, Edmund Algidasovich." Tanya was the only laboratory assistant capable of properly pronouncing his intricate name, the product of a Polish-Lithuanian and, rumor had it, Jewish mix.

"Aren't you being a bit hasty, Tatiana Pavlovna?"

He stood up, and Tanya's position atop the stepladder became even more ridiculous. The professor stood right in front of her, and she found herself pinned in a corner between the bookcase and the chair piled with books. Tanya turned her legs so as not to touch his hip.

"You made such a good start at your work. I have to admit that I had already decided to take you on and to give you a research topic. It's very important for a person to begin their research career early. Next year you could publish your first scientific article already . . ."

Tanya did not understand very well what he was saying insofar as she was distracted by the feel of his cool lab coat against her bare leg and the unpleasant rustling of his hand in his pocket, visible through the cloth of the coat.

"You've mastered the technique of experimental hydrocephaly," he continued. "MarLena Sergeevna told me that she could trust you with any stage of the work. I just don't understand why you want to leave."

Now he gripped the side of the stepladder with one hand, while the second accidentally, but with absolute assuredness, lay on her hip. Like any well-brought-up person trained not to notice an interlocutor's faux pas, Tanya pretended not to notice.

"You have three years of classes left, and in that time you could succeed not just in writing a course paper and your diploma thesis, but half your dissertation."

He looked her in the eye: his expression was absolutely matter-of-fact and even stern. He took his hand off her hip and stuck it between the buttons of his lab coat, beneath his belt, and rummaged about. Tanya followed his manipulations out of the corner of her eye.

"There is this substance called auxin." His heavy hand went for her tightly closed knees, then slid up her leg.

Tanya was ready to faint. Not because his hand had firmly and precisely penetrated under her panties and the pads of his closely manicured fingers were pressed against a place never before touched by a foreign object, except soap, but because his stern and professional demeanor stood right before her and his powerful voice hypnotized her with its multivalent "auxin," which had no relation whatsoever to what was taking place at the moment.

"This growth hormone wonderfully stimulates capillary growth; the introduction of, let's say, five milliliters increases the number of developing capillaries by one hundred to one hundred twenty percent . . ."

He undid the lower button of his lab coat, and Tanya, completely petrified and incapable of turning her head away, saw with her peripheral vision the swarthy pink bulb with the longitudinal slit in the middle that he held in his broad freckled hand. He had already positioned himself between her spread knees, preparing to enter her with one hand, while moving Tanya closer with the other, pressing on the back of her waist . . . Tanya's lockjaw ended the moment he stopped talking about auxin and said equally authoritatively and matter-of-factly: "Spread your legs a little wider and throw your shoulders back."

Tanya shoved him in the chest.

"Sit still!" he bellowed, but she had already jumped from the stepladder and run for the door, grabbing it by the round knob that was exactly like his bulb. The door would not budge.

"The pig, he locked it!" Tanya thought, and bashed her fist with all her strength against the glass insert. The glass flew out with a clang, but the door still did not open.

"Idiot," he said calmly. "Turn the handle."

He closed his lab coat over the flash of his bare chest and academician's bulb in the unfastened fly of his light-colored slacks . . .

Tanya flew out of the institute like a cork out of a bottle and ran as fast as she could from the temple of science with all its nastiness, filth, and sleaze.

THE YAUZA WAS CONSOLING, ESPECIALLY IF YOU DID NOT look at the factory buildings along the bank, which almost since the time of Peter the Great had taken their water from the river and dumped their sewage back . . . The potters, tanners, the first industrialists . . . But the river remained untainted, alive . . .

Tanya ascended the hunchbacked bridge that hung over the river and peered into the morosely green water.

Her slashed hand hurt. The bleeding had already stopped, but the bandages had managed to soak through. At the drugstore she had chanced on a kind pharmacist. Without saying a word, the woman had taken a sterile pad and some gauze and tied a very professional bandage. She bound Tanya's middle and ring fingers with surgical tape. The deepest cut was between the fingers in exactly the same place as her mother's scar from the fishhook—wasn't that weird?

Tanya had no money on her—she had left her bag in Gansovsky's office, hanging on the back of the chair piled up with medical books that Tanya would never read in this lifetime. A good idea would be for her father to pick up her bag from Gansovsky. Lay it out just like that: Gansovsky tried to screw me, but I got away. And ask him what he thought about proprieties and all that bunk he so respected. Actually, there was no way she could say anything to him. Though he was a well-mannered person when it came to forks and knives, "thank you," and "good-bye," if she told him this story, he would simply murder Gansovsky. No, not murder. Beat the hell out of him. Make hamburger out of him. Tanya laughed, picturing to herself how her father would trap Gansovsky in the same corner where Tanya had sat on that stupid stepladder, and pummel his dyed head with his heavy fists.

"Poor Liza!" she said aloud, peering for the last time at the Yauza's water. "No drowning for us."

She no longer trembled from excitement, and she had the urge to tell someone right away about her adventure. But there was no one to tell. She, it goes without saying, had tons of girlfriends, but her closest friend, with whom she had studied in the same class, had married immediately after graduation, quickly gave birth, and was now sitting at their dacha with her baby. Tanya did not know the address of the dacha. Two of the nicest girls in her year at the university had set off for the Caucasus mountain region for vacation. Toma in this case was out of the question. Besides, she was not Tanya's friend. Discussing this adventure with the young men who flocked around Tanya by the dozen would be uninteresting, and impossible. In addition, for all the sleaziness of what had happened, the whole business madly excited her. That bulb had made an impression . . .

"Seems I've fallen behind . . . That old coot is vile, but he got to me somehow . . . It's about time . . . That's nonsense: I don't like anyone, and I certainly don't love anyone . . . All my girlfriends already have lovers . . . I could use some advice from a knowledgeable older woman, but there aren't any around . . ."

Without noticing, she had turned off the embankment onto a tidy street completely atypical for Moscow, planted with old lindens at regular intervals. There were military hospitals, antiquated and semiantiquated yellow buildings, maybe barracks or dormitories. The street was called Hospital Rampart. This was Lefortovo, and Tanya was here for the first time in her life.

Since morning she had had nothing to eat, but she did not want to go home. All her money was in her bag.

"It's much better to have no money at all than not enough," the thought suddenly occurred to her. It was a strange awakening: whatever else there hadn't been, she had always had money. She had her own salary, and there was the tin in the kitchen from which anyone could take however much they needed. (Vasilisa was constantly amazed how quickly the money disappeared and had attempted to organize their spending.) For the first time in her life Tanya had not a kopeck, which she found amusing and gay. She knew perfectly well how to get home without paying by sneaking on board trolleybuses and trams, or she could simply take a taxi and pay the fare at home . . .

She also, however, was without keys: they too were back in her bag. That new skirt was nice in all other respects—Italian-made, a rusty orange color, with studded snaps, but it had no pockets. I will never buy anything without pockets again . . . She also enjoyed being hungry today: it made her feel light and free . . . Wait, wait, something important had finally come to her, about freedom. What, for example, had made her decide that she wanted to study biology? As a child, she used to draw, and people had praised her; then she took up music, and people had praised her. She started reading her father's books, and they praised her again. That's what she wanted really—praise . . . She tried, and she studied, and she pored over her notebooks so that her father would praise her. She'd been bought on praise, the good girl . . . Enough! Over! From now on my actions will no longer depend on whether they please my father, my mother, Vasilisa, anyone. Only me. I am my own judge. Freedom from the opinion of others. What if I asked Dad if Gansovsky's opinion means anything to him? Of course, it does. They all want to be liked by each other. That is, not all, but by everybody. Circles. Castes. Closed societies . . . Rat-killers. Obedient. We, intelligent human beings . . . What banality . . . Not for me . . .

It never entered her head that the entire student population at the time, in the 1960s, in Paris and London, New York and Rome, all thought approximately the same thing. But she had arrived at this on her own, without anyone's suggestions or cheat sheets. Independently . . .

She walked along the high cemetery fence behind which stood tall grave markers under tall trees . . . She stopped at the gate: VVEDENSKOE

CEMETERY. Right. This was the former German Cemetery where all the Kukotskys lay buried, Tanya surmised, and entered.

The path crossed the cemetery perpendicularly, from one gate to the other, with graves and grave markers extending in all directions. Antiquated ones, with German Gothic inscriptions, and ones that were just old, without Latin script. Chapels, marble angels, plaster vases, crosses and stars, stars and crosses ... Amazingly, in all her twenty years Tanya had never been to a cemetery. She had never once been to a funeral, unless you counted Stalin's. She had been in a crematorium once or twice, but had not really understood what went on there. But here it was beautiful and sad—neglect lent the place charm. She walked through the old part of the cemetery, studying the inscriptions on the monuments: the Kukotskys had to be here somewhere. But she encountered none of them.

She found herself once again at the fence, this time at the other end of the cemetery. Two men sat near a newly excavated grave. There was a pile of shoveled earth on one side, and the two workmen sat in the low bushes of the grave site to the other side. Their simple fare was spread out in front of them on a newspaper: a round of stone-ground bread, a pale piece of sausage, and some yellowed green onion. The bottle of vodka was propped against two bricks for stability.

One of the workers was elderly and wore a cap; the other was younger and bald, and wore a cap folded from newspaper. Neither of them looked at Tanya. The freedom that had fallen to her today prodded her to ask them for some bread.

Barely looking at her, the elderly one grumbled: "Go ahead."

The one who was younger made a fuss: "What about earning it?"

"I cut my hand." Tanya trustingly raised her palm with the bandage coated from below and the side with darkened blood.

"I wasn't talking about with your hand," the young man retorted.

"Take it and get lost." The old man looked with a disapproving eye at both Tanya and his partner, and even at the opened bottle.

But the younger one would not let up.

"Pour you some, maybe?"

"No, thank you." She took a large hunk of bread and small piece of sausage, bit off a piece, and spoke as she chewed.

"My grandfather is buried here. Kukotsky's the name. I can't find the plot."

"Go to the office, they'll tell you," the elderly one said more respectfully than earlier. The girl might be a prostitute, but she was one of theirs, a client . . .

Thanking them, Tanya left, leaving the two of them with their bottle.

"You amaze me, Senka," the old man said thoughtfully. "You're supposed to be married, and you've got a decent woman, and a kid. What do you need that stick for? Phoo!"

Senka snorted. "Uncle Fedya, what's so bad about it? I would have screwed her right here on this grave. What's so bad?"

Tanya walked past the office. The path led her out through the other gate onto a ramshackle street toward a dried-up pond or foundation pit overshadowed by a sprawling center of so-called culture further in the direction of the tram lines. The tram was a good mode of public transportation suitable for freeloaders. It was already turning dark, but something was not right with the time: the day was turning out to be too long. She looked at her watch, a present from her father, and it showed two thirty. It had stopped.

A completely empty tram, the No. 50, approached. She did not have time to see where it went. Most likely, to some metro station. The tram was long in transporting her alone; then an elderly couple got on. They crossed the Yauza. The last stop turned out to be the Baumanskaya metro station. It was nearly ten, but she didn't feel like going home . . . Tanya circled the large cathedral and found herself on Olkhovskaya Street. The courtyards on this street of almost entirely one-story buildings were good dirt yards, with gardens and benches, children's sandboxes, and swings. There were no new buildings, just old lower-middle-class dwellings. Only one of them had five stories, a Moscow moderne building from the early 1900s. Tanya felt tired, walked into the first courtyard, and saw— what a gift!—a gazebo. Inside the gazebo there was a crude table and two benches set into the dirt. A place for playing dominos.

Tanya lay down on one of the narrow benches and turned her head in order to see a piece of the sky thick with stars. From somewhere came the sound of radio music mixed with the sounds of a proletarian argument.

"I am a very, very free person," Tanya said to herself, admiring the phrase, and fell asleep without noticing. She woke up from the cold. There was no telling how long she had slept. Not long, it seemed. In the meantime, the moon had come out, filling everything with its artificial light. She still had no desire to go home, but it was time . . . On the earthen parapet of a completely rural-looking house in the depths of the courtyard sat a boy. With concentrated attention he was conjuring over his wrist.

Tanya walked up closer. He heard her steps, turned around, and froze, grasping the wrist of his left hand with his right hand.

"Beat it," the boy said rudely.

Tanya just stood there without moving. Half of a razor blade shone in the strong light of the moon. Understanding, she said to him: "That's not going to work."

"Why not?" He raised his head, and she saw a pale face that seemed tear-stained, with a fresh black-and-blue mark swelling under one eye.

"You need to do it in the bathtub, in warm water . . . ," she said, sympathizing. "It won't work otherwise."

"How do you know?" the boy asked glumly.

"I'm a vein specialist. I spent two years studying veins. That's going to drip for a bit and stop. You're better off jumping from the roof—Bam! And it's over."

"Not for me!" The boy smirked. "I need a machine. Understand, I don't have a machine. But if I cut it wider, I can stick a vial inside . . . If you're such a specialist, maybe you have a machine on you?"

Now Tanya did not understand him: "What kind of machine?"

"A syringe, idiot!" he explained.

"Oh, a syringe. I have one at home." Wonder of wonders, she had lived her whole life being so smart, but today had spent the whole day playing the idiot . . .

"You live far away?" The boy lit up with interest.

"Far away."

"Then what are you doing here?"

"I'm out for a walk. I like to walk around at this time of night." She sat down alongside him and noticed that he was older than he had at first seemed. "Let's go for a walk. I like to look inside windows . . ."

She pulled him by the sleeve of his checkered shirt, and he obeyed. He wrapped the razor blade in a piece of paper, stuck it in the pocket of his shirt, and hurried after her. She led him out into the street, then turned confidently into a passageway between two houses that led to a barely visible walkway toward an illuminated window. A dirty lightbulb streaked with whitewash hung naked on its cord. A chair stood on a table, and there were sawhorses as well. The room was being remodeled. Obviously, they had forgotten to turn off the light. The window was open. The first floor.

"Let's crawl in," Tanya proposed.

"No, I've already done time for a shop. That's enough for me." The boy scurried ahead. "What if we go to your place?"

"I lost my keys . . . And, in general . . ." Tanya was at a loss. Everything was a bit topsy-turvy.

"All right, let's go," the guy proposed magnanimously, and they set off to wander further.

They walked with their arms around each other, then, in some courtyard, they kissed, then they wandered about a bit longer, and then it turned out that they were standing in a large entranceway, pressing against each other with their arms and their hollow stomachs and hands that were sticky from the little bit of blood that had managed to flow through the tiny cut across his vein.

They went up to the last floor of the very same Moscow moderne building that Tanya had noticed at the beginning of her journey along Olkhovskaya Street. A light burned on the fourth floor, but beyond that lay mysterious darkness. A story above the last floor, near a padlocked entrance to the attic, there was a small semicircular window with flowing casements that cast curvilinear shadows in the strange light. They kissed a bit longer, standing at the wide windowsill. Then she sat down on the windowsill and did everything that Gansovsky had wanted of her.

"Gansovsky ordered that stepladder especially for that kind of stuff!" Tanya guessed as the boy pulled her onto himself.

With neither a thrill nor inspiration she bid farewell to her senseless virginity, imparting absolutely no significance to the event whatsoever. The boy accepted this unexpected gift in total bewilderment.

"You still got your cherry? You're my first. And do you know how many broads I've had?"

Tanya laughed at his street slang and shook her bandaged hand.

"What a bloody day I've had today . . . And you too . . ."

266

Then he sat down alongside her on the windowsill. Though wide, the windowsill was too short for them to lie down on.

Ten minutes later he was telling her about some girl named Natasha who had played with him for two years—because all broads are bitches—and about his deferral—he was going to join up during the fall draft as a border guard—and some other gibberish about real men . . . Tanya had no interest in this whatsoever. She jumped off the windowsill and waved to the little chump.

"I'm out of here!"

And she flew down the stairs, clicking distinctly with the heels of her flats.

By the time he slowly figured out what had happened, she was already two floors down.

"Where are you going?" he shouted after her.

"Home!" she replied, without slowing down.

"Wait! Wait!" he shouted, dashing after her. But she was already out of sight.

3

PAVEL SENSED MORE THAN KNEW: CALL IT STARS OR whatever, but there was something beyond human beings themselves that guided human life. He was convinced of this most of all by the "Abraham's" children, brought into this life through his, Pavel Alekseevich's, hunch about a connection between cosmic time and the innermost cell responsible for the production of progeny . . . He allowed that other aspects of human life could be influenced by the cosmic clock—that bursts, as well as slumps, of creative energy were governed by this same mechanism. Determinism—so obvious in the development of, say, an embryo from a fertilized egg—satisfied him entirely; what was more, he regarded it as the principal law of life. But he was unable to extend this strictly predetermined movement beyond the physical course of ontogeny. His freedom-loving spirit protested. However, a human being was formed not just from certain more- or less-known physiological processes; many other completely chaotic factors interfered, as a result of which identical seven-pound sucklings developed into spiritually diverse human beings, some of whom achieved great deeds, others—crimes, while some died in birth of scarlet fever and others on the field of battle ... Had a plan been preprogrammed for each of these innumerable millions? Or was fate a grain of sand on the seashore? What unknown law dictated that two out of three Russian soldiers would fall under fire during the war, and of those who remained a part would perish in prison camps and another part drink itself to death ... One in ten had survived ... Who regulated this mechanism?

As far as he himself was concerned, Pavel Alekseevich knew that his fate was headed downhill. He still worked, and taught, and operated, but gone from his life was the intense pleasure of the incipient moment, the sensation of being one with the times, with which he had existed for many years. His home life too preserved only its general designs, an empty shell of their former family happiness ... Gone was the feeling that had overcome them in evacuation during the war and had lasted a whole decade, until 1953, that like a sunken ship with stolen gold had descended to the bottom of memory to be replaced by a monastic and laconic union built without touching and almost entirely on understanding glances alone ... Something was happening to Elena: her eyes were covered over with a thin film of ice; if they expressed anything at all, it was an anxious and strained lack of understanding, like that of a small child still unable to speak just before it is about to start crying for some inexplicable reason.

His relationship with Tanya had fallen apart. Just as before, she was rarely at home, but earlier her absence had signified a kind of accumulative activity, a nutritional acquisition of skill, whereas now, after she had abandoned everything, Pavel Alekseevich wondered with what sort of activities she filled her day, evening, and—not infrequently—nighttime hours spent away from home. He was chagrined by what he suspected to be an empty waste of time mostly because he so valued the special quality of each young person's time, before fatal automatism had set in and when each youthful minute was muscular, capacious, and commensurate with the acquisition of knowledge and experience in their purest form ... As opposed to his—an old-man's—time, which slid by, weightless and even more worthless ...

What had once been the burning content of life—those birth mothers transparent as aquarium guppies with all their pathologies and complications, and his teaching, through which Pavel Alekseevich passed on to his students not just techniques but that tiny unnamable entity that comprises the heart of every profession—was becoming more and more automatic and losing its value, if not for those around him, then for Pavel Alekseevich himself.

"The relative weight of time decreases with age" was Pavel Alekseevich's diagnosis.

Fatigued, he returned from work and first thing headed for his study, drank three quarters of a glass of vodka, and only after that emerged for supper. Elena, who had been waiting for him, also came out of her room. She sat down at the table Vasilisa had set, placed her thin hands with their enlarged joints alongside her eating utensils, and sat, her head lowered, as Vasilisa recited the appropriate prayer—to herself, on her own behalf as well as for all those present, repeating it as many times as there were people at the table. Pavel Alekseevich, who knew nothing about this ritual of hers, also hesitated, waiting for the wave of alcohol to spread through his body, and on feeling its warmth, he uttered his usual "bon appétit" and started in on Vasilisa's thin soup. Tanya rarely ate supper at home. Toma, who had embarked on further studies, came home after eleven four times a week, and if she ate with the family, she was silent most of the time. They exchanged the most insignificant and necessary words: pass the salt, thank you, very delicious . . .

After supper Pavel Alekseevich retired to his study and over the course of the evening drank the remainder of the bottle, leaving two fingers at the bottom for his morning dose. This was now his way of fighting with time: his sad attempt to kill it.

Ilya Iosifovich, by contrast, had entered the happiest streak of his life. In the beginning of the 1960s his life had taken a turn: he was given a laboratory that operated as an independent research institute, and the lab had attracted several young people who were committed to the sciences to their last drop of blood. For his monograph on the nature of genius he was awarded a doctorate in biological science without having to defend. True, many years later Ilya Iosifovich acknowledged that those two dissertations he had been unable to defend owing to yet more arrests more aptly fulfilled the requirements of a doctorate. But at this particular moment he was enamored of his own work and had not yet reconsidered his hardly genial achievements in the field of genius research. Ilya Iosifovich existed in a state of euphoria: genetics had been allowed, Lysenko was done, and the same people who earlier had not let him in the door now flatteringly shook his hand and smiled phony smiles at this former foot soldier from the front lines who out of the blue had entered the ranks of heroes.

The main event in Ilya Iosifovich's life—long kept secret from everyone—was named Valentina II. A graduate student from Novosibirsk, Valentina Moiseevna Gryzkina, an athletic type of girl, the complete opposite of the deceased Valentina, had fallen in love with her dissertation adviser with the singularity of purpose of a basketball forward. In point of fact she was the best shooter on her university women's basketball team, and her athletic vigor benefited from the inner resolve of an Old Believer: she was descended from a family of schismatics. One of her ancestors had accompanied Archpriest Avvakum on his famous journey, and since that time for more than two hundred years now, the family had settled in Siberia, and in the face of all sorts of persecution, persisted in its faith and produced strong and numerous offspring. It was to these folk, tempered by centuries of struggle, that Valentina, in the sixth grade or so, had announced that humans had evolved from apes. For starters her parents thrashed her with all their patriarchal ferocity and forbade her from going to school. But the little girl turned out to be worthy of her parents: they had met their own match. One faith against the other . . . Following two years of devastating struggle for the dignity of humankind descended from apes, Valentina left home, bearing on her already broadened shoulders her grandfather's curse. Next came boarding school, evening school, and university—who knew on what money, with no financial aid whatsoever, living only on her paltry stipend. In her last year she read several articles by Goldberg in the journal *Genetics* and chose him to be her mentor. She arrived in Moscow with a recommendation to graduate school—she'd graduated with honors after all!—sought out Ilya Iosifovich, and passed her entrance exams.

To Goldberg's credit, a long time would pass before he noticed the amorous charge emanating from his new graduate student. He did, however, note her self-discipline, resourcefulness, and excellent knack for work: she deftly maneuvered heavy crates filled with test tubes and quickly taught herself all the techniques for working with flies, which were the principal object of the laboratory's investigations.

The main thing was that Valentina had no idea that Ilya Iosifovich measured female attractiveness by one single criterion: the extent to which the subject under consideration approximated the image of his late wife. It needs to be noted as well that during her life Valentina I had never struck him as the ideal, but after her death, over the course of the years, he idealized her more and more in his memory.

The broad-shouldered, droll graduate student with two sharp bumps under her sweater in place of the massive soft hills expected in this broad expanse, in her men's shoes and dark-blue lab coat, in no way inclined Ilya Iosifovich to thoughts of his inveterate loneliness, his unsettled bachelor life, or, even less likely, of the youthful frivolity of falling in love or of sexual conviviality . . .

Valentina endured and endured, and then confessed her feelings. Ilya Iosifovich was perplexed and flattered, but with Onegin-like craftiness he mumbled something appropriate to this classic declaration against the background of a maidens' chorus: "When old enough to be a father, my pleasant destiny dictated I become a spouse . . ."

After which they both started thinking. Valentina—about transferring back to Novosibirsk; and Ilya Iosifovich about the sweet girl who had avalanched on his bald head like Siberian snow . . . And the more he thought, the more he liked her. The first symptoms of lovesickness occurred simultaneously with the arousing thought of the obscenity of having relations with a) a graduate student in general, and b) a graduate student who was almost forty years his junior . . .

Gansovsky, of course, would have just smirked and backed the hussy into the corner of his bookshelves on a specially designed device . . . But Gansovsky would never have cause to experience but a shadow of the happiness that Goldberg achieved following a half-year of semiromantic torment when, on a trip to the biology school in the semisecret city of Obninsk, following a long cross-country ski trip, Valentina remained with him in his cold hotel room . . . For all her awkwardness to disappear without a trace, Valentina needed only to get on her skis; in her

271

dark-blue Olympic ski suit and ski cap pulled down to her shining eyes and wedging at the bridge of her nose she was for Ilya Iosifovich a streak of amazing lightning. (She was ranked nationally in skiing as well as in basketball.) His joyous amazement was fated to be long-lived—the first few years in great, but poorly kept, secrecy . . .

Pavel Alekseevich, had he known, might have reflected on the hormonal nature of creative inspiration. He and his friend saw each other not very often, but no less than once a month. Usually Goldberg arrived at Novoslobodskaya Street at around ten in the evening, and Pavel Alekseevich would pull out a bottle of vodka, and they would carry on their purely man-to-man conversation until the wee hours of the night. Not about war, or horses, or drinking exploits, but about population genetics, the gene pool, genetic drift, and problems Ilya Iosifovich would label with the previously unknown term *sociogenetics* . . . Although Goldberg loved abstract, philosophical-biological conversations, he also knew how to formulate an experiment both competently and cleverly, as well as how to extract with maximum economy a direct answer to a precisely formulated question. His students worked productively, at a state-of-the-art level, and many of them were publishing articles in international journals. Everyone knows that Russians always do well in those fields of science where it's possible to do the work in your head, on your fingers, and without serious financing.

For all their disagreements—which over the course of the many years of their conversations constantly, like a cat in a bag, made themselves known—Pavel Alekseevich and Ilya Iosifovich coincided unconditionally in one regard. They shared a clear sense of the hierarchy of knowledge, of which raw data collection (weight, shape, color, number of chromosomes or legs or veins on the wing) was the most primitive but also formed the very foundation. In the ancient and descriptive science of data collection, approximation was not allowed, and answers had to be unequivocal: yes or no . . . Speculation of a theoretical nature—about the cosmic clock or the evolution of some biological species—had to build precisely on reliable knowledge measured with a ruler, a thermometer, or a hydrometer . . . And so, Goldberg based his calculations and speculation about genius on levels of uric acid in blood. Goldberg's new ideas struck Pavel Alekseevich as interesting, but completely unfounded. Goldberg insisted that the construction of a model of a process was also in many cases its proof. Pavel Alekseevich did not want to hear anything of the sort.

After three terms in the camps, having lost the intelligentsia's innate sense of guilt before nation, society, and Soviet power, Goldberg had arrived at his latest idea: that over the course of fifty years of Soviet power the sociogenetic unit formerly, before the revolution, known as the "Russian people" had ceased to exist as a reality, and the current population of the Soviet Union that bore the proud name of the "Soviet people" was in fact a new sociogenetic unit that differed profoundly from its predecessor in a variety of parameters—physically, psychophysically, and morally . . .

"Okay, Ilya, I am prepared to agree that in physical appearance great changes really have occurred: hunger, wars, the massive displacement of peoples, miscegenation . . . Ultimately, it is possible to conduct anthropometric research. But how can you measure moral qualities? No, that's rubbish. I'm sorry, but it's unprofessional . . ."

"I assure you, there are ways. They're indirect still, but they exist." Ilya Iosifovich defended his theory. "Suppose the human genome consists of one hundred thousand genes; that's a plausible figure. They are distributed across twenty-three pairs of chromosomes, right? Although we know a lot about the various mechanisms of intrachromosomal exchange, we still have grounds for dividing all genes into twenty-three groups by chromosome affiliation. Well, of course, that's impossible to do today, but a hundred years from now, I assure you, it will be doable. And just imagine: the gene responsibility for, say, the blue color of the iris is located in direct proximity to the gene that determines cowardice or bravery! There's a good chance that they will be inherited together."

"One gene for one quality, you're saying?" Pavel Alekseevich objected. "It seems unlikely that such a powerful and diverse quality as courage would be determined by a single gene."

"What difference does it make: let it be ten genes! That's not the point! The point is simply that eye color could turn out to be linked to another gene. Crudely put, a blue-eyed person has a greater chance of turning out to be heroic," Ilya Iosifovich raised his index finger.

"Great idea, Ilya," Pavel guffawed. "A blue-eyed blond is brave, while a black-eyed brunet is a coward. And if the black-eyed fellow also has a hook nose, then he's a Judas, for sure! Genetically speaking . . ."

"You're a typical provocateur, Pasha!" Ilya Iosifovich wailed. "I had something totally different in mind. Listen! In 1918 the White Army—nearly three hundred thousand healthy young men of reproductive age—left Russia. The aristocratic, select part of society—the more educated, the more honest, and unwilling to compromise with Bolshevik power!"

"Where are you going with that? Ilyusha, that's going to get you a fourth term!"

"Don't interrupt!" Ilya Iosifovich dismissed him. "Nineteen twenty-two. The year they deported all the professors. Not that many, around six hundred, it seems. But again: the select! The best of the best! With their families! The country's intellectual potential. Further: the anti-kulak campaigns claim millions of peasants, also the best, the hardest working. And their children. And their unborn children as well. People disappear and take their genes with them. They remove them from the gene pool. Party repressions knock out whom? Those who have the courage to express their own opinion, to object, to defend their own point of view! The honest ones, that is! The most honest! Priests were systematically exterminated over the entire period . . . The bearers of moral values, teachers and educators . . ."

"But at the same time, Ilya, they were also the most conservative people, no?"

"I won't deny that. But allow me to point out that nowadays conditions in Russia are such that a conservative—traditional, that is—mentality presents less danger than a revolutionary one," Goldberg noted with a haughty smile. "Let's keep going. World War II. Exemption from military service is granted to the elderly and the infirm. They're the ones given an extra chance of surviving. Prisons and camps consume the larger part of the male population, depriving them of the chance to leave offspring. Do you sense the degree of deformation? Now let's add to that Russia's famous alcoholism. But that's not all. There is one more extremely important consideration. We're constantly discussing whether or not evolution is a directed process, whether it has its own goals. Within the current time span, a very short one from the point of view of evolution, we can observe an exceptionally effective mechanism of directed evolution. Insofar as the evolution of a species is aimed at survival, we are within our rights to put the question as follows: which qualities offer the individual greater chances of surviving? Brains? Talent? Honor? A sense of self-esteem? Moral resolve? No! All of these qualities have impeded survival. The carriers of these qualities either left the country or were systematically exterminated. And which qualities facilitated survival? Caution. Caginess. Hypocrisy. Moral irresolution. Lack of self-esteem. Overall, any illustrious quality made a person conspicuous and immediately put him at risk. Gray, average, C students, so to speak, found themselves at an advantage. Take a Gaussian distribution. Remove the center, the area of more pronounced carriers of any quality. Now, taking all these factors into consideration, you can construct a map of the gene pool that claims to be the Soviet people. And you say?"

"In view of the general atmosphere these days—five to seven years," Pavel Alekseevich commented.

Ilya Iosifovich laughed. "That's what I've been saying: the nation has become flatter, the chimney lower, the smoke thinner . . . Before it would have been worth ten to fifteen . . ."

Pavel Alekseevich always liked his friend's wit and fearlessness, although inside he often disagreed with the results of his high-keyed mental work. The brutal picture of national degeneration Ilya Iosifovich had drawn demanded verification. Pavel remembered perfectly his father's social circle in the last years before the revolution. In a certain sense, Ilya was right: the doctors of the highest rank, university professors, and leading clinicians at the time were people with European educations and broad interests extending beyond the bounds of their profession. Among the people who visited their house there had been military men, lawyers, and writers . . . He had to admit: it had been a long time since Pavel Alekseevich had encountered people of the same intellectual level . . . But that didn't mean that they didn't exist . . . They could exist—in secret, without announcing their existence . . . "No, no, that's nonsense," Pavel Alekseevich cut himself short. That only supports Ilyusha's idea: don't stick out, hide in a corner, and that means denying your own identity . . . A serious objection lies somewhere else . . . Of course, with children. In newborn children. Each is marvelous and unfathomable, like a sealed book. Goldberg's ideas are too mechanistic. According to him, if you subtract a couple dozen genetic letters from a hundred thousand, new children—the daughters and sons of informers, murderers, thieves, and perjurers—who carry their parents' qualities alone, will populate the world ... Rubbish! Each infant holds enormous potential; it represents the entire human race. When you come down to it, Goldberg himself wrote a whole book about genius and should have noticed that genius, that rare miracle, can be born of a fisherman, a watchmaker, or a dishwasher ...

The natural greatness of mountains and oceans with all that they contain—their fish, their birds, their mushrooms, and their people—stands above Ilyusha's reasoning, and the wisdom of the world surpasses all, even the most outstanding, human discoveries. You can sweat, pant, stand on your toes, and strain yourself to the limit, but all you'll get is a mere reflection of the true law. Of course, those hundred thousand genes are a great puzzle. But that puzzle does not contain the whole truth, just an insignificant portion of it. Its entirety lies inside the newborn still slippery with vernix, and even if each of them bears all one hundred thousand potentials, it cannot, it must not be, that nature intended some massive aberration that would turn an entire nation into an experimental herd ...

Pavel Alekseevich said something of the sort, in short, to Goldberg, but the latter resisted.

"Pavel, human beings stopped being governed by the laws of nature long ago. A very long time ago! Already today certain natural processes are regulated by humans, and within a hundred years, I assure you, humans will learn how to change the climate, control heredity, and discover new forms of energy ... Soviet man will also be reshaped, the lost genes reintroduced. And, in general, imagine: a young couple have decided to have a child—that's your field—and they are able to designate in advance their child's genetic makeup, combining the parents' best qualities with desired qualities absent in the parents' genome!"

"It wouldn't be a bad idea to ask the child." Pavel Alekseevich frowned.

Ilya Iosifovich was angry: Why couldn't the old gynecologist understand such simple things? Why didn't he share his joy for the inevitable beauty of a future world enhanced through science with precise calculation and without all the pesky imperfections of a marvelous design?

"When are you going to resurrect the dead?" Pavel Alekseevich quipped.

"Not yet, but life expectancy will increase at least twofold. And people will be twice as happy," Ilya Iosifovich claimed with exaggerated passion. All his discoveries and ideas required a dispute; without polemics they lacked something . . .

"Maybe twice as unhappy? No, no, that kind of world is not for me. Then like Ivan Karamazov, I'll return my ticket . . ."

Father and daughter, stepfather and stepdaughter, had not grown so far apart from each other after all.

4

Elena's Second Notebook

I NEED TO JOT DOWN MY NOTES AT THE SAME TIME EVERY day and to tell Vasilisa to remind me. I used to keep a notebook like this, but I don't remember where it's disappeared to. For absolute certain I hid it somewhere, but I don't remember where. I tried looking for it, but couldn't find it anywhere. I remember well what it looked like: a general-purpose school notebook on some subject that Tanya had started and then abandoned. Light blue.

Today my head is clear, and my thoughts are in order. Sometimes there are days when I can't think a single thought to the end and I lose it. Or I lose words, and everything is filled with black holes. What a disaster!

At first the doctors thought that I had some sort of disease that affected the blood vessels in my brain. Then PA took me to the Burdenko Institute, and they tested me with all their various apparatuses. PA didn't leave me for a second, and he looked so lost. He's too good for words. There, at the Burdenko Institute, they said that my blood vessels weren't great, but that nothing terrible was happening to them. It turned out that in fact they had been looking for a brain tumor and were happy not to have found one. Of course, there wasn't supposed to be one. I am absolutely sure that there's nothing in my head that shouldn't be there; just the opposite, something necessary is missing. A psychiatrist examined me as well. He also found no disease. Still, I spent a month and a half on sick leave, then went back to work. Everyone was very glad to see me, Galya and Anna Arkadievna as well. Galya had been doing all my work and says that she'd had a rough time. Kozlov brought his drafts and asked me to do final copy. As always, I found lots of mistakes in his work. It's just amazing: he's such a talented engineer, but has absolutely no spatial imagination.

I feel best at my drafting board: I don't forget anything, and my work, as always, consoles me.

Tanechka of late has become more kind. Although basically nothing has changed: she isn't looking for work and quit the university. PA says that I shouldn't pester her about that. He says that she's an intelligent girl and we should trust her judgment. Yesterday (or the day before?) Tanya dropped in on me in the evening when I was already in bed. She kissed me, sat down on the bed, and asked if I remembered how we had all gone to Timiryazevka to ride the horses. We spent a long time recollecting that winter day. I remember all the details: how PA's nose kept dripping. (He'd forgotten his handkerchief at home and kept asking us to turn away, blowing his nose soldier-style between his two fingers. With a trumpeting sound.) How happy we were in those days! I remember perfectly all the details of that day, the kind of car we rode in, what kind of coat Tanya had on, even that famous purebred black horse with the small head. Only I couldn't remember its name, and Tanya reminded me: its name was Arab. I don't remember why PA was so cheerful that day. He still didn't drink then.

No, that's not right. I'm mistaken: that was precisely the year he started to drink. He keeps worrying about my health, but he ought to think about himself. He can't drink that much at his age. But I can't say anything to him. Still he's the best. Despite the fact that we've lived as if we've been divorced for ten years. Or not divorced?

Another memory slip again. This time at work. During lunch I was in the cafeteria. I was eating salad when I suddenly couldn't figure out what was in front of me: some red pieces of something that I had no idea what to do with . . . I came to, like last time, the next day in my bed. Then Anna Arkadievna came and told me what had happened to me. I stayed in the cafeteria with my salad until the cafeteria lady said that it was time for her to close, but I didn't answer her. She even got scared. And so on.

Anna Arkadievna didn't call an ambulance, but got a cab and drove me home. She says that I was very obedient but didn't respond to questions.

PA resigned me from my job. He speaks very tenderly to me, but unnaturally, as with a little child. I have tried to explain to him that I am absolutely healthy, that certain pieces drop out of my memory, but that in all other respects everything's the same. I am not insane, and I understand perfectly what's happening to me. I really can't go to work in this condition, but I would like to get work from the institute to do at home. We have an arrangement for people who work at home. Otherwise, I'll just be bored. It's not like Vasilisa and I are going to start making soup together. So he and I made an agreement.

Yesterday Tomochka said that she's planning on entering trade school. Good girl! She's also very tender with me.

This morning I drank tea, ate a piece of bread with cheese, and then forgot and went back to the kitchen to have breakfast. Vasilisa yelled at me, saying that I got in the way of her making dinner. I said that I wanted to have breakfast. She said that I had already eaten breakfast. What a nightmare! I'm turning into an old woman who never walks away from the refrigerator, like Anna Arkadievna's crazy mother-in-law. I'm going to have to write down what I did and didn't do.

I ate breakfast. I ate dinner. I worked after dinner. The doctor from the polyclinic came by. It's cold in my room.

I ate breakfast (or was that yesterday?). PA came home and scolded me for not taking my pills. Now Vasilisa is going to give me my pills three times a day because I forget. That's very funny. It would be hard to find anyone less suited for that assignment. Today she woke me at six in the morning—to take my medicine. "My dear, why so early?" I asked her. "Later I'll be busy and forget!" It's so funny you want to cry! This isn't a family; it's a madhouse. Poor PA, what will happen to him if I lose my memory entirely?

I ate breakfast. I couldn't remember if I washed up or not. I went to wash up, but my towel was wet. That means I'd already washed. There was dinner: vegetable soup and chicken for the main dish. Was there chicken yesterday too? And the day before?

They brought my drafting table from work. It fills half my room. I asked if it couldn't be moved. It turned out that they had brought it last week. I was amazed. I didn't tell them the worst of it: it turns out that I had already done some work, drafted something, but I don't remember a thing. And it would be awkward to ask. I'm trying hard to behave correctly. Because I'm afraid of constantly revealing my memory lapses I've almost stopped talking with people at home and try to answer with as few words as possible. I watch TV more. Reading gives me no pleasure. I picked up my old volume of Tolstoy. It's probably the only reading that doesn't depress me. I know his work so well that I don't have to strain.

Today my head is exceptionally clear. I had Vasilisa change my bedding. She has never liked to change bedding. If you don't remind her, she'll never do it on her own. I took a bath and washed my hair. While sitting in the tub I remembered a recent dream with an enormous amount of water in it. Suddenly I realized that I had not stopped having dreams; I'd simply stopped remembering them. I have to try to write everything down.

PA sat with me for a long while in my room. I feel so good with him. He simply sat down in the armchair next to me and said nothing. Then he took me by the hand and played with my fingers for the longest time. I love him very much. He probably knows that.

I ate breakfast. I took my pills. I ate dinner. Kozl. has two mistakes in his drafts. It's much more plesnt working with constructors. They have mch more competent staff.

It turns out it's already May. I must start writing down the date. Otherwise, time is like mush. PA said that he wants to rent a dacha. That seems excessive to me. What does he imagine: Vasilsa and I will move there, and he'll come to visit on Saturdays and Sundays, and the girls, who knos if they'll come even once the whol summer. And who's going to take care of the whole apartment in Mocsow. Vasilis's also against it. She left for some prayer service for several days, and the apartment just simply fell apart. Only in the evening PA came home and life begagagan. One day I didn't even get otuof bed. Everything in the kitchen has been rearranged, I don't know where the pots are, or where . . . Or maybe I simply forgot?

I ATE BREAKFAST. AND SO ON.

Vasilisa sad that she's leaving for Ss. Peter and Paul day. The twelvth July?

Strangers. More strngers. Why are so many strangers cming here? someone died DIED

I don't understand, but it's uncomfortable asking: it seems we've moved to a new aprtment. Everything is different. A long cordor.

Tanya came by today. Or Toma. No, it was Tan. She's beautiful.

No one home. Yesterday no one. TANYA PA

Vasilisa gave me tea

BREAKFAST DINNER SUPPER

PA said yesterday that he gong on a busness trip. Three days. Vasilisa dosn't give me breakfst.

BREAKFAST Nothing hurts. Nothing thing hurts. DIED who

TANYA TANYA TANYA TANYA

HOSPITAL BREAKFAST NO

PAVEP A PV PA

WHITE brkfast

Happning awfal ask PA WHERE

WPER WHER WRE HERWHERWH

I Elena Grgeva N Kukts 1915 PA who ded de tnya

5

ILYA IOSIFOVICH'S WORK GREW LIKE A TREE: THE OLD AT the roots, the new in the branches. With many, many new offshoots. Anthropology, evolutionary genetics, demography, statistics, and even history all came in handy, everything went into the mix, and everything was made to work. Ilya Iosifovich was both plowman and poet. Sometimes in the evenings, having spent ten hours straight at his desk, he experienced the pleasant muscular fatigue that occurs after a mountain hike or skiing. Besides its sixteen staffers, his laboratory had a whole troop of volunteers—students, librarians, pensioners—who helped him assemble huge amounts of information that he tallied and built into a system similar to Mendeleev's periodic table that explained not the structure and properties of elements, but the structure and properties of nations.

He cast his nets so broadly that the most varied fish—from the *Brockhaus and Efron Encyclopedic Dictionary* to *The Gulag Archipelago*, from

Anaximander of Miletus to Theodosius Dobzhansky—were part of his catch. The grandness of his designs made his bald head spin, and he was constantly giving papers for various research societies, at institutions of higher education, and at the private seminars that blossomed in those days through an oversight of, and in part overseen by, the organs of state security, which had slightly relaxed during the Thaw. It was here he performed as an inspired poet in the Romantic sense of the word. Pavel Alekseevich, who happened to be present at one of his performances, gave him a rather sharp review.

"Ilya, you may have some important points, but you get too carried away, like some David Garrick . . ."

Goldberg could not contain his passion: he had made an earthshaking discovery and hastened to share it with his contemporaries: politics absolutely had to be considered as one of the most significant components in the evolutionary process. In the slice of time he had studied, from 1917 until 1956, in a concrete geographic region—within the territory of the USSR—this factor had exerted a negative influence on the evolutionary process. A convinced Darwinist, Goldberg considered evolution as a phenomenon having a moral aspect: positive evolution, in his opinion, was directed at the preservation, improvement, and expansion of the habitat of a species, while negative evolution aimed at the weakening and degeneration of a species. At its core Soviet power, in Goldberg's opinion, was progressive, but in the concrete historical situation it functioned as a negative factor.

His fundamental treatise, something like "Political and Genetic Foundations of Population Theory," had not yet been written, but "Essays on the Genetic Ethnography of the Soviet Nation" already existed on paper.

Other papers also existed, collected in a tidy green folder with a two-digit number: numbered, bound sheets of paper bearing the reports of regular and nonstaff employees, copies of book requests from the Lenin Library and the Library of Foreign Literature, and tape recordings of Goldberg's impassioned presentations. Filed under its own separate number was the typescript of "Essays on Genetic Ethnography" with the author's own notations: it had been lost accidentally by one of the especially talented staffers in his laboratory on the No. 110 bus . . . Likely owing to the same accident, the thick folder also contained Valentina

II's report on her trip to Novosibirsk. The graduate student had reported on the work of Novosibirsk geneticist B on the "domestication" of silver foxes, animals that were both aggressive and dangerous. It turned out that with consecutive selection and crossbreeding, by generation X the most obedient animals evidenced a sharp decline in the quality of their fur, and having become obedient and trusting, the foxes began to bark like dogs. Thus, the only foxes suited to adorn the collars of generals' wives were those who failed to conform to good relations with human beings. Foxes that behaved badly. Those that learned to lick the hands that fed them were no good for any other purpose.

Captain Seslavin, who was conducting detailed research on Goldberg's own behavior, was an outsider: after graduating from the Institute of Veterinary Medicine, having already become a specialist, he was invited to serve in the security system in the section that oversaw the sciences. The work of the Novosibirsk scientist made perfect sense to him, but there was something suspicious about it.

Considered on its own, this amusing fact from the life of the animal kingdom perhaps might not have attracted the attention of the vigilant Seslavin, but the attached protocol on Goldberg's presentations contained the following statements made by him: "I ask you to note that what we have here is a reverse correlation between acquiescence and fur quality. Which we also observe in our own society: the more acquiescent a person, the less valuable he is as an individual . . ."

This Jew with three prison terms rubbed Seslavin the wrong way. At one time there had been Weissmanites and Morganites at his veterinary institute, who had been dealt with accordingly, and the students were taught Marxist-Leninist biology, with its grass-rotation system and without any of that bourgeois heredity stuff. Because existence, as they say, determines consciousness. Had Seslavin had his way, he would have hauled this estimable personage off for a fourth term to let life in the camps straighten out his crooked consciousness. But there were no orders from above . . . Ilya Iosifovich energetically compiled his dossier on the Soviet people, while Captain Seslavin in the duty of his office resourcefully and painstakingly compiled his dossier on Goldberg.

Both turned out to be hardworking and systematic, and both hoped to achieve their desired results. For this reason Ilya Iosifovich contrived to deliver the manuscript of his "Essays" to a visiting American scientist by passing it through a long chain of friends, acquaintances, and sympathizers indirectly to a performance of *Swan Lake*, where its transmission for eventual publication in a scientific journal took place to the accompaniment of Tchaikovsky's music and the synchronized movement of the muscular legs of the world's best corps de ballet.

Captain Seslavin, knowing nothing about this ideological diversion, had a gut sense for his ward's maleficence, and aspiring no less than Ilya Iosifovich to achieve effective results, approached his administration with a report on the wrongheadedness and overall unreliability of this frigging philosopher. His superiors scratched their collective head and promised to think about it. The first thing they thought up was to summon Ilya Iosifovich for a conversation, which privilege they accorded Seslavin. An experienced hand, Ilya Iosifovich should have demonstrated great restraint in his intercourse with the captain. But the demon of scientific garrulity overcame him, and he blathered the entire two and a half hours almost without interruption. The sheer mass of Goldberg's loquacity made it almost impossible for Seslavin to insert any questions. Goldberg was extraordinarily pleased with himself, and it seemed to him that he had managed to interest the inspector in his ideas and now, like the clever Odysseus, he was already figuring what a stroke of luck it would be if he were able to attract this powerful organization to his side . . . His three terms in the camps had taught Ilya Iosifovich nothing, absolutely nothing.

At 9:30 P.M. Seslavin interrupted Goldberg with unanticipated rudeness, and, contrary to his first impression, it turned out that Goldberg had not succeeded in acquiring a new ally. Just the opposite: Seslavin suddenly stopped nodding understandingly and snarled.

"Here's the deal. You can work with flies as much as you want: that's none of our business. But all those ideas you have about the population— you're going to bring them here first," he knocked on his desk, "and if you don't, you're going to be in major trouble . . . You're better off not arguing with us, Ilya Iosifovich . . ."

As Goldberg deliberated how best to react to the unanticipated situation that had evolved, the secret search and not-so-secret robbery of his apartment was drawing to an end. Arriving close to midnight at the new apartment on Profsoiuznaya Street he had received last year from the Academy of Sciences, he found the door jimmied and the apartment replete with evidence of crude pilfering—the TV, the tape recorder, and the coffee grinder were missing—and vulgar hooliganism: a pile of shit lay in the middle of a room . . .

It looked like Goldberg, with his innate uncontrollable optimism, had grossly overestimated the temperature of the Thaw. But because he had already received news that his essays would be published by a well-known American press, he called Seslavin the next day, met him near the KGB club on Derzhinskaya Street, and handed him the next-to-the-last remaining copy of his "Essays." For all intents and purposes his "Essays" were of no interest to anyone since they were already recorded with their own number; what was important was Goldberg's willingness to cooperate, and Goldberg had demonstrated it: he had brought them what they had told him to.

This time the attack on Goldberg came from an unexpected direction: an audit of the laboratory's financial records was to be carried out. Over the past two years of its existence the laboratory had acquired no small quantity of equipment and various other technology including, for example, raisins for fly food, alcohol for histological work, paper for writing maleficent essays, glassware, chemical reactants, et cetera, et cetera . . . Officially, Goldberg figured as the laboratory's head, but to economize on appointments in favor of research personnel, he had charged an experienced elderly laboratory assistant, Natalia Ivanovna, with keeping the books, while he himself bore legal financial responsibility . . . An Academy audit elicited no emotions except irritation: two drones showed up and dug around in useless paperwork, getting in everyone's way. For two weeks this pair—a fat woman bookkeeper and her skinny assistant with a soldier's posture—dug through papers. And dug up enough for a laughable accusation of embezzlement. Frightened out of her wits, Natalia Ivanovna quickly submitted her resignation, and disappeared without a trace. While Ilya Iosifovich and the staff joked about the affair, the case was handed over to the prosecutor's office. Ilya Iosifovich, with his extensive past, should have taken a moment to reflect, but his recklessness was so great that he realized what hit him only on the day of the hearing when he found a delayed summons in his mailbox in the morning. Even then he failed to realize what sort of threat hung over him. The hearing was set for 3:00 P.M., but all that Ilya Iosifovich succeeded in accomplishing in the fast-ticking hours before lunch was to speak over the phone with a famous lawyer who had just recently acquired the reputation of a human-rights advocate. The lawyer fretted, having recognized the enemy's trademark.

"Under no circumstances should you go to that hearing today," the perceptive lawyer advised. "Your best bet is to go to the polyclinic and get permission to take a sick leave, and then we'll think. They are obliged to reschedule the hearing . . ."

Ilya Iosifovich did not go to court, but he also had no intention of going to the clinic: he felt uncomfortable taking sick leave when he was healthy. However, the morning of the next day, at 9:00 A.M., a visitor with the unmistakable look of a gumshoe awaited him at the lab and introduced himself as an investigator. The embezzlement case quickly took a new turn, the hired lawyer who quickly became a friend at first laughed, then pondered, and finally, following extensive mental effort, decided that the best strategy would be a scrupulous defense on each of the eighteen charges of financial irregularity layered at Goldberg with an insignificant admission of financial wrongdoing, such as an unrecorded check, for propriety's sake, that is, for public censure . . .

The scheme was clever, but failed. Pale and teary-eyed, Natalia Iva-novna gave phantasmal testimony, and Ilya Iosifovich received—as befit the gravity of the financial crime—a full three years in corrective-labor camps. He was taken under guard directly from the courtroom before the eyes of his stunned and indignant staff.

Goldberg's book was already at the typesetter's, but neither the author nor Seslavin's organization knew anything about it. For Goldberg, who had managed yet one more time to outsmart his own fate, a trip north to all-too-familiar territory lay ahead . . .

6

TWO YEARS HAD PASSED SINCE TANYA HAD LEFT HOME, living in various places, with new friends—in the studio of an art-ist acquaintance on Shabolovskaya Street, in a winterized dacha of someone's parents near Zvenigorod, or in caretaker quarters her janitor-caretaker girlfriend inhabited on Molchanovka Street . . .

The last six months a jeweler friend, Nanny Goat Vika—an enormous, unattractive woman with an aristocratic surname and commoner's manners—had sheltered her. She was a cool woman, and Tanya lived with her as sort of an apprentice. As befits an apprentice, she did the housework and ran errands. Nanny Goat's studio was in a half-basement on Vorovskogo Street, and her apartment in a new construction area. Her family of old Muscovites of God knows how many generations had been resettled from Znamenka Street to the Cheryomushki district, but Vika, after moving her mother, two grandmothers, and son, just could not tear herself away from her old neighborhood, and went home to the new apartment only to sleep, and that not every night. Tanya settled herself in a corner room the size of a closet formerly heaped full of pieces of expensive old furniture rescued from local trash bins.

Nanny Goat had hands of steel, a heart of gold, and the mad sensibilities of a truth-seeker. Ages ago she had graduated from radio-engineering trade school, where she had learned how to dexterously manipulate a soldering iron to just the right place on a circuit board. After having casually repaired a few antique rings and earrings for some elderly acquaintances on the Arbat, friends of her two grandmothers, she turned this otherwise unexciting skill into a new profession. She had a ton of work: fix this, create a setting for a stone, or make some simple earrings . . . After a while she discovered that repairs and resettings demanded highly developed intuition and more experience than creating new pieces. She went to study with a famous jeweler, an artist, and owing to a confluence of various strange circumstances, including those related to housing, married him. A few years later he left her, pregnant, but with compensation: his workshop. Along with the studio Nanny Goat inherited his marvelous bohemian lifestyle, which included the drinking, and the parties, and the interesting people from all sectors of society: prim little customers, various fans of just hanging out, self-declared musicians, poets, and philosophers who had strayed from the path of Marxist-Leninism, simply pleasant do-nothings, and, finally, the night people Tanya had observed during the adventures of her first year of freedom—estranged, belonging to no one, like peculiar animals that lived only at night and disappeared to no one knew where during the day. Tanya, however, now knew where they spent the daytime, which was so dangerous for them: in shelters like Vika's studio . . . Tanya came to love the visitors to Vika's studio all at once, in a bunch, almost without making distinctions among them and without studying their faces especially, sensing acutely how different they were from the people she had met at the university and in the laboratory, in stores, and at the conservatory. She learned to distinguish in a crowd those who might show up at Vika's studio.

"Our kind of people," Vika would say with a grin, and no more explanations on the subject were necessary. What precisely did that possessive pronoun entail? Neither social origins nor national identity, neither profession nor level of education, but something elusory connected in part, but not only, with an aversion to Soviet power. In order to be "our kind," you also had to experience a certain discomfort, a certain dissatisfaction with everything that was possible and allowed, and discontent with the existing world as a whole, from the alphabet to the weather, to the Lord God himself, who had done such a lousy job of putting things together . . . In a word, that sense of Russian metaphysical melancholy that came to the surface, like grass at a springtime trash dump, after the permissive Twentieth Party Congress . . . Those who studied the properties of capillary development in the brain, Chinese grammar, or metal spark machining had no chance of becoming "our kind." Although their ranks also included secret adversaries of Soviet power, they practiced the rules of disguise: in the morning they tied their ties, did their hair up, and, most important, kept a loyal expression on their face for eight working hours a day, for precisely which reason they remained in the category of "clients."

"Our kind" of person was uncombed and unkempt and arrived at Vika's studio toward midnight with a bottle of vodka, a guitar stuffed with "our kind" of songs, a new poem by Brodsky (or one's own), or a pinch of hashish, and stayed to spend the night either with Nanny Goat or with Tanya, however the cards fell. "Our-kind-of-ness" trumped personal sexual attraction. Occasionally casual affairs would sprout within their own circle, which required the implementation of certain unwritten rules. Nanny Goat herself was a businesswoman who despised all that lovey-dovey stuff and, having been burned when she was young, extirpated all sentiment from her own life and successfully trained Tanya to do the same. Tanya liked these rules, according to which courting rituals of the variety the Goldberg boys had managed to spread over an entire five-year period were abolished, matters being decided in the short span of an evening at the table, and relations by morning either exhausted or continued, with no obligations attached for either of the dallying parties.

Overall, Tanya's apprenticeship was exceptionally successful, her already disciplined hands readily and joyously acquiring new skills and techniques. She would extract an ingot of silver, formerly a teaspoon, from its soapy mold, pound it with a mallet, heat it on a burner until it turned cherry red, release it, and press it through rollers. Then she pulled it through a wire rolling mill, out of which emerged new thin silver wire ... The work was not complicated, but Nanny Goat turned out to be a strict teacher and monitored Tanya's work to make sure she did everything by the rules, as her former husband, a tiresome pedant, had once taught her. Tanya worked with a passion and quickly converted the entirety of Vika's silver supply into millimeter-sized wire. Now Vika had no choice but to teach Tanya the next important stage of jewelry making, soldering. Here Nanny Goat Vika was a professor. Although she withheld none of the secrets of her craft and generously shared all the mysteries of soft and hard soldering and the slightest differences in color by which to measure the temperature of the melted solder, Tanya never achieved Vika's level of mastery. On the other hand, she quickly mastered the torch: with a deft and lightning-fast movement of her left hand she raised the versatile flame to shoulder level and affixed it to the stand. She never once burned herself. Time passed, and Tanya began to learn how to do settings. She almost wore her thumb down to the bone with a needle file before she learned how to finish a piece for sale. But it appealed to Tanya that her hands—which she used to care for, growing long nails that she manicured—were now covered with grazes and scars of varying degrees of newness, just like a boy's ... She turned body and soul toward masculinity—cut her hair short, slipped on her first pair of jeans, which would replace all other options, bought two boys' plaid shirts at the Detsky Mir department store, threw out her bras, and gave Toma all her blouses with their round collars and lacy inserts sewn to her mother's taste . . . A unisex Chinese jacket lined with crude dog fur, dark blue, like everything working-class Chinese, and a rabbit fur cap with earflaps completed her new image, and people on the street would address her as "young man," which she also liked. Even Tanya's gait changed, became more abrupt with a swagger to her shoulders . . .

She had already turned twenty-two, but seemed to be experiencing her teenage years anew. Although her nocturnal sorties had ended almost entirely, she still treasured nighttime the most, especially those solitary nights when Vika would leave for the evening for Cheryomushki, hauling two bags of food from the Prague restaurant carryout store for her elderly female relatives, to kiss and shower presents on her little Mishka, fight with her mother, make peace with one of her grandmothers, and argue with the other. Relations in their family were stormy: they couldn't let a day pass without tears, verbal abuse, and passionate kisses. On returning from Cheryomushki, Nanny Goat was always very invigorated and slightly aggressive, as though family turmoil opened up new sources of energy in her.

Tanya visited her own family infrequently. She usually arrived toward evening. The apartment, which had once been very light, now seemed gloomy at all times of day. Tomochka's tropical vegetation consumed the light. The place was dusty and faded; only the ever-green leaves Toma was never too lazy to wipe down with a damp sponge gleamed with a waxy shimmer. Her mother, sitting in an armchair that had shaped itself to her lightweight body, rustled the woolen yarn that she either knitted—her knitting needles tinkling rhythmically—or undid with a quiet electric-like whirr. Balls of old wool covered with knots and the tails of knots turned softly at her feet. Two striped cats, Murka-mother and Murka-daughter, lazily pawed the rolling gray balls that picked up clumps of the cats' shed fur and dust balls from the poorly swept floor.

Tanya would sit down alongside her mother, on the spinning piano stool. Elena Georgievna happily smiled when she saw Tanya.

"My little girl, I wanted . . ." Elena began to say, but did not finish her sentence.

"What, Mommy?"

Elena fell silent, having lost the thread of her passing desire. Unlike the broken wool that she caught and knotted together, she could not reconnect either her thoughts or her sentences at the point where they split, and pained by this, she attempted somehow to hide this terrible condition from those around her.

"Would you like me to bring you some tea?" Tanya offered the first thing that came into her head.

"I don't want tea . . . Tell me . . ." And once again she fell silent.

"What are you knitting?" Tanya made a new attempt at communicating.

"Here . . . I'm knitting this for you . . . ," Elena answered in confusion and smiled guiltily. "I undid it a bit . . ."

Elena did not know what she was knitting. When her work turned into a rectangle and she needed either to drop a stitch or pick up and knit the collar, she would become confused, undo the whole thing, and start all over again . . . Tanya quickly tired of the strain of their conversation, of the impossibility of communicating: her mother, of course, was sick, but her sickness was something very bizarre . . . A kind of slow deterioration . . .

"Do you want to go for a walk?" Tanya offered.

Elena looked at her in fright: "Outside?"

Following those awful lapses of memory that had happened to her outside the apartment, she completely stopped going out. It was difficult for her even to leave her own room. When she needed to make her way to the washroom or the kitchen, she would pick up a cat, because the cat's warmth would lend her a sense of balance. Thoughts of the world that lay beyond the confines of their apartment evoked a wild terror in her. She was ashamed of this terror and attempted to hide it.

"Not today," she would say childishly, and searched with her eyes for one of the Murkas. Her helpless and almost infantile intonation and convulsive searching for a cat flustered Tanya as well.

"Tell me something . . ." Elena asked vaguely.

"About what?" Tanya hid behind the empty words because it was impossible for her to tell anything about her current life.

Elena smiled pathetically. "About something . . ."

Their conversation about nothing lasted half an hour, then Tanya went to the kitchen, put on the teakettle, took note of the household's degeneration and desolation, the unscoured pots and poorly washed cups . . . But there was food in the house: in the evenings Toma would bring home what she had managed to grab between work and her evening classes.

Then her father would arrive and, he too, instead of his former strength and power, emanated aging and decline ... His field of energy, at one time so powerful and magnetic, had grown exhausted, and Tanya felt uncomfortable looking at him: it seemed as if he had committed some shameful act and wanted to hide it.

Pavel Alekseevich had shrunk and grown thin, his shoulders drooped, and his forehead and cheeks were deeply furrowed, as if his skin had become a size larger. He was happy to see Tanya, and at first his boxer-looking face would light up with all its doglike furrows, but it quickly paled when he saw Tanya's sadness and poorly disguised pity. He suffered, like an abandoned lover, but out of pride never initiated the conversation: the easy, happy dialogue that could arise at any point between two people who understood each other no longer existed between them ...

Vasilisa, now totally blind, would emerge from her pantry. She felt so sure of herself in the kitchen that her blindness was almost not noticeable. She set the table, warmed up soup for Pavel Alekseevich, and even placed a grubby three-ounce shot glass next to his plate ... She made her way around the apartment by running one hand along the wall, her rummaging hands having traced the dark band of the trajectory of her movements on the blue-and-yellow wallpaper. She moved soundlessly on the mended soles of her old felt boots, and it was amazing how she still preserved her village smells—a combination of sour milk, hay dust, and even, it seemed, a whiff of smoke from a wood-burning stove ...

Her parents' house depressed Tanya and saddened her. She rarely ran into Toma these days, but each time she dropped by the house she would leave her a present: a ring with a cornelian, a pendant, or a package of cheap cookies.

At the end of February Tanya had her first sale: she made real money for real work. Fifty rubles for a silver ring with a transparent black smoky quartz, a tender oval stone she had worked on for two days. At one time her salary as a laboratory assistant had been thirty-eight rubles and fifty kopecks, so the jewelry sale seemed like easy mad money, and she decided to spend it all on presents for everyone.

She borrowed a shopping bag from Nanny Goat and did as her mentor: she loaded a bag with pedigree goods from the Arbat—Indian tea, cakes, cookies. For some reason that day they had put on sale a rare shipment of English cosmetics and German cigarettes. She bought those as well. She bought her father a bottle of Armenian cognac, although she knew he preferred vodka. But cognac was classier.

She was met by Pavel Alekseevich, who had already consumed his evening dose. He pressed her head in its gray rabbit fur fitfully to his chest and winced.

"Tanya, there's been such trouble ... They beat up Vitalik Goldberg. Genka came in from Obninsk and called. I just came back from the Sklifosovsky Hospital. His condition is serious. I talked to the doctor. He has a skull fracture. His arm is broken, his nose too. He still hasn't regained consciousness ... Ilyusha's book has come out in the States ... It's a mess ..."

Tanya did not even set the heavy bag on the floor, but just stood there in the doorway, stunned by the news. Although of late she had hardly any contact with them, the Goldberg boys were more relatives than friends.

Tanya set the bag on the floor and began to cry. Pavel Alekseevich pulled the wet rabbit cap and heavy jacket off his daughter.

"The KGB?" Tanya suddenly asked soberly.

"Looks like it. He got pounded by professionals. They didn't want to kill. If they had wanted to, they would have."

Vasilisa stood in her usual place in the corridor near the corner between the kitchen and the entrance hall, and seemed to be looking in their direction.

"Tanya, is that you?"

"It's me, me, Vasya. I brought presents."

"Presents? For what?" Vasilisa was amazed. It was Lent, hardly the time for presents.

"I bought you some Armenian cognac." Tanya smiled with moist eyes, and Pavel Alekseevich perked up, not at the cognac, of course, which to this day his patients brought him in quantities that exceeded human consumption, but at Tanya's smile, just like before, her usual former smile, as if all the recent years of alienation had not happened between them.

"Let's go see Momma, and then you and I will drink some of your cognac. Okay?" Pavel Alekseevich proposed and nudged Tanya in the direction of her mother's room.

"Did you tell her about Vitalik?" Tanya asked in a whisper.

Pavel Alekseevich shook his head: "We shouldn't."

They sat together, the three of them, for the first time in several years. Elena in her armchair, Tanya on her bed, which smelled either of cats or stale urine. Pavel Alekseevich drew closer, together with his round stool.

"So should we have a little drink, girls?" he asked buoyantly, then suddenly stopped short. Elena looked at him with horror.

"Have a drink, have a drink, Mom," Tanya shouted unexpectedly, instantly bringing her cognac in from the corridor.

Pavel Alekseevich went to get glasses.

"Do you think that . . . Is it true . . . Pavel Alekseevich says . . ." Elena uttered uncertainly and incoherently, but doubtless in protest.

"Mom, one glass . . ."

Pavel Alekseevich stood in the doorway with three unmatched wineglasses. It turned out that Lenochka had not forgotten everything on earth: she had just remembered that her husband was an alcoholic. The sight of the bottle made her nervous for her husband . . .

"It's good for you, Lenochka. It's good for your circulation." Pavel Alekseevich grinned.

Elena extended her hand uncertainly and awkwardly clutched the wet green wineglass. Her knitting slid off her knees and fell to the floor. Murka Jr. pawed it immediately. Elena got upset, the wineglass tipped, and a bit of cognac spilled out.

"Look, Tanya . . . It's all fallen down . . . Like that . . . Wet . . ." She was not able to put down the wineglass and pick up her knitting: that was too complicated a sequence of actions . . . Pavel Alekseevich picked up the knitting and placed it on the bed. He poured for himself and for Tanya.

"To your health, Mommy."

Elena moved the wineglass in the air in front of her, Tanya leaned the glass toward her mouth, and she drank it. They sat together for almost an hour, silent and smiling. They slowly drank the cognac and ate the cakes. Then Elena suddenly uttered completely coherently and distinctly, as she had not spoken for years already: "What a nice evening it is today, Tanechka. How nice it is that you came home. Pashenka, do you remember Karantinnaya Street?"

"What Karantinnaya Street?" Pavel Alekseevich was surprised.

Elena smiled, the way adults smile at children who don't yet understand. "In Siberia, remember? The place you brought us from to the hospital . . . We had a good life there. At the hospital."

"We don't have it too bad now either, Lenochka." He placed his hand on her head and stroked her cheek. She caught his hand and kissed it . . .

The strangest things would happen: Pavel Alekseevich could not remember any Karantinnaya Street. But Elena remembered. How could memory be so whimsical? Twenty years spent living together, of which one of them remembered one thing; the other—something else. To what extent had that life been spent together, if their memories of one and the same thing were so different?

Gena Goldberg arrived shortly after. He told what little he had found out about yesterday's incident. His brother had returned home late and was beaten up in the entrance to their building. He had been found only in the early morning by a neighbor of theirs hooked on jogging who had come out after six in the morning to perform his athletic feats. Vitaly's coworkers said that over the past week he had received several threatening phone calls.

"Did they call you?" Tanya asked.

"What's the point of calling me: I'm far away from all that." Gena seemed to be justifying himself.

By all appearances the matter appeared to be linked with the fact that Vitaly had just returned from Yakutia, where he had been gathering anthropological data on northern peoples. He had been summoned by the security services and requested to hand over all the material he had collected on his research trip on the grounds that his topic was about to be classified as secret. He refused. The secret had been known to the whole world for a long time already: ethnic groups in the North were drinking themselves to death, and the populations of Yakuts and other tribes had shrunk four times over the last twenty years. All of this fit Ilya Goldberg's theory about the genetic decimation of the Soviet people perfectly logically, but it did not fit the conception underlying that golden wonder at the All-Union Agricultural Exhibition known as the "Fountain of Friendship of Nations."

A bit later Toma arrived. They invited her to drink together with everyone else what was left at the bottom of the bottle. One glass made her drunk and she began to laugh loudly. The evening was ruined. Tanya kissed her mother and her father, put on her Chinese coat, and remembering Vasilisa, went already dressed to say good-bye to her. She entered the tiny pantry and switched on the light. The lightbulb had burned out long ago, but Vasilisa did not know that. She turned her head at the sound of the switch.

"Tanya?"

Tanya kissed Vasilisa on the crown of her head, covered with her black headscarf.

"Tell me what to bring you?"

"I don't need anything. Just bring yourself," Vasilisa answered disagreeably.

"I do come by . . ."

Tanya walked out into the street with Gena. He wanted to see her home.

Toma led Elena into the bathroom to replace with a dry layer the multilayered rags rolled into a soft pad inside her old bathing suit stretched over even more spacious underpants. Toma paid not the slightest attention to her shamed resistance: she did this every evening, and every evening she chanted her tongue twister, without the slightest note of reproach.

"Now hold on, Mommy, hold on. We have to change the wet ones . . . You're making it difficult for me."

Then she washed and dried poor Elena, doing it all dexterously and roughly, like underpaid attendants in hospitals. Elena was so ashamed that she closed her eyes and just switched off. She had this little, subtle movement called "Imnothere." Then Toma nudged Elena ahead of her, led her into her bedroom, and tucked her in. After that she called Vasilisa, who sat at Elena's feet and took to muttering her evening encomium—a long, scrunched prayer pasted together from scraps of prayer formulas, psalms, and her own vociferations, the most frequently reminisced of which was "a Christian death, peaceful, painless, and without shame . . ."

With bright eyes that from year to year grew lighter and lighter, at one time having been deep blue and now turned smoky gray, Elena looked out from one darkness into another . . .

7

AS FOR HER RELATIONSHIP WITH THE GOLDBERG BROTH-
ers all that Tanya could say was that was the way it had turned out. Since
childhood both of them had crushes on her and competed agonizingly
for her. Tanya turned out to be a severe test of their bonds as twins, the
closest of bonds that connect human beings: in the human world where
immaculate conception is attributed only to Mary of Nazareth, even
mother and son cannot achieve the same degree of proximity in biological composition as monozygotic twins. So said Goldberg's exact science
of genetics.

The Goldberg brothers withstood the test honorably: by unspoken
agreement they always visited the Kukotsky household together, calling first by phone to announce "it's us, the Goldbergs," even though the
technical capabilities of telephony always dictated that only one of them
spoke. If they invited Tanya to the theater or the cinema, they unfailingly
traipsed together as a foursome, with the bland Toma as compulsory
addendum to Tanya's knockout charm. They never spoke about Tanya
between themselves, unless to make a statement or indirectly.

"Let's go to the Kukotskys' on Saturday . . ."

"I bought tickets to the theater for next Sunday . . ."

And that was the end of the conversation.

Each of the boys individually had all the makings of an intolerable
child with a superior intellect and egocentrically deformed personality,
but the presence of Tanya in their lives in some strange way counterbal-
anced the dangerous circumstance of their being one step short of Jewish
Wunderkinder with an ineradicable and almost justified sense of superiority over everyone else around. In the bitter years of their early manhood
and later in their lives they would be forced to make sense of the particular significance of that "almost." Tanya would give them a good run
in this respect. Curly-haired, cheerful, and absolutely unconcerned with
how those around her felt about her—likely because she had lots of evidence of being surrounded by people's love from all sides—Tanya was
beyond competition, if only for the reason that she was two grades behind
them in school. There was two years' difference in age between them and,
in addition to everything else, she belonged to a different, female world,

plus, at least until they were fifteen, she was taller than they were, and stronger—and it never would have occurred to either of them to match their strength against hers: for all these reasons they both were willing to submit to her, to serve her, and to provide her various pleasures commensurate with their age . . . In passing, with a flourish of the angled hem of her checkered skirt, she, without knowing it herself, had dismantled the strict intellectual hierarchy in which the still unmarried Ilya Iosifovich for the moment still held first place, followed, nose to nose, by the brothers, who were breathing down his collar, with everyone else left in their wake. Except Tanya . . . She was beyond . . . to the left or right. Her game was, essentially, not quite honest, as if during a game of chess she changed the rules without telling her opponent and won by shooting all her opponents' pieces off the board and onto the floor with the snap of her thumb and middle finger . . . It was precisely this about Tanya that delighted the Goldberg brothers, and not her ash-blond curls or vigorous pounding on the piano . . . A hierarchy of intelligence turned out thereby not to be the only scale by which values were determined . . .

From an early age the brothers' tastes and preferences had been similar, but their mother had known almost from the moment of their birth that one of them, Gena, who was born twenty minutes later—the younger one, that is—cried just a bit harder and laughed just a bit louder. His needs were more dramatic and his fears more explicit. In any case, it was precisely five-year-old Vitalik, the relatively older one, who would ask Gena: "What kind of cereal do we like more?"

And Gena would decide that they preferred buckwheat . . .

Their worship of Tanya to a certain extent spared them from the comic role of *Wunderkinder*: they voluntarily, if not entirely appropriately, relegated first place to Tanya. The school in Malakhovka was unable to appreciate the boys' talents—A students were all alike. Through the hardships of postwar existence to the day of her premature death, ingenuous Valentina—who worked as a laboratory assistant until 1953, when, in the heat of antisemitism, she was fired—never discerned her children's talents, while their egocentric father, himself descended from a breed of *Wunderkinder*, for precisely that reason regarded his boys' rare abilities as entirely to be expected. In addition, the brothers raised the bar for each other not only in relation to Tanya, but in physics, chemistry, and mathematics. For

Tanya, basically, it was more interesting talking to Vitalik insofar as he was inclined toward medicine and they had more topics in common, but to tell the truth, as boyfriends she much preferred other boys who might not possess such exceptional knowledge in the field of the natural sciences but knew how to cut loose, boogying to the rock 'n' roll that had filtered through the pores of the Iron Curtain . . .

Now, after Ilya Goldberg had been arrested and appeared—unlike in previous years—to be an innocent suffering hero (it was the middle of the sixties!), his sons were illuminated by their father's reflected light. Especially after Vitalka's nighttime beating in the entranceway . . .

Tanya and Gena walked out of the Kukotsky apartment a little after eleven o'clock. Gena knew that Tanya was not living at home, and over the past year they had not seen or called each other. Tanya seethed with compassion for Vitalka and immediately wanted to take part in hospital vigils over him. Gena, for the first time in many years, was alone with Tanya, and unexpectedly a completely new configuration arose in which Vitalka existed separately, while he and Tanya were together, unified entirely in their sympathy and compassion. While Vitalka—entangled in tubes, with freshly placed stitches along his cheekbone and the bridge of his nose, in plaster cast and with an IV drip—half-slumbered behind the glass divider of his isolation ward, Gena, having seized her by the dark-blue sleeve of her jacket, led Tanya to the metro, attempting to persuade her to spend the night on Profsoiuznaya Street, in order to be able to rush off to the Sklif first thing in the morning without losing time . . .

Tanya hesitated a bit: ordinarily she warned Nanny Goat in advance if she planned not to spend the night in the workshop. There was no phone there. Tanya wavered; Gena was resolutely determined . . . Generally speaking, leaving him was not a good idea, and she headed off for Profsoiuznaya Street, where she had never been before.

The two-room apartment in a Khrushchev-period five-story panel building looked as if the search had ended only a couple of hours ago. More accustomed to order than to cleanliness, having, essentially, rebelled against the inflexible logic of order and spent two years wandering around chance apartments and finding shelter ultimately in a workshop among small metal parts, old canvas stretchers, and heaps of broken furniture, Tanya stopped dead in her tracks at the sight of the elemental chaos of scribbled paper that flooded tables and chairs and cascaded in broad waves onto the floor. Footpaths had been marked out among the papers—one to water and another to food, one to the table and another to the bathroom—with newspapers spread over the scribbled paper; tea fields had formed with troops of variegated teacups brown from tea stains on the inside and dirty on the outside. Peaceful herds of fattened cockroaches grazed the scientific pastures.

"How can you live here?" Tanya, by now used to everything, was amazed.

"It's not a problem. For the most part I'm in Obninsk. And Dad and Vitalka are here. But we don't let anyone in the apartment so as not to scare anyone." He flashed his big teeth, resembling white beans. "It's even worse in Malakhovka. When Mama was alive there was some order. How she maintained it I have no idea . . ."

"No, no, this is impossible." Not yet having removed her jacket, Tanya tried to decide which side they should begin cleaning from. "We'll start with the kitchen," she announced.

The decision turned out to be the right one. There were fewer papers in the kitchen, and the usual household dirt did not demand as close attention as the paper trash. Multilayered deposits peeled off the stove in sheets; the sewage-gray linoleum easily washed clean thanks to a packet of laundry detergent found in the bathroom. The main rooms went more slowly: the papers begged to be read, and from time to time some particularly intricate sheet would inhibit their progress. The effort required was more than Herculean: horse manure could be thrown out blindly.

From midnight until four thirty in the morning they merrily cleaned four-hand. They chatted, giggled, and recollected childhood secrets; everything was easy, and the filth flowed down the toilet, while the papers got stacked in drawers, which was also rather funny: the desk drawers had all been completely empty. The people who had conducted the quasi-robbery search had taken only what was in the desk; the other papers, of more recent vintage, spread in massive layers on all work and nonwork surfaces, had been left untouched . . .

"Your brother's strange," Tanya announced toward the end. "Ilya Iosifovich has been in prison for half a year already, and he still hasn't cleaned the apartment."

"You don't understand: this is a memorial, an apartment-museum . . ."

At half past four a couch covered with a dusty horse blanket emerged from under multiple layers of paper deposits. Tanya collapsed on it, raising a cloud of dust.

"Enough. Time to sleep," Tanya commanded, and Gena, who had spent several hours suppressing various urges—from sweet tenderness to bestial desire—did not keep himself waiting . . .

After spending the full reserve munitions of a young warrior and not having slept for two full days, he sank into sleep, continuing all the while to be amazed by this state of acute tenderness and equally acute beastliness . . .

"Where does that feeling of having done something underhanded, of some sort of guilt, come from?" he managed to think as he fell asleep. A voice within him answered sternly: "She's your sister, after all . . ."

Tanya thought of nothing of the sort: the fellow she had been sleeping with most recently was a hard-core geologist, promiscuous to the point of sainthood, with an innumerable number of children by café waitresses and academicians' wives, and no worse and no better than this sweet little friend of hers since childhood. Tanya saw nothing particularly charming about a roll in the sack in and of itself and was always surprised by her older girlfriends and the way they went crazy over men: in bed all are equal . . . At the time she still did not know that this was not quite so.

They arrived at the Sklif not by nine, as they had planned, but toward noon. At first they could not wake up, then Gena reaffirmed his new rights. By that time Vitalka had been transferred from intensive care to a regular ward: his condition had improved and he had regained consciousness and no longer intended to die.

8

A YEAR HAD PASSED SINCE A MURKY FILM HAD TOTALLY clouded over Vasilisa's sole eye and darkness had occluded her vision. Blindness, a misfortune and terrible threat for the elderly, had liberated her from constant labor.

So began her lawful release from work, beyond which blind Vasilisa envisioned her final unlimited and boundless recumbency. Her constant activity directed outward now turned inward. Before she had prayed to icons. She had several: a dark three-tone Theotokos from Kazan executed in cursory traveling merchant style, an Elijah the Prophet split in half by some stupid ax and crudely glued together so that the Prophet's face had been preserved, but the cape that hung from the chariot for the most part did not fall in Elisha's arms, having broken off to remain as a chip in the village church and to burn up along with it. There was also a Saint Seraphim of Sarov with an earless bear, and a drowning Peter—halo shifted to one side and arm extended toward a Savior walking past him in the opposite direction. Now it was as if she were deprived of all these protectors. She stood on her knees in her usual place where the rug was bald from her kneeling and attempted to resurrect them in her memory, but could not. The darkness that enveloped her hung like a smooth wall with no shades or points of light whatsoever. This went on for a rather long while, and Vasilisa grieved: it seemed to her that her prayers hung in the stale air near her head and rose neither to the Lord, nor to the Lord's Mother, nor to God's saintly miracle workers. Then something like a flickering candle flame began to cut through the darkness. The flame was so weak and so unsteady that Vasilisa feared that it might be some charm of her imagination. But it was so alluring, that bright spot, it so gladdened her, that Vasilisa beckoned it from within and tried to hold on to the image of light a bit longer. And the unsteady light grew and became stronger, and shone, visible to no one, in her private gloom, moving her to incessant and almost wordless prayer. Her prayers now were only about the "little flame," as she called it, that it not leave her. Even in her sleep her prayer did not abandon her, as if it dozed alongside her, like the old Murka who had long ago chosen for her night lodgings the space alongside Vasilisa's skinny, cold legs.

So it was that Vasilisa thought that she had found a completely new, easier life for herself without her usual never-ending chores—without all those excessive, by her understanding, purchases of food, without washing large loads of hardly soiled laundry, and without enormous deck-swabbing housecleanings—leaving herself only her almost ritual duties of washing Elena in the morning and meeting Pavel Alekseevich after work. The larger part of the day she spent in her pantry in subtle meditation comprehensible only to Eastern monks ... A blend of prayer-filled contemplation, spiritual communication—with the abbess, Mother Anatolia, with whom, of late, thanks to her blindness, she had grown even closer than before—and loving reminiscence of all those living and dead, close and distant, beginning with her own parents and the eternally memorable Varsonofy and ending with the nameless faces of the nuns of the N monastery, long ago deceased ... by the light of that tiny flame that she had learned to fan within herself, as she would a coal in a stove ...

Every day, as he accepted from Vasilisa's hands his pauper's dinner, completely indistinguishable from the hospital dinner the practical nurse brought him at work, Pavel Alekseevich reproached himself for not being able to overcome Vasilisa's stubbornness: he was convinced that all she had was just a banal cataract that could be removed and her sight at least partially restored. He was not some absentminded professor incapable of turning on a gas burner. He could warm up his own food, he could even prepare it, but to deprive Vasilisa Gavrilovna of performing her duties he could not, yet to accept the services of a blind servant was also untenable ...

Again and again he spoke to her about an operation. Vasilisa, though, did not want to hear about it, invoking God's will, which determined everything for her ... Pavel Alekseevich got angry, could not make sense of her, and tried, using her logic, to convince her that God's will lay precisely in that a doctor given the call to operate on the blind would perform an operation on her, and she would be able to see the light, if only to sing the praises of God ... She shook her head, and then he got even angrier, accused her of cowardice, illiteracy, and playing the holy fool ...

Each time he drank just a bit more than usual, Pavel Alekseevich started in anew with Vasilisa. But no line of reasoning could move her. Then once, Toma, without at all having spoken with Pavel Alekseevich, but simply having hauled an enormous bundle of linen from the laundry up five flights of stairs (the elevator was not working that day) and completely drained, accidentally uttered the only words that would convince her.

"Look, Aunt Vasya, you're so strong and healthy you could haul water, but all you do is pray ... Why don't you at least come with me ..."

Despite her scrawniness, Toma in fact came from a hardy breed: she spent whole days on end pottering with her green babies, pushing her nose to the ground, tirelessly digging and weeding. The blood of the peasant had spoken in her: what she had not wanted to do for trite beets and carrots she did with tenderness and passion for rhododendrons and choisya.

She had never liked doing housework, which now required more and more of her time, and now she was enrolled at an evening trade school and in fact very busy.

For a whole day Vasilisa carried this reproach—vented by Toma in a fit of temper—inside her. As always, she thought slowly and assiduously, calling upon Mother Anatolia for help. Finally, on Sunday evening, after supper, she informed Pavel Alekseevich that she was agreed to an operation.

"But you didn't want to do it." Pavel Alekseevich was surprised. "First we need to show you to an oculist. For a consultation ... Maybe they won't agree to do it ..."

"Why not? I'm agreed. Let them cut ..."

The doctors found no contraindications. Two weeks later Vasilisa Gavrilovna was operated on at the eye institute on Gorky Street. Sixty percent of her sight was restored, and Vasilisa returned to her former household chores—once again she did the shopping, stood in lines, cooked their food, and did the laundry. Only her step remained unsure, wary, as if she were carrying some fragile precious object—her only seeing eye. Pavel Alekseevich's words about God's will effected by the hands of doctors had touched her heart. Although she remembered perfectly the entire operation—performed under local anesthetic—from the first acutely painful shot in her eye until the moment when they removed the bandage and she saw people, vague and quivering, like trees in the wind, she was constantly reminded of the New Testament story of Christ healing the man blind from birth, and she linked the doctors' fiddling with her numbed eye with the Savior's touching of the young blind man's dead eye.

No one in the house guessed the extent to which Vasilisa's attitude toward herself changed after she recovered her sight: she became filled with respect for her strong, eternally virginal body, for her muscular, calloused feet and hands, and especially for her unseeing, tearing eye which had upped and begun to see. The inner light that had illuminated her in times of total blindness had left her, and now, in her restored sightedness, she could not see it at all. She longed for her lost "little flame," but remained strongly convinced that it would return to her again when her temporarily resurrected eye would once again go out.

Having reacquired her lost sight, she understood in what vain and fruitless fear for her last eye she had spent the larger part of her life. Only after having lost what remained of her sight was she able to liberate herself from that fear, and now, after the operation, having seen God's earth anew, she found new faith not in God—her faith in God had never required reaffirmation—but in God's love directed at her personally, at bent, stupid, and ignorant Vasilisa. She began to respect that same Vasilisa as the object of God's personal love ... Now she knew for sure that the Lord God set her apart from the enormous human multitude ...

A completely new, outlandish thought crept into her head: that God loved her even more than others ... Take Tanya: beautiful, wealthy, talented from birth, but she had left home to live the life of a vagabond, in other people's spaces, and not out of need, but of her own free will ... Or Pavel Alekseevich: what an imposing, famous man, the doctor of all doctors. How many children had he done away with: countless numbers, over his head in sin. Plus he drank, like a lowlife loser, like her deceased brother, God be with him ... There was nothing to be said for Elena: what had happened to her was obvious as the palm of your hand. Kind, and quiet, and compassionate, she felt sorry for every last cat, but had forgotten about Flotov! Wasn't that on her conscience? What else was God punishing her for? He'd taken away her mind and all her senses. She lived like an animal ...

Vasilisa now treated Elena condescendingly, like a domesticated animal that needed to be fed and cleaned ... She spoke with her as with a cat: into the air with inarticulate words of approval or discontent ... No, there was nothing to discuss here—if the Lord had singled out anyone, it was she, Vasilisa. First He had taken her eye away, and then returned it ... How else could you make sense of it?

9

TANYA WENT TO THE HOSPITAL EVERY DAY AND ASSISTED Vitalka with his needs, from bathing to eating. His right hand was in a cast, and with only the left he had a hard time reading—turning pages was a challenge . . . He somewhat exaggerated his infirmity and allowed himself even to be capricious. Every day, with Vika's shopping bag—which she had not yet returned—Tanya traveled from Profsoiuznaya to Sklifosovsky Hospital. Friends of the Goldbergs contributed a pile of money, and Tanya translated it into various culinary delicacies. Her workouts at the stove entirely replaced her exercises in jewelry-making. Tanya dropped in at Vika's studio only once, grabbed three pairs of underpants, woolen socks, and her notepad—everything she owned.

Every Saturday Gena came in from Obninsk. They would eat supper, drink a bottle of Georgian wine, sleep on the couch pressed flat by bony old Goldberg, and travel together to visit Vitalka at the hospital. The childlike ease of their relations perplexed Gena: it was as if they were five years old, playing on swings or at blindman's bluff, guessing in the dark, touching the face and shoulders of whoever happened to fall into their casual embraces . . . Nature had provided them each other for their needs, and no superfluous words occurred between them . . .

Vitalik lay in the hospital for a month and a half. His injuries ultimately proved to be not as grave as they were complex. His broken nose was reset, the new one no worse than the old, and his concussion also was nothing out of the ordinary, but his broken elbow required some serious tinkering. They performed one operation, which turned out not as well as it might and led to pseudarthrosis. The doctors had to perform a second operation, after which the joint lost all flexibility. Either those masters of fisticuffs really knew how to produce the worst possible fractures, or Vitalka's particular brand of bad luck had been at work.

Be what may, they released him at the end of winter, and Tanya brought him home with a great deal of celebration and even arranged a small party for close friends to mark the occasion. The next Saturday, as usual, Gena arrived from Obninsk. Vitalik had been home three days already. Crossing the threshold, Gena immediately sensed that he had been replaced. He was madly disappointed, but not surprised. He looked Tanya right in the eye, but she felt not the least discomfort. The three of them ate dinner together. On the table there was a fat yeasty pie that breathed warmth and homey comfort. Tanya served Vitalka as if he were a child, and Gena understood that his brother, apparently, had had a stroke of luck. He also wondered whether his brother understood that he had stolen his lover . . .

Meanwhile Tanya washed the dishes and declared that she would be spending the night at home.

"Besides, you probably have things to talk about without me hanging around . . ."

The brothers indeed had things to talk about. The laboratory their father had directed had been closed because of those mythical financial violations. Goldberg senior had been informed of this in camp. What worried him was both the laboratory's future and the problems his staff inevitably would have, Valentina in particular. She had already been fired from the laboratory, deprived of her temporary residence pass in the graduate school dormitory, and after dragging her from office to office in the ministry, they ultimately had shipped her back to Novosibirsk, where no one offered her a position of any sort. A letter from Goldberg to his sons had arrived several days earlier. The letter contained a clumsy and long overdue declaration of love for Valentina, plaintive phrases about his love for their deceased mother, and an abashed declaration of his intention of marrying.

Obviously, the announcement contained nothing new for the young men: they had known everything about their father's affair, but their father had not considered it necessary to inform them of anything until just before he had been shipped off. Most likely, he had had no intention of marrying Valentina, and the idea had occurred to him only in prison. Visitation was allowed only for spouses, and, it seemed, there was an official means for them to legalize their marriage in the camp. Precisely in this regard Goldberg asked his sons to contact his lawyer and find a clever way to tackle the problem. He would say nothing to Valentina of his intentions until he was sure that their marriage was at least theoretically possible.

"I don't want to cause anyone any needless concern, my dears, but I ask you to take this clarification on yourselves insofar as V—a strong and exceptionally noble person—is nonetheless a woman, and I am completely sure that for her to approach a lawyer with this question would be unbearably humiliating."

"She's our age?" Vitalik pointed to the spot in the letter Gena read aloud.

"She's only two years older than us. Maybe three."

"Our stepmother." Vitaly smirked.

Vitalik, who had not yet entirely comprehended the new happiness bestowed on him, would have liked to inform his brother that he himself was ready to get married, but he held his tongue. They had competed for Tanya for too long—almost their entire conscious lifetime—for him to just come out and announce his dazzling victory, which signified simultaneously the unconditional defeat of his other. He even felt pain for his brother, almost as if he were Gena. For the time being the subtle question of why Tanya had preferred him did not concern Vitalik. She had turned out to be an unexpected prize following everything he had undergone. But, ultimately, even if he had been forced to undergo even greater hardships in order to win her, he would have agreed to them willingly.

Gena had the advantage of having been first, but he was not talking. Probably, Vitalka would not be very pleased by the news that his brother had spent six Saturday nights, passionate weekend nights, from Saturday to Sunday, here with Tanya ...

In keeping with the unspoken agreement between them, they did not talk about Tanya. But they did talk at length about their father and his endless and old-fashioned naïveté. And about his courage. And about his talent. And about his honor. And about how lucky they were to have such a tremendous father.

Then, Gena, as the elder, took action. In the evening he set off for Obninsk, having told his brother that he had an appointment scheduled with his department head the next day.

At eleven o'clock, after shutting the door behind his brother, Vitalik immediately dialed the Kukotskys' number and even prepared that little phrase from their childhood: "It's us, the Goldberg brothers ..." Tanya, however, was not at home. She had not been there at all that evening ... She was sitting at Nanny Goat's and matter-of-factly relating the story of the twins, which had occurred completely by chance and entirely to no purpose ... Vika laughed resoundingly, recollecting Shakespeare,

Aristophanes, and Thomas Mann, while Tanya drank Georgian wine and grimaced . . .

"They're like brothers to me. We grew up together. I love them both."

Vika raised her round womanly shoulder, pouted her dry lips, cupped the soft rolls of her breasts squeezed in pink knitted fabric in her rigid, iron-stained palms, and bounced them up and down as on a scale.

"So take them both. Only together. That'll be a high."

Tanya looked at her seriously as if at a mathematics lesson.

"You know, that's a thought. It's not the high itself that interests me especially. But at least no one would feel left out . . . And it would be honest."

Vika doubled over with laughter.

The next Saturday Gena did not come in from Obninsk. Tanya barely managed to get through to him on the phone. He informed her dryly that he was extremely busy and unable to visit in the foreseeable future. She quickly gathered her things and set off for Obninsk. March was in its final freezing days, and Tanya froze numb in the suburban train. She searched a long time for the dormitory and found it only near evening. Gena she found in bed: he had an awful cold and was covered with two blankets and someone's old overcoat. The room was desperately cold; water spilled on the windowsill had turned into an icy crust.

"My poor, poor boys," Tanya mumbled, warming Gena's hands on her breast. He had a temperature of just under 102 degrees, and it seemed to Tanya as if her hands lay on a frying pan.

"You're frozen to the core." Gena laughed, having reached the limits of the possible.

"Yes," Tanya agreed. "Thoroughly. But you're very hot."

Gradually their temperatures balanced out.

Gena went to the communal kitchen to put on a teapot. He had an immersion heater, but the high voltage blew out the fuses. The entire dorm was heated with electric ranges and heaters.

They drank their tea. There was no food, and no place to buy any. The half-empty stores had closed long ago. They warmed each other up again. Toward morning Gena asked Tanya if she wanted to make a choice.

"I've already made one," Tanya answered seriously. "I've chosen the Goldberg brothers."

"There are two of us."

"I know that."

"And?"

"And nothing. I don't see any difference. You or Vitalka, it's all the same . . ." Tanya waved her arms. "Essentially, I love your father a lot too."

Gena sat up from his pillow.

"You can leave our father out of it. He's engaged."

"I'm not making claims on anyone . . . You're the one who's insisting that I make a choice. You also have an out, by the way: you can tell me to leave." Tanya laughed.

He pressed her head to his bony shoulder and fluffed the short hair on the back of her head.

"Remember how we used to visit you in Zvenigorod? When we'd go down to the river . . . And go boating . . . And play badminton . . . And then you grew up and turned into a bitch."

"What?" Tanya was surprised. "Why a bitch?"

"Because it makes no difference to you who you screw."

Tanya stirred, making herself more comfortable.

"It does make a difference. There are some I'd never sleep with, not for anything. But with the Goldberg brothers—anytime."

"I'll think about it. Maybe I'll let Vitalka have you."

"It's precisely for their nobility that I love the Goldberg brothers so much," Tanya hemmed and fell asleep . . .

Gena was still saying something and was profoundly amazed to discover that Tanya was sound asleep. Miraculously, his cold had passed, and he felt completely healthy and totally unhappy. Apparently, he needed to talk not with her, but with his brother. Only about what?

10

AT ABOUT THE SAME TIME A STRANGE LETTER ARRIVED addressed to Elena Georgievna. Vasilisa pulled it out of the mailbox together with the newspapers. She brought it to Elena. Elena took the official white stamped envelope into her hands, made no attempt to figure out what it was, and sat that way with the unopened envelope in her hand until evening, when Pavel Alekseevich dropped into her room. She handed him the letter.

"Here. Please . . . An envelope . . . For Tanechka . . ."

Pavel Alekseevich took the envelope. It bore the impressive stamp of INIURKOLLEGIA. The pale letters printed on white paper spelled out that the International Legal Collegium writes to inform of its search for the heirs of Anton Ivanovich Flotov, who died January 9, 1963, in an oncological clinic in the city of Buenos Aires and bequeathed half of his estate to his wife, Elena Georgievna Flotova, and to his daughter, Tatiana Antonovna Flotova. The office of the International Legal Collegium similarly reports that documentation of a change of surname and of an adoption had been obtained from the civil registry office of the town of V, and summons Elena Georgievna to discuss registration of inheritance as well as to provide more complete information about the status of her daughter Tatiana Pavlovna Kukotskaya . . .

Pavel Alekseevich put the letter on the table and walked out. The news was mind-boggling. According to this official letter written in typical bureaucratic style, Anton Ivanovich Flotov had not at all perished during the war, but somehow had made his way to South America, where he died twenty years later. What worried Pavel Alekseevich was neither the death of this man he had not known and to whom he had only an indirect relationship, nor the information about some mythical inheritance . . . What had crashed down on him was the inevitability of having to tell Tanya that her birth father was someone else, and of having to tell her that now, when their relationship was already falling apart.

In his office he sat down at his desk, having forgotten for a moment what he had come for. Automatically he rummaged with his hands along the shelf next to the desk: his hands remembered his needs better than his head, and he pulled out a half-bottle of vodka and small—"just the right size," as he liked to say—glass and drank. A minute later everything was clear. Right now he would tell Elena everything, and then he would call Tanya and reveal to her the secret of her paternity and let her decide at that point what she wanted to do about the inheritance. He had forgotten about Vasilisa, the only other person besides Elena who had known Flotov. His life as a father, once so happy, was drawing to an end in the most banal and trite way: the real father had turned up, dead by the way, and upset the entire set of lies. His heart was crushed, like a finger in a door. He winced and drank the remainder.

He returned to the bedroom. Elena was sitting in her chair, the younger Murka in her lap purring loudly like an oncoming suburban train and it seemed that at any moment a whistle would blow. Catching sight of Pavel Alekseevich Murka fell silent and tucked her fluffy tail under herself.

"You know, Lenochka, that letter contains a message about the death of your first husband, Anton Ivanovich Flotov. According to the letter, he did not perish at the front, but, probably, was taken prisoner and then wound up in South America . . . He died only a few months ago . . ."

Elena responded briskly and unexpectedly: "Yes, yes, of course, those huge cactuses, those prickles . . . That's what I thought. They're prickly pears, right?"

"What prickly pears?" Pavel Alekseevich became alarmed.

Elena absentmindedly gestured with her arm, confused.

"You won't tell anyone, will you?"

"About what?"

She smiled an unbearably pathetic smile and grabbed the cat the way a child grabs the hand of its nurse.

"They're huge, with prickly thorns, on the reddish earth . . . And there was a horseman, that is, first he didn't have a horse . . . Now I think that it was him . . ."

"You didn't dream that?"

She smiled a condescending smile, like an adult to a child.

"What are you talking about, Pashenka! It's more likely that you're a dream for me."

Elena had not called him Pashenka for a long time. Elena had not spoken with such a firm voice for a long, long time. Ever since that last attack—an unquestionable and long seizure, a complete prolapse of memory that she herself had noticed as well as those around her—her voice had sounded insecure, and the intonation of her speech was that of inquiring doubt. Does this mean that all her prolapses of memory are accompanied by a sense of derealization . . . What was this? Pseudo-memories? Hypnogogic hallucinations?

He took her by the hand.

"And where did you see those cactuses?"

She grew confused and upset. "I don't know. Maybe in Tomochka's room . . ."

Pavel Alekseevich took the letter in hand and ran his eyes across it one more time. Why at the mention of the death of her first husband had she started talking about cactuses? There was no connection. Except perhaps mention of Buenos Aires . . . What a peculiar array of associations. And now was she trying to conceal her train of thought by supplying a false argument? The cunning of the mad?

"Lenochka, Toma hates cactuses. She doesn't have a single cactus. Where did you see cactuses? Maybe you dreamed them?"

She bent her head even lower, practically snuggling the cat, and he saw that she was crying.

"My little girl, what's wrong? Are you crying because of Flotov? That all happened a long time ago. And it's good, isn't it, that he wasn't killed . . . Please stop crying, I beg you . . ."

"Those stinging prickles, there they are, those stinging prickles . . . No, not in a dream . . . Not at all in a dream . . . In a different way . . . I can't explain it . . ."

Oneiric confusion syndrome, perhaps? Dreamlike delusional derangement of the consciousness: is that what it's called? Find the details in the psychiatric literature. The most tenuous, most vague of the medical sciences, psychiatry . . . His wife's illness put Pavel Alekseevich at a loss because he could not understand it. A derangement of consciousness . . . A particularly malicious form of early dementia? Alzheimer's disease? Pre-senile dementia? What were the limits of this disease? . . . One way or another, though, today had been one of the better days: she was reacting and answering questions. It was almost full-fledged communication.

"It's possible Flotov was taken prisoner and became a displaced person. Thousands of Russian soldiers did not return home, you know that. Perhaps it was all for the better. If he'd returned, they would have sent him to the camps . . ." Pavel Alekseevich spoke insignificant words only so that her speech mechanisms would not shut down, as frequently happened with her.

"No, you don't understand . . . Flotov was a Baltic German. His great-grandfather was from Königsberg, von Flotow, and he had a lot of relatives who had stayed behind. He hid who he was . . ."

313

"What are you saying, Lenochka? That's simply amazing . . . That means he was one of the guilty? When I was young, everyone in my circle of acquaintances, well, perhaps except for a few idiots and bastards, knew that they were guilty of something, and they hid who they were . . ."

"Yes, of course. I remember how I felt it the first time. When my parents took me from my grandmother and brought me to a colony near Sochi, in the spring of 1920. That's when I first saw the vegetation in the South . . . And that's when I understood that something bad made us colonists different from all other people . . . A portrait of Lev Nikolaevich Tolstoy hung in the communal dining room. Done in oils, a clumsy portrait, his bare forehead shining and his beard fluttering in the wind, and, what really annoyed me, the frame was crooked. And no one noticed . . ."

Pavel Alekseevich listened to his wife's story, a coherent and detailed narrative with precise details. With an analysis of the situation, criticism, and an ability to arrive at meaning. Not a shadow of dementia. There could be no thought of dementia here . . . So why, two hours ago, had she been sitting with the cat and the unopened envelope, answering with irrelevant information, with nonsense answers typical of the insane, unable to control even the simplest movements, and at times forgetting how to hold a spoon. No, she hadn't quite forgotten entirely, but was experiencing obvious difficulty dealing with the simplest of things. She couldn't remember what she'd eaten for breakfast . . . If she had even eaten breakfast . . . The picture more likely suggests pseudodementia. A seeming loss of the simplest skills. A sui generis game of hide-and-seek of the mind with itself . . . No, I could never solve this puzzle. Maybe I should read Freud. In 1912 my dead mother had traveled to Vienna for psychoanalytic sessions with one of Freud's students. What a shame I know absolutely nothing about that. It seems my mother had some variety of hysteria . . . Pavel Alekseevich frowned. Silly Vasilisa: his sin lay not in aborting fetuses, half-ounce clots of high-potency protein with enriched potential, but in the stupid rigidity with which he had rejected his mother's second marriage, and his mother herself, a fair-haired beauty who had grown old with dignity and died in Tashkent in 1943 from ordinary dysentery.

With the acuity of the mentally ill Elena noticed the lightning speed of Pavel Alekseevich's frown and fell silent.

"Yes, yes, Lenochka. The frame was crooked . . . Tell me more . . ."

But she had fallen silent, as if someone had switched off the power. Once again she sank her fingers into Murka's fur, charged with live, slightly crackling, electricity, and withdrew entirely from the conversation and from the letter that had served as the indirect reason for the conversation, and from Pavel Alekseevich, who just seconds ago she had called "Pashenka" . . . Once again her face resumed its expression of "Imnothere."

Pavel Alekseevich knew that no force could bring her back. She would wake up to communicate again in a week, a month, or in a year. Sometimes these glimmers lasted hours, sometimes days. These temporary glimmers threw him for a total loop because Elena would become herself and even resemble herself in those mythological times when their marriage had been complete and happy.

The exact same thing had happened last time, three months ago, when she had spoken to him about Tanya, as if she had wakened from her illness, and she had spoken bitterly, almost in despair about alienation and loss, about emptiness and the torturous loss of sensation that afflicted her, about her indescribable confusion at not being able to recognize the world around her . . . And then her speech had stopped in the middle of a word, and she buried herself in the cat.

"Always the cat," the thought entered Pavel Alekseevich's head. "Next time when she begins to talk again, I'll chase the cat into the corridor . . . How strange: the cat is like a conduit to madness . . ."

"Lenochka, you and I were talking about Flotov . . ."

"Yes, thanks much . . . I don't need anything . . . Yes, everything's completely fine, please, don't worry . . ." Lena babbled, addressing either the cat or someone else who existed imaginarily inside her dusty, unkempt room.

11

LIKE ALEKSANDR SERGEEVICH PUSHKIN, TANYA WAS MIS-erable in spring: she felt wiped out, fatigued, and caught colds that refused to go away. This time her usual spring indisposition was complemented by an insuperable somnolence and aversion to food.

She was living on Profsoiuznaya Street now, in the Goldbergs' apartment. As soon as his medical leave ended, Vitalka was immediately fired from his job as part of a supposed staff reduction. He eked out a living as a translator. Like his father in the old days, he found what work he could writing for several scientific review journals, usually under someone else's name, and attempted to write articles for popular science magazines. Two short notes of his about new technologies in the West appeared in *Chemistry and Life*. Also with the help of acquaintances.

Barely able to withstand her nausea from kitchen smells, Tanya cooked food and slept fourteen hours straight. Occasionally coming out of hibernation, she went to Obninsk to see how Gena was doing. He was finishing his quick-fire dissertation and awaiting trouble at any minute from his institute's internal security office, but his adviser, a friend of Goldberg senior, a physicist who like Goldberg had done time in the camps, supported him one hundred percent. Yet, for all his authority and scientific achievements, the adviser was neither tsar nor god, and it was unclear until the very last moment whether or not Gena would be allowed to defend . . .

Tanya spent a day or so strolling through the still-transparent April woods underlit by varicolored buds ready to open, and returned a couple of times again in May to look at the young greenery. The fresh air quickly made her tire, and she fell fast asleep, thinking little of the fact that Gena lay down alongside her when he returned from the laboratory. Their friendly intercourse had no more significance than their communal breakfast, after which he accompanied her to the bus, then ran off to his laboratory . . .

Having spent a couple months living this way, Tanya suddenly woke up, made a few female calculations she had never before condescended to, and arrived at an interesting conclusion. In the five years of her experience in bed nothing similar had ever happened, and the discovery at first stunned her.

Nanny Goat Vika's girlfriends constantly discussed issues of applied gynecology connected with contraception, abortions, and means of dealing with the pain. During these discussions Tanya maintained an expression of total disinterest, as if she were a virgin or an old woman. For her, pregnancy was neither a joy nor an affliction, merely an interesting event. After making her discovery, she slept almost a full day straight, in her sleep reconciled herself with this entertaining circumstance, and announced it to Vitalka, who just happened to be at hand.

"Oh you devil," he rued. "I'm a jerk, of course, but you're to blame too . . . But a kid, in the present circumstances—that's too much."

"You think so?" Tanya surprised herself by taking offense, although she had not yet decided how she should feel about the possible appearance of a child. "So should I have an abortion?"

Vitalik said nothing. For too long.

"It seems I don't want it." Vitalka's long pause turned out to be decisive, because a minute before that Tanya had not at all known what she wanted. "We don't need a kid," Vitalik announced rather decidedly. "And my arm doesn't straighten completely . . ."

That was when Tanya suddenly took mortal offense on behalf of her future child, raised her splendid eyebrows, and smirked.

"I'll have to ask Genka. Maybe he wants it?"

Having assumed in the depths of his soul that Tanya belonged principally to him and visited Gena out of tradition and with his, Vitalka's, tacit agreement—a kind of sexual philanthropy on behalf of his brother, Vitalka gazed at Tanya with a look of stupefaction: he hadn't expected this turn of events. It had somehow never occurred to him that the alleged child might turn out to be his nephew . . .

"Listen, so who's the kid's father?"

Having made it a rule never to hide her thoughts and always to tell the truth, Tanya smiled a bit more broadly than usual.

"The Goldberg brothers, Vitalik. The Goldberg brothers. Under the present circumstances, it seems to me, you won't have as hard a time dealing with it together."

Then, not saying another word, Tanya began to collect her bag. Vitalik, also without saying a word, saw her to the bus that she usually rode to Obninsk.

Gena's reaction was more circumspect and mature.

"I'm completely at your disposal, Tanka. The only thing I can't do right now is leave Obninsk before I finish this damn dissertation. As for everything else, you call the shots. If you want, you can move here, at least until autumn. If you want to get married, we'll do that here, not in Moscow."

"Why not in Moscow?" Tanya asked, expecting some catch.

"I'll lose two days on my dissertation. I told you, there's a huge rush."

"Ah." Tanya nodded, satisfied.

Gena did not mention Vitalka. That pleased Tanya. She was ready to marry one of the Goldberg brothers, and the choice had now been made for her: Genka . . .

But things did not turn out according to plan. When Tanya returned from Obninsk three days later, Vitalik was preoccupied with a new problem that had been dumped on him: a notice had come from the draft board . . . It was obvious that this was their way of punishing Goldberg senior.

The answer proposed itself: a draft deferment lay right in Tanya's belly. All they had to do was get married as quickly as possible and have her pregnancy certified at the polyclinic.

"If that's the way it has to be . . . What's there to talk about, Vitalik? Just keep in mind, though, that my choice of husband is Genka."

Vitalik smiled a crooked smile.

"Are you trying to tell me that ours is going to be a fictitious marriage?"

"I didn't put it that way. But if you want, we can call it that."

The rest of the evening they spent battling wits on the subject of who would be related to whom and how as a result of their matrimonial operation. Tanya designated Vitalik a verbal adjective, the future child a half-nephew, and their marriage a Triple Alliance.

Having laughed their full and eaten supper, they lay down on the same distressed couch with its iron ribs sticking out and fell asleep in a close embrace, entirely oblivious to whatever moral dilemma might be seen by any outside observer, but not by the members of this particular family.

The next day they ran down to the civil registry office and submitted an application. Their wedding was set for the beginning of July. Vitalik did not go to the draft board. As a precaution it was decided that he should leave Moscow for a while. He quickly gathered his things, stuffed his bag with dictionaries, and grabbing half of a German textbook on clinical biochemistry—one of his father's staffers had shared this sweet morsel of a translation with him—set off for his maternal aunt's house in Poltava. Without calling or otherwise alerting her . . .

Everything turned out to have been calculated flawlessly. Two days after Vitalik left, another summons arrived, and on the next day, at seven in the morning, there was pounding at the door. Tanya admitted three men—two military and one policeman—into the apartment. They had come to take Vitalka into the army.

"The owner's on a trip. I don't know a thing. I think he went to the Urals to look for work . . ." was all they were able to extract from Tanya.

Following Vitalik's departure Tanya fell in love with her pregnancy. Not with the child that was supposed to be born, but precisely with her condition of fullness, contentedness in the literal sense of the word. Usually inattentive to her health, she now obeyed her body's slightest whim and resolved to indulge herself by doing everything that was pleasant and wholesome. In the morning she drank juice—not store bought, but hand-squeezed; she set up her own kefir production on the windowsill using some especially curative dairy culture; she spent several days a week in Obninsk with Gena. There she would stroll through the woods for hours on end, acquiring in the process a warm brown tan, hemoglobin, and a pleasant fatigue. Her somnolence was replaced by morning sickness. In the morning she would suck on sour hard candy; her nausea usually let up later in the day. To Tanya's great chagrin her belly had not grown one bit, although she constantly experienced a kind of taut fullness inside her that had nothing in common with the vulgar condition of someone who has eaten two dinners at one sitting. Her breasts, on the other hand, had enlarged noticeably; her nipples stuck out like doorbell buttons, and turned from pink to brown. Tanya scrubbed them with a coarse loofah: somewhere she had read that that was the way to prepare breasts for nursing. Gena sucked at her darkened nipples. He liked the way her nipples hardened from his touch. Tanya also liked this entirely new sensation.

Two more notices addressed to Vitaly arrived from the draft board. Some captain called, threatening and attempting to scare her. Tanya played the idiot.

On rare occasions Tanya would visit her family. She announced that she was pregnant and was planning to get married. But Elena did not react to the announcement at all. It seemed to Tanya that her mother had not heard. But that was not quite true, because in the evening of that same day Elena told her husband that Tanya would give birth to Little Tanya. Accustomed to the chaos of her mental processes, Pavel Alekseevich did not attach any special meaning to this vague bit of news, thinking to himself about the complex processes taking place in his wife's mind: apparently, the message about Flotov had stuck in the deep layers of her cortex and she had remembered the time when she herself had awaited a daughter. She was identifying herself with the grown-up Tanya.

The letter from the International Legal Collegium remained unanswered. Elena was in no condition to express her opinion about the inheritance, let alone answer. And Pavel Alekseevich had not said anything to Tanya about it: he just couldn't find an appropriate moment. For him it was a question not of inheritance but of something much more important.

On one of those late light evenings at the beginning of July when, having found her father in a pleasantly intoxicated state, Tanya informed him of her forthcoming marriage, he made up his mind to talk to her about that ill-starred inheritance. He sat her down in his study, placed the slightly pawed envelope in front of himself, and before handing it to her told her how he had met her mother, how he had operated on her and married her soon after she recovered.

"You moved to my place, Tanya, the very same day that a telegram arrived with information about the death of the man who had been your mother's husband before me."

Tanya's eyes burst out of their sockets: she had never thought about her mother having been married to someone before Pavel Alekseevich.

"You were two years old then, Tanechka. Your biological father was Anton Ivanovich Flotov. I adopted you immediately after we got married. Probably I should have told you about this earlier . . ."

"Daddy, what difference does it make?" She saw Pavel Alekseevich's anxiety, and all her childhood love, like the sun in the sky, shone down upon him at that minute . . .

She hugged his bald round head, kissed him on his fuzzy eyebrows, and on the nose. She inhaled his smell, which she had always liked—a combination of medicine, war, and alcohol—squeezed her eyes shut, and whispered: "Who cares about Flotov or Boatov . . . You're crazy . . . You're my real, my favorite elephant, Daddy, you old fool . . . You and I are terribly alike; you're all the best in me . . . I'm sorry that I abandoned you . . . I love you terribly, and I love Mama. I just can't live with you . . . Dad, I'm pregnant, I'm going to give birth to your grandson soon . . . Cool, huh?"

He had never had children of his own. He had heard about this moment from others, although many, many times men desperate to have children had learned of the event from him and had become fathers owing precisely to his demiurgic intercession. His adopted daughter had just informed him that she was going to give birth, and his chest filled with the warmth of happiness, and the future child turned out to be at once both desired and long awaited.

"My little girl: is it really true we lived to see the day . . . Will I really deliver my own grandson?" Pavel Alekseevich said in an old man's weakened voice, and Tanya suddenly saw how he had aged over the last few years, and, moved to tears and immediately angry at herself for that reason, she remonstrated.

"So why don't you ask me who I'm marrying? I'm marrying the Goldberg brothers."

"What difference does it make? So it's the Goldbergs. The main thing is that you be happy." He in fact could barely tell the brothers apart and was always joking that one of the brothers was a tad smarter and the other a tad more handsome, but he always forgot which one was which . . .

He sensed nothing amiss in this piece of news. For the first time after many years downhill, of decline—both at home and at his job—he sensed an upsurge of joy: Tanya had not rejected him, and his life's renewal was promised by the child, who would be his and Ilyusha's grandson. Wasn't that a miracle?

"Here's the official notification of your inheritance." He handed her the envelope. "Your father, Flotov, as we found out not long ago, did not perish at the front, but somehow wound up in Argentina, where he died not long ago. They're looking for his heirs."

"So, like, he remembered me only after he died? What about earlier? No, Dad, I don't want anything. I don't need anything." She pushed the envelope away and never thought of it again in her life . . .

12

IN THE MIDDLE OF JULY THE GOLDBERGS GOT MARRIED: Vitalka and Tanya signed at the Moscow Wedding palace, while Ilya

Iosifovich registered his vows with Valentina in a camp in Mordovia. At the camp they completed the formalities without ornamental witnesses—in the presence of the camp's regimen officer and the Moscow attorney who had managed to obtain permission for a prison marriage. Gena and Toma served as witnesses for Vitalik and Tanya. Toma—in a pink dress and white shoes on stiff heels—looked like the bride. Tanya had not thought of dressing up, but one could not say that she had totally ignored the importance of the moment: she had marked it with the purchase of three absolutely identical yellow and white striped men's shirts, and in these shirts the three of them looked like they were all from the same children's home—shorn short, thin, identically dressed, and the same height, five feet seven inches.

Toma was disappointed—no reception, no gifts, and no merrymaking. She wanted grand solemnity and a huge party, but all that was precisely what Tanya could not bear. Their sole wedding gift was an orange-pink orchid, for which Toma the day before had traveled to the home of a friend from the Botanical Gardens and which replaced the traditional *fleur d'orange*. The mental picture of the brothers Goldberg with Tanya between them bearing a languid wobbly branch with three large drooping flowers—lion's heads with manes, mouths, and side petals forming a lighter-colored halo, "a rarity of rarities"—would remain in Toma's memory for the rest of her life.

Vitalik did, though, get one more present. After the newlyweds received their marriage certificate written out on iridescently patterned official paper, Tanya pulled out of the pocket of her yellow-and-white shirt a certificate, folded in half, from the obstetric care center certifying that she was in her eighteenth week of pregnancy. Together these two documents gave Vitalik the right to a deferral from military service.

Having resolutely refused all services offered by the state, from Mendelssohn's "March" to expensive champagne, and accepting only the pompous congratulations of the Nonna Mordiukova look-alike beneath the red flag with the red suit and the red satin ribbon across her fat chest who had conducted the ceremony, the kids descended the grand staircase of the Wedding Palace, sat down on the steps, and drank a bottle of cheap, sour Rkatsiteli, after which Gena hailed a passing cab, he and Tanya got in, and they drove off.

Toma, stunned and unaware of the true state of affairs, asked the melancholic young husband, "Where are they going?"

"To Obninsk. She's planning to spend the week there . . ."

Tanya spent not one, but two whole weeks in Obninsk. Back in Moscow, she immediately stopped in at home. She missed them.

She found Elena in her former condition, but very pale and limp, and she even tried to persuade her to go outside for a walk. Elena was so frightened by the offer that what had started as a coherent conversation suddenly came to a halt as she babbled pathetic and incoherent words.

"If it wouldn't be too much to ask . . . Might I possibly go there . . . You have to ask Pavel Alekseevich. Isn't that so?"

Tanya was horrified. Her mother's illness was something unique, unlike anything else, and getting used to it was impossible.

Later Pavel Alekseevich arrived and was delighted to see both Tanya and her belly, which had just begun to show.

"Come on, I'll tell you about our little boy."

Neither of them doubted for a minute that Tanya would give birth to a boy, and each time they met, Tanya would ask her father to tell her how the child must look at that point.

She made herself comfortable on the couch, tucked her legs under her, and loosened the button of her jeans. He sat down on a round stool alongside her.

"So, tell me," she said.

"So, now. First of all, I'm certain that he already feels something. Folk belief has it that the soul enters the child at the midpoint of pregnancy. That is, he begins to move and to feel simultaneously."

"No, I felt a lot earlier that he was running his finger along inside me," Tanya objected.

"Well, that means our little boy is an early developer. I'm telling you what happens in the average situation. Your little one is floating now and has no idea of up or down. He's like this, about a foot long. His head is large and covered with hair, which, if it was light before, has now darkened. He is relatively grown, has acquired more than half of his height, but weighs only a pound and a half. A skinny little thing. And his skin right now is very wrinkled, without any hypodermic fat. But he doesn't need fat right now. He's covered with down, and the vernix caseosa is already forming. His face has acquired distinct features. He already resembles you, that is, I hope he resembles you. But the main work going on right now is taking place in his nervous system. A very complex program has to set in for his organs to begin working. It's forming right now. How? I don't know. And don't ask. No one knows.

"There's a lot I don't know about what's taking place in there. But some things I do know. It seems to me that he has already acquired awareness of himself and that precisely in these last few days his sense of 'I' has been born. His sense of being apart from the rest of the world. The 'rest of his world' is you, my joy. Because until he's born he'll know no other world. With men that never happens. Men are never the cosmos. But a pregnant woman—in the second half of her pregnancy, at least—represents the entire enclosed cosmos of another human creature. You know, my dear, it always seemed completely natural to me that there could exist a species of animal where the female would die immediately after giving birth. The cosmos gives birth to the cosmos: who needs this imperfect world? That's me talking nonsense. He's floating right now like a rowboat tied to a pier, back and forth. Suspended from a mooring by the cable of his umbilical cord, and listening, probably, as the dense waves come and go, the thick moisture flowing about his sides and his tucked-under legs. They're crossed, almost in a lotus pose. And the nails on his feet are already forming. And the auricles of his ears have already formed, but they're still only skin, without any cartilage. And you know, those little ears of his are big. I wonder if he can hear what we're talking about. You know, I don't rule that out. Your mother was certain that the larger part of what she knew, even about drafting, she learned before she was born. I can't say anything of the sort about myself. But then men are much more crudely constructed creatures than women. In biological terms a woman, as I see it, is the more perfect creature. I think that our little boy already experiences changes of mood. Sometimes he's dissatisfied, sometimes happy. For example, when you eat something tasty, an hour and a half later he can already taste strawberries or grapes."

"Can he smile already?" Tanya interrupted her father.

"I don't think so. The mimetic muscles begin to function later. As a rule, as I've observed, fetuses have rather poor and somewhat chaotic

324

facial expressions. There is, though, one certain expression they have—one of concentration and withdrawal—I know that one very well . . ."

"And what would give him pleasure? What do you think? Maybe I should take him to a concert?"

"Give yourself as much pleasure as you can—I think that will be pleasant for him as well," Pavel Alekseevich advised his daughter. He could have had no idea in what direction his innocent recommendation would lead Tanya.

13

NANNY GOAT INHERITED A FORTUNE FROM THE ELDEST of her aunts and blew it immediately. More precisely, she blew only the packaging, a pudgy silver Fabergé jewelry box with a pseudo-Greek female profile and three yellow diamonds on the lid. The jewelry box was late moderne, ornate, and the embodiment of a butler's concept of true luxury. The box's contents, however, were charming pieces of jewelry of pearl and amethyst, not of great value, but marvelous pieces of work with a pedigree: they had been presents to her great-grandmother from one of the Yusupov princes.

The jewelry box brought Nanny Goat big money, approximately one one-hundredth of what it ultimately went for at an auction in London. But Nanny Goat never found out about that, while five hundred rubles were ooh-la-la what a sum of cash. Handed the money directly by an acquaintance, the director of a commission shop, she took a taxi to the dacha she had rented where her son Misha was stuck with her two remaining aunts and his own grandmother, Nanny Goat's mother. She picked the kid up, and—paying almost twice the face value—bought train tickets to the South.

Tanya arrived at her place the next day in the morning, having missed her cheerful banter. There were still six hours before the train departed, and Nanny Goat persuaded Tanya to go with her.

"The ticket's not a problem. If worst comes to worst, we'll fix it so you can sleep in the conductor's compartment." Nanny Goat waved a fat bankroll before Tanya's nose.

At eight in the evening they were sitting in the train. An hour later, after all the tiny suburban stops had winked good-bye and remained behind, they found themselves luxuriously ensconced in a compartment of their own, having resettled the inhabitants of the entire sleeping car. Among Nanny Goat's many talents was the ability to set down roots instantly, and blithe to the effort it cost, she had dragged along a whole suitcase of things that, from Tanya's point of view, were entirely superfluous: little napkin placemats, coffee cups from home, and even a copper crank coffee grinder . . . Tanya's lean bag held a bathing suit, some underwear, and a spacious dress with enough room for her future belly. She hadn't even taken a towel, planning to buy one once they got there . . .

It was not quite clear to her where "there" was. One of the Goat's customers, an actress, who had dropped in the night before to show off her deep, still somewhat reddish, suntan, had sung the praises of the Dniester Estuary, from where she had just returned. Nanny Goat, white and freckled and never in her life ever able to get a real tan, was struck with envy and decided to try the same estuary sun, and now they were traveling to approximately the same places that the exiled Ovid had cursed . . .

Their route took them through Odessa. At a transfer point in Odessa they were supposed to meet the mother of one of Vika's girlfriends, who would put them up for the night and the next day put them on a bus through Bilhorod-Dnistrovsky to a sandbar between the Dniester Estuary and the sea . . .

They arrived in Odessa toward evening. Waiting for them was a huge—couch-size—woman, Zinaida Nikiforovna, swaddled in flower-patterned silk. Next to her the buxom Goat seemed like a sparrow, and the woman immediately took to them with indulging tenderness. She dragged them down to her "ah-paht-ment," two connected rooms in a communal apartment that had seen better times. A mirror in a gold-leaf frame occupied the space between two Venetian windows and reflected the ranks of five-pint canning jars of tender fruit boiled alive and intended for speedy consumption. The house burst with food and drink, and before they could wash up, their "open-ahmed" hostess started piling food on the table . . . Little Misha was falling asleep at his plate. Zinaida Nikiforovna waved him off in disappointment and told them to put him to bed. Like all seaside denizens, she had a stash of folding cots and bedding for the innumerable relatives who came to visit. While their hostess made up a cot for Misha in the next room, Goat whispered to Tanya:

"We're in for it now . . ."

But they had no idea what adventures lay ahead.

Little Misha fell asleep immediately. Zinaida Nikiforovna declared that they should all call her "Mama Zina," that right now she had to go to work, and proposed that they take a stroll through evening Odessa, because there was no other city like it on earth . . .

They walked out onto the boulevard submerged under a flood of people, taking in the overabundant denseness of the southern evening, the warm air weighed down by cachinnate voices, and the waves of food and beer lightly seasoned with the smell of vomit. Above all this floated the sounds of Odessa-Soviet radio music—crude thieves' cant, but not without its own charm.

The crowd on Deribasovskaya Street respectfully circumvented Mama Zina, splitting into two streams as they approached her cephalothorax, while Tanya and Vika, moored to her powerful right and left sides, occasionally exchanged glances, barely able to contain their laughter. Never closing her mouth of gold teeth for a second, Mama Zina spoke about literary Odessa.

"We'll take their Babel and Ilf and Petrov, even Bagritsky and Kataev, and even Margarita Aliger and Vera Inber. If we subtract them, who's left? Do we need that Sholokhov of theirs? Their Fadeev? Bunin lived here. Even Pushkin spoke on behalf of Odessa! Right here!" she proclaimed, having stopped at the respectable entrance of the Hotel London. "Here's where I work. We'll go through the staff entrance."

It was a sailors' club. International. Hard currency. A nightclub . . . And Mama Zina was in charge of the beer . . .

"They're with me," she said, squeezing into the narrow corridor, to a whitish man who looked like a packing trunk and who had appeared from a dark corner. He nodded. They entered the main room. It was air-raid dark, and the pianist played quietly. Several sailors who had not yet had their fill lazily drank their beer, while two painted working girls sat at a corner table and lushly sucked something through straws.

People spoke quietly, and the place did not smell of fish. Even Mama Zina sort of partly faded behind the bar counter. The beer was domestic, but the money was real—hard currency. Not just anyone got hired for this kind of work, only the most trusted. Mama Zina was precisely that kind—every seam of her, down to her uterus, checked by state security, even before the war, a partisan and a member of the underground. Here too her watchful party eye insured nothing got out of hand. As for the girls, the friends of her daughter who'd split to the capital, let them sit here and take a look, have some fun with the sailors, dance a bit . . .

The pianist picked quietly at some song that was definitely not of the domestic variety, but soulful in its own way. It used to be that Zinaida Nikiforovna did not like this newfangled music, but then it grew on her. They played jazz here.

The drummer arrived and set up his drums. He started to warm up. The really hot one was the one with the horn. But he was running late.

It grew dark outside, and lights went on in the club. People started showing up. There was rarely a crowd here.

Tanya felt more and more like sleeping. The piano gloriously purred out one and the same tune, but in different variations, which was rather interesting musically and slightly intoxicating, and she had no desire to get up. Then the horn's voice rang out. It cut through the piano's murmur with a dramatic and bitter sound. Tanya turned toward the stage. A not very tall, thin boy held a saxophone with both hands, and it seemed as if the instrument wanted to tear itself from his grasp as he tried to hold it back. What torturous music it was—sweetly painful, bitterly salty, sadly joyous . . . These were improvisations on Miles Davis's old album 'Round Midnight, the saxophone following Coltrane's dramatic lead, but at that moment Tanya knew none of this.

The musicians played as if slightly out of sync, the drummer holding back, the pianist heading off ahead then slowing down, while the saxophone followed its own separate road, and occasionally they all came together as if accidentally, carrying on an exchange at the point they met, a question-answer session—about something important, but incomprehensible . . . They all played very precisely and subtly, but the saxophonist was the best of all . . . The wind spun around him, fluttering his straight, blond hair, and Tanya had the urge to place her face right under the sound of his horn . . . She didn't even notice that Nanny Goat went off to dance with a foreign sailor who looked too scrawny and intelligent for so masculine a profession. Some creep approached Tanya, and she jolted in fright: no, no. He went away. Nanny Goat continued dancing with scrawny-guy and was even communicating something in a mix of German and French, which somehow overlapped with his English and Swedish . . .

"Why did I give up music? Dad was right: sit at the piano; it flows from your fingers; you're just a container, a mechanism for making the transfer from sheet music to sound . . . I don't remember why I gave it up . . . Because of Tomochka, that's why . . . The Komsomol consciousness of the idiot . . . It wasn't the right music anyway. Music like this I'd never have given up . . . That and that," she thought, noting the sighs of the saxophone and the heartbeat of the drummer . . .

"Whatever dragged me into that scientific rat's nest? I could have studied music . . . How expressive that saxophone is! I never realized that it had the intonations of a human voice. Or is the musician that talented? Yes, probably the latter . . ."

The Swede escorted them back to Zinaida's place. The two of them liked each other, but it was clear that this evening would be the end of something that wasn't even started. He gave Nanny Goat a present, a notepad that already had writing in it, with a black leather cover—really classy. He didn't have anything else. He wrote his address on the first page. Rune Svenson. And that was it. Because the next morning his ship was heading out to who knew where and forever. What a shame!

They were let in by Zinaida's sister, who lived in the same communal apartment and had kept watch over Misha's sleep. By the time Mama Zina, who worked until three, returned, everyone was asleep. In the morning she saw her guests to the bus station, and they set off on the flat, dusty road. Sitting in the jolting, sweltering bus, Tanya remembered that that night she had had a dream with yesterday's music in it, but in proportions larger than life, and it was performed by unusual sounding instruments . . .

Odessa and its suburbs ended about forty minutes later, giving way to a dusty, bumpy road, to fields annihilated by heat, to burned-out corn, and to feather grass. Nanny Goat was the first to get sick: she and her Swedish comrade had got carried away not just dancing, but with an exotic combination of cocktails that wrenched her Russian stomach even without the jolty road. Then little Misha threw up. Tanya held out the longest, but three hours of jostling suitable only for cosmonauts in training and not for delicate beings—particularly pregnant ones—unglued her as well.

They crawled out of the bus near a string of whitewashed peasant huts turned gray from the dust of orchards and tomato gardens. This miracle of nature was called Kurortnoe, "Resort Town." Only there was nothing of a resort about it. Just more of the same dusty fields, with the sea nowhere in sight. In short, there was nothing there but heat and ferocious sun. They asked a woman passerby with a bucket full of tomatoes where the sea was.

"Over yonder," she waved in no particular direction. "You lookin' to rent?"

"Yes, to rent."

The woman led them toward her place. Along the road they ran into two more women. They stopped and chatted quickly in not quite understandable Russian. After which the first woman passed them on to one of the others, and she led them off in a different direction. Sickly cypresses came into sight, with something resort-looking behind them. It was a resort hotel, behind which more little white houses appeared, and the new arrivals were taken to one of them. They rented a separate little house in a garden alongside a wooden outhouse with a tin sink attached with a huge rusty nail to a ridiculous lone wall—all that remained of a demolished shed. Beds of tomatoes stretched around the little house: they were "oxhearts," a rare variety, huge lilac-crimson beauties, sooner fruit than vegetable . . . This was the sole local tourist attraction, the sole local delicacy, and almost the only food there was for people, pigs, and chickens. The tomatoes were used to make borscht and jam; they were boiled down into paste, dried, and left to rot. As the new arrivals figured out the next day, the local store had no bread, no butter, no cheese, no milk, no farmer's cheese, no meat, and no lots of other things, but they did sell a low-grade flour, vegetable oil, canned fish, and chocolate candies . . . For the time being, having consumed the travel rations Mama Zina had provided, they set off to find the sea, which they still had not set eyes on and about which their landlady had said, waving in a certain direction, "over yonder."

They set out in the indicated direction along a beaten path through the feather grass and arrived at a steep cliff. The land ended, and the sea began. It lapped—invisible and inaudible—far beneath their feet and merged with the sky in the blinding gray haze seamlessly, without even a hint of a horizon.

An earthen staircase haphazardly reinforced with wooden posts led to the water. Down it Tanya and Nanny Goat led a recalcitrant Misha, who was a bit cowardly and rather lead-footed. Having overcome about a hundred feet of crumbling steps, they found themselves on a sandy shore that was peopleless and touchingly sad, like the shore of an uninhabited island.

"Awesome," said Nanny Goat.

"The end of the earth," Tanya confirmed.

"There's nothing here," Misha whined in disappointment.

"What's not here?" Nanny Goat said in surprise.

"Where they sell ice cream, and in general," Misha explained his disappointment.

The sea was shallow, warm, and gray . . . It pretended to be calm, tame, as if it never battered the local shore with its autumnal storms that eroded many miles of barren, but hard earth . . .

They went in for a dip, gave Misha swimming lessons, built a maze out of wet sand, then fell asleep, waking up only toward evening when the sun had relented and a breeze blew from the sea . . .

Their landlady, a cook at the local resort hotel, turned out to be simply a treasure. In the evening she took them to the kitchen and showed them the cellar, whose shelves were lined with jars of butter preserved in salted water and pyramids of stewed meat—Soviet man's daily bread.

"Take what you need and then we will figure it out. You have a child with you," the landlady proposed generously.

Their vacation was working out sumptuously. Never in their lives had they eaten such quantities of stewed canned pork and butter as they did in those two weeks vacationing in the South. As for tomatoes, there was nothing to be said: that summer taught them that the product sold under the name of tomatoes in all other places had no relation whatsoever to the real thing.

But their principal discovery was made three days later, when having had their fill of looking at the sad, barely live sea, they made their way finally to the estuary.

The sandbar—overgrown in places with reeds and wormwood—stretched many miles, washed on one side by the languid sea and on the other by the estuary's standing water, rather, that of one of its long inlets, which during spring high water was connected with the river's main stream, but for the larger part of the year was entirely cut off. In a surprising way this small sandbar represented the entire local region: abandoned, almost nameless, cut off from its own history and alien to the present. This was the edge of the Bessarabian steppe, the setting for ancient civilizations trampled by Scythians, Gets, Sarmatians, and various nameless tribes. Once the outlands of the Roman Empire, it was now the wasteland of another, contemporary empire. Unfortunate, forsaken by all the gods, the motherland of white feather grass and fine suffocating dust . . .

Already sunburned, in long sundresses, their crimson backs covered with towels, Tanya and Vika dragged little Misha in his pajama bottoms along the unpopulated shore as they attempted to find a place where they could take cover from the direct rays of the sun. The round sand dunes, which had stopped growing short of full size, offered no shade. At noon, no one went outside except vacationers: the locals lived by the laws of the South, burrowing off for siestas at this time of day, regardless of their work schedules . . .

They found a small hill with three bushes with a trembling hint of shade underneath. They lay down on the hot sand. At this place the sandbar was about three hundred feet wide, the path running close to the estuary; having rested for a bit, they dipped themselves in its fresh water. You couldn't say the water was warm; it was hot. They found a half-submerged dinghy in the reeds, which kept Misha busy for quite a while. Ducks with their adolescent ducklings scurried along the shore, accustomed to the heat, the warm water, and the abundance of food. The shallows, like a can of sardines, teemed with minnows. Only without tomato sauce. The thickets of reeds were filled with a live rustling: something there scurried by, started a ruckus, and emitted various sounds. Unidentifiable paws of various sizes had left their tracks along the tiny sandy shoal, and Misha bent over them, studying their script.

Tanya folded her arms across her stomach and tapped with her finger.

"You good in there? Satisfied?" She understood that yes, he was good . . .

The ever-prepared Nanny Goat, who in addition to water and food had hauled along a chubby volume, leaned her head into the scanty shade and opened her book. She started to read aloud.

"He thought that the mountains and clouds looked completely identical and that the particular beauty of the snowy mountains, about which he had been told, was as much an invention as Bach's music and a woman's love—none of which he believed in—and he stopped waiting for the mountains to appear. But the next day, early in the morning, he was wakened by the fresh air in his cart and looked casually to the right. The morning was perfectly clear. Suddenly he saw—about twenty steps away, as it seemed to him at first glance—the pure white colossi with their gentle outlines and the whimsical, distinct aerial line of their summits against the distant sky. When he comprehended the true distance between him and the mountains and the sky, the full enormity of the mountains, and when he sensed the full infiniteness of this beauty, he became frightened that it was all an apparition, a dream. He shook himself, so as to wake up . . ."

Tanya glanced over her shoulder. "You rereading Tolstoy? What for?"

"Honestly, I don't know. I feel like it. Almost every year, and certainly in the summer. Like this, on the beach. On a train . . . In the yard, in the kitchen garden . . . Like visiting a relative. Out of a sense of duty. But love too. It's a bit boring. But necessary."

"Yes, yes. I know. My mother has read Tolstoy that way all her life. Her father, my grandfather, was a Tolstoyan or something like that. He was shot."

"Are you kidding? They arrested Tolstoyans too?" Nanny Goat was surprised.

"How else? Absolutely . . ." She closed her eyes. She saw an unexpectedly lustrous picture—pure white colossi with their gentle outlines and the whimsical, distinct aerial line of their summits against the distant sky. "I don't care for him. No, that's not so. He writes that he doesn't believe in the music of Bach or a woman's love, in the beauty of mountains, and you're prepared to agree with him. Then he ups and suddenly writes three sentences about the beauty of the mountains that hit you right between the eyes . . . And it all gets turned upside down."

She rolled off her back onto her stomach and leaned on her elbow in the sand.

"Thank you for hauling me out to this hole. This place, of course, is awesome . . . Nobody around . . ."

In fact, there were lots of vacationers, who could be observed in the morning at the local market: people from Zaporizhia, Donetsk, and Kishinev. Many vacationers arrived particularly toward the weekend. But they all gathered amicably on two beaches—the resort hotel's and the so-called public beach . . . The Moldovans with their hanging mustaches, Ukrainian mine workers who succeeded in covering their coal-dust-darkened faces with crimson suntans, their full-bodied wives, and screaming children laid out their domestic supplies along a littered strip of shore where they drank warm vodka, played circle volleyball, splashed about in the shallows, then left, leaving behind stinking mountains of trash to be washed away by the cleansing storms of autumn. No matter what they called themselves, they were the true descendants of the extinct barbarous world.

Neither the sandbar nor the wild seashore down the staircase interested anyone. Walking past the feculent public beach, Tanya and her companions would come out on the sandbar, and a quarter mile later the remains of the barbarians' campgrounds disappeared. If they followed the turn of the sandbar and walked another two to two and a half miles, they found themselves at such a remove, in such an uninhabited world, as was impossible to imagine . . .

On the second Saturday of their stay on the estuary, the pain of their sunburns having already subsided, they made their way to the very middle of the sandbar, where the remains of some indeterminate stone structure were still preserved. Likely the winter waves reached these ruins, but the vacationers did not, which meant that there were no broken bottles and no tin cans among the roots of the pathetic bushes that had sprouted under the cover of the heaped-up stones . . . They walked over toward the ruins and caught sight of a tent made out of a white sheet strung in seclusion among the rocks: there were several young men inside the tent.

"It's the musicians from the club." Tossing a quick glance in their direction, Tanya recognized them immediately.

"What club?" Nanny Goat wondered.

"The sailors' club, where our Mama Zina . . ."

"I hadn't paid any attention to them. Tanya, you have an incredible visual memory. How did you remember them?" Nanny Goat continued to be amazed.

The pianist, the eldest of them, thick-nosed and hairy-legged, waved cordially.

"Welcome, ladies, welcome!" he shouted in English.

Everyone called him Garik, but his real name was something Armenian and difficult to pronounce, and whenever he drank his first shot of whatever, he immediately switched to English, which he knew in the particular context of jazz—exclusively by way of musical terminology and classical blues lyrics. Jazz musicians at the time were totally insane, but until today there had been none in Tanya's circle of friends. The saxophonist sat almost with his back to them, but Tanya recognized him by his light straight hair of a length considered in those days a challenge to the social order. He looked around, looked at Tanya, and she immediately seized her stomach: the child kicked about with unusual force.

"What's with you?" Tanya asked him. He kicked about another time, and then fell quiet. Everything's all right.

Tanya and Nanny Goat were still trying to decide whether they should turn in their direction or pretend that they were going somewhere else, but Misha had already run up to the musicians and declared: "You're sitting in our spot. We always sit . . ."

So they did not walk on, but stopped . . . The forty feet between Tanya and the saxophonist passed as if in slow motion: he raised a slow hand to his temple, and a lock of long hair shifted in a protracted agonizing movement. He touched his hair, stopped, slowly turned his neck, smiled with the corners of his mouth, which flowed upward, revealing his large upper teeth and the small lower ones that resembled a young puppy's. It all happened in enlarged close up. He smiled at Tanya, and he looked at her with the same slow gaze, and Tanya already then, it seems, had guessed that at that moment her fate was being decided.

The musicians were drunk, but within reason. In the evening they were supposed to play at the local resort hotel and were observing their work regimen. They had been playing together for half a year already, and they knew perfectly well how much wine would improve the music, and when it became destructive. The drummer started making moves on

Tanya. Tanya couldn't take her eyes off the saxophonist. At six o'clock, when the sun's heat had abated, they set off together in the direction of the resort hotel. The guys had left their car at the entrance. Nanny Goat and Misha headed home to eat supper. Tanya squeezed into the back seat and went off with the musicians. She liked Sergei something awful. Like no one and never before.

The concert went off with great success. After the concert people danced for a long while to tape-recorded music. All the musicians got very drunk. Sergei did not dance. They sat behind the do-it-yourself stage and kissed till stupefaction, until he said that there was a room reserved for him but he didn't remember the number. The key, though, just happened to have attached to it an oilcloth ticket with a violet number 16 penned on it.

14

TANYA DID NOT WAKE UP, SHE CAME TO. THE ROOM—A shoddy double with a pair of wooden beds and a bedside table between them—was filled with hot dense light, like an aquarium filled with water. There was not the slightest movement, not the least flutter, and none of the bustle that often occurs in the early morning. It was as quiet as noon, at the hour when the sun is at its peak. An instant of life in freeze-frame was what it was.

"And I'm at my peak." Tanya smiled, placing her palms on her convex belly and stroking it from the sides. "We're at our peak!"

The high point of life, the top of the mountain, and the mountain of her belly—all these things were related.

"Do you feel it?" she asked her belly.

"Do you feel it: you and I have fallen in love . . ."

Her belly for some reason was her accomplice. She looked at Sergei sleeping alongside her. She had been studying his hands since the night before: not large, with the distal phalanxes bent upward, with enlarged joints under the horizontal folds of skin on his knuckles, fingernails with white spots—signifying either some sort of vitamin deficiency or an unexpected present prepared for him by destiny . . . She squinted to the side:

336

his hand, opened trustingly palm upward, lay on her shoulder. In the middle of the flesh of his mons pubis she found a deep scar. There was another one on his forearm. There were many more details of this boyish body that she had not managed to note the night before, but already loved. The big toe on his foot stuck out forward, the foot itself was narrow and not large, like a woman's. There was the plush of thick white hair on his shin . . . He lay on his side, one leg bent at the knee. In the shadow of his private parts, among the light curly hairs, lay his sleeping tool, and it was not at all without its own character. Previously it had seemed to Tanya that men's penises differed only slightly in size, but in all other respects were absolutely identical. This one had a characteristic bend that replicated the line of his lips and expressed naïveté and a capacity for self-oblivion . . . With her hand Tanya touched his milky-white skin, the small strip on his hip not covered with a suntan. His skin was as soft as a woman's. His chest was covered with soft growth, light-colored, like sun-bleached moss. She touched the scar on his palm. "This will be my favorite place."

He rummaged his other hand along his side, then pressed her to his body.

"Where are you going? Don't leave . . ."

"Never," Tanya laughed. "But can I go to the bathroom?"

"No way."

He pressed her to himself: everything fit wonderfully. Never before had he experienced such a coincidence. Without opening his eyes, he asked her: "Where did you come from?"

"Nowhere. I always was." Tanya laughed.

"Apparently," he agreed, running his hands over her neck, breasts, and stomach.

"Open your eyes," Tanya said.

"I am afraid." He smiled, but opened them.

"And?" Tanya got up and edged away slightly.

"Terrific," he said to calm her and, perhaps, himself. "Everything was terrific, only I just couldn't remember your face. You know, once at just this point I had a terrible trauma. I woke up, and alongside me . . ."

Tanya clamped her hand over his mouth.

"Forget it. Immediately forget everything that ever was before. You are Sergei, I'm Tanya, and nothing else matters."

Sergei chuckled. "Good. But I just happen to have a wife."

"And I have a husband. Two, even. And I'm going to have a baby soon . . ."

"In what sense?"

Sergei pulled himself up and leaned on his elbow. Tanya took his hand and placed it on her belly.

"In three, three and a half months."

Her belly was taut, full. Sergei pulled back his hand as if he had been scalded by a teapot.

"For real? Nothing like that has never happened to me before . . ."

"Or to me either." Tanya laughed. "There's always a first time . . . This is the first time I've ever been with you."

He got up and went to the shower. He stood under the thin warm stream for several minutes. Then he drank some of the nasty water from his palms.

"The girl's nuts. I'm going to kick her out right now," he decided, and stepped out of the shower. She was already standing alongside the door and slipped inside. She had a wonderful figure, and breasts, and waist. Her belly was not large, but entirely noticeable.

He went back to bed and lit a cigarette.

"Get dressed and leave," he requested when she sat down next to him on the bed.

She shook her head.

"What, are you scared? Everything is all right. I'm not going anywhere."

"You've got a child inside you, and I could break something in there. Are you supposed to be screwing in your condition?"

"Did it seem to you that I shouldn't be?"

"No, I just didn't notice."

"Well, I think that I'm very much supposed to. After all, I came to the South in order to make life pleasurable for him." She clasped her belly with her arms.

"In what sense?"

Tanya laughed.

"Go swimming, roll around in the sun."

She dove into bed under the sheet and hugged him around the neck.

"Everything I like, he likes. Word of honor."

She was a wonderful girl, and his fear had passed, while his desire remained. And in fact there was even a certain appeal to that taut belly of hers, those tense nipples, and the intensified womanliness that derived of her being pregnant. They spent the whole day in the hotel room, leaving only once to get mineral water . . .

In the evening the musicians gave another concert, and Tanya could not take her mind off Seryozha's music for a minute—it was the continuation of their new love. Then they spent the night together, collected some very respectable money for their performances in the morning, and left. Tanya ran over to Nanny Goat's place for a minute, grabbed her travel bag, planted kisses on the top of Misha's head and on Vika's cheek, and disappeared from Nanny Goat's sight forever.

15

THE JAZZ TRIO'S TOUR RAN FROM THE MIDDLE OF SUM-mer until late autumn. They called themselves GAZ—Gabrielian, Aleksandrov, Zvorykin. It was their first year as a group, they were still just learning to function as a single organism, and things were just beginning to come together. Every day they made a new discovery. Although they did not give up their usual drinking habits, they essentially got drunk not on wine, but on the high that came from the music they made. The eldest and driving force behind the project was Garik Gabrielian, the only professional musician among them, who had been expelled in his last year from the Leningrad conservatory and effected a mind-boggling escape from the castle of classical beauty into the free zone of jazz improvisation. The drummer, Aleksandrov—a former engineer, mad with exotic ideas and at that particular moment preoccupied with levitation, but also having an unhealthy predilection for abominable snowmen, aliens, and extraterrestrial civilizations—banged out signals to unknown forces on his four booming drums and multitude of percussive rattles and clappers. He assured all that with proper percussive technique flight was as natural a phenomenon for humans as, for example, swimming. He had never, by the way, learned how to swim. Seven years later he chanced upon the golden vein of shamanism and ultimately flew off into the great beyond straight from his cot at a wretched psychiatric hospital on the outskirts of Leningrad . . .

Saxophonist Sergei Zvorykin also belonged to the breed of musical maniacs. By this point he had abandoned his studies at the Technological Institute in Leningrad, and having quarreled irrevocably with his father, a professor of communist philosophy, left home and married a forty-year-old retired ballerina, thereby driving the last nail into the coffin of his reputation as a sane human being. That was Tanya's chosen man and his friends. It turned out that the people Tanya had taken so close to heart, the people for whom she had so longed, were not doctors, like her father, the best of the best; not scientists, like MarLena Sergeevna, armed with scissors and tweezers for poking around in the depths of a pregnant rat's uterus; not tenacious and inspired dissidents, like old Goldberg and his sons; not Nanny Goat Vika's loud and clueless semibohemians, but precisely these men of few words and vague thoughts—or rather no thoughts at all when it came to crucial real-life issues, be they moral, social, or political. They did nothing, they sought to achieve nothing, and they aspired to nothing: they simply played their music, played at their music, and entrusted it to speak for them, taking joy in that fact that it, their music, turned out to be so good at doing that . . .

Tanya listened closely, not only at rehearsals and concerts, but all the time, from morning until night, from night until morning. It turned out that the music never stopped; it sounded not just in those moments when keyboards were pounded or horns blown.

She told Sergei about her discovery. He just nodded his head.

"Why, of course. And in dreams too. Especially in dreams . . ."

Tanya strained her memory, or imagination, or some other organ responsible for nocturnal consciousness, and recollected, that yes, dreams do have music, only it's impossible to remember it . . . From that day on a musical sound track appeared, running parallel to the world in which she was a participant, a stream uninterrupted and ever changeable, just like the view from a train car, inseparable from the movement of the train itself . . .

The jazzmen's music was but a component part of everything that moved alongside it, that lived and sang in the rustling and splashing and sounds of human speech—not in the dull sense of words, but in the timbre of voices, their banter back and forth, their intonations and rhythmic patterns ... The sounds of machines and the natural voices of the sea, the wind, the rain—receding and approaching—existed like background noises, occasionally gathering strength and assuming the lead part ... This lasting music had no preconceived plan; it existed beyond the limits of the chorus form, was full of arbitrariness or chance, but was nonetheless music, not musical chaos, and for all its uninterruptedness and infiniteness, it ultimately resolved to a cadence, culminating at logical points and taking off once again from almost any chance note ...

Once, when lying on the warm sand of a rather filthy beach, Tanya attempted to express this sensation verbally. Sergei nodded matter-of-factly.

"Aleatoric. It is called aleatoric music. Chance contains a wealth of possibilities."

"Like fragments of glass in a kaleidoscope?" Tanya brightened.

"You could put it that way. Talk to Garik, he's a wiz at music theory; I've just picked up what I need along the way."

"Man, everything's been figured out already," Tanya said in dismay. "No matter what you discover, it's been studied and described ..."

"You're silly," laughed Sergei. He stroked the rolling hill of her firm belly.

"You're not going to overheat, are you? Let's go sit in the shade, huh?"

In the space of two weeks he had grown as accustomed to Tanya and her belly as if he had spent the last six years with her and not with the retired ballerina Elvira Poluektova, who was totally devoid of female bulges or softness, which, it bears mentioning, he liked a lot.

Following two more weeks of gigs in Odessa, the trio headed for the Caucasus mountain region.

"First we're going to put you on a train, and then we'll head out," Garik announced to Tanya.

Tanya asked them not to send her off and to let her stay until the end of their tour. Sergei added: "At least for one week, Garik. We'll do Sochi and send Tatiana from there. Besides, it'll be easier to get tickets by then."

This was absolutely true: train or air tickets were hugely difficult to obtain at the end of August.

"What about her belly?" Garik frowned. He had two children, and he was the only one of them who knew from firsthand paternal experience that pregnancies inevitably ended with birth.

Tanya folded her thin arms over her belly.

"Garik, honey, I still have two more months ahead . . . Don't banish me now. I'll be good for something."

Garik raised his hands in defeat.

"You're just like the Frog Princess . . . Ultimately, it's Seryoga's decision. Not mine."

Garik was a classic Caucasian womanizer, who considered it his sacred duty to bang any and every big-busted blond at the same time he idolized his bright and scholarly wife, a Georgian woman grown old before her age, with a Ph.D. and a letterless bra size. He was prepared to approve of any of Seryoga's affairs, particularly because he couldn't stand that stuck-up and stupid ballerina, but Tanya's pregnancy was a dilemma for him.

"Are you sick, Seryoga? Tanka's a nice little girl, but how you can fuck her with another man's goods inside, I'll never know."

Tanya's belly in fact excited Sergei terribly. His marriage to Poluektova, who was abstractly sexual and barren as a rock, had been concluded coldly and straightforwardly. At the outset he had rented a room from her, then he started to bring home kefir and walk her two borzois, then somehow accidentally he found himself in her bed, and married her as a demonstration to the world, mostly his parents, of his total independence from everyone. At one time the retired ballerina had attracted him with her complete lack of resemblance to anything he had known before; Tanya now attracted him with her perception of the world, which coincided entirely with his, as did the course of her thoughts, the turns in her emotions, and, most of all, her protestant thirst for the truth, which in practice played out as protest against any kind of falsehood, be it official or everyday.

"We have total synergy at the molecular level." Tanya stated this surprising fact, and Sergei agreed.

The tiny thing in the middle of Tanya's belly got in absolutely no one's way. Tanya said that her son was happy because she had found him a proper father. Sergei did not object to this either.

There was also one other, profoundly intimate circumstance. For all her impudent spirit—being with a child that had resulted from a charitable act and touchingly uninhibited in her examinations of male anatomy, to which she had not condescended in her earlier experience—Tanya, as she candidly admitted to Sergei, until that summer had never known the not exclusively human delight that any living creature from earthworm to hippopotamus experiences as the direct result of the friction of mucous glands against mucous glands, producing a powerful release of the central nervous system.

"It's the most fundamental difference between men and women: men can achieve it with anyone and at any time," Tanya philosophized drowsily.

"You're mistaken, I know a lot of women who can achieve it with anyone," Sergei objected.

"But for some reason I don't want to continue exploring how many men in the world I can achieve it with. I think I'll stop with you."

"Just keep in mind that others have already stopped with me." Sergei laughed.

From time to time Tanya called Vitalka and her father in Moscow. It was impossible to get through to Obninsk: Gena's laboratory had one landline for the entire floor, and the person on duty in the dormitory would not call people to the phone in the evening. It was precisely Gena Tanya really wanted to talk to, to tell him that she had fallen head over heels in love and was not planning to return to Moscow. She didn't have the resolve to tell either her father or Vitalka that: Vitalka was too vain, and her father too logical and serious. As it was, he was demanding that she return immediately, shouting into the receiver that the end of the seventh month was particularly dangerous, and that she was putting the child at risk.

"He's doing well, Daddy! And I'm doing well! We're so well! We're going to stay here just a little bit longer!" She held the phone with one hand and Seryozha's hand with the other.

"Should I send money?" Pavel Alekseevich asked.

"No money. Don't send any money. Day after tomorrow I'm going to Sukhumi!" she shouted joyfully, while Pavel Alekseevich, once the phone call was over, went to his study to down a glass of tranquilizer. He in fact was very worried: Tanya had her mother's build, the same narrowness of the lower pelvis, and there was danger the pelvic bones might separate. She should be confined to bed rest.

It could never have entered Pavel Alekseevich's head that she would not return to Moscow to give birth, but would remain to deliver her child in some other city, into a stranger's hands.

But that was precisely how it happened. The tour, having begun successfully in Yalta and met with even greater success in Odessa, achieved the pinnacle of success in Sochi. In Sukhumi they were received considerably less enthusiastically, and in Batumi they gave only two of the four scheduled concerts. Scorching Adzharia gave them a cold reception, partly because it was the beginning of the tangerine harvest season, and so they left, breaking their semilegal contract. Garik was anxious to send Tanya home, but she kept finding pretexts not to go, until he just gave up.

Over the past month Tanya had noticeably put on weight, and the child would go for days without making himself known, then suddenly make such a fuss inside that it felt as if there were a whole pack of children in there. At night Sergei would put his hand on her stomach and feel a heel or a fist thrashing and with entirely distinct outlines.

"I could give birth to twins," Tanya threatened Sergei, but he was lighthearted and without a care.

"What difference does it make? If it's twins, it's twins. One gray, one white, two happy geese." He clapped her on her swollen side, pressing his lips to her thin skin stretched to its maximum from within, and his attraction to the future child's domicile not only did not wane, but, on the contrary, increased.

"I like it so much, I love it so awfully much. You will always be pregnant and having babies with me . . . Like Natalia Nikolaevna . . ." Like all Petersburgers, he did not invoke Goncharova's surname—there was no need. "Abortions are abominations. When she was young, Poluektova got herself scraped every three months. Ballet dancers don't have babies. But you and I will never do that . . . Never . . . It's so beautiful. Carefully . . . very carefully . . . I won't hurt you . . ."

Up until the moment she gave birth they were unable to tear themselves apart from each other.

Tanya did not return to Moscow. She flew to Leningrad at the end of October. They had no place to live. Initially they crashed with Tolya Aleksandrov, the drummer. Long ago his family had been allotted communal living space in the former living room (with three pseudo-Italian windows) of a grand apartment on the corner of Pestel Street and Liteiny Avenue, but the huge room had already been partitioned off with wooden walls into four long pencil cases with three-fourths of a window in each. True, following the deaths of his mother and grandmother Tolya came into two whole rooms, and now he let one of them to his friends. The money earned on the tour quickly ran out, and so they lived together with Tolya as one needy family. Tanya fried potatoes, did the laundry, cleaned the neglected rooms, and listened to the music, that same unceasing sound track that she had learned to hear during their travels . . .

In the middle of December an ambulance took Tanya to a maternity hospital. They did not want to accept her without documentation from a women's clinic. All she had with her was her passport with her Moscow registration and labor pains. While admissions was scolding her for being so irresponsible, her water broke, and there was nothing left to do but place the woman in labor on a cart and take her to the delivery room. The baby was delivered by one of those midwives taught by Pavel Alekseevich at advanced qualification courses at the institute, and, seeing the renowned last name on a hastily written piece of paper, the midwife asked Tanya if she was related to Doctor Kukotsky. Once she learned that she was his daughter, the midwife never left her side and at the end of the tenth hour of labor—which was good, even quick, for a first delivery—received her little girl with rather long black hair.

When she heard that she had a daughter, Tanya cried bitterly. Never had she been so profoundly disappointed . . .

The midwife who had performed the delivery called Moscow, tracked down Pavel Alekseevich's home phone number, and congratulated him on the birth of a granddaughter.

16

PAVEL ALEKSEEVICH PUT DOWN THE RECEIVER. HIS HEART suddenly drained, skipped a beat, then burst into a drumroll.

"Oh-ho, one hundred eighty beats a minute," he estimated. "Paroxysmal tachycardia . . ." He reached for his watch—half past four. A night girl. Born between midnight and late sunrise. December 16. The darkest days of the year. Close to the solstice.

The second hand of his old—wartime—Swiss watch was completing its meticulous circle, and Pavel Alekseevich automatically counted his pulse. One hundred ninety beats a minute.

He lowered his legs from the bed. Dry sinewy sticks. He pressed his finger against the ball of his foot: not a hint of edema.

"All right, thank God, I have a granddaughter. No more feeling offended. My disappointment is of no significance."

He sat for a rather long time, waiting for the rhythm of his heart to settle down. "Most likely it's sinus arrhythmia." Pavel Alekseevich quickly arrived at a diagnosis.

He stood up and did his nighttime rounds, checking the apartment in which he had lived almost twenty years. A massive old man with a shaved head dressed in old military long johns, his back hunched, made his way along the corridor and turned on the light in the anteroom: the place couldn't have been more run-down. At first he looked into the girls' room: there were two beds there. Toma was sleeping on one, while the other, Tanya's, was piled with a mountain of unironed laundry. Dark masses of leaves billowed disagreeably in the room's twilight; it smelled of damp earth . . .

He turned down the corridor to the left and looked into their former bedroom, Elena's room. There was a complex smell of hospital, dust, and some sort of bitter herb.

It was filthy. Their place had become very filthy. Vasilisa's vision was poor, and she never really had known how to clean right. Toma worked and went to school: the girl had a heavy load. He should ask Praskovia, the cleaning woman in their section, to come by. No, that was impossible: Vasilisa would take offense . . . But you couldn't put a child in this room. In my study. That's the optimum choice. And I can clean my place up myself. A crib in the center of the room—there's plenty of space. I'll bring a changing table from the section. And immediately apply for retirement. How fortunate, I've already turned sixty-five . . .

Elena was not sleeping. She looked at the dark silhouette in the doorway. The light burst from behind his back, and the semblance of a halo had formed around his head and shoulders.

"Is that you?" Elena asked.

Pavel Alekseevich sat down at her feet. Elena had always loved to sleep on high fluffed pillows. Earlier, when he used to sleep on this wide bed, her pillows had stood upright in the left part of the bed, while his little flat one lay on the right ... He stuck his hand under the blanket and stroked her feet in their silky socks.

"I just got a call from Leningrad: Tanya's given birth to a little girl."

"No, no," Elena interrupted him softly. "I'm the one who's had the little girl."

"Tanya has grown up, gotten married, and given birth to a little girl," Pavel Alekseevich reiterated.

Elena's eyes flashed brightly in the semidarkness.

"It's too early. It's too dark. Where is Tanechka?"

"In Leningrad."

"Tell her to come in here. I haven't seen her in a long time ... Is she at school?"

"Tanechka finished school a long, long time ago. She's in Leningrad. She's given birth to a daughter," Pavel Alekseevich repeated patiently.

"Say something else, Papa," Elena requested. "I don't understand that."

Pavel Alekseevich moved his round stool to the head of the bed. The young Murka, who had arranged herself under Elena's hand, started and opened one eye. Pavel Alekseevich sat down next to his wife and took her by the hand. Her hand was dry, cool, and almost weightless.

For many years they had called him PA. At work they had pronounced it *Pee-A*, such was the fashion in those days—to refer to superiors by their initials. At home in the better years of their family life he had been called Pah. But now Pavel Alekseevich wondered whether Elena had taken him for her own father. He held her hand, stroked her fluffy uncombed hair, and decided not to find out who she took him for. It wasn't all that important ...

"I'm leaving for Leningrad right now, to see how things are there, and I'll try to bring them back," he informed Elena.

"That's nice," she sighed. "Tell Tanya to come in."

Pavel Alekseevich continued, ignoring Elena's inability to keep up a coherent dialogue.

"It seems to me she's having some trouble with her husband. Perhaps he offended her somehow. I don't know. And I don't intend to ask. Last time Vitaly called was last week. He asked about Tanya, and I told him that she was in Leningrad and was planning to return soon, but that she hadn't given me her address. What do you think about that?"

Elena was perplexed and began to fret.

"I don't know, what do you think . . . You yourself . . . I don't . . ."

"In any case it's better for her and the child to be at home than just anywhere, don't you think?" He asked a question that required no more than a nod of the head.

But Elena no longer heard him. She swept her hands anxiously at her sides, and he guessed that she was looking for the escaped Murka, whom she developed a need for whenever she found herself in a difficult situation. The cat sat in a chair, at some distance. He picked it up and put it on the bed near Elena. Elena squeezed it with both hands and smiled. As soon as she touched the animal, she seemed to abandon the space of the bedroom: her gaze became not quite vacuous, but focused somewhere without, beyond the bounds of the here and now . . .

Pavel Alekseevich sat a bit longer, then went to his study and called the information line. It turned out he had plenty of time to make the day train to Leningrad. He took his briefcase and packed a toothbrush, his white hospital coat, and the military flask with diluted alcohol that he always kept in stock at home. He decided not to tell anyone he was leaving, and to call in the evening from Leningrad. He was not worried about finding a place to stay: he had an old friend at whose place he could always stay, and there was the Academy's hotel on Khalturin Street, where they would always find a room for him . . . He set out for the train station, bought a ticket unexpectedly quickly, and managed to drop in at his clinic as well: there was a woman there in critical condition whom he wanted to check on and give the attending physician instructions for . . .

The Leningrad day train traveled an absurdly long time, and Pavel Alekseevich turned out not to have a single book with him. He cast a curious eye toward his fellow travelers—a young couple that kissed surreptitiously—and tried to figure out whether they were older than Tanya . . . Probably they were even younger. Until the darkness set in he looked out the window: the pleasant flickering outside distracted him from his oppressive thoughts. When he was young, his sense of righteousness had been exceptionally important, and many of his actions had been determined precisely by that inner sense. Now he was at a loss: Tanya had acted completely irresponsibly. You have to admit: she abandoned her ailing mother—with no explanation whatsoever. Now, with a kind of maniacal consistency she was making everyone sick with worry—her husband, her father, even Vasilisa . . . She had given birth recklessly and thoughtlessly who knows where; it was unclear where she would go to live with the child, and how she would support it . . . The girl was wrong on all counts.

He, Pavel Alekseevich, could not seem to find himself guilty of anything, but that was irrelevant. He took her wrongfulness on himself and was going to her in order to set wrongs right, to correct what had gone wrong, the abnormities in her life that had come about, after all, through his, Pavel Alekseevich's, entirely imponderable fault. He reproached himself for his inability to put their lives in order: his wife was ill, his daughter had left home . . . Every time his circular anxious thoughts returned to this juncture he opened his briefcase and took a big gulp from the canvas-covered flask. It was an automatic reaction that had formed at the end of the 1940s when a summons to the ministry or to a meeting at the Academy had promised trouble . . . The hydroxyl group (–OH) near the saturated carbon atom, bless its heart, protected him in its usual way from troubles both external and internal . . .

In the evening, when the train had moored at the Moskovsky train station, the flask was bone-dry and his heart once again rumbled double-time, but inside he felt relieved, because over the course of the trip—while observing out of the corner of his eye the young couple that kept trying to touch each other with a shoulder, an elbow, or a knee—everything had come together of its own in his head. The sole plausible explanation for Tanya's unreasonable—no matter how you looked at it—behavior was a new romance. He recalled a similar tragic incident in '46–'47, when a woman confined to bed rest toward the end of her pregnancy—Galina Kroll was her name, a beauty, a colonel's wife—fell in love with the department assistant, Volodya Sapozhnikov, within a few days of when she was to give birth. Their affair was so wild that by the time Galina and her child were to be released from the hospital she refused to return to her husband and moved in with Volodya. Her husband tracked down the home wrecker and filled him with lead. The poor woman was left with no husband and no lover: one had been murdered and the other put in prison ... About five years later she came back to see him. After the infertility center had already been founded ... Galina had married a second time, changed her surname, and spent three years in treatment before she could conceive again. She came to Pavel Alekseevich to give birth to the baby. Her second labor was complicated: a breach presentation ... For some reason his memory held hundreds and hundreds of cases ... Thus Pavel Alekseevich prepared himself for a meeting with his daughter and consoled himself with the fact that Vitalik would hardly track anyone down ...

From the train station Pavel Alekseevich took a taxi; twenty minutes later he was at the maternity hospital. The chief doctor was awaiting him: it wasn't every day academicians visited an ordinary maternity hospital. He washed his hands and put on his white coat. They took him to the ward where on the second bed from the door lay his thin, dear little girl—who looked more like a teenager, perhaps even a teenage boy—with deep circles under her eyes and swollen lips ... He did not recognize her immediately, but she, seeing her father, quietly "oh-ed" and flew straight out of bed onto his neck.

They held each other tight: there was no question of either being offended.

"Dad, it's great that you've come ... You're a real ... Tell them to show you our little girl. How's Mama? What's Tomka up to?"

He stroked her short-shorn little head, her shoulders, and his hand was amazed by her thinness, and his fingers savored the feel of her sharp shoulder blades ...

"My silly little girl," he whispered. The other women in the ward were all eyes. Tanya was a special bird in their ranks: although she had said nothing about herself, over the course of the day public—if not opinion, then suspicion—had formed that the girl was unmarried, a drifter, and something about her was not right ... Now it turned out that she was special in addition because her father was someone famous ...

THEY GAVE TANYA A DRESSING GOWN, AND THE TWO OF them set out for the nursery ward. White swaddled bundles just slightly larger than loaves of bread lay in miniature beds that resembled a doll's.

"Go find her, show her to me," Pavel Alekseevich whispered.

The local doctor was about to extract herself from the hastily formed procession around him, but he signaled to her: don't.

It was not much of a riddle: there were little plates with the mothers' surnames on the cribs, but Pavel Alekseevich peered into each tiny face, hoping to recognize his own among them.

"Here," Tanya pointed to a baby. Their name was written in violet letters at the foot of the crib . . . The little girl slept. Dark bangs fell on her high forehead, her face was a bit yellow, her nose big, her mouth small and tightly shut. "Beautiful, isn't she?" Tanya asked possessively.

Pavel Alekseevich lifted the swaddled bundle out of the crib, and his heart ached: our baby . . . Then he stuck his little finger into the corner of the diaper folded inward from the back, and placed the bundle on the changing table. The little girl opened her mouth with a little smack and squeaked. Pavel Alekseevich extracted her from her diapers, pulled aside her undershirt . . . straightened out her legs, leveled them, turned her over on her tummy with the same dexterous movement women use to turn pancakes on a frying pan, compared the folds under her barely defined buttocks, probed her pelvis joint—he knew this was a genetic weak spot—and held the little girl up by her legs . . . He ran his finger down her spine, probed the nape of her neck, the top of her head, then once again turned her on her back. Then he felt her protuberant stomach and pressed his finger alongside the bandaged stalk of her umbilical cord.

"Fresh as they come," he murmured. "Her liver is slightly enlarged—infantile jaundice, nothing terrible. You haven't forgotten everything yet? Do you understand what's happening there? The fetal hemoglobin is breaking down . . ." He placed three fat fingers on the left side of her chest. Then he took the tiny hand, straightened the fist, and touched the soft nails, which were bent at the edges.

"Stethoscope," he tossed out into space, and immediately, as if out of thin air, a metal disk with ear tubes appeared.

He listened for a minute.

"Normal. It seemed to me at first that her little nails were a bit blue. But her heart is just fine. At least there's no defect."

The little girl grabbed at his finger, looked at him with her milky—like a kitten's—eyes, and moved her upper lip. Tanya watched all these manipulations as if bewitched: her father with the infant in hand somehow reminded her of Sergei with his saxophone—the same tenderness and assurance in the way they held them, the same freedom of movement and ease of touch . . .

"A marvelous little baby. I like this kind the best: tiny, firm, and with good musculature . . . You know, she's not of your breed. She's a Goldberg. I'm going to send a telegram to the camp to tell him, make him happy," he whispered quietly in Tanya's ear. "Congratulations, my little girl . . . In a day or two we'll gather your stuff and take you home."

Tanya had not thought of going to Moscow, but at that moment—either out of postpartum fatigue or owing to her father's total assuredness and belongingness in this place alongside the newborn little girl—she agreed readily.

"We'll go, but not for long. I'm moving to Piter. I have a . . ." she pondered for a minute how to explain to her father what precisely she had here. "Everything I need is here."

Pavel Alekseevich nodded understandingly. "That's what I thought."

17

Dear Sergei!

How my hand enjoys writing your name! How your name suits you; it's the only one for you. But it could have been Vitalik or Gena . . .

Greetings, Sergei!

Congratulations to you on having me and to me on having you. Everything about my existence today is different from yesterday. I had a little girl. It looks like we were terribly deceived, and she got substituted for a little boy. But she is very beautiful, everyone says, she looks like me. Keep in mind, I'm going to need a little boy soon. A little boy who looks like you. The fact that the little girl doesn't resemble you and could not resemble you makes her a not very interesting creature for me. That is, I like her. They brought her to me today. She is touching and darling, but in some way—I can admit this to you—she is particularly dear to me as a witness to our love, as a witness to your caresses. As a secret participant even. I think that she will love you terribly, in a way that will be torturous for me.

I am jealous of you. Jealous of your former life, of all the things you touch, especially your instrument, but also the towel you wipe your face dry with, the teacup you touch with your fingers. Of all the women you caressed before.

Since you appeared, the world has changed so awfully much. Because I used to look at everything from one point of view, but now I look at things from two: I ask myself what would you think? I kiss you wherever I want. This time in the little indentation under your neck and on the scar on the left. Our little girl says hello. I don't have any milk, but they say it might still come. Bring kefir and a big towel. It hurt, but went quickly.

Tanya

SERGEI READ THE LETTER, NEATLY REFOLDED THE SHEET of paper along the crease, and placed it in the inner pocket of his jacket. He had just delivered to the mustached receptionist behind the little window a bouquet of tea roses, some food, and a note. He had asked where the windows in Tanya's ward looked out, and it took him a long time to figure out how to find them. He had known since evening that Tanya had given birth, and he had spent the whole night drinking with friends on that occasion, but now he suddenly wanted terribly to see Tanya, not through the window, but in person. He walked away from the information desk and headed for the staff entrance. A door guard was sitting there.

"Where do you think you're going?"

"I'm here to fix medical equipment," he improvised. "Someone in the second section called me to come in and fix the proton synchrotron. Where can I leave my coat?"

The proton synchrotron that had for some reason rolled off Sergei's tongue thoroughly satisfied the door guard.

"The coatroom attendant's out sick; take off your coat and hang it up yourself. No one will steal it. We all know each other here." The door guard let him pass. Removing his jacket, he took the absent cloakroom attendant's blue work coat off its communal nail and rushed up the stairs. The door to the section was closed, so he rang the bell. A while later a nurse opened the door.

"What do you want?"

"They called me about fixing some equipment," Sergei answered, trying not to breathe wine fumes at the nurse.

"You have to talk to the head nurse, in room seven," the nurse barked and disappeared.

Sergei immediately spotted the door he needed, ward four. Tanya was standing alongside the window, her back to him, in a blue hospital gown—very tall and very thin.

"Tanya," he called to her. She turned around. He had never seen her not pregnant, and she seemed like a stranger and terribly young.

The bouquet lay on her bed stand, not yet put in water. It was obvious that having received his parcel she had immediately run to the window to look for him.

"How did you get in here?" Tanya asked, somewhat embarrassed and freeing herself from his embrace. The women in the beds stared at them, their eyes popping out of their heads.

"I got called in. To fix the proton synchrotron," he continued the game, and not in vain, because one of the women, almost elderly, who had just given birth to her fourth, was already planning to complain, because visitations were not allowed . . .

"They just took the children away. Too bad. If you had shown up about twenty minutes earlier, you could have taken a look at her." Tanya smiled the silliest of smiles.

At that moment Sergei seemed to her to be dazzlingly handsome and unbearably her own. She had long ago and permanently forgotten that the child had no relation to him, and she passionately wanted to brag. After Pavel Alekseevich had praised her daughter yesterday evening, she had started to like her a lot more.

"Let's go out somewhere before they throw me out . . ."

The section at that hour was quiet. They pulled at one door, then a second, and found an empty linen room, and Tanya pushed him inside. Here they buried themselves in each other, whispering passionate silliness in each other's ears, locking themselves to each other with lips and teeth, and, between kisses, informing each other of various important things. Tanya told him that after they let her out she was taking the child to Moscow for a bit. He told her that he had been to see Poluektova and told her that he had a daughter, and that Poluektova had been invited to conduct ballet classes at the Perm Choreographic School and she had offered them her apartment to live in . . .

"In your wife's apartment?" Tanya was taken aback.

"What's the big deal? It's normal. We'll keep an eye on her place, walk her dogs, and feed her old cats . . ."

Tanya pressed his wrists.

"All right. We'll decide that later. But on the whole it's pretty cool that she's so . . . magnanimous, is it?"

"No, you don't understand. It's just easier for her that way. She has two borzois, and they're not easy to deal with . . . But they listen to me . . ."

They buried themselves in each other once again, and with her tongue Tanya traced the hard spot inside his lip—from the saxophone mouthpiece . . . For a whole hour no one bothered them in the linen room as they checked to make sure that nothing had changed now that Tanya did not have a belly anymore . . . But everything was just as it should be: the hot places were hot; the damp places—damp; and the dry—dry . . . And their love, as it turned out, had not diminished one single bit . . .

18

THREE DAYS AFTER GIVING BIRTH TANYA FELT AS IF SHE had been born again, as if the birth of her daughter had infused her with a certain quality of newness as well. Essentially, that was what had happened: she was a newborn mother and, although she still knew nothing about the lifelong burden of motherhood, about the immutable link between a woman and her child that alters a woman's psyche—often to a painful degree—a thought had already awakened inside her that she wanted to share with her daughter before anyone else. She lowered her brown beanlike nipple into the child's delicately opened mouth and tried to imbue the tightly swaddled bundle with the idea that they loved each other, mother and daughter, and would take joy in each other, and belong to each other, but not solely ... that she, Tanya, would have her own separate life, but, in exchange, when she grew up, Tanya would give her freedom and the right to live the way she wanted, and that she would be the older daughter, and then there would be a little boy, and another little boy, and a little girl ... And our family will not be like those others where the daddies yell at the mommies and fight over money and the children scream and take each other's toys ... And we will have a house in Crimea, and a garden, and music ... Tanya fell asleep without finishing her picture of the happy future, while the little girl continued to suck. She had an amazing little girl who emanated sleep like a campfire emanates warmth ... Tanya had never known such strong and powerful sleep ... The practical nurse collected the fed infant and carried it away, while Tanya, though she noticed some movement around her, had not the will to wake up ...

A week later Tanya was released, and Pavel Alekseevich delivered her and the baby to a large cold room in an expensive hotel. The little girl was set down perpendicularly on the immensely wide bed made of Karelian birch and covered with a woolen blanket and then a cotton-stuffed one. Soon after, Sergei showed up with a bouquet of frozen roses, champagne, and his saxophone. He pulled off his jacket filled with damp cold and rushed to the child. He sat down on the bed to look at the new face in its multilayered packaging.

"Oh my gosh, she's so small. And how she makes you want to sleep!"

"She's a terribly soporific girl, that's for certain," Tanya agreed. "As soon as they brought her into the ward, I would conk out."

Essentially Tanya was not planning to go to Moscow, but things turned out not quite as she had wanted. Poluektova was scheduled to leave for Perm only at the end of January, while a long drawn-out scandal had erupted at Aleksandrov's communal apartment with the neighbors, who had no intention of putting up with a tiny child on the other side of their plywood wall ... Sergei refused to travel to Moscow to Tanya's parents' place: he had had enough of his own parents. Tanya's departure upset him mainly because he had already managed to telephone everyone in town that he had a daughter, and no little vodka and dry wine had been drunk over the past week in that connection, but now he had no one to produce as proof.

Tanya hastily introduced her father to Sergei and asked if he would let her and Sergei go for a walk. Pavel Alekseevich let his daughter go for three hours, until the next feeding, and stayed with his little granddaughter. Five minutes after Tanya left, having been exposed to the infant's soporific energy, he fell into a deep sleep, not to wake up until his daughter returned. He dreamed that he was asleep, but in the dream inside his dream it was summer outside, and a large group of children was getting ready to go to a pond. He was the eldest of the children, who included his younger sisters, nonexistent in real life, but who were very convincingly played by Lenochka in the role of an eight-year-old and Toma as a two-year-old. The other children were familiar, but also refashioned from adults he had come to know in the later years of his life. The duality of these people, however, did not at all surprise Pavel Alekseevich. What troubled him, rather, was that one of the boys was someone he did not know at all. Only at the very end of the dream, when the crowd of them poured out of their old dacha in Mamontovka, did it become apparent that the unknown little boy had been Tanya's Sergei in disguise, after which Pavel Alekseevich stopped worrying and woke out of his deep sleep into a more shallow slumber and pressed the bundle swaddled in a thick blanket to his chest, thought for a minute about whether or not he wanted to go down to the pond with all these masquerading children, but decided not to return to that place . . .

The next day at eight fifteen in the morning, Pavel Alekseevich, his daughter, and granddaughter were home on Novoslobodskaya Street. Toma had not yet set off for work, Vasilisa crawled out of her pantry and stood with old Murka at her feet in her usual pose of greeting facing the corridor from the kitchen, propping herself with one hand against the wall. Out of the half-opened door into Elena's room, Murka Jr. poked out first, followed by Elena in a robe thrown over her shoulders.

"Tanechka, I've been waiting for you for so long," Elena said coherently and joyfully, and Tanya, passing her daughter to a perplexed Toma—who still did not know what to say and what to do—kissed her mother, while the latter pushed her away and reached for the bundle:

"Tanechka . . ."

"Momma, that's my daughter."

"That's my daughter," echoed Elena, anxious consternation forming on her face.

"Come with me, Momma, and I'll show her to you . . ."

Tanya spread the child on her mother's bed, while Pavel Alekseevich was relieved that Tanya was acting the right way, not scaring poor Elena, but drawing her into the new event.

Tanya undid the layers of clothes and extricated the tiny body. The little girl opened her eyes and yawned.

Elena looked on tensely and as if with disappointment.

"Well, do you like her?"

Elena lowered her head in embarrassment and looked the other way.

"That's not Tanechka. That's another little girl."

"Mom, of course it's not Tanechka. We still haven't decided on a name for her. Maria, maybe? Masha, huh?"

"Evgenia," Elena whispered barely audibly. Tanya did not hear what she said.

Vasilisa repeated: "How else? Evgenia. After your grandmother . . ."

Tanya bent over the little girl, who was pushing her little fist into her mouth.

"I don't know . . . I have to think about it. Evgenia?"

While the women crowded around the baby, Tanya was swept upward, as if by a tidal wave, held there for a minute, then lowered down . . . She rushed about the apartment, looking into every cluttered corner . . .

"Dad, we're remodeling," she said to her father fifteen minutes later.

"Yes, actually, we're long overdue," Pavel Alekseevich agreed, "only now, I think, is not the time. There's a baby in the apartment. Maybe in the summer, when you all go to the dacha . . ."

"No, no, I'll leave for Piter later, we need to do it right now. We can start with the nursery . . . Then the common spaces, your study, the bedroom . . ."

In the evening, when Toma arrived home from work, half of her flowers had been distributed among the neighbors, half discarded, the furniture was stacked in the middle of the room, everything was covered over with a drop cloth, and a deal had been struck with the painters . . . Pavel Alekseevich got the feeling that their dilapidated abode, which had stood like an abandoned ship at anchor, had moved from its spot and set off sailing toward its destination, its sleepy crew awakened, and even the limp and sunken-in furniture lined up in formation and standing at attention . . . Vasilisa, who never threw anything out, surrendered to Tanya's pressure and carried out of her pantry in her own two hands the decayed blanket given to her as a present by Evgenia Fedorovna in 1911, when it had already been not very new. But even that seemed not enough for Tanya, and with a cheerful sweeping movement she carried the chipped plates, burned pots and pans, and empty glass jars stored up just in case—Vasilisa's entire collection of pauper's-and-hoarder's household goods—out to the trash heap.

The nameless little girl abided the orchestrated chaos almost without a peep, getting in no one's way and demanding practically no attention. Tanya settled her in a laundry basket she had first lined with clean cotton print fabric, and for a while hauled the basket from room to room. Then Elena asked that the little girl be left near her bed, which formed a quiet corner that Tanya did not touch for the time being. The speed with which the apartment metamorphosed was amazing: the former girls' room was redone in a week, and although Toma's jungle suffered substantial losses, the surviving plants sparkled fresh against the background of sand-yellow wallpaper that recalled the heat of African deserts.

The next week was devoted to the kitchen and the bathroom. Cooking at home was cancelled. Tanya bought incalculable quantities of inexpensive food at the takeout store, fed the workers and her family as well as acquaintances, who dropped in from time to time. Vitalik telephoned on the third day, and Tanya greeted him with indifferent gladness. He came over immediately, frowning, with an insulted look on his face, but she did not trouble herself to notice. She showed him their daughter, as if she were her own private trinket. To his proposal that she move to Profsoiuznaya Street Tanya responded with a hurtful smile, but promised to visit him as soon as she finished her household affairs here.

"Valentina's living with us now." Vitalik reported his principal news.

"Why didn't you bring her along?" Tanya asked with surprise.

"She'll come. She frequently comes to visit Pavel Alekseevich. You know, all the legal hassles . . . Perhaps they'll parole him early. The crime is the variety they usually serve only two-thirds of their terms for . . ."

"I should have done something about Ilya Iosifovich's affairs . . . The whole lot of them, after all, are so amazingly inept," thought Tanya. But that was unjustified: Valentina was entirely competent, and whatever she did she thought through carefully and carried out to the letter . . .

Tanya slept in Pavel Alekseevich's study between the laundry basket holding her daughter and the telephone: Sergei called at night, and they would talk at length about everyday nothings, about the little girl, who had not yet been given a name, about the remodeling, and about Poluektova's borzois, then Sergei would turn on a tape recording so that Tanya could hear the music he had played that day . . . That week he played a lot, almost every evening, because there were New Year's parties everywhere, and they had a lot of gigs lined up—at institutes, clubs, and cafés . . . On the morning of December 31, Tanya was about to set out for one night in Piter, having tricked Sergei into telling her where he was playing and even bought a ticket for the day train. But such a fierce freeze set in the evening before that Tanya, not having told Sergei about her secret plan, cancelled her trip. She remembered how cold it had been in the train when she returned to Moscow with her newborn daughter. She was frightened that the little girl might catch cold . . . The decision turned out to be more than wise, because Sergei, following the same logic of caprice, or surprise, arrived to spend New Year's Eve in Moscow and killed the few hours in between at a restaurant at the Leningrad train station . . .

By this time the remodeling had engulfed the entire apartment like fire. The place smelled of paint, glue, and roast goose. The table was set up in the former nursery. Toma, on Tanya's orders, decorated the seven-foot fatsia (referred to by laypeople as fig tree). At the head of the table sat Pavel Alekseevich; next to him Elena, whom Tanya had dressed for the occasion, sat with a childlike, happy face. Vasilisa had donned her carpetlike yellow and crimson headscarf, which made her as self-conscious as if she had come out with bare shoulders. Toma, on the other hand, had put on a dress with a deep plunging neckline, the same one she had sewn for Tanya's wedding, and had piled her hair so that her little head resembled a big sheep. The guests included the three Goldbergs—the two brothers and Valentina (maiden name Gryzkina), the young stepmother of Tanya's retired husbands. The basket with the little girl stood at a distance, on Toma's bed—she was the star that night—and Pavel Alekseevich understood perfectly that were it not for her, Tanya would not have come home or organized this huge, wonderful perturbation.

At a quarter to twelve the doorbell rang, and Tanya ran to open the door, having prepared in advance a snide phrase for their neighbor Roza Samoilovna, who had come by at least fifteen times today and by this time had managed to borrow positively everything there was in the house, from salt and a stool to candles and napkins ... In the doorway, wearing a light cloth jacket and a huge fur cap, saxophone and sports bag in hand, stood Sergei.

This was the most bizarre family holiday one could imagine. Except for Tanya and Sergei—happy and unconcerned about either the past or the future—each of those present experienced a profound loneliness and a piercing sense of alienation from the others. As if their natural ties to each other had been severed, scrambled, then retied in some perverted way: Pavel Alekseevich's wife had long ago become his child, while his daughter over the last two weeks had turned out unexpectedly to be the true head of the family; Elena, who sat at a crowded table for the first time in three years, experienced a nauseating form of anxiety caused by all the familiar people who had completely lost their names. Even her daughter Tanya, who more or less resembled her old self, was slightly doubled because the little girl lying in the basket was also Tanechka, but not entirely, only in part, as in a cutaway or cross-section, where the invisible, internal contours of the object usually indicated by lines of dashes were those of the little girl revealed by the cutaway ... Vasilisa, with her eye resurrected from darkness, saw bright spots of light and the colored contours of bodies against a flat background, and Tomochka's light-blue spot was the only one that was reassuring. Fluttering about the table like a thin gray bird, placing food on everyone's plate, and dropping her, Vasilisa, a piece of ferial goose—in total disregard for the Orthodox Christmas fast—Tanya kept disporting herself and touching the young long-haired fellow in black (a member of the clergy?) as she went, all in the presence of her husband and just as Elena had done during the war, while her husband sat and watched, as if he didn't care, and was this good . . . Filled with disgust by the picture before her, Vasilisa entreated: Lord, have mercy, Lord . . . Establish, O Lord, my unstable heart on the rock of Thy commandments, for Thou only art Holy and Lord . . . The words flew off and fell downward, the pieces of the psalms and prayers that Vasilisa had preserved in her failing memory were forgotten and jumbled, and all that remained was her remorse for her dear ones, all of them living incorrectly, committing sins, and not observing God's commandments—both temporal and spiritual, no matter where you looked . . . Sins, all our mortal sins . . .

Valentina Goldberg, raised in Old Believer purity in everything, from body, hut, and habits to thoughts and actions, and having deviated from her ancestors not in the slightest degree—despite her total and final estrangement from their unintelligent and outdated religion—observed Tanya mournfully. She had become acquainted with Pavel Alekseevich only after Ilya Iosifovich's arrest, come to trust him, and to love him, and now she found it impossible to connect the dots between the well-known story of their children's strange marriage, their indecent family triangle, the appearance of this long-haired musician (obviously, Tanya's lover), and Tanya herself, whom she was seeing for the first time, having taken a dislike to her in advance, and now on seeing her, for some reason feeling somehow sympathetically disposed toward her . . . although what else should this girl elicit except protest and indignation with the way she carried about, thinking of nothing, and destroying the relationship between the two brothers . . . She was promiscuous, promiscuous . . .

The Goldberg brothers—or husbands—conducted themselves appropriately, but they hardly "didn't care," as Vasilisa had surmised. Both of them were pained by the appearance of the pretender. For the first time in the last year they both felt one and the same thing—a condition familiar to them since early childhood, perhaps, one of their first conscious experiences—that of the disappointment and justice of defeat . . . It had already struck twelve, and they were late with the champagne. Tanya had forgotten the bottle in the refrigerator, and by the time she brought it out and Pavel Alekseevich opened it . . . The New Year had already begun, and they drank a toast that all be well, that Ilya Iosifovich be released, and that everyone be happy and healthy, especially the brand-new baby girl . . . They all talked noisily, interrupting each other, clanking their forks against their plates, while only Tanya and Sergei sat silently, looking at each other, well, staring at each other like two icons. Everyone saw that this musician was a perfect match for Tanya, you could see they shared the same nature, lived on the same planet, or whatever . . . What in Tanya was singular and slightly enigmatic was written all over him in full color. The Goldberg brothers had absolutely nothing to do with this and understood that perfectly. Especially when the musician unpacked his saxophone and asked Tanya to accompany him a bit, and she immediately, without mincing, cleared the stack of newspapers off the piano, warned that she had never heard a more out of tune piano, and sat down without protest, and he showed her the left-hand accompaniment on the bass, and she picked it up. Pavel Alekseevich immediately guessed that she had been practicing on and off over the past months . . . Sergei first extracted out of that horn of his some prospective trills, and Tanya harmonized, going right, then left, until they bumped into each other in some indeterminate place, and then Sergei sang long jubilant tidings on his saxophone that ended with such a happy wail that the Goldberg brothers exchanged understanding glances and felt like they were back in the schoolyard in Malakhovo during recess among those hostile rural, small town, and children's home kids from whom they suffered particularly for not belonging to any of those groups . . . At the first sound of the saxophone Elena dug her fingers into the cuff of her husband's house jacket: she heard—rather, saw—the music as a set of French curves running from the dark core of the instrument's metal throat: the principal curve, taut and matte like fresh rubber, first flattened itself, then rolled into a harmonious Archimedean spiral that kept expanding, filling the entire room, and then with a flip of one of its arms whipping out the window . . . The sound itself, it turned out, was the projection of something unknown, unnamed, but produced with obvious effort by the long-haired youth with the familiar face . . .

Pavel Alekseevich was amazed at how skillfully Tanya accompanied; she had obviously not forgotten her music lessons—and this gladdened him.

Sergei diminished the sound, blowing the remnants out of the saxophone, and Elena saw the French curves topple, fade, and dissolve. The young man's face was not just familiar, but as familiar as if she had memorized it: his thick light brows in a single line, his upper lip hanging slightly over the lower . . . He placed his saxophone alongside the laundry basket, shook his head, ran his fingers through his hair, then threw it back with a familiar gesture . . . His hair is full of sand, Elena thought.

Then Tanya carried the basket with the sleeping baby girl into Pavel Alekseevich's study, where she and Sergei closed the door behind them, and the guests, passing through the corridor past the door to the bathroom, could hear them laughing. They chatted and laughed for two hours. In the morning Sergei left while everyone was still asleep. Pavel Alekseevich had put Elena to bed and lay down to sleep in the bedroom, in his former spot, without undressing, and slept until late in the day: the night before he had had a lot to drink. Elena practically did not sleep and lay with her eyes open as she recollected where she knew that musician from, and seemed to have remembered . . .

By the end of January the remodeling was finished. The apartment had been renovated, and Vasilisa now could not find anything: the pots, and plates, and vegetable oil all stood in new places, and she so tired of constantly searching that she ultimately took the bread into her pantry, wrapped it in a towel, and kept it in her nightstand. Tanya turned the household over to Toma, stocked up on grains and macaroni, sugar, and flour. She hung new curtains and bought a washing machine . . . Then she announced to Pavel Alekseevich that she was leaving.

"Mama's grown accustomed to her, leave her with us. When you get your life in order in Leningrad, you can take her," Pavel Alekseevich implored.

In the space of time that his granddaughter had spent at the apartment he had understood that he had lived to the point in his life when this little baby girl was capable of replacing his entire professional life, his students, his mentees, and, most of all, his patients. No matter what he did at the section—follow the quivering lines of a cardiogram, poke his seeing hands into a hemorrhaging uterus rupture, or palpate a ripe belly—he never forgot for a minute the little girl in the wicker basket. He mentally kept track of her newborn, still not rich time: now she was sleeping, already waking up, sucking, belching, stretching and kicking her little legs, performing the grave act of defecation, then falling asleep again . . . His sole and constant desire was to be alongside her basket, alongside the little girl who emitted infantile radiation and sweet slumber. She still had very little individuality, but her family heritage was beginning to show through: her eyebrows were long, and several little hairs stuck out in that same place where the family brush would eventually grow. She sort of reminded you of a hedgehog: a long nose and locks of hair clumped together in little needles . . . But her forehead was Goldberg's high forehead . . .

Tanya had been two years old when she had come into Pavel Alekseevich's life, and she had been a beautiful and tender child, kindhearted and trusting, while this tiny mite was almost without any character at all; she did not have to capture her grandfather's heart, she had simply from birth been imbued with power over Pavel Alekseevich, and he relished sitting alongside her basket, helping Tanya bathe her, touching her little red unwalked-on feet. It was a purely natural feeling that needed neither justification nor explanation, like a lion loving a lion cub, a wolf a wolf pup, and an eagle an eaglet . . . At this point, he discovered, pedagogy of any sort is nonsense and cold rationalism, and when pedagogy begins, what recedes is this natural feeling, this profound animalistic sense of love for one's young . . . The lowest of all high emotions . . .

"I say that absolutely seriously. We'll match her up with donor breast milk. Tomorrow I'm turning in my resignation . . ."

"Dad, what are you saying?" Tanya gazed at her father's wrinkle-lined face and caught an expression she had never seen in it before—entreaty. It made her feel uneasy, and she became indignant: "What are you talking about? I can't imagine you retired! You're going to make her porridge, are you? Take her for walks in her stroller?"

He nodded. "Uh-huh. With pleasure. Tanya, I've spent too little time on the family. And now's just the time. Mama and I will take her for strolls."

"Mama's totally out of it," Tanya responded gloomily.

"I don't know. I'm not sure . . ."

Tanya embraced his neck and tickled him behind his ears.

"Dad, you're fantastic, really. I'll bring the baby girl to you, for sure. You know I want to have a lot of children. Girls and boys, five of them."

Pavel Alekseevich clenched Tanya's hands, wasted on laundry and remodeling, kissed them, and went to the kitchen to down an absolutely necessary dose: three-fourths of a medium-size, broad-faceted glassful.

The gears were turning in his aging head: why of all the tens of thousands of children he had brought into the world, saved, and even planned through his own intuition, was this baby girl and the other two or three Tanya planned to have so dear? I can't even say that it's *blood* . . . There's no blood, no parentage, nothing but the irrational, inexplicable, capricious, and good-for-nothing call of the heart . . .

Tanya was in a hurry. She had a whole list of things to do, which she crossed out one after the next—the ineradicable habit of a responsible and organized human being . . . The most expensive and labor-consuming task was replacing all the plumbing fixtures, including the bathtub, which had become unusable of late because of a constant leak; the most delicate task was getting her daughter baptized. Vasilisa was commissioned as expert to arrange this sacred procedure, with Toma as godmother. For starters, Vasilisa flatly refused to go to the St. Pimen Church, which was closest to their house, because it had—in Vasilisa's mind—besmirched itself in the past with "revisionism"; she suggested they go to some rural church in the far reaches of the Moscow region where a "proper" priest served. Tanya dealt with Vasilisa's principles with surprising ease, telling her that she would not travel that far and that she was not sure herself how she had got it into her head to baptize the child in the first place, and if there were going to be complications, then she was prepared to give up the notion entirely. At that, Vasilisa pursed her lips and began changing from her trimmed felt boots, which served as house slippers, to her street felt boots with the rubber galoshes . . . The sacrament of baptism was performed at the Church of St. Pimen. From that day on the little girl was designated Evgenia, and Tanya struck the thin cross from her list. All that was left was to give Elena a bath in the new bathtub. It had been more than a year since they had last used the bathtub, taking showers instead, not plugging the drain and rinsing off as quickly as possible so as not to flood the neighbors downstairs.

Tanya filled the tub. Elena pressed her elbows to her side and feebly resisted.

"You have to get undressed. Look, Mommy, there's already water in the tub . . ." Tanya coaxed her, and reluctantly she obeyed.

Her mother's gauntness was painful, and it was not a matter of her being underweight: Tanya herself weighed less than 110 pounds. Empty folds of flesh hung from Elena's shoulders and arms, and at the sight of her mother's nakedness Tanya was struck by the thought of how sad and sexless the human skeleton was, and how what lent women their charm and men their strength and even made for the difference between men and women were merely pieces of fat-streaked flesh. Of her mother's former womanhood all that remained were her pale breasts and the vague shadow of her almost hairless pubis.

At long last Tanya sat her mother in the warm water. Elena lay back and stretched out her legs.

"How good it is . . ."

"I'm like Ham," Tanya laughed to herself as she lathered the sponge. Looking was indecent, but washing, trimming, and wiping dry was quite all right . . .

"Wait, Tanechka. I want to lie here for a bit. It's such bliss . . . Was the bathtub broken before?" Elena asked in a very hale voice.

"Yes. Now it's fixed."

Elena closed her eyes. Her hair slipped into the water and got wet. Tanya moved it to the side.

"Everything changes in water. My head is a lot better in warm water. I don't want you to live at home. I don't want you to live with me. I forget everything, and it seems to me that now I've forgotten more than I remember. But soon I'll forget even how much I forgot. Don't be frightened, I don't have anything terrible in mind, I am simply dying in the most usual way, from the middle of my head. Right now I feel very good. I haven't felt so good in a long time, and I want to say good-bye to you. I'm being consumed by a hole. For some reason what's happening to me is very shameful. And I don't know if anything will remain at the very end. Tell me, how old am I?"

"Soon you'll be fifty-two . . ."

"And you?"

"I'm twenty-three."

"Good. The water has cooled. Add a little bit more hot . . . I'm not sure of anyone or anything. Sometimes strangers come, and sometimes people I know . . . At times there's Vasilisa, with someone else inside her . . . I'm not even sure of myself . . . You know about that."

"No, Mommy. I don't know anything about that . . ."

"Never mind, whatever. I wanted to tell you that at this minute I am I and you are you, and I love you very much. And now I'm going to say good-bye to you. And then you soap me up . . . And then leave . . ."

Tanya wanted to object, but her tongue refused, because all she could have said would have been pathetic, meaningless words. She lathered her mother's hair, leaning her head back slightly so that the soap would not run into her eyes, scrubbed her scalp, and directed the stream of water from the shower head to rinse off the suds . . . She washed all the sagging folds of Elena's narrow body, dried her dry, and covered her skin with baby cream. Then she dressed her in a long flannel shirt and took her to her bed. It was nearly nine in the evening. Pavel Alekseevich arrived soon after: that day he had delivered evening lectures at the institute of continuing professional education. Tanya was all packed. They ate supper together, and he saw the girls off to the station.

The Moscow period of Tanya's life was over.

19

DURING HIS LAST PRISON TERM LUCKY GOLDBERG SPENT not a single day doing general labor: they immediately put him to work as an attendant in the camp's sick bay. The head doctor—an elderly, real shit, Lord forgive, of a woman who had lazed herself into a lump—drowsily dumped half her work on him. For all of her rottenness—having logged twenty years doing prison camp medicine, which less than any other branch had the right to call itself medicine—the head doctor lazily defended before the administration her right to keep Ilya Iosifovich on, and at least twice she managed to spare him from getting transferred to general labor . . .

Had there been a male doctor in her stead, Ilya Iosifovich would not have tolerated—even in spite of her protection—her sleepy indifference toward the patients, her thievery, and her petty underhandedness. What reconciled him with the head was compassion, which went beyond all his principles: perpetually grazing at the doctor's side was her twenty-year-old mentally disabled daughter whom she was afraid to leave at home alone. This woman's biography—bitter, Soviet, and as ineluctable as an unburied corpse—tagged behind her . . .

Perhaps for the first time in his life, Goldberg's public insistence on the truth—as indecent as a patch on the seat of one's pants—held its tongue. Over the past two-plus years he had drudged away as attendant in name and assistant chief physician in fact, he never once bothered her with stormy discussions, never called her on anything, never tossed a mug at her, and never yelled . . . When they were saying their good-byes, she uttered to Goldberg words that amazed and even shamed him: she turned out to be smarter and better than he had thought. But perhaps the matter lay precisely in the fact that Ilya Iosifovich's presence, his old-fashioned magnanimity and comical gentility—usually taken for impracticable ridiculousness—had for a brief moment elevated the doctor to his level, and she clumsily pronounced her unprepossessing words, worthy of a dying man's last confession, then asked how she could help him . . . After which she sat her fat ass down on her red plush upholstered chair to spend another twenty full years at her boring job, because somehow she had to feed her impaired daughter and send money to her widowed sister, with a house full of kids, whose husband had long ago been swallowed up by the same system she worked for . . .

In a word, Ilya Iosifovich said good-bye to Elizaveta Georgievna Witte (there it is again, the unburied corpse!) and marched toward the gate. It closed behind him, and he marched farther toward the train station, a small bit of money and his release papers with him . . . The local train stopped at this station—to be found nowhere on any map—in the evenings, rather, did not even come to a full halt, but slowed down, and just at the moment when it should have stopped, it picked up steam again . . . An hour before the train was to arrive, Elizaveta Georgievna Witte—"the lump," as Goldberg had come to call her to himself—dropped into the plywood pavilion and gave Ilya Iosifovich a parcel of food. A notebook of sheets of paper sewn together lay between a loaf of bread and two cans of stew meat . . .

"All moral foundations have been undermined, Pasha. The moral foundations of life, the moral foundations of science . . . But the human being is alive." Goldberg held his bony palm on the notebook of pieces of paper that had been kept separately and bound together only on the eve of his release.

Once again, three years later, they sat in Pavel Alekseevich's study, friends turned relatives by the whim of their children whom there was no figuring out, except that baby Evgenia, their granddaughter in common, was alive and well and living in Leningrad with Tanya and the long-haired jazz player who had enthusiastically assumed the not insubstantial cares of paternity . . . The old men drank, first with toasts, then simply after raising their glasses slightly higher than their noses and stopping the motion of their arms for a second . . .

"Your health . . ."

"The hole of holes, Pasha, the hole of holes . . . But the head doctor ordered journals for me from Novosibirsk University. American, German, French . . . From the 1930s forward. I think, Pasha, that I've closed the gap that opened when the Center for Medical Genetics was shut down. This book is not so much for scholars as it is for doctors specializing in what is not yet a specialization . . . A textbook that's not a textbook . . . An introduction to medical genetics . . ."

Pavel Alekseevich reached for the bottle, which was already light . . . What a wreck I've turned into . . . Ilyusha's as strong as an ox: thin with a neck like a plucked rooster's, even his bald spot has wrinkles, and where does he get the strength, the energy . . .

More than two weeks had passed since Goldberg had shown up in Moscow. In that period of time he had managed to meet with a dozen colleagues, caught up with what was going on in the scientific world, delighted at the serious level of thinking taking place—although he saw no new great achievements—visited two publishing houses, presented a project description of the book he had already written, and realized that there was no hope of publishing it soon. Khrushchev's fall, which had occurred while Goldberg was doing his last term in prison, interested him only insofar as it signified the final defeat of Lysenko and his henchmen. The most significant event that had taken place in his absence was the formation of the Institute of Genetics. Naturally, he rushed off first thing to visit the new director, whom he had known since before the war, a well-trained geneticist nicknamed Bonya, short for Bonaparte . . .

The first forty minutes of their meeting Goldberg sang like a nightingale, generously casting his pearls hardly before swine . . . The beast who sat before him looked at him with stern blue eyes; it had jaws of steel, an iron grip, and a diamond-hard fortress of ambition to match his nickname ... But the two of them also had a lot in common: great mentors, a flawed family background—if a Jewish lumber dealer can be compared to a Siberian factory owner—experience in the camps, and top-quality brains ... The director listened with the highest degree of attentiveness, but gave no indication of his thoughts either in word or with movement of his eyebrows.

Only forty minutes later did Goldberg sense the ice-age frost creeping toward him across the long, T-shaped desk from the direction of the bald podge ensconced at the head of the desk in Buddha-like fixity in the center of his large office at the epicenter of rejuvenated genetic science. Goldberg fell silent, stunned by a grim presentiment. The director also was silent. He knew how to hold a pause. Goldberg did not.

Ilya Iosifovich halted the stream of his outpourings, all of them concerning medical genetics—from general assertions on the need for structural reorganization connected with Pavel Alekseevich's project for creating a center for genetic consulting to the most abstract of ideas, the realization of which would require about thirty years ... Interrupting himself, he got straight to the point.

"Kolya, are you going to give me a laboratory or not?"

The director's face did have something of Napoleon's about it: diminutive facial features, a chubby chin that flowed softly into a massive short neck. The insignificant face of exceptional significance ... His brain was hard at work, but the look on his face said nothing. Should he stave off saying *no*, and leave it to this cocked fool to figure out for himself with time that in some cases *yes* signifies nothing more than a variation of *no*, or cut him to shreds immediately ... They were already enemies anyway, and they would become even more bitter enemies, that the director understood for certain. There was nothing to calculate here whatsoever; it was merely a matter of personal satisfaction. For that reason he maintained his absolutely neutral pause for a while longer—in moments like this his graduate students would be struck by spasms of diarrhea—and, having tried on in his mind several variations with differing degrees of derogation, he bared a pseudosmile of new, too-white plastic teeth, and answered.

"No, Ilya. I have absolutely no need for you ..."

All of this Ilya Iosifovich related to his friend.

"It turns out, Pashenka, that he has no need for me, or Sidorov, or Sokolov, or Sakharov. He doesn't need Shurochka Prokofieva, Belgovsky, or Rappoport. Timofeev-Resovsky he especially has no need for. Instead he's hiring small fry, *Landsknechts*, and starry-eyed kids hatched only yesterday. And now, my friend, I return to the beginning of our conversation: all moral foundations have been undermined. Immoral science turns out to be worse and more dangerous than immoral ignorance . . ."

At this juncture Pavel Alekseevich perked up.

"There you go again, your usual tendency to lump everything into one big heap. You're confusing concepts. There is no such thing as moral ignorance. A semiliterate can be moral. And an entirely illiterate person, like our Vasilisa, can be moral. What follows from your words is that science is the antithesis of ignorance. That's mistaken. Science is a way of organizing knowledge, while ignorance is the rejection of knowledge. Ignorance is not a lack of learning, but a position. Paracelsus, for example, knew less about the workings of the human body than the average doctor today, but there's no way you could call him an ignoramus. He knew about the relativity of knowledge. Ignorance knows nothing, except its own level, and precisely for that reason there can be no such thing as moral ignorance. Ignorance despises everything that it cannot access. It rejects everything that demands intensity, effort, and changing one's point of view. And, by the way, as far as science is concerned, I don't think that science has a moral dimension. Knowledge does not have moral nuances, only people can be immoral, not physics or chemistry, and especially not mathematics . . ."

Goldberg chuckled, and the last of his surviving premolars peeked out of the corners of his mouth.

"Pashka, maybe you're right, but that kind of rightness is not for me. If there is progress, the good of humankind, it means that science directed at achieving a certain conditional good is moral, while that which has no good in mind can go to the devil. It's a reliquary."

"I'm sorry." Pavel Alekseevich made a helpless gesture. "By your logic science can be Marxist-Leninist, Stalinist, bourgeois, and even workers'-and-peasants'! Give me a break!"

They started in for what would be half the night, picking apart science in general, theory and practice in particular, the not-so-distant past, and the bright future. They cracked jokes, swore, chuckled, and drank a second bottle. Toward daybreak Ilya Iosifovich slapped himself on his bald spot and cursed.

"What an old fool I am! I forgot to call Valentina."

So he called Valentina, who all this time had been sitting on the edge of her chair, hugging her high belly, which had been growing since the time of her three-day visit to her husband in the camp. She had already constructed a detailed plan of what she would do tomorrow, and the day after tomorrow, and had intended first thing in the morning to go to Pavel Alekseevich's, where no one was picking up the phone—which meant a search was under way and they were not allowed to pick up the phone—and from there to the regional KGB office, and then to the lawyer's. Or first to the lawyer . . . The main thing was to pick up the main manuscript of the book at the typist's and hide it in a safe place . . .

Ilya Iosifovich picked up the phone: there was no dial tone.

"Your phone's broken: there's no dial tone. Valentina is going crazy. She, Pasha, is in her seventh month, you know . . ." Goldberg seemed to be apologizing.

Pavel Alekseevich attempted to dissuade Ilya Iosifovich from going home. It was almost five in the morning. And only after his intractable comrade had slammed the door behind him did Pavel Alekseevich realize at long last that dear awkward Valentina was giving birth to a baby from no one other than old, stooped, and withered Ilya, and that—say what you will but—the real question had nothing to do with science or with whether it was moral or not very. The main thing lay in the infant—its little nose tucked inside its crossed palms, covered with lanugo, slippery with vernix, and not yet having acquired full pigmentation and for that reason yellowish-colorless—that floated, concentrated and totally complete in and of itself, in the crammed space of its first home, in Valentina's uterus, the child of old age, but also of love, with all its physiological accoutrements—kisses, embraces, erection, friction, and ejaculation . . . Pavel Alekseevich sighed: the seminal glands, the adrenal cortex . . . and androgens, several varieties of steroids . . . He tried to remember the formula for testosterone . . . And for this very reason, because of the activeness of his endocrinal system, Ilya Iosifovich was smitten by global interest in the moral foundations of gnosiology, while he, Pavel Alekseevich, having suppressed forever his hormonal surges, was tormented solely by his worries about Tanya, about his granddaughter Zhenya, and about his wife Elena, whom he would leave with Toma and Vasilisa when he left that Saturday for Piter to visit his dear little girls ...

20

IN LENINGRAD LIFE SEEMED TO TANYA TO BE MORE PEDIgreed, with interesting roots, and somehow better accoutered in all respects—the streets, and things, and people had more substance to them, was that it? The past peeked out from under every bush, and you had to be a complete numbskull, like dear Tolya Aleksandrov, to put a hot frying pan on a wood mosaic table and never once in twenty years wonder to whom the table had belonged before. It had belonged to Zinaida Gippius, who had lived in precisely this room, having moved in as a young girl with her young husband. The city was a marvel of perpetual history, but the scars of the frying pan were also visible everywhere, which occasionally invoked a certain melancholy. There was no time, however, for melancholy: their little child did not allow it. Morning and daytime life were filled with things to be done, their bohemian, artistic life ensuing in the evening. They hired Aunt Shura, who for not very much money agreed to babysit Zhenya in the evenings and sometimes through the night. Tanya and Sergei dashed to friends' or to the cafés—no small number of which had cropped up in those days—drinking, smoking, and dancing. From time to time Sergei would perform. Their trio had not only not broken up, but, just the opposite, was becoming more and more well known in the world of the city's younger generation, but—it goes without saying—that fame was of the half-underground, private variety.

During her second Petersburg winter Tanya began to experience a wearying drowsiness and sluggishness, which she battled unsuccessfully, sleeping with little Zhenya up to twelve hours a day between December and February. But when winter's gloom began to recede a bit, she set herself into calculated motion, and already in February managed to lease a rather decently equipped workshop. There she planned to begin making strange jewelry from wire and cheap Siberian stones that a geologist friend brought from the Urals.

Tanya's daughter was blessed with a marvelous disposition, amused herself, never got bored, and it was enough to put a toy, a spoon, or a piece of string in her hands for her to spend hours of total delight investigating it, gnawing at it with her fresh tooth, sticking it in her pocket, spinning it, and deriving from it masses of interest. Sergei came to love the little girl in the most natural of ways, just as Pavel Alekseevich had once come to love Tanya, so that few of their friends knew that the little girl was hardly Sergei's daughter or Tanya—his wife. The couple did not bother with the issue of matrimony. Technically, neither of them was officially free: Sergei was married to Poluektova, and Tanya was married to Goldberg. The only problem that could possibly arise was that Tanya lacked a residence permit, which was required to get a job or to have access to health care. But Tanya had no intention of getting an office job and was completely healthy. Were anything to happen to her little daughter, she would immediately jump on a train and the next morning place the sick child in the best hands on earth . . . But nothing of the sort happened, not even a cold.

Tanya rose early, like a working woman, fed Zhenya, dressed her in her little fur coat, hat, and the stuffing underneath that one was supposed to put on children in those days before down snowsuits and hygroscopic diapers had been invented, and, with the heavy bundle loaded into her carriage, traveled—no matter what the weather—from the south mainland bank of the Neva to the checkered Petrogradsky district, where she had managed to lease a studio on the west bank of the Nevka, right next to the house of the artist Mikhail Matiushin, of whom, at the time, she knew absolutely nothing, although she quickly sensed the bizarre springs of avant-gardism that poked through the local decaying bogs.

The route from home to the workshop took at least an hour, which made for a good walk, after which Zhenya slept for an hour in her carriage, which had become a tight fit. Tanya constructed large, deliberately crude jewelry pieces with black jet and smoky quartz, which she intended to make fashionable on the Neva's left bank among her pretentious contemporaries, lovers of Petersburg jazz. Since childhood she had been aware of a special quality she had: when she put something on, all of her classmates immediately imitated her . . . For that reason, the first thing she needed to do now was to drape herself with as much of her own handmade beauty as possible, hang out, and wait for customers.

At lunchtime Sergei would arrive, having taken care of his morning responsibilities—walking the dogs and communing with his saxophone. He brought food from a takeout store and kefir for little Zhenka. Although she was more than a year old, she loved baby food and obviously preferred liquids to solids. Tanya set the teakettle on the electric hot plate, and Sergei steeped tea. Opinion was that he did that better than anyone else. They ate student-style. Like a true Petersburger he referred to white bread as buns and was careful not to waste food: the blockade had left its mark, although he, a sickly little boy, had been evacuated that year over the ice . . .

Afterward he either left to hang out with the guys, to practice, or just shoot the breeze and drink, or they spent the rest of the day together until evening. When he stayed, he would lie down on the filthy couch and play with Zhenya.

Their dinners together concluded with after-dinner games, considered harmful from the point of view of digestion. He would hoist the little girl dancing in his arms into the air, trying to catch the rhythm of her movements and tooting intermittently with his lips, while Tanya pounded out her own working beat with her mallet—metal against metal. Sergei delighted in how rhythmically conceptualized their existence was—filled through and through with musical meaning, while they themselves formed a kind of cool trio with a bass line, a lead, and a sub-lead, just as in a jazz ensemble, and even their acoustic space was divided into distinct niches, like the three melodic voices in New Orleans Dixieland . . .

"We're having a terrific jam session," Sergei said to Tanya, who, beating out another cascade of blows, objected.

"No, we have a marvelous family music box."

"Are you kidding? Music boxes make dead music . . ."

"You're right, you're right," Tanya agreed instantly.

They did not reflect on their happiness, just as the blissful pair in the never-ending Summer Garden had not a care for their daily bread, their health, or their bank accounts. Even the question of where to live did not faze them: they were living for free in a pricey bourgeois apartment in exchange for services rendered to their hostess, also for free—feeding and walking the two stupid, handsome borzois. This was work, but Sergei was used to it, knew where to buy bones, what kind of meat to add, and who to get vitamins from. Two enormous pots never left the stove top, and there were times when Tanya and Sergei served themselves from the dogs' pots, adding salt to taste.

Of course, this improbable idyll was not without problems. For example, the climate. It was cold. Or, for example, where to buy a bottle of vodka at night? From a taxi driver? Go all the way out to the airport? And there was the political order, which was disagreeable and at times downright dangerous. On the other hand, politics was everywhere, and where there was no politics there were either mountain precipices or wild beasts and venomous snakes. And other inconveniences . . .

Everyone had it bad, while for these kids, in the 1960s, life was a wonderful time.

That is difficult to believe—convincing evidence is required, a survey of eyewitnesses, the testimony of onlookers. Over the many years since, a lot has been erased from memory, and each remembers his own: Goldberg—the insides of the camp; Pavel Alekseevich—Elena in her strange transitional state as she slowly departed the world of living people; Toma—long lines for food that she had to stand in despite the food rations PA brought home from work. Others remembered the invasion of Czechoslovakia. Searches and arrests. The underground. Gagarin's launch into space. Radio-buzz and tele-pandemonium. Memories of how closed-in life was, of fear dissolved in the air like sugar in tea.

But these kids at play had a wonderful time. In their frivolity they lived without day-to-day fear, taking fright instead only for minutes at a time. Then, shrugging off their fears, they took up their redemptive music, which not just made them free, but was free in itself. This was where the invisible divide existed between Sergei and his parents. This was the very thing that had jarred the two of them—Sergei's Marxist-Leninist father and the father's musician hooligan son—apart. They were like sulfuric acid for each other . . . The child's attachment and the parent's love hissed and went up in acrid smoke, leaving neither pity nor empathy in the burnt-out hole . . .

Sergei and his parents had cut each other off long ago. His father referred to his son as none other than a bum and a renegade. His mother could not forgive her son's betrayal, although she was unable to explain whose faith he had violated with whom. Funny, but it couldn't have been with music! From Sergei's neighborhood friends his mother learned that he had a daughter. She yearned for reconciliation but, fearing her husband, lacked the courage to take the first step. Sergei's disgust with his parents was stronger than hatred. He had not seen them for eight years already, since his grandmother's death, having left home as soon as he finished school.

"There is nothing human in them. Everything that they think and say and do is one big lie. Nothing human." Talking about them wrenched his guts.

His mother sent Sergei's former classmate—Nina Kostikova, one of the neighborhood girls who had had a crush on him since first grade—to visit him. She had a mission: to set up a family reunion.

"What's the big deal?" Nina petitioned on Sergei's mother's behalf. "You could show them Zhenya."

"Tell her that the kid isn't mine, and she'll calm down." He took the baby in his arms, pressed her little forehead to his own, and cooed "ooh-ooh-ooh." Zhenya jumped with joy. "Tell her that someone dropped her on my doorstep. In her mother's lap." He chuckled as if he were being God knows how witty.

Tanya arched her brow. "So what's wrong with my lap? All right, next time I'll deliver the kid right into your arms . . ."

She had not forgotten about a new child. Several times it had seemed to her that she was pregnant, but each time she was mistaken. She loved her little daughter very much, but she wanted a little boy, and this desire had a strange persistence, as if she were obliged to give birth to a boy for the sake of some unknown higher goals. From the vantage of their everyday existence a second child would be insanity. But the first one had not been any less so. They were completely bereft of so-called material resources. Although money came in from Sergei's performances, and Pavel Alekseevich, who came to visit his children once every six weeks or so, also always left them money. This weighed slightly on Tanya, but she hoped that soon she herself would begin earning money. However, both of them—Sergei and Tanya—ruled out as an option the sweaty servitude of working for someone else, figuring that money for their livelihood should come about of its own, in the process of their free play . . .

In the meantime Tanya had become increasingly more engrossed in music. She even got herself a recorder and conversed with it occasionally, on the sly from Seryozha. The instrument was poor, but the sound was touching and childish . . . Tanya did not miss a single one of the performances of Sergei's trio and went with him to hear other jazz groups, of which no small number had formed in Piter at the time. There were not that many truly worthwhile musicians: you could count them on one hand. Sergei's idol at the time was Germann Lukianov, a Muscovite with conservatory training, of a different social breed entirely—a snob in black tails who played multiple instruments (at the time, principally the flügelhorn), and was an interesting composer as well. Later Sergei became disenchanted with him and got hooked on Vladimir Chekasin . . . But in general everyone was mad over Coltrane and Coleman. Each new album was a celebration; Sergei even celebrated the anniversary of the first time he had heard each album. He and Garik sucked every note dry and discussed every turn, every chord progression, every rhythmical shift, every tempo change, and the asymmetrical phrasing. Though Tanya far preferred listening to live music rather than these hours-long analyses, she completely understood what they were talking about: though it was not extensive, she did have musical training.

The most fortunate of their circumstances was the complete confluence of the components of their lives, which usually only somehow coexist, sometimes pulling a person in different directions. Tanya's love, family, creative, and routine household interests all flowed in a single line, her everyday life lived "musically," by the same laws as a musical composition—a symphony, for example—was organized. The analogy amused her, and early in the morning when Sergei was still asleep and Zhenya was already cooing in her crib, she would give herself over to a sonata-like allegro, a dual-themed harmony in which the first theme, Sergei's, was initially stronger and more voluminous, then subsided and conceded to the child's line, which was burbling and joyful. She caught the andante on the dark street, pushing the carriage ahead of her, and its tripartite form corresponded to the geography of the streets, with the last part, so to speak, the most indistinct, beginning at the Petrogradskaya embankment.

At her workshop the music initially stopped: she undressed her daughter, fed her water from a bottle, sat her on her pot, and tucked her back into her carriage for a nap before lunch. After that Tanya smoked her first cigarette of the day and went to her workbench. Here she was overtaken by the scherzo, which amused and lightly urged her on, rushing her as she lived for the finale, which led to the rondo, where the coda arose, a tender coupling of the morning's theme connected to the sleeping Sergei, who would arrive toward lunchtime. A ring of the doorbell, and a very sweet recapitulation: AEACADAE.

In spring the music season began. Tanya wanted to go with Sergei to the jazz festival in Dnepropetrovsk and then to Crimea. Toward the end of the winter two or three of the Petersburg jazz clubs started to get boring, and the trio's relationship with one of them, The Square, soured. Sergei did not suffer from ambition, was easy going and friendly, but Garik would periodically get into some stupid conflict with one of the city's jazz elders, first with Gologhin, then with Lisovsky. Tanya, by that time already familiar to a certain extent with the ins and outs of jazz life and having made the acquaintance of many musicians, thought that Sergei should leave Garik. They played great together, but Garik never gave Sergei the amount of freedom he had grown to deserve. Sergei did more and more composing. Garik looked down his nose at these exercises and made light of them, but once, when they had been drinking, he said sternly and unambiguously: "As long as you're playing for me, we're playing my music . . ."

Sergei was bitter. Tanya—all the more. It even seemed to her that the moment had arrived for her to get involved and direct the situation a bit. In the winter Sergei had been invited to play with Dixieland. Why not play with someone else? Garik wasn't the only show in town . . . She called her father and asked whether he was still burning with desire to take Zhenya for the summer. If so, the two of them would come and live for a while in Moscow so that she got used to everyone . . .

In the middle of May Pavel Alekseevich met Tanya and Zhenya at the Leningrad train station. He neatly finished off all of his duties at work by the end of the month. Now he wanted only one thing: to stay at their dacha with his granddaughter, feed her porridge in the morning, take her for walks, try to figure out her incoherent words and first thoughts. The women in his family were all falling apart: Elena got up from her armchair only unwillingly, Vasilisa had become decrepit, and her vision, despite the successful operation, was very weak. Toma helped him as much as she could, but her evening studies took a lot of her time, and Pavel Alekseevich could only quietly wonder why precisely Toma, with her very average abilities, banged her head so zealously against the sciences, while Tanya sat in a half-basement, molding something with her skilled hands, while her wonderfully organized head went completely unused.

His granddaughter, whom he had visited in March, had not forgotten him and stretched out her little hand and turned her check for him to kiss. He kissed her creamy skin and was filled with hot air, like an aerostat . . .

Tanya spent a week living at home. She did a deep cleaning of the place, digging out all the corners. She washed the windows. She was very tender with Vasilisa and took her to the public bathhouse: Vasilisa recognized no other form of bathing, but she was afraid to go on her own after she had slipped on the bathhouse's stone floor. Toma rarely agreed to accompany her. In addition, Vasilisa did not recognize bathing on any day except Saturday, while Toma usually had her own plans for Saturdays. The bathhouse was not far away, on Seleznevskaya Street, and Vasilisa always brought her own basin, loofah—wherever did she get them?— smelly tar soap, and fresh change of underwear. For the first time in her life Vasilisa accepted Tanya's help. First Tanya helped her peel off her thick coat, which was somewhat binding in the sleeves, then bent down and removed her all-weather felt boots. Nowadays she dressed year-round for the winter, just like a real old woman from the village. Vasilisa had stopped wearing shoes several years ago . . . Vasilisa grimaced and said in self-deprecation: "Well, miss, I've lived to see the day . . ."

Then Vasilisa herself quickly unbuttoned her flannel house robe and removed her gray patched underwear. Her nakedness was as abject as her clothing. A gray, wrinkled body, knotty long legs with inky veins and a red rash of tiny vessels, and a withered, spiderlike rib cage with a big crucifix that hung down almost to her navel. Looking at Vasilisa was discomfiting, but her vision was so poor that she did not sense Tanya's gaze, and for all her innate prudishness Vasilisa at the bathhouse took off her inhibitions along with her clothes. Tanya noticed hanging between her legs a rosy-gray fist-sized little sack that was relatively disgusting to look at . . .

"Vasya, what's that hanging between your legs?"

Vasilisa bent over slightly, squatted a bit, and with an awkward movement stuck the hanging little sack back inside.

"It's my child parts, Tanechka. It ripped off. In 1930, when we were pulling a cart . . . It's nothin', nothin' . . . It doesn't get sick . . ."

Tanya sat her down on the bench, put the basin with hot water under her legs, took a bathhouse basin full of water, and started to wash her with the loofah. Vasilisa moaned a bit, and groaned, emitting various degrees of pleasure . . .

Awful, just awful . . . She worked for us all her life, carried bags, washed windows, ironed laundry with a two-ton iron . . . Reinserted her prolapsed uterus and climbed up the stepladder . . . In the house of the country's leading gynecologist . . . Should I tell Dad? Awful, just awful . . . Standing in her rubber shower flip-flops on the slippery bathhouse floor as she scrubbed the old woman's boney back, Tanya mumbled: "Lord, what am I supposed to do with you all? Vasenka, am I supposed to move back home . . . Why are you all grown so old . . ."

The place was noisy with voices and flowing water, and Vasilisa did not hear her.

"Enough. We've had our good time. Now we have to get back home," Tanya said to herself. And she despaired at the horrible prospect of life in their old house between aging Vasilisa and her out-of-her-mind mother, with her daughter, and with Seryozha . . . The most intolerable thing was the smell of stale urine, both human and feline, of soured food, dust, grime, and dying—even after the most painstaking cleaning . . . Poor Dad, how does he bear it all? Then she remembered his chilly office and the ever-present empty bottle between the desk's two columns of drawers . . . What if she were to have Toma quit her job and take care of the house? Then she realized immediately that she should be ashamed at the thought.

When Tanya brought steam-mellowed Vasilisa back home and sat her down next to the teakettle, her mind was made up: she was going to the dacha right now to prepare it for the summer season and make a deal with some local woman to help out with the housework, then move them all out there and leave them there till fall. In the fall, after she returned to town, she would move to Moscow. With Sergei . . . The last point was still up for question ... But, ultimately, they could rent a room ... And people played jazz everywhere!

21

TOMA DID NOT LIKE CHILDREN. SHE DID NOT LIKE childhood—her own or anyone else's—or anything connected with having children. One doesn't need Freud to understand her profound repulsion for everything in that sphere of life where sexual attraction resides—be it innocent petting in some corner or the wretched panting that accompanies coitus, to which she had been witness since childhood. Her mother's festering bed—where the mystery of love occurred and where it claimed the life of the janitor whose name had long ago been forgotten by the people in the courtyard—and her undignified death were the stuff of Toma's nightmares. Whenever Toma fell ill and her temperature climbed, it seemed to her that she lay in the family lair. She would open her eyes, and there would be Elena Georgievna alongside her clean starched bed, crocheting with a large hook something gray or beige; seeing that Toma had woken, she would give her warm tea with lemon and wipe her wet brow ... Pavel Alekseevich would drop in in the evening with some surprise: once he brought her a transparent glass rabbit the size of a real mouse. Later she lost the rabbit at the dacha, or one of their dacha neighbors had stolen it, and there was much grief. Another time Pavel Alekseevich brought her a little box with scissors, tweezers, and a sharp thing she didn't know what to do with. He brought Toma the present and kissed Elena Georgievna on the head as she sat alongside the bed. To Toma it was absolutely apparent that although they were husband and wife, there could be none of the wretched muck from which her poor momma had died between these two clean, fine-smelling, and beautifully dressed people. They even slept in different rooms.

A lot of what Toma saw in the Kukotsky household she interpreted in the most fantastic ways, but in this case she was not mistaken: no such muck took place between husband and wife, in fact not since the moment she had entered their home ...

As for the manicure set, it has survived to this day and not lost its significance: when the girls were ill, he brought little presents every evening, and these daily treats reconciled them with their illness. When Tanya was ill, Pavel Alekseevich brought two presents, for both girls, the sick one and the healthy one. But if Toma was ill, he brought nothing for Tanya . . .

For that reason, Toma was certain that Pavel Alekseevich loved her more than Tanya. Her understanding of fairness, whereby everything was distributed equally by weight, size, and quantity, had remained with her since infancy, although occasionally it was shaken by suspicion that things were not that simple. But Toma had always preferred simple things to the complex . . .

In the Kukotsky household there was no talk of fairness. And nothing was divided equally. At dinner everyone was apportioned two meat patties. But Tanya frequently refused the second. Vasilisa did not eat meat at all. For a long while Toma thought that Vasilisa was not given meat "out of fairness," that is, because she was a servant. Later it turned out that Vasilisa herself did not want the meat. But, after having spent several months in their household, Toma stalked Vasilisa and uncovered that she had her own special food that no one else in the house ate: in her pantry she kept dried white bread cut into tiny pieces, which she ate in the morning, in secret from everyone. Which meant that there was a certain kind of fairness here. Toma once crept into the pantry and found the bread wrapped in a rag and tried a piece: it was absolutely tasteless. There was absolutely nothing special about it at all.

Living with her mother and brothers, Toma had constantly been involved in divvying things up: her little brothers always grabbed the larger and better pieces, and they fought constantly over food. Her mother also argued with everyone on various counts, and the arguments—even fistfights—were always over fairness. With the Kukotskys everything went contrary to fairness, which amazed her, especially at the outset. In the summer at the dacha Pavel Alekseevich would drop the first strawberry from his own plate onto Elena Georgievna's, and she, laughing, poured her berries onto the plate in front of Vasilia, who would get upset.

"I'm not going to eat your slush! Give it to the children . . ."

Just as with meat patties, Tanya did not care for strawberries, and the berries would end their circular journey around the table on Toma's plate . . .

Now, though, after Zhenya had appeared in the household, Toma finally came to understand the joy of giving. It was amusing that Toma experienced this for the first time at the same dacha with the same first strawberries grown in their "own" garden. There were only eleven of these first, red but not quite fully ripe, berries from Vasilisa's planting, which Vasilisa placed proudly on the table one Sunday morning, saying: "The first are yours . . ."

Pavel Alekseevich gave everyone two berries each, placing the very last one on Zhenya's plate. Once again, just as when Toma had been a child, the berries went from plate to plate. Pavel Alekseevich placed one in his mouth and another in Zhenya's. Zhenya popped her berries into her mouth, comically screwing up her face but smacking her lips in delight . . .

Vasilisa muttered something that sounded as if strawberries were also included in her fast. And here, watching Zhenya's gastronomical pleasure written on her berry-juice-smattered face, Toma understood how she would get more enjoyment watching the child eat them than eating them herself . . .

And so it happened, unnoticed by all, that Toma came to love Zhenya, her niece, as she called her . . .

The little girl was living at her grandfather's house for a second year. Pavel Alekseevich thought that the child should be with them until Tanya got her life in order. And so it came to be that last year's dacha season had stretched over a whole year. Tanya was not able to move to Moscow. She had come to visit rather frequently for several days at a time, but only now, toward the beginning of July, had things begun to settle down. Just before retiring, Pavel Alekseevich had managed to obtain rights to a one-room apartment in a new academic cooperative building—for Toma. The former girls' room returned to Tanya's ownership, although, truth be told, the ownership was not hers alone, but her family's, together with Sergei and Zhenya.

The separate apartment Pavel Alekseevich had managed to arrange and pay for with his own money was a fairy-tale fantasy come true for Toma. The building was not entirely completed, but she had already made several trips to Leninsky Avenue, the far end, and walked around the already finished construction and even stood alongside the entrance to her future front door. She had been given an estate, her own island, as a result of which she reevaluated in her head everyone around her in relation to herself: her own worth, it seemed to her, had grown immeasurably . . . Among her coworkers, especially those her age, she knew no one who possessed a similar treasure. What was more, she still could not understand why the apartment was being built for her, and not for Tanya, their own daughter, who, in addition to everything else, had a family of sorts of her own.

Certainly, the same idea had occurred to Pavel Alekseevich before it had to Toma. Moreover, he had discussed it with his daughter during one of her visits to Moscow. He had begun the conversation precisely by proposing to Tanya that they build a two-room apartment for her family. But Tanya, without a minute's hesitation, had refused: her sole motivation for returning to Moscow was "our old girls, who are falling further into decline, and I'm moving here in order to take care of them . . ." Pavel Alekseevich was hurt by Tanya's condescending use of the word "old girls" in reference to both Elena and Vasilisa . . .

Breaking with Piter was difficult: Sergei had had a breakthrough, and he was mastering one instrument after the next, playing unusual chromatic double-voice pieces on a handmade double recorder, then trying his hand at the basset horn, then, finally—following in the footsteps of Roland Kirk—he got caught up in the completely exotic musical practice of playing two saxophones at once. And he succeeded at all of it. His musical path spiraled upward, and with increasing frequency Sergei extracted his own compositions from this musical rumble. After long drawn-out doubts, Garik began playing one of his compositions—"Black Stones."

Tanya worked a lot: her black stones were becoming stylish, in part with the help of Poluektova, who had come from Perm for the holidays. True, during her visits Sergei, Tanya, and Zhenya would have to move to the workshop, which Poluektova herself did not insist on: jealousy was not in her repertoire. She even liked Tanya, and her own life in Perm was on a steady rise. Her classes were considered the best, she had moved from stage repertoire teacher to choreographer, and her love affair with the most talented of the school's graduates lent her energy, spirit, and a certain dose of good nature that was entirely out of character. Tanya presented Poluektova with a pair of her creations, and the latter modelled them very successfully at the Mariinsky Theater, where she had danced before retiring, and the entire corps de ballet lined up for Tanya's jewelry. Tanya barely managed to keep up with the orders. Tanya herself had become an item as well: she and Sergei were constantly invited to all the hip events, from theatrical premieres to closed at-home concerts. Tanya now wore short black dresses, and her dyed brown hair, which grew with amazing speed, she wore long: after two years it covered her sharp shoulder blades. Tripping constantly along music's shore as though along the sea's edge, her body was poised and transmitted a kind of hidden movement even when she stood completely still. But the main event was taking place in the dark and where no one could see: Tanya was pregnant, thrilled immeasurably, and so far had said nothing about this to anyone, except Sergei—not even to Pavel Alekseevich. It was decided that her last two months free of household responsibilities she would spend together with Sergei touring Crimea and the Caucasus Mountains; after the tour ended they would travel to an international jazz festival in the Baltic region, and then, after quickly packing their rather impoverished stuff and drawing the line at the end of their Petersburg life, they would move to Moscow—to give birth to a son, raise Zhenya, and take care of the old folks. That the difficulties in all this promised to be enormous only fueled Tanya's resolve: she was so full of happiness and strength, so fearless and carefree, that she even rushed time a bit. Which in no degree got in the way of her finding pleasure from day to day . . .

The tour began—which was especially delightful—in Odessa at that same International Sailors' Club where Tanya had first seen Sergei. Here they celebrated the theoretical third anniversary of their union. There were no performances in Kurortnoe this year, but they hired a car for a day and went out there. Nothing had changed, and everything stood in its old place: the dusty whitewashed huts and the tomato plantations. They descended the precarious staircase to the colorless sea. Over those three years it had washed away even more shore, and now a dangerous hole gaped between the lower part of the staircase and the slope of the cliff.

"Not for the tipsy," Tanya noted. Sergei offered his hand. She took his hand, even though she felt completely sure of her footing.

They went for a swim and decided to take a look at the dunes. The driver waited for them up above. A native Odessan, he was morose and gloomy and of few words, a walking refutation of common stereotypes about Odessans. He dropped them off at the sandbar, at the same place where three years ago Garik's car had got stuck. Tanya and Sergei headed for the sandbar. It was a weekday, there were practically no people, no one was sunbathing near their memorial ruins, and only a few empty bottles lay scattered, half-covered with sand. It wasn't as hot, as burning sticky hot as it had been then. A breeze blew in from the sea. It fluttered Tanya's red sundress—she had put it on especially so that everything would be as it had been. They skinny-dipped. They lay down on the sand in the half-shade of the half-ruins . . . Tanya embraced Sergei, and he immediately responded. Now everything was different. They had matured and grown careful. They feared disturbing the infant that floated inside and had already begun his first stretches, thrashing from inside with a foot or a fist, and their lovemaking—pianissimo and legato—was of an entirely different variety from their first stormy and unconscious time. But both ways were good . . .

Placing Sergei's hands on her stomach, she whispered in his ear.

"Our little boy is going to be big, not like Zhenka, the potbellied squirt . . ."

Then Sergei took a bottle of wine, two tomatoes, some eggs, and greens from his bag. The green onion was yellowed and mature. The bread crumbled. Tanya chewed a limp stalk, salted a crust of bread, and bit off a piece. The food would not go down. She drank two gulps of wine, and, after collecting the remains, they headed back to the car. As they walked, Tanya's nose began to bleed. Sergei dampened the red sundress in the estuary's water, and applied a rather warm compress. The blood stopped quickly. They had to hurry, because there was a performance in the evening.

They arrived an hour before it began. Tanya was nauseated, and her head and leg muscles ached. She wanted to put on her evening dress—the green one with the thin straps, a gay little number that stretched over her stomach—but at the last minute decided to stay in the room. She lay down and fell asleep immediately. But she quickly woke up from the pain. She placed her hands on her belly and asked: "So, how are you?"

The little boy did not answer. Apparently, everything was okay with him. She should probably take an aspirin. But, first of all, there was none, and second, Tanya did not really want to take any pills. Just before Sergei returned, the nosebleed began again.

"Maybe we should call a doctor?" Sergei began to worry.

Tanya puckered her lips: she did not want medical care. During her last pregnancy she had not even bothered to register at a clinic, had not had any of the prescribed tests done, and was even a bit proud to have avoided all the ado women today make over so natural and healthy an affair as having a baby . . . A bit later Garik and Tolya—already slightly drunk—dropped by with two bottles: an open bottle of wine and a sealed bottle of vodka. Tolya did not consider wine alcohol, while Garik had an acute sense of style: he thought only a hopeless alcoholic would drink vodka in the South in the summer. Winter was a different matter . . .

"I don't like the way you look, old girl," Garik announced from the threshold. "You're not jumping or hopping, just bitter-bitter sobbing . . . Think what you will, but I'm calling an ambulance . . ."

He headed resolutely for the phone. The phone was dead.

Tanya stopped Garik.

"Let's wait until morning . . . I'd like to drink some tea with lemon. And, to hell with it, bring me some aspirin . . ."

They brought Tanya her tea, and after taking the aspirin she felt better. She fell asleep. She woke up at four o'clock in the morning, vomiting. This time Sergei did not hesitate, went down to the reception desk, and called an ambulance.

An elderly Jewess quickly examined Tanya and said that she was taking her to the hospital right away. She spoke in vexation, even threateningly, and Tanya took a deep dislike to her, but her muscles were killing her, her head was pounding, and pain was spreading along the wall of her belly.

Tanya tried to object, but the old doctor would not listen to her, as if she were a senseless child, and turned instead to Sergei.

"Her liver has descended by almost more than two inches. I refuse to accept that kind of responsibility. What did you bring me out here for?

To talk? If you want to get medical help, you have to hospitalize her immediately. Explain to your wife that she could lose the child."

For some reason she did not take a liking to Tanya either and did not even look in her direction.

Tanya was taken away, and after that all hell seemed to break loose. A pipe broke in the club, closing it for technical reasons. Their performance was canceled. They spent the whole day with only their worries, and Tolya Aleksandrov got drunk as a result, which in and of itself was nothing terrible, but he got into a fight in some beer hall and was socked hard right in the eye. Sergei shagged back and forth to the hospital three times a day: they told him nothing, and for two days straight he was unable to track down the attending physician, who had either just left or not yet arrived. Then the weekend came, and there was no physician in attendance whatsoever, only a doctor on call, whom Sergei also was unable to track down: he was either eating dinner or had been summoned to care for a critical patient. All the staff knew perfectly well that he was on a drinking binge and not coming to work.

No one was allowed in the pathology section: it was quarantined. Everything stopped and was put on hold. Even the weather deteriorated, and it started to rain.

Tanya was getting sicker and sicker, and the moment had come when she herself began to get scared. She discovered a black-and-blue mark on her left forearm, and a similar bruise on her side. The back of her head continued to throb. Her belly hurt with an unusual burning metallic pain. Nurses came and took her temperature, felt her belly, and measured her blood pressure . . . Her temperature was normal.

Tanya felt worse and worse; on the third day she decided to summon her father.

She got paper and a pencil from her neighbor and wrote a note to Sergei asking him to call her father in Moscow and tell him to come. Notes were passed by tossing them out the window. On Saturday morning Sergei picked up Tanya's scribbled missive: it was laconic and desperate. He immediately headed for the post office and sent Pavel Alekseevich a telegram.

Toward evening Sergei came to Tanya's window with his saxophone. Usually visitors called up to their Veras and Galyas from the dusty lawn below, and the women would hang their milk-swollen breasts and victorious smiles out the window. Among the dozen or so local, fresh-baked poppas—sailors, criminals, and merchants—Sergei was the only one who was thin, long-haired, and sober. Moreover, what he experienced was not the collective joy of childbirth, but his own personal alarm and terror, which had settled at the bottom of his stomach, apparently, because his ulcer, healed over long ago, did not exactly hurt, but was sending ominous signals . . .

Tanya was on the third floor, but Sergei decided not to shout from the lawn. He took his instrument out of its case, put the reed to his lips, and made it speak slowly.

Tan-ya . . .

Tanya heard, but was not able to come to the window right away. When she lifted herself from her pillow, her head started to spin, and a wave of nausea came over her. But her stomach had been emptied long ago, and enduring the sharp and pointless spasms, she dragged herself to the window. Her legs ached desperately with each step, while her belly seemed to be filled with lead . . . She popped her head out the window only after Sergei had extracted his mournful "Tan-ya" for the third time from the thin metal throat of his instrument.

At first he did not recognize her: she had piled her hair in a bun on the top of her head, just as her mother had worn hers all her life. And the hospital gown–prison shirt made her seem strange and bulky . . . She waved her hand: the gesture was Tanya's own, imitable by no one. Looking at him from above, Tanya recognized her favorite moment: when he took his instrument in hand, and this cute but nondescript young man metamorphosed into a musician in the same way a horse turns a person into a rider, and weaponry turns a man into a warrior: when the sum of human and inhuman exceeds the value of each separately.

Sergei held his saxophone in his hands. His right hand was below, fingers on the keys, his left hand higher up, on the octave pin near the crook of the metallic body, his chin pointed upward, and his lower lip protruded—right inside was that tender callus she could touch with her tongue . . . He held the saxophone—a generally silly creature, the fantasy of an instrument-maker, a hybrid of wood and metal with a piece of plastic thrown in, that in terms of shape was far from perfect, its keys protruding not very elegantly from the body, and the bell, likely, too sharply turned outward . . . Among the wind instruments there were no few beauties: the flute with its ancient simplicity, and all its ingenuous relatives—from the syrinx to the tsevnitsa; the maple bassoon with its vestigial bell and beaklike head; the ascetic trombone that looked like something out of an apothecary; the pedantically curled brass cornet with its silly valve mechanisms; and the snail-twirled stately French horn . . . And what about the oboe's bell? Or the funnel of the trumpet, curled back to the depths of its soul? The saxophone, of course, was not the most perfect, but the overtones of its voice could transmit human gradations of tenderness, triumph, or sorrow. And, in addition to everything else, they—Sergei and his saxophone—mutually resonated each other . . . Together the two of them were capable of uttering that which Sergei never could on his own. He placed the reed between his tensed lips, pressed his teeth up against the fold inside his lower lip, worn with years of playing, and a velvety deep-blue A-note said: "Let's begin!"

And they, Sergei and his "Selmer," began—lightly, easily, and without having to think about what they wanted to tell Tanya that was so important. It was Coltrane's "Giant Steps," and Tanya immediately recognized the breathless music that progressed through major thirds—C–E–G♯— the key changing three times over the course of the theme, but Sergei did not play to the end, swerving off into his own solo, then progressing by way of rising arpeggios to the top, looking back, and ascending once again to the point where the saxophone's possibilities ended, and then carefully descending down the blues scale, and Tanya began to recognize something vaguely familiar, something she had heard many times . . . perhaps Haden's "Always Say Good-bye" . . . or something like it . . . or Seryozha's . . .

She remembered how she had written him a letter full of grandiloquent nonsense from the maternity hospital three years ago, in Piter, when she had given birth to Zhenka . . . About how wonderfully they— Sergei and his instrument—got along without any words, and about how now, if this entire episode ended well, she would never again talk nonsense, because talking nonsense was shameful when there was music, which never spoke nonsense . . . Now the music spoke distinctly, gravely, and not at all glibly . . . , as it might seem to someone not fluent in its clear and transparent language: say good-bye, say good-bye ... always ... forever say good-bye ... The small sounds—sharp, jagged, metallic— were just as unrelenting as they were marvelous ...

Tanya held her pain-wracked belly with both hands. Would he really die, their little boy, with his palms folded under his chin, his soft ears, his mouth still sealed shut, blond, resembling Seryozha, with an upper lip that hung slightly over the lower ... Poor Pavlik ... Poor unborn Pavlik ...

Sergei did not see Tanya alive again. Nor did Pavel Alekseevich. He arrived from the dacha and found two telegrams stuffed in the door: one from Sergei with a request that he come; the second, written two days later, with the notarized signature of the chief physician, informing him of the death of Tatiana Pavlovna Kukotskaya.

A day later Pavel Alekseevich stood alongside a table covered with spotted tin, and it was the bitterest moment of his life. The delicate flame of life, the greenish tinge of a working heart, the clots of energy produced by the various organs, were already all shut down. She was an olive-plastic color, his suntanned little girl, with hematomas on her forearms and calves, with autopsy sutures of the like to indict these so-called doctors of a grave crime against nature. He had already seen the forensic report. They also showed him her backdated case history. The entire hospital—from the chief physician down to the last nurse—froze in horror, awaiting retribution. With a single glance Doctor Kukotsky had determined that over the first two days following admission to the hospital no diagnosis had been made and no treatment administered, that the required tests had been done too late, that pregnancy had only made the situation worse ... and that he would have been able to save his little girl, had he arrived from the dacha not on Tuesday, but on Friday ...

Tanya's resemblance to her mother was incredible and tormenting. A quarter century ago he had stood exactly the same way over young Elena, close to death, and had seen her gathered chestnut hair, her thin nostrils, and her brushy brows from precisely the same angle.

"Never. Elena will never know about this," he thought, and was stunned by an instantaneous epiphany: might Elena have departed for her empty, enigmatic, mad world so as never to learn about what her prophetic heart had glimpsed long ago ...?

He proceeded to the chief physician's office and asked him to gather the section heads. The chief attempted to object, but Pavel Alekseevich cast him such a general's look, that he rushed to call his secretary to invite them all immediately to his office. Five minutes later six doctors sat in the office. The forensic report and the patient's history lay before Pavel Alekseevich.

"This case demands a special investigation," uttered Pavel Alekseevich. The doctors exchanged glances. "The quantity of blunders, errors, and medical crimes exceeds all bounds. A patient with a communicable infection was placed in the pathology ward. No biochemical blood tests or bacteriological analyses were performed. No diagnosis was made. I am assuming that what we have here is Weil's disease, *Morbus Weili*. If it is leptospirosis, then immediate measures need to be taken."

The forensic pathologist—a deformed little Asian with dyed whiskers, was terribly nervous.

"Excuse me, colleague, but we have no grounds for such conclusions. You saw the report, and we gave you an opportunity to conduct an examination of the . . . corpse? body?" Whiskers hesitated for a second, "Patient? What grounds do you have?"

"Focal degeneration with hemorrhaging in the muscles, petechiae. The patient's records correspond to nothing. There was toxicosis. Intravenous infusions, indicated here, were not administered. I examined the veins . . . I am left to conclude that no treatment whatsoever was given. But that's not the issue right now. Your maternity hospital is infected with hepatitis."

Pavel Alekseevich did everything he would have done in any other situation: he called the city health office, summoned the head of the health inspection service, and the chief epidemiologist. A fever ran through the city's medical administration from top to bottom, to the extent that janitors started scrubbing down toilets twice a day, midlevel medical personnel stopped getting drunk on night duty, and the kitchen kept an eye out to make sure stolen butter and meat were not taken from the premises.

Pavel Alekseevich spent three days at the hospital. On the fourth he boarded a train together with Sergei—who had fallen into spiritual lockjaw and total stupefaction. In the train's baggage car there stood a zinc coffin with a small rectangular window through which multiple folds of white gauze were visible.

With Garik's last money—Pavel Alekseevich had spent everything he had, Sergei also—they bought four bottles of vodka. They drank the warm vodka a long time, slowly, a little bit at a time, snacking on pieces of crumbled cookies straight out of the package—there wasn't anything else—in silence . . . Then Sergei lay down on the lower berth, hugged the case with his instrument hidden away inside, and slept until they reached Moscow. Pavel Alekseevich never closed his eyes once the entire thirty-six hours: he sat opposite the sleeping young man and looked at his tormented face. He was fair-skinned, his eyelids and nose tipped with redness. His thin white stubble broke through the tender skin of his cheeks, forming tiny pustules . . . The corners of his crusted lips twitched. In his sleep he stroked the case and mumbled something. Pavel Aleksee-vich did not catch the words. He was thinking about how their life had changed when two men had appeared in their home: this dear young man and the little one who was not to be . . . He also thought about what had happened to his daughter: from the moment when a restless spiral had landed in her stomach together with the local rotten water, been absorbed by her mucous membranes, dispersed by the bloodstream throughout her entire body, nested in her highly oxygenated muscles, and poisoned her blood to such an extent that her poor liver, already over-taxed by her pregnancy, had been unable to filter it . . . Pavel Alekseevich needed no auxiliary clairvoyance now: the accursed picture, crude and clear as a picture from a child's primer, stood before his eyes . . .

Everything had been arranged. Vitalik Goldberg met them at the Kursk train station. At the German cemetery the family burial plot was already open—two steps away from Doctor Haass. There lay Pavel Alek-seevich's grandfather and great-grandfather. And now, interrupting the natural order, Tanya would be placed to rest there. No one besides Tanya's father, husband, and lover was present at the burial.

Sergei wanted to leave immediately, but Pavel Alekseevich asked him to spend the night. Sergei did. The apartment was empty, summery, dusty. Pavel Alekseevich gave him some sort of pill. They drank vodka. Then Sergei lay down to sleep on Toma's couch. He, Tanya, Zhenya, and the lit-tle boy were supposed to have moved into this room several months later.

22

IN PITER, SERGEI TOLD NO ONE OF HIS ARRIVAL. HE immediately went to the workshop. He did not have keys: they were back in Odessa with Tanya's things. He easily picked the lock. There was the same mess they had left when leaving. A coffeepot abandoned in haste stood unwashed in the sink. A mysterious flower of fungus sprouted from the teapot. Tanya's black dress hung on a wooden hanger on the wall. Her high-heeled shoes that made her a half-head taller than him stood alongside the narrow couch, one on top of the other ... On the eve of their departure they had gone to a party at the house of a young director who intended to invite him for some sort of vaguely enticing staging ... Lord, and the bed wasn't made either, the striped sheet hanging from the foot of the bed, and the only pillow, which each of them in their sleep dragged to their own side, preserved the indentation of their heads ...

Sergei sunk his face into the pillow, and the smell scalded him. She was still here. On the white pillow lay one of her dark hairs curled in a spiral. Under the pillow lay her tiny black underpants, pushed to the side. Still dressed in his clothes he lay down on the couch and fell asleep.

He woke up after an indeterminate length of time, drank some water straight from the tap, and pissed in the sink: the toilet was on the stair landing—one for all four basement apartments—and locked. The key to the toilet hung on a nail near the entrance, but Sergei for some reason decided that it was on Tanya's key ring in Odessa.

He lay down to sleep again, this time having undressed. Tanya's smell intensified each time he crawled out of the bed and returned to it again. All that remained were her smell and the bunched up nylon underpants. He would keep them for an indeterminate number of days and nights. He fell asleep, then woke up. He drank water from the tap. He pissed in the sink. He had no appetite. His unfed stomach idled.

At long last he crawled out from under the blanket and sat down at Tanya's workbench. He touched her tools and her moldings. The metal said nothing to him about Tanya. But when he opened the motley tin box with the black stones, he could not tear his eyes from them for a long time. They seemed to have preserved the touch of her hands: polished layered agate, blackish-blue magnetite, rough black nephrite, and his very favorite—the translucent obsidian ... He selected two at random and put them in his jeans pocket. Then he grabbed his case and walked out of the workshop. The door, not fastened with a hook from inside, flapped in the doorway: the lock was broken. He turned back, found a hammer with a nail remover, and a large nail. He hammered the nail from the outside into the doorframe and with a strike of the hammer bent it so that the door seemed locked. Then he put the hammer under the doormat so that there would be something to extract the nail with when he came back. A strange thought ran through his head: but will I come back?

Poluektova—whom everyone considered a world-class shrew, but whom Sergei knew was still a human being even though she really was a bitch—had assumed that he was stuck in Moscow. Garik had called Piter from Odessa and informed everyone of Tanya's death. He also had said that Sergei had set off for Moscow with the coffin. All of Seryozha's friends were certain that he would remain there.

Sergei seemed to have lost the keys to Poluektova's apartment. In any case, he rang the doorbell, not at all sure that anyone would open the door for him. The door was opened by the mistress herself in full make-up and with hair-sprayed black ballet bun at the top of her head.

"What do you want?" she asked and stopped short. She had not recognized Sergei at first. He was thin with long stubble or a patchy beard, pale and slightly jaundiced, and looking totally deranged. Gray bounded toward him to lick him on the lips ... He stood in the door, as if he had come there unconsciously, on autopilot.

Poluektova gasped and began shouting in an ugly high-pitched voice, bombarding him with her silly prattle.

"So you couldn't call, could you? I'm leaving today. Damn, it's all so stupid, stupid. Don't dare say anything. I know all about it. Anything but about that ... I'm taking the dogs with me. That's it. Why didn't you call, scarecrow? I've rented the apartment. Maybe, I should have left it for you? Don't dare say anything to me!"

She hugged his shoulders: her boy, her—who knew what—student, old lover, nephew, pal ... It always happened that way with her, between genres, never anything reliable, definite, or socially upstanding ... That is, at just that moment, it seemed as if someone like that was about to bite ... How to avoid jinxing it? A man with no artistic inclinations whatsoever: exactly what she needed. Gremin, Gremin. An honest-to-goodness general ...

She stroked Seryozha's dirty, disheveled locks, which he had not pulled back with an elastic band (he'd lost it), patted him on the back, and pushed him away.

"Go take a bath. I'm making you something to eat."

He went to the bathroom, turned on the water, which streamed sumptuously from the faucet, and realized that he had not bathed since Odessa ... He lay down in the almost unbearably hot water and began to sob ...

Poluektova-the-bitch called her general in Perm and in a squeaky voice most ill-suited to her mighty martial spirit, informed him of a change of plans: he did not need to meet her train; she was returning her tickets and staying on for at least a week. Her former husband, who had just been widowed, had dumped himself at her place like an avalanche, and she was going to have to take care of him, because there was no leaving him alone in this condition ...

The Siberian general nodded into the receiver, said drily "yes, yes, yes," and marveled at what a proper, strong, and real woman he had found himself, even if she was a ballerina with a flat hard chest and a back as muscular as a new recruit's. He smiled and quietly relished the resuscitation occurring below his belt: never in his life had he had such a woman; he had never even thought that they existed ...

A week was not enough for Poluektova. She cared for Sergei for almost a month, fed him food and pills, turned on his favorite music, forced him to go for walks with the dogs, and gradually he returned to himself and began to play. The very same day when, after the long hiatus, he was scheduled to perform at the club, Poluektova flew off to her gray-haired lover who, although he wasn't quite tall enough, was in all other respects the most proper of husbands even for a prima ballerina and who, in the course of his unplanned extended wait, had reached a final decision to put an end to his drawn-out widowerhood and to marry this exceptional, outstanding woman with the past of a whore and the future of the grand dame of a region large enough to accommodate fifteen Belgiums, eight Frances, and five Germanys all at once ...

23

WHILE ON DUTY ONE NIGHT AT THE PRECINCT, KUPCHINO resident Semion Kurilko, a militia officer and squadron leader, beat the shit out of a prisoner. Not more than usual, within limits, but toward morning the guy died.

The guy turned out to work at a museum. And all because of that skinny-pants faggot, that pansy dick-licker, Semion got into so much trouble that his whole life took a left turn. They kicked him out of the militia, adding: you ought to be thankful they didn't put you in the slammer . . . His wife left him and moved with their daughter to Karelia. Then his mother—the only person who had stood up for him, not to mention fed him—died. Then, after all this, Semion himself got sick: in a fit of rage he axed to shreds a brand-new, just constructed children's playground, with a little house for crawling into, a sandbox, and a carved wooden bear. They strait-jacketed him right there alongside the mangled bear and took him to the mental hospital. He was treated for almost a year, then released back to his room in Kupchino. While he was sick, his neighbors cleaned his place out, taking his blankets and his "Spidola" radio receiver left over from better times.

Semion had served eight years in the militia, joining right after the army, and he had no other profession. They gave him a disability pension, but a small one. Fortunately, he didn't drink, because the pension barely covered food. He had a good appetite that didn't match his pension. In the hospital he had put on a lot of weight, and now he needed more than before. The way he saw it, a skinny guy doesn't need as much nourishment as someone with meat on his bones. He would have looked for a job somewhere—as an armed guard someplace, for example, but they wouldn't take him because he'd been severed from the militia. He tried to get a job as a loader at a print shop, but they fired him for a—you have to admit—really stupid reason: smoking was forbidden on the premises, but he kept lighting up out of habit. They caught him once, twice, a third time, and then the foreman, a young kid just out of university, the same kind of skinny-pants shit as that museum worker the whole ruckus in the militia was about, fired him.

Once again Semion was left with nothing. That was when he was overcome by enormous anger at those skinny young guys, all those brainy boys, who had messed up his whole life. That was when Semion picked up his shiv. Thin, sharp, thicker than a knitting needle, but thinner than a file. He'd kept it at home for a long time, since his militia days when he took it away from a thief they'd hauled in. Why he pocketed it, he didn't know. He stuck it in his sleeve, tucking the blade under the band of his wristwatch. The watch was broken and hadn't worked for a long time, but now it came in handy. It was a crafty setup.

Semion lived near the Memorial Cemetery of the Victims of January Ninth, located on an avenue with the same name, in a building with a deep courtyard formed by three two-story barrack-type apartment buildings, about twenty minutes by foot from the suburban train station. On May 1, 1961, his favorite holiday, when the militia was up to its ears with business—drinking brawls, slashings, and other cheerful entertainments—he completed his first mission. He strolled down to the train stop, got on a suburban train, and rode to the Vitebsk train station. From there he turned left down Zagorodny Avenue, and, not hurrying, checking out the passersby, set off in the direction of the Technological Institute. There in the walk-through courtyard with a huge trench running through it that deprived it of its walk-through functionality—people peeked in, went as far as the trench, then returned to the archway they had come in through—he sat down on a bench and sat until evening, because things were not going as he had planned: either people walked together in groups, or the lone passerby was not of the right type he needed. It was only after eight that a skinny faggot in narrow-legged pants (with a thin little briefcase) came by. He was drunk as well. He wasn't looking for a way to exit to the other street; all he needed was a secluded spot, a dark corner, to release the fast-flowing beer. After he had splashed his load in a suitable place, Semion approached him from the back and stuck the shiv right where it was supposed to go, slightly to the side and between the ribs. At first the shiv seemed to hesitate, as if it had run up against a dense film, but after that it was like cutting butter . . . In, and out. The guy oohed, fell nose-first against the wall, and dropped without even turning around. Semion didn't even look at the briefcase, wiped the shiv neatly with a kitchen rag taken with forethought from home, stuck the instrument back up his sleeve under his watchband, and exited the courtyard with the new gait—stiff and manikin-like—that he had developed after his hospital treatments.

His next mission took place November 7, also without a hitch. Now he already knew that next year on May 1, he would celebrate his holiday as his heart desired: he'd shiv that shit, the skinny faggot, that worthless kike . . .

He'd been coming to this courtyard for three years. The trench had been covered over long ago, and people came through not in big streams, but in trickles. In May when it was light—more; in the November darkness—fewer. Semion was always lucky: one time the guy had a bouquet of flowers; another one—a tape recorder; the third was carrying two cake boxes tied together with string. Some he'd already forgotten. First he'd track one of them down: he recognized the type immediately. Then he'd catch up with him, stick to him for a second, then grab him with his right hand by the shoulder and strike with his left. Semion was a lefty retrained at school so he wrote with his right hand and did other things with both, but more easily with his left.

He had already scored seven when once, while in line in a store, he overheard two women talking about a murderer who'd appeared in town that the authorities hadn't been able to capture for ten years already, and that the maniac killed only on holidays—all red-letter days, killing men on all the holidays, except for March 8, once a year, when he killed women. At first Semion was surprised, but a few seconds later he figured out that they were talking about him. They exaggerated, of course, the number of years and about the holidays. But basically they had it right. Two weeks later, passing by his former place of work, he saw a large poster reading: "Wanted . . ." There were three photographs—two men and one woman con artist, with names; the fourth was a sketch, an artist's rendering instead of a photograph. The only thing in common between the sketch and Semion were the steep arches over the eyebrows and the buzz cut.

Semion got scared, went into hiding, and didn't come out of the house for a week until he had eaten his last piece of macaroni. It was close to November, and he decided that year not to go out of the house on the seventh. The manhunt didn't just scare him, it also provoked him. From the seventh through the eighth he sat at home, barely able to control himself, his hands even shaking. On the ninth he went out. And carried off his mission quite well and successfully. The guy had nothing in his hands, but on his face he had this chi-chi little beard, and he was for sure a stinking faggot . . .

After each mission Semion always felt better. He was even earning money now from time to time in a furniture store as a loader. Only just before the holidays he would begin to get jittery and attempt to recollect where he had hidden the shiv. He hid it at home, each time in a new place; one time he forgot where he'd hidden it, and turned the place upside down before he found it. He'd put it under the oilcloth tablecloth where the table ran up against the wall . . . Now he decided that he was going to detour the holidays, going out two or three days earlier or later . . . The militia was nothing but a bunch of idiots, that Semion knew well. They'd been told to search on the holidays, and there'd be no getting them out on any others.

In November of 1966 number ten's turn had come. But Semion came down with a bad cold—he had a cough, his body ached—and so he put things off not for three days, but for a whole week. He even thought that maybe he would skip this time. But it didn't work out that way. The urge to go hunting beckoned. Only on the fifteenth he put on his cherished watch, loaded the shiv, and left the house when it was still light, right after three. As always, he rode the train to the Vitebsk station and headed down Zagorodny Avenue. Instead, though, of turning in the direction of the Technological Institute, he went in the other direction, toward Moskovsky Avenue . . .

He didn't know Leningrad well: he had been born in Kupchino and rarely made his way into the city. His mother always used to say it that way: we'll go into the city . . . In school they took them on field trips several times. And his army service stationed him in a village, at a prison in the Kursk oblast. So he wound up neither an urbanite nor a villager, but a lifelong outlier, who couldn't saddle a horse or find his way to the football stadium . . . Before serving in the militia, he hadn't been able to cross the street without almost getting hit, and to this day he lost his way in unfamiliar places . . .

Moskovsky Avenue led him to a square. He looked at the last house: the sign read PEACE SQUARE. It was crawling with people. There were lots of stores here. The square was odd-shaped, with lots of little side streets coming into it. Turning into one of the narrower and quieter ones, he thought to himself that he'd been wrong not to go to the Techno-logical Institute, where he knew his way around. But the lane he was moving down now was, overall, just what he needed. Semion dropped into one courtyard, then another: they were all deep as wells, and not one of them had two exits . . . Then he walked into a deep archway and stood near the door of a former servants' entrance that exited into the arch-way. PAWNSHOP read the modest little sign on the securely closed door. Occasionally people passed by, but his view was blocked and he couldn't make anyone out. Furthermore, there were mostly women with shop-ping bags. It occurred to Semion that more young guys came out on the streets during the holidays, while there were mostly only middle-aged women on weekdays.

Then he tried a different tactic: he started walking up and down the side street from corner to corner until he sighted "his man." He was walk-ing toward him, and Semion simply began to tremble he was so right . . . By comparison with this one, the nine before simply didn't count. The guy wore a jeans jacket that was too big for him; he was skinny, and for sure worked at a museum. A blond girly-style ponytail swung down his back. And he was walking slowly and real laid back. Semion even man-aged to notice his shoes, which were special, not regular shoes . . . In his hand he carried a little suitcase, also not the usual kind, not like regular people carried. Semion's heart thumped. It was like love at first sight, like a flame of recognition. Semion had never experienced such a piercing sensation. At that moment he felt no hate; he was overwhelmed by the ecstasy of the hunter enraptured by his beautiful quarry . . .

But this quarry was dragging himself pretty slowly and people kept walking around him. Semion was walking behind him now, several steps behind. He got the urge to look at his face again and crossed over to the other side of the street, got in front of him, then walked toward him face-to-face. His little snout was the size of a fist, a fox's, and he was deep in thought. Faggot, now I'll get you . . .

Semion walked behind him again. They passed one courtyard entrance, and while they were approaching the next one, the one with the ser-vants' entrance in the archway, Semion focused himself and pulled the end of the shiv out from under his watchband. When they were even with the archway, Semion placed his right hand on the guy's shoulder, and set the shiv in motion with his left. The interference was minimal; the jeans jacket slowed down the movement of the blade, but Semion's swift and experienced hand sensed that it was going in well, and then it passed through the usual spot where the membrane between the ribs squeaked with resistance, and then the shiv slipped on smoothly, softly, with a slight pull . . .

The guy sighed, lurched initially upward, then began falling forward, but Semion did not let him fall, grabbing him with both hands by the shoulders and shoving him into the archway.

The guy wanted to drop, but Semion dragged him deep into the archway and wanted to leave him in the courtyard, so that the body lying on the ground would not be visible from the street. But just then the door of the servants' entry opened, and a huge, decent-looking man came out and looked inquiringly at Semion.

Semion dropped the guy and leapt out of the archway. He ran straight ahead, along the deserted lane, with no route in mind and only one thought in his head: he'd not managed to retrieve the shiv.

TWO CIRCUMSTANCES SAVED SERGEI'S LIFE. THE FIRST was the shiv, which had stuck in his heart. The second was the decent-looking man who had come out the door, the director of the pawnshop, formerly a medico. Holding Sergei upright, he shouted into the open door for someone to call an ambulance and to bring down a bandage . . . The doctors who revived Sergei from clinical death and sutured his punctured pericardium told him later: "It was a miracle, Seryozha, a miracle. One in a million."

Sergei asked them to give him the shiv, but that was impossible, because it had been made physical evidence, and so he never even saw it.

Semion was arrested two days later. He was accused of twenty-six murders, three of them involving rape. He confessed to his "own," but denied and refused to admit to the others. But it had already been decided on high that all the militia's "cold cases" be hung on him. They gave him the death penalty, which was implemented a half-year later. No appeal was entered, and no psychiatric testing was performed . . .

PART
FOUR

1

EVERY TIME ZHENYA STOPPED IN FRONT OF THE DOOR OF the apartment where she had spent her childhood she experienced the most complex of emotions: affection, anger, melancholy, and tenderness. The door was battered and chipped, the bronze plate with her deceased grandfather's surname was tarnished. Alongside the door, to the neighbors' aggravation, stood a broken chair piled high with sacks stuffed with Toma's crap. It reeked of destitution and a communal apartment.

Zhenya had not had keys since they changed the old lock. It just happened that way: they hadn't taken her key away, they just forgot to give her a new one. Zhenya asked once, but they ignored her request . . . She rang the bell. Toma hobbled down the corridor, tapping with her cane. The poor thing's arthritis had flared up again.

"Zhenechka, is that you?"

She opened the door. And gasped. "How round you've got!"

Mikhail Fedorovich—smelling of Chypre aftershave, sweat, and, for some reason, old leather—peeked out of Granny's room. "How unfair I am toward them after all," she reproached herself. "They don't stink on Sundays. They take baths on Saturdays."

Zhenya's inner smile showed slightly on her lips.

"How are you, Mikhail Fedorovich?"

All the time he had served in the army, he had always greeted his senior officers first. Now, in civilian life where there were no lieutenant colonels, he decided as he saw fit whom he was supposed to greet first— the director, the deputy director for operations (not the deputy director for research), and the head of the polyclinic he was assigned to . . .

Mikhail Fedorovich nodded with self-importance, ". . . day." With no name. And remained standing in the doorway. Which was unusual.

Zhenya removed her shoes, bending over her stomach first from the right side, then from the left. With a sense of repugnance she put on some old, crudely stitched house slippers and set off down the corridor to Granny's room. Toma stopped her.

"Zhen, we've done some rearranging. Rozina's relatives gave us their big bookcase. It didn't fit in there, so we had to put it in here . . .

Mikhail Fedych's collection fit perfect, so we moved Granny to Vasilisa's room . . ."

The blood rushed to Zhenya's head. By hook or by crook. They'd chucked Grandma out into the pantry.

"What do you mean?" Zhenya's chin trembled with rage. Mikhail Fedorovich's collection was mind-boggling idiocy: newspaper and magazine cuttings about aviation . . .

"What difference does it make to her? She didn't even notice. It's peaceful and quiet in there. We took out Vasilisa's chest and put a table in. She can eat there too. Vasilisa, rest her soul, always ate there."

Mikhail Fedorovich remained standing in the door of Granny's room ready to step in at any moment.

Zhenya held back and said nothing. She went to the kitchen without even looking into the room that last week had been her granny's and would always be Granny's . . .

She walked through the kitchen and opened the pantry. They had not changed anything in there since Vasilisa's death. There were the two large icons she had known since childhood, the Mother of Kazan and an Elijah the Prophet that had been either rent by a Red Army ax in times immemorial or had split from age, with a crude seam of glue running down the flying red mantle and separating it from the swarthy hand . . . So where are you now, all you helpless helpers?

Granny was sitting on a bentwood chair with a hole cut through the seat, her face toward the tiny window that looked out onto a solid brick wall. A bucket stood under the chair. The pantry smelled of urine and aged infirmity. One gray cat slept on the blanket that covered the trestle bed. Elena Georgievna held a second on her lap, her fingers with their unevenly trimmed nails lying on the cat's striped side.

Zhenya kissed her thinning hair with the two wisps at the temples, where young Lenochka had used to stick bobby pins. The old woman stroked the cat's side.

"Hi, Babulya. Why did you . . ." Zhenya began agonizingly, because she knew that it would be better for her to keep silent in this shameful, intolerable situation. "We're going to take a bath now . . ."

The old woman silently stroked her on the hand. In the kitchen water was flowing and knives were chopping. Toma and her husband divided everything in half, the housework included. They peeled the four potatoes in pairs: two for him, two for her. For reasons of family fairness.

Zhenya headed for the bathroom. As she passed through the kitchen she noticed that Toma and Mikhail Fedorovich were now sorting the buckwheat—they'd finished with the potatoes.

The bathroom was, as always, beyond description. Wet laundry hung on lines. Saturday was bath day. Half the day they prepared, and half the day they washed. And then they relaxed—with tea, candies, and ginger cookies. A patriarchal family scene. Everything totally serious. On Sunday morning, before Zhenya's arrival, the week's laundry was done in the tiny washing machine Mikhail Fedorovich had bought for the needs of his small family. He was squeamish, and washing Granny's nasty linen in the machine was not allowed.

Zhenya pulled a washbasin out from under the old footed bathtub. From the zinc container with the bent lid she pulled out shabby rags and pieces of sheets, all of them damp and soiled. The disposable diapers she used to buy had gone unused: Toma thought that they were synthetic, and Mikhail Fedorovich did not tolerate synthetics. Zhenya had stopped bringing anything into the apartment for Granny long ago: Toma would immediately take away anything new, saying: "Oh, Zhen, what a swell nightshirt this is: good enough to get buried in . . ."

At moments like this Zhenya did not know whom to pity more: Granny, who had shattered her own psyche so as not to notice what she could not battle, or Aunt Toma with her mousy snout and arthritis-stiff knee, happy with her marriage, proud of her past, present, and the future toward which she was making slow but steady progress. She was writing her candidate's dissertation on the viral infections of her evergreens and considered herself the spiritual successor of her famous mentor, Pavel Alekseevich Kukotsky. That might possibly have been the case . . .

Zhenya sorted the pile on the stool-bench, where she would sit Granny for her bath. Old washbasins, one inside the other, jars, and raggedy loofahs. How close-fisted they were . . .

Turning her nose aside, she soaked Granny's rags in the largest basin and pushed it under the bathtub. After the bath would come laundry. She cleaned out the bathtub. The faucets dripped, and water collected under the tub. Everything was shabby, but cleverly fixed to get by. Mikhail

Fedorovich was a genius when it came to tying clotheslines, twisting wires, filling holes, and making patches. Wonder what he did in aviation?

At long last, everything was ready. The water was a bit hotter than needed. It would cool down while she got Granny ready. At the last minute she dripped some shampoo into the water. To make foam. Toma never used anything that Zhenya brought into the house. She and Mikhail Fedorovich did not use shampoo: they couldn't stand anything foreign. Patriots they were. Not soap, not medicine, not clothing. Their line for everything was "ours, made in the . . ." How pathetic . . .

Zhenya lifted her grandmother from her chair.

"Let's go, Babulya, everything's ready."

Elena Georgievna obediently stood up. Her back was straight, her legs thin and long, slightly bent by old age . . . Zhenya held her by her fragile shoulders and led her off. Granny walked well, but her torn house slippers with their unglued sole got in the way. Three pairs, if not more, of new ones were in Toma's room. Oh, how grudging . . .

They went inside the bathroom. Granny pointed to the latch with her finger. Zhenya locked it. Slowly Granny undressed. She seemed to want Zhenya to help her, but resisted at the same time. She fought with the button of her robe. She had forgotten how to undo buttons. She was straining to remember. She couldn't.

Zhenya helped her to undress.

Damn, what was Toma thinking of when she invented those idiotic elastic bands under her knees. Why couldn't she put diapers on her, or at least put a diaper underneath her?

They undressed.

"Okay, now raise your leg. The right one. Hold on to me."

Zhenya's stomach was in the way. A lot in the way.

"Now the other . . ." Elena Georgievna lifted her long legs easily. Her foot was awful. The nails were covered with yellowish-gray fungus. Her bunion stuck out. How could someone who had worn only house slippers for more than twenty years have developed a bunion? Elena Georgievna stood knee-deep in water and could not figure out how to sit down. Her figure . . . Her bone structure was highly symmetrical. Her waist small, her sides angled. Her breasts were small and not at all droopy, and her nipples were fresh. Her stomach was flat, her navel hidden inside a

410

horizontal fold. Another fold hid a scar beneath her navel. Her body was hairless, white, and completely wrinkled, like crushed cigarette paper. Her face was white too. The only hairs growing were under her chin. Zhenya used to tweeze them, but now she just cut them with scissors. There wasn't enough time. There was too little time. She had no idea how she was going to manage when the baby was born . . . Probably, she'd have to take Granny to her place on Profsoiuznaya, as soon as Dad moved to his new apartment. In Dad's old apartment with the two connected rooms there was room for all of them. But Toma might object . . .

"Sit down, sweetie, sit down." Zhenya pressed her grandmother lightly on her back. Granny cautiously sat down. Zhenya directed the stream from the shower over her. Granny moaned with pleasure. Now what would happen was what had brought Zhenya here weekly for the last ten years. Ever since her grandfather had died and she had moved to her father's.

"Thank you, my child," Elena Georgievna said. Toma was certain that Elena Georgievna had forgotten how to talk. That wasn't so. She knew how to talk. But only here, in the latched bathroom, when Zhenya sat her in the warm water. There was an inexplicable closeness between them. Zhenya had been raised by her grandfather. Granny had always been silently present and observed her tenderly. For as long as Zhenya could remember, her grandmother had been sick. And they had always loved each other, if love without words or actions, purely in the air and hinging on nothing else, could exist at all. Zhenya stroked her head.

"Feel good?"

"Bliss . . . Lord, what bliss . . . In Siberia we all used to go to the bathhouse together—Pavel Alekseevich, Tanechka, Vasilisa . . . With birch branches . . . There was so much snow . . . Do you remember, child?"

"Who does she take me for?" Zhenya thought. But essentially that did not make any difference. Once a week Elena Georgievna would utter several words. For but a few minutes her link with the here and now would be restored.

"Why did you move into the pantry?" Zhenya asked.

"Into the pantry? What difference does it make . . . Let it be." Then confidentially: "Why didn't you bring Tanechka with you?" She shuddered and seemed confused.

Zhenya suffered most at those times when she sensed that her granny was confused and bewildered. Zhenya soaped her sponge and ran it along the jagged vertebrae of her spine. How should she answer? Sometimes it seemed to Zhenya that her grandmother took her for her deceased daughter. That, probably, was what it was, because in her moments of confused speech the name Tanya would slip out addressed to her . . . But it also happened that Granny would call her "Mama . . ."

"Is the water okay? It hasn't cooled down, has it?"

"Very good . . . Thank you, child." She thought and added in a whisper: "Today some man shouted at me."

"Mikhail Fedorovich? Mikhail Fedorovich shouted at you?"

"No, child, he would never allow himself to do that. Someone else was shouting."

Zhenya pulled her head back slightly and placed her hand on her forehead.

"We're going to wash your hair. Squeeze your eyes tight so no soap gets in."

Elena Georgievna obediently closed her eyes.

While Zhenya washed her hair, she gathered water in the cup of her hands and poured it on her shoulders and chased it with her fingers: she was playing, just the way children play, except without the rubber ducks and the little boats . . .

Then she said unexpectedly: "Don't be angry with Tomochka. She's an orphan."

Zhenya had already rinsed her hair and now pulled a plait of hair upward and stuck in a hairpin so that it would not get in the way.

"And who am I? And you? We're all orphans. I don't understand why she in particular needs to be felt sorry for."

"My head is one big hole. It's difficult," Elena Georgievna complained.

"Mine too," Zhenya admitted. "Yesterday I turned the whole house upside down and spent three hours looking for my documents. I couldn't remember where I'd put them. Stand up, please. I'm going to rinse you with the shower, and then we're done . . ."

Zhenya helped Elena Georgievna get out of the tub, wiped her dry with a bath towel that was disintegrating from age, coated her legs and her intimate creases with baby cream against diaper rash that threatened with time to turn into bedsores, dressed her in a clean nightshirt and a clean robe. She wrapped the towel into a turban, and wiping down the steamed mirror, she told her grandmother to take a look at herself.

"See how beautiful you are."

Elena Georgievna shook her head and laughed. There in the mirror she saw a completely different picture . . .

2

THE NEXT SUNDAY ZHENYA WAS NOT ABLE TO COME: THAT evening, her husband had taken her to the maternity hospital. During the same Sunday after-dinner hours when Zhenya normally would be combing and drying Elena's gray and no longer wavy hair, her cervix dilated and the fetus began to be pushed out: the baby's head crowned. They—Zhenya and the baby—still constituted a single whole. The rise and fall of their muscle spasms were coordinated, but the moment was already approaching when the baby would begin to undertake its first independent movements . . .

When she could no longer stand the pain, Zhenya screamed, and the pain receded, then rolled in again. "If Granddad were alive, he would probably do something so that it wasn't so painful . . ." she thought in those moments when she was capable of thought. This was heavy collaborative work—for her, the child, and the midwife, whose face she completely forgot. What did remain in her memory, however, was her commanding and tender voice: "breathe deeper . . . put your hands on your chest . . . count to ten . . . don't tense up . . . now shout . . . shout . . . good . . ."

It was the most imperfect of all natural mechanisms of giving birth— human childbirth. No other animal suffered as much. The pain, the duration, and sometimes the danger for the health of the mother were signs of human beings' special status in this world. The two-legged, straight-backed, forward-looking, freehanded, and sole creature in the world conscious of the connection between conception and childbirth, between corporeal love and that other variety, known only to human beings. The price of walking straight up, some thought. Recompense for original sin, claimed others.

413

The child had already bent its head so that the posterior fontanel faced forward, turned it slightly, and, straightening its head, entered the pubic arch. The pain was so unbearable that Zhenya's world went black.

The midwife slapped her, saying, "Hey, Mommy! Everything's fine . . . Just a little bit longer," while commenting to someone on the side, "Left occiput anterior position."

Tears and sweat streamed over Zhenya's face. The head tore through. He was already turning his shoulder, and the midwife, grabbing the wet, elongated head with both hands, coaxed the front shoulder forward . . .

3

ELENA DOZED ON HER BENTWOOD CHAIR WITH THE humiliating hole in the seat. She dreamed a dream: one bright spring day when the buds had already opened on the trees but each separate leaf was still small, pale, and not yet its full color, she was walking down Bolshaya Bronnaya Street and turned into Trekhprudny, tilted her head back, and saw a crowd of people standing on the semicircular decorative balcony under the polycircular window of their old apartment on the top floor of the building. She wanted to look more closely to see who was standing there, and she found herself level with the balcony and even slightly above the balustrade and saw that there on a cot lay her grandfather—very old with a not entirely live face—and alongside him her grandmother, Evgenia Fedorovna, Vasilisa, her mother, her father, her young brothers, and all of them were waiting for her in order to tell her something important and joyous. In addition to her own family—the Miakotins and the Nechaevs—in the receding distance that widened like a wedge with the crowd she saw the adult bald Kukotskys with their exotic wives, Toma's relatives from Tver, bearded Jews with a Torah at their head, and some completely unfamiliar people. What was so surprising was how many people could fit on that tiny balcony. More and more of them appeared, and suddenly, in their midst, there appeared two people—a young man who was tall with a head of thick hair, not very clean skin, and a puffy mouth, and a girl resembling Tanechka or Zhenya or Tomochka, with an infant in her arms. This couple was at the very center of this geometrically improbable composition, and Pavel Aleksee-vich took the infant into his arms and turned it so that it faced Elena ... And this infant emanated light, sense, and all the joy of the world. As if in the middle of a sunny day another sun had risen ... This infant belonged to them all, and they to it. And Elena Georgievna sobbed with perfect happiness, just a tiny bit amazed that she could sense both the salty sweetness of her tears and her total disembodiment ...

4

ON THE EVENING OF THE SAME DAY VITALY SET OUT FOR the Central Telegraph: for certain reasons he did not call America from his home phone. He and his father were connected very quickly. Ilya Iosifovich picked up the receiver, heard his son's voice—quick, business-like, without "hello" or "how are you doing."

"Zhenya gave birth to a son. Congratulations! You've got a great-grandson." With no superfluous comments.

He did it within one minute. Then it took him twenty minutes to get through to Leningrad. He told Sergei that everything was all right. She'd had a boy, without any complications.

"Can I come to see her?" Sergei asked.

"Call Zhenya when she gets out of the maternity hospital. Figure it out with her."

He felt no particular weakness for this long-haired musician and was even a little jealous of his relationship with Zhenya. Whatever connec-tion they shared was completely incomprehensible ... Sergei also did not know what connected him with this girl who had been his daughter for a few years. But he didn't think about it. He took his instrument and began to play his old composition, "Black Stones."

5

ILYA IOSIFOVICH HAD DECIDED LONG AGO THAT HE WOULD go to Moscow when his great-grandson was born. The visa was ready.

Valentina at first was categorically against it, but then gave in—under the condition that she go along. All that was left to do was order the tickets. Their older daughter, born four months after Zhenya, had her own place. The younger one, the sixteen-year-old, brought from Russia when she was just an infant, they never left alone. She was a shy, rather strange little girl who loved cats and aquarium fish. They decided that it would be good for her to spend ten days living on her own.

There was a bit of difficulty with Valentina's job. She taught at Harvard University and could not just up and take a vacation. But her class was over in three weeks. As for Ilya Iosifovich, he had retired long ago, and although he was an honorary member of a dozen or so various societies and editorial boards, he could pick up and leave whenever he wanted.

The last three years he had been reading the Torah in German and English, upset that his parents had not sent him to heder as a child. Learning Hebrew at eighty-six was not easy. On the other hand, he'd never been frightened by difficulties. He didn't have and would never again have a conversation partner like Pavel Alekseevich. He spoke and even argued with him frequently in his head. Although he had to admit that a certain rapprochement was taking place between them: Ilya Iosifovich was now inclined to believe in the existence of a Universal Higher Reason and was toying with the idea that the Bible represented a grandiose encryption, that Universal Higher Reason's cosmic message to humankind. But humankind had still not matured to the point where it could decipher this encryption. He constantly attempted to discuss questions of theology with Genka, who lived in New York, but Gena had a decided preference for all varieties of Eastern hogwash—beginning with Chinese food and ending with karate. When he found out that Zhenya had given birth to a son and his father was planning to travel to Moscow as a result, he was alarmed.

"A trip like that at your age! You're better off sending her the money! And I'm ready to . . ."

But Ilya Iosifovich said firmly: "Don't teach me how to live! The girl has a grandfather. I have a great-grandson. Too bad Pasha didn't live to see the day."

TRANSLATOR'S AFTERWORD

THE HISTORY OF THIS TRANSLATION IS WORTHY OF THE notebook of Chekhov's Trigorin: "an idea for a short story." But that is not what this afterword is about, or at least not entirely. I first read *The Kukotsky Enigma* in its debut incarnation, which was titled *Journey to the Seventh Dimension* (*Puteshestvie v sedmuyu storonu sveta*) and published in the Moscow literary journal *Novy mir* in 2000, its place of publication a recommendation in its own right. In 2005, along with millions of Russian television viewers, I watched Yuri Grymov's twelve-part eponymous adaptation of the novel (on which Ludmila Ulitskaya collaborated), and my disappointment—despite the film's talented actors and clever cinematography—was not atypical. As film adaptations often prove, there is more to a great novel than the love story at its core.

The love stories in *The Kukotsky Enigma* certainly deserve twelve episodes and great actors. Ulitskaya weaves wonderfully complex tales with unanticipated turns, and her storytelling has made her work popular among readers as diverse as her cast of characters. Tanya Kukotskaya's Soviet hippie friend Nanny Goat Vika or Vasilisa's intellectual monastic mentor, Mother Anatolia, both would have liked *The Kukotsky Enigma*, but for very different reasons. Certainly, the love story has attracted millions of Russian readers to this novel, now in its fifteenth printing and at the same time available free of cost online in Russian in the Russian Federation. But readers who focus on the love story alone will miss Ulitskaya's true artistic innovation in this work.

On the odd chance that someone will read this afterword before embarking on the novel and in any event not to diminish readers' pleasure in solving *The Kukotsky Enigma* on their own, the only clue to be provided here is that the core of this novel lies in your, the reader's, experience, particularly of part 2. Throughout the rest of the book, Ulitskaya's narrator, like Elena Kukotskaya, leaves little notes to her readers to assist them in deciphering Elena's and the other characters' experiences in part 2. There Ulitskaya veritably re-creates for her readers an experience of the novel's fictional reality as if they themselves were victims of Alzheimer's disease. The process of memory (or the thwarting thereof) comprises the principal mechanism that makes reading possible and pleasurable, and Ulitskaya has given that process a twenty-first-century name.

The novel's title merits comment. In an interview given shortly before the first book edition emerged (published online in Russian by Tatyana Martyusheva in a posting titled "A Mondial Hodgepodge or *The Kukotsky Enigma*" Erfolg.ru. http://www.erfolg.ru/culture/ulizkaya.htm), Ulitskaya confessed that she had changed the novel's title because she had tired of explaining what she meant by *Journeys into the Seventh Dimension*. Perhaps similar confusion had led Ulitskaya's German publishers to release the novel as *Reise in den siebenten Himmel* [Journey to Seventh Heaven]. In Russian, *Казус Кукоцкого*—the title the novel bears to this day—is marvelously alliterative and polysemous. The first word, derived from the Latin *casus* (as in *casus belli*) in Russian conveys: "an incident that occurs independent of the will of any person and cannot be anticipated under certain conditions; a condition or noteworthy occurrence or event or meeting that involves complications; an extraordinary occurrence, particularly from a legal standpoint; a particular incidence of any particular disease or illness; a cause or reason," and "something inexplicable." Clearly, the English word "case," which has been used in English-language references to this novel, does not convey the wealth of meanings implied by the Russian *kazus*. Neither does "enigma," entirely, but at least it suggests the novel's core mechanism and encompasses all of the events contained within it—each in its own way an explication of one of the definitions above.

As with many great novels—including Tolstoy's *War and Peace* and Bulgakov's *The Master and Margarita*, two literary predecessors as "Moscow" novels that are directly and indirectly referenced by Ulitskaya—*The Kukotsky Enigma* contains so many references to cultural phenomena, Russian, European, and worldwide, that annotating this novel would require a companion publication twice its size. In my translation, I have tried to elucidate references for English-speaking readers without spelling them out, knowing that those so inclined will do extratextual research.

The majority of work on this translation was completed in Moscow, in an apartment five minutes' walking distance from the Kukotskys' building (a real place that housed very real doctors and academics) and across the street from the church where baby Zhenya was baptized. Most of the sites Ulitskaya mentions in the novel were very familiar to me; many of them are surrounded by legends and linked to particular stages in the city's history. Some of the places Ulitskaya names no longer exist, although their legacy remains in street names that now refer only to a memory. Each part of Moscow mentioned adds a dimension of characterization to events in the novel. The same is true of places named in Leningrad–St. Petersburg (Piter), which include the building where Dostoevsky located his pawnbroker's apartment in *Crime and Punishment*. Literary tours of Russian cities are a staple of the tourist diet; perhaps someday tours will be given of Ulitskaya's "Novoslobodskaya," a traditionally mixed (working-class and intellectual) neighborhood in Moscow that has finally found its poet.

In Russian, Ulitskaya's prose is, for the most part, unlabored and easy to read. She is also a master of dialogue. The accessibility of her language, though, can be misleading, encouraging readers to slide over references the same way some of her characters stroll past cultural monuments oblivious to their significance, in a kind of cultural amnesia. To the extent possible I have striven to style the language of *The Kukotsky Enigma* to mirror Ulitskaya's idiom, and this has also involved shifts to more complex syntax or unusual lexicon to signal disjunctions in the original Russian. American spellings and punctuation have been used throughout, following style guidelines specific to Northwestern University Press. Transliteration from the Russian generally follows the Library of Congress system, simplified for readability. Names ending in the letter *i kratkoe* (й) are spelled with an *i* (e.g., Serge*i*); names ending in the letters *i* (и) or *y* (ы) and *i kratkoe* are rendered as *y* (Gennad*y* and Vital*y*); names including the soft sign, *miagkii znak* (ь), have been transliterated using *i* (e.g., Vital*i*evna), whereas names including so-called "soft" vowels with or without a *miagkii znak* (e.g., я, ё, ю) have been rendered as *y* plus phoneme (e.g., Tan*y*a and Il*y*a). The metric system in some cases has been replaced by the U.S. system of measurements. Place-names have been transliterated, but words such as "street," "lane," and "monastery" are supplied in English.

This is the third translation project I have published with Northwestern University Press, and the third that freelance editor Xenia Lisanevich and I have collaborated on. Not a few of the "enigmas" in *The Kukotsky Enigma* derive from Ulitskaya's creative choices, some of which are inexplicable even on repeated readings. The translation and editorial team, headed by Anne Gendler at the Press, aided by graduate assistant Jessica Hinds-Bond, turned what could have been agony into an intellectual project, as the four of us have worked to coax out layers of meaning in this very tricky (not to repeat "enigmatic") text. To Xenia, Anne, and Jessica this translator owes much. Any infelicities that have eluded their scrutiny are my responsibility. And, finally, to Ludmila Evgenievna: thank you for your marvelous work.